Andrew Lang

The Life and Letters of John Gibson Lockhart

Volume the First

Andrew Lang

The Life and Letters of John Gibson Lockhart
Volume the First

ISBN/EAN: 9783744765473

Printed in Europe, USA, Canada, Australia, Japan

Cover: Foto ©Raphael Reischuk / pixelio.de

More available books at **www.hansebooks.com**

THE LIFE AND LETTERS

OF

JOHN GIBSON LOCKHART

BY

ANDREW LANG

FROM ABBOTSFORD AND MILTON LOCKHART MSS.

AND OTHER ORIGINAL SOURCES

With Fifteen Illustrations

IN TWO VOLUMES

VOLUME THE FIRST

LONDON

JOHN C. NIMMO

NEW YORK: CHARLES SCRIBNER'S SONS

MDCCCXCVII

Printed by BALLANTYNE, HANSON & CO.
At the Ballantyne Press

TO

THE HON. MRS. MAXWELL SCOTT

OF ABBOTSFORD

THESE MEMOIRS OF HER GRANDFATHER,

Her Illustrious Great-grandfather's

Son-in-law, Biographer,

. *and Friend,*

Are Dedicated

PREFACE

THIS Life of Mr. Lockhart has been compiled under many difficulties, some of which I foresaw, while others I did not anticipate. The book grew out of the publisher's wish that I should prepare for him an edition of Mr. Lockhart's "Life of Sir Walter Scott." An introductory chapter on the author of that great work seemed desirable, and the chapter swelled into a biography of Mr. Lockhart.

The book had not been in hand for more than two or three months, when I found that there were impediments which a fuller knowledge of Mr. Lockhart's professional career would have taught me to anticipate. As regards his relations with Mr. John Wilson Croker, and with the *Quarterly Review*, documents exist which, perhaps, may some day be given to the world. Their absence from this work is touched on later, in the appropriate place. I am inclined to think that my information, derived from Mr. Lockhart's familiar letters, is adequate for the purpose of his biography, though there ought to be much interesting matter in his letters to Mr. Croker, of which but a very small part, apparently, has been given in Mr. Croker's published correspondence.

Indeed, my own regrets in this matter are concerned with my apparent, though perfectly unintentional, slight to the successors of Mr. Lockhart's old allies and associates, rather than with the loss of biographical materials.

Other difficulties have occurred ; Mr. Blackwood, I doubt not, would have given me every reasonable access to the archives of his house, but these were already in the hands of Mrs. Oliphant for editorial purposes. Mrs. Oliphant has most kindly allowed me to consult her for the avoidance of errors in matters of fact, and Mr. Blackwood gave me a list of many of Mr. Lockhart's later articles.

Mr. Lockhart's letters to Mr. Southey I have been unable to trace. Mr. Southey's side of the correspondence, preserved at Abbotsford, is of very little interest or literary importance ; it deals with business between editor and contributor.

A large collection of private letters from Mr. Lockhart to a lifelong friend was destroyed many years ago by its actual possessor. To a portfolio of caricatures, of which a few were published more than thirty years ago in Mrs. Gordon's "Christopher North," access has been denied me, but Mr.

Brewster Macpherson has kindly lent me his collection of Lockhart's sketches.

I have to thank, first of all, Mrs. Maxwell Scott of Abbotsford, without whose aid this biography of her grandfather could never have been attempted.

All the manuscripts at Abbotsford and Milton Lockhart have passed through my hands, and Mrs. Maxwell Scott has assisted me in every possible way, by revision of the book before and after it was in type. The chief documents are eleven volumes of letters to Mr. Lockhart, including two volumes of letters from Mr. Croker, of which, for obvious reasons, I have made no use, beyond a remark on Mr. Croker's character as revealed in these papers. The volumes of letters to Sir Walter Scott include a few (in addition to those from Mr. Lockhart) which have been of service. From Sir Walter's two volumes of letters to Mr. Lockhart I have made selections of such as are not anticipated in Scott's Letters or Journal. Mr. Lockhart's letters to his own family, to his wife, his children, and his son-in-law, Mr. James Hope Scott, have supplied much material. Much more might have been extracted had it seemed desirable *celebrare domestica facta*. Mrs. Lockhart's letters have also been sparingly used.

For the important though incomplete series of

letters to Mr. Jonathan Christie, Mr. Lockhart's lifelong friend, I have to thank the kindness of Mr. Christie's daughter, Mrs. Herrick.

For permission to quote the *Quarterly* article on Mr. Lockhart, by his old friend, the Rev. Mr. Gleig, and for the sight of a complete list of Mr. Lockhart's articles in the *Quarterly Review*, I am indebted to the kindness of Mr. John Murray of Albemarle Street. Mr. Gleig's article is the only authority on the boyhood of Lockhart.

To Mr. J. H. Stevenson and the Dowager Lady Foulis, the representatives of Mr. Cadell, the publisher of the " Life of Scott," I owe many valuable documents. Colonel Gleig has also provided such materials of his father's, the Chaplain-General of the Forces, and author of " The Subaltern," as he possessed.

My friend, Mr. Ernest Hartley Coleridge, has allowed me to see and extract from a MS. diary of a Scottish Tour in his possession, containing a description of Mrs. Lockhart before her marriage.

Miss Bessie Wilson has gratified me with a view of some letters by Mr. Lockhart to her grandfather, Professor Wilson, for the most part already published.

Mr. and Miss Carruthers of Inverness have kindly lent me letters to their grandfather, Sir Walter's friend, Mr. William Laidlaw.

My friend, Mr. Falconer of Dundee, has lent me, and even more kindly copied out for me, an important letter of Sir Walter Scott's, and a few letters from Mr. Lockhart, in the collection of his brother, to whom my thanks are no less due.

Mr. S. L. Davey, of Great Russell Street, has aided me with all his wonted generosity to authors, in the attempt to collect scattered documents.

Mr. David Douglas, the publisher of Scott's Journal, has helped me in the most generous manner, by his great knowledge of Scottish literary history, and by the loan of rare books and pamphlets.

To Mr. Archibald Milman, whose generosity has been of the highest service, I owe the use of Mr. Lockhart's important series of letters to Dean Milman, without which one aspect of Mr. Lockhart's industry and character would have been most incomplete.

To my dear kinswoman, Mrs. William Sellar, I am indebted in this, as in all things, for much aid and encouragement. Mr. Alexander Carlyle not only lent me Mr. Lockhart's letters to his celebrated uncle, but permitted the publication of Mr. Carlyle's letters, and gave information as to the high regard and affection in which Mr. Lockhart was held by him. General Lockhart and other members of the family have ungrudgingly lent all the aid in their power. Mr. James Traill, son of Mr. Lockhart's lifelong friend, obliged me with some interesting notes : the Dean of Salisbury, also, was kind enough to add to what he had said in his charming volume of Reminiscences.

I must not omit to acknowledge my debt to the anonymous writer who, in *Temple Bar* for June 1895, suggested the compilation of this work, and indicated many useful references. His name is still unknown to me, but he is "the onlie begetter" of this work.

Without the generous labours of Father Forbes Leith, S.J., in the Abbotsford MSS., nothing could have been done to any purpose.

I have to thank Miss Violet Simpson for examining the unpublished correspondence of Mr. Macvey Napier in the British Museum, and for discovering, not without labour, the account of the Scott-Christie duel, published by Mr. Horace Smith.

My friend, Mr. Edmund Gosse, has greatly obliged me by reading the proof-sheets, and by discovering "Mr. Flatters" (vol. ii. p. 195), though I would not try to shelter any oversights due to myself under his authority.

To Mr. Maitland Anderson, and Mr. Smith, of the University Library, St. Andrews, I owe more than I can easily say.

It is not easy to write the Life of a man whom

few living people remember, and whom none remembers in his prime.   On the other hand, the
lapse of years makes it possible to say much that
a contemporary biographer might feel obliged to
keep in reserve.   Mr. Lockhart's character—too
complex to be easily construed—was also so strong
as to leave its leading traits deeply and permanently
marked.   His letters best reveal him, and though
much has perished, much is left.   Through the
letters we can see Mr. Lockhart as he really was,
not as he exists in hostile report and erroneous
legend.   The compiler will be more than satisfied
if a portrait, however slight, takes, in the gallery of
great Englishmen (including Scots) of letters, the
place of a shadowy set of caricatures.

I am aware that, in several passages, this biography may seem to resemble a speech for the defence.   But Mr. Lockhart has been so vehemently
attacked, and often so unjustly misrepresented, that
a defensive attitude was sometimes unavoidable.

                              ANDREW LANG.

July 1896.

CONTENTS

CHAPTER I

GLASGOW, 1794–1808

CHAPTER II

OXFORD, 1808–1813

CONTENTS

CHAPTER III

GLASGOW, 1813–1815

CHAPTER IV

EDINBURGH, 1815–1817

CONTENTS

CHAPTER V

EDINBURGH, 1817–1818

CHAPTER VI

EDINBURGH, 1817-1819

CHAPTER VIII

EDINBURGH, 1819-1820

CHAPTER IX

EDINBURGH, 1820-1821

CHAPTER X

CHIEFSWOOD, 1821-1824

CHAPTER XI

EDINBURGH, 1817-1824

CHAPTER XII

CHIEFSWOOD, 1821-1825

CHAPTER XIII

LONDON, 1826

LIST OF ILLUSTRATIONS

VOLUME THE FIRST

xxiii

LIST OF ILLUSTRATIONS

LIFE OF J. G. LOCKHART

CHAPTER I

GLASGOW, 1794—1808

"EVERY Scotsman has his pedigree," says Sir
Walter, in the Autobiographical fragment where
he traces his own. The interest in our ancestors,
"without whose life we had not been," may be
regarded as a foible, and was made matter of re-
proach, both to Scott and his biographer, the story
of whose own life is here to be narrated. Scott
"was anxious to realise his own ancestry to his
imagination; . . . whatever he had in himself he
would fain have made out a hereditary claim for."

In this taste there is not wanting a domestic piety ; and science, since Sir Walter's day, has approved of his theory, that the past of our race revives in each of us.

For these reasons Scottish readers, at least, may pardon a genealogical sketch in this place. Or, if they be unkind, we may say of Lockhart, as he says in the case of Thomas Campbell, " He was a Scotsman, and of course his biographer begins with an ell of genealogy."

The pedigree of Scott's biographer and son-in-law, John Gibson Lockhart, was hardly inferior in historical interest to Sir Walter's own. Both Sir Walter and his son-in-law were descended from cadet branches of noble houses. If Harden was the "fountain of the gentry" of Scott, Lockhart of Lee was, as we shall see, in all probability, the source of the "gentry" of Scott's biographer.

In the Upper Ward of Lanarkshire is the parish of Symington, bounded on the east by the stripling Clyde, and rising in the south to the crest of Tinto. The whole district lies high, but, save for Tinto, is not hilly. The waters of the land, except Clyde, are but burns, which, in later life, Lockhart remembered with all a Scot's personal affection for his native streams. There is a warm wooded look, considering the height of the general elevation, and the parish is best known, perhaps, for Symington Railway Station, on the Caledonian Railway. The old official name of Symington is *Villa Symonis*

Lockard, Symon's town, whence Symington. This name is understood to be derived from Symon Loccard, who, in the reign of Malcolm the Maiden, was lord of the parish, and founded the village and the church. The name Loccard also occurs, it is believed, in Lockerby, in Dumfriesshire (Locardebi), and certainly in Craig Lockhart, and Milton Lockhart, which is still in the possession of the family.[1] A man of Symon Loccard's importance must necessarily have had forefathers of no mean estate. I have not had the opportunity to trace, through documents, this Loccard (probably derived from "*de Loch Ard*," a territorial designation) to the house of Saint Lys, and the companions of the Conqueror, but it is a mistaken etymology which accepts Lockhart of Lee as a corruption of Loccard de Saint Lys.

Whatever the truth of the Saint Lys theory may be, the eponymous hero, so to speak, of the Lockharts, Symon of Symington, founded his parish church about 1153. He also held lands in Ayrshire, and gave his name to Symontown in Kyle. He appears as a witness to charters and other deeds as late as 1190, and was succeeded by his son Malcolm.

The Lockharts of Lee, now the chief house of the family, soon eclipsed the parent branch of Symontown, which disappears in stormy times. In 1300 (*circa*) we find Richard Hastang, an Englishman,

[1] "Lockhart" was only added to "Milton" some seventy years ago.

writing to Edward I., "praying for the lands of
Simon Locard," in Ayr, "and in the Leye, in the
county of Lanark." This Simon Locard of the Lee
was knighted by Robert Bruce, and took his side
in the resistance to England. After Bruce's death,
he sailed with the good Lord James Douglas, to
carry the king's heart to the Holy Land. Douglas
fell, fighting the Saracens in Spain; all the world
knows how he threw the royal heart into the
mellay, crying, "Lead on, as thou were wont to
do!" Sir Simon then took the command, rescued
the heart of Bruce and the body of Douglas, and
returned to Scotland. His acquisition, in Spain,
of the famous "Lee penny" ("The Talisman"),
part of the ransom of a Moor, is well known.
The Locards now added to their bearings a heart
within a fetterlock, and took the name of Lockhart.
"Did you ever hear of such a name, Master Hugh?"
asks Scott, in his "Tales of a Grandfather," written
for "Hugh Littlejohn," the son of John Gibson
Lockhart.

While the Lockharts of Lee, themselves originally
of the Symonton or Symington family, thus came
to honour, the Symonton branch dwindled and
vanished. Probably they took the English side,
for Bruce, soon after his accession, conveyed
the barony of Symonton, as crown property, to
"Thomas fil Dick" (*Thomae filio Ricardi*), probably
Thomas Dickson of Hesilside, who helped the
Black Douglas to surprise the English garrison

of Castle Dangerous, on a famous Palm Sunday.[1]
Thus the headship of the Lockharts was now settled
in the patriotic and illustrious house of Lee.

From 1339 to 1440, the history of the Lockharts
of Lee (as far as printed documents go), is somewhat obscure. In the latter year (1440) we find them
settled in their lands by a charter to Alexander
Lockhart, who was followed by his son Sir Allan,
knighted by James III., and succeeded, in turn, by
his son, Sir Mungo, who died before 1489.

Now in the days of this Sir Allan Lockhart of
Lee comes on the stage a Sir Stephen Lockhart,
who owned the lands of Cleghorn in Lanarkshire.
About the parentage of this Sir Stephen Lockhart
of Cleghorn, who was the direct male ancestor of
John Gibson Lockhart, uncertainty prevails. A
scholar who has aided me by his researches[2] says,
" He may have been a cadet of the Lockharts of Lee,
whose history at that period is not well known, and
family tradition takes this view, though it has not
found support from public documents." On the
other hand, the authors of " The Upper Ward of
Lanarkshire"[3] (to which most of the information
given here is due) find a Sir Allan Lockhart in
possession of Cleghorn in 1441. " He," they say,
" was undoubtedly a cadet of the Lockharts of Lee,

[1] See Scott's novel, " Castle Dangerous."
[2] The Rev. John Anderson.
[3] " The Upper Ward of Lanarkshire." By G. V. Irving and A.
Murray. Glasgow, 1864.

but the pedigree of that family is involved in considerable obscurity in the latter part of the fourteenth and the early portion of the fifteenth centuries." And they represent our Sir Stephen as the son of this Sir Allan Lockhart of Cleghorn. His own son was named Allan. The account already given, however, is, I believe, correct.

The connection of Sir Stephen with the main stem of the house, the Lockharts of Lee, would not satisfy a strict genealogist, but no Lockharts of any other stem are likely to have flourished in Lanarkshire, so near the centre of the race. Sir Stephen frequently appears in charters and other documents ; he was armour-bearer to James III., he went on an embassy to the King of the Romans, he adhered to his king in the rebellion which ended in that monarch's death near Bannockburn, he was member for Lanarkshire in 1491, and was altogether a stirring and notable man. He died about 1518.

Sir Stephen's son, Allan Lockhart of Cleghorn, married twice. His second wife was Marion, daughter of John, third Lord Somerville, by whom he had a son Stephen, who acquired Waygateshaw, or Wicketshaw, in Lanarkshire. The Wicketshaw Lockharts were addicted to manslaughter, having a feud with the Hamiltons. In 1539, Alexander Lockhart of Wicketshaw was pardoned for the slaying of James Hamilton. The laird of Lee, in 1572, as head of the house, was security for the appearance, to stand his trial, of Stevin Lockhart of

Wicketshaw. In 1605 the Hamiltons, pursuing a
feud of at least seventy years' standing, had their
turn, and the Rev. John Hamilton of Crawfordjohn
was indicted "for a savage assault on Alexander
Lockhart, tutor" (uncle and guardian of the heir)
"of Wicketshaw." Probably these Lockharts of
1572 were king's men, as the Hamiltons were of
course for Queen Mary, in the Douglas wars.

In 1606, we find Stephen Lockhart of Wicketshaw, "Goodman thereof,"[1] marrying Grizel Carmichael, a sister of the first Lord Carmichael, by
whom he had three sons—(1) William Lockhart of
Wicketshaw, whose line failed in 1776 ; (2) Robert,
who, about 1665, purchased the lands of Birkhill
in the parish of Lesmahagow ; (3) and Walter, laird
of Kirkton.

Two of these three brothers were urged, by such
dragoonings as Scott describes in "Old Mortality,"
to fight for the Covenant, under the Banner of
Blue. From the second, Robert Lockhart of
Birkhill, the subject of this biography was directly
descended.

Of Robert Lockhart of Birkhill, Colonel Wallace
writes thus, in his contemporary "Narrative of the
Pentland Rising :"—"We marched close by Robert
Lockhart's house, where Mr. Robertson was with
Mr. Robert Lockhart. None of them came out

---

[1] I have observed "Goodman" used of Grahame of Netherby :
the phrase need not indicate a mere "bonnet-laird." See also
"Memorie of the Somervilles," i. 496.

(though it was but three or four paces from the house), to countenance us so much ; yet some of our company, in the by-coming, spoke with them, such as Mr. Brysson, Sundaywell, and old worthy Robert Bruce of Skellietoun, *who most freely and faithfully acquitted themselves to them.*"

However, on this occasion the descendant of the guardian of the heart of Bruce declined to follow a Robert Bruce, on the weary tramp through the wet moors to the places of testifying at Rullion Green and the Grassmarket.

What a picture of the scene might Scott have drawn : the straggling "drookit" company of small lairds, farmers, farm-servants, "Knockbreck's two sons, with a few others ; these were the hundred men we had heard were coming from Galloway, for we saw no other,"—the disorderly array of muskets, swords, and scythes, the closed windows and doors of Robert Lockhart's little château, the faithful contendings and flytings of Mr. Brysson, and white-haired Robert Bruce of Skellietoun, and looking on with his arms pinioned, and the smile of the scorner on his lips, the Royalist captive, Sir James Turner,—"the motion of pistolling him was slighted, alas, it is to be feared too much."

It is not, perhaps, the most glorious page in the history of the Lockharts, for the watchword of the godly was, " Though we should all die at the end of it, we think the giving of a testimony enough for all." However, even Mr. Alexander Peden, the prophet, kept out of this rising, as foreseeing the end of it.

Lockhart of Wicketshaw, on the other hand, is said to have joined his little troop to that of the wild Galloway Whigs, among whom the rising began, at St. John's Town of Dalry in the Glen Kens. As to Lockhart of Birkhill, if he once let the Banner of the Covenant pass his door unaided, it is fair to say that he had already tried to prevent its followers from coming so far, and had "earnestly dealt with Mr. Brysone to follow the business no further, ... but to dismiss the people, the fairest way and the handsomest we could, and let every one see to himself, until the Lord gave some better opportunity."[1]

In 1679, after the murder of Archbishop Sharp, Lockhart of Birkhill seems to have thought that the Lord *had* "given them some better opportunity." He turned out for the Covenant, and led the Lanarkshire Whigs, at the battle of Bothwell Brig, his brother Walter fighting under Claverhouse for the king. Tradition relates that Birkhill fled from the field with Dalyell's men after him, and accompanied by some friends of his own side. Thinking that they had escaped pursuit, the rest of the party deemed it convenient to sing a psalm. Lockhart remonstrated, but they would sing, so he privily withdrew himself and climbed up a tree.

---

[1] Wallace's narrative of the Pentland Rising, in Dr. M'Crie's " Memoirs of Veitch and Brysson," pp. 399–404.

His tuneful friends below were arrested, and he escaped, but only to die of privation and fatigue.[1] In later days (1825), the Rev. Dr. M'Crie edited a work containing references to these forebears of Lockhart's, who, in the too renowned "Chaldee Manuscript," had named Dr. M'Crie "The Griffin," he himself being "The Scorpion." By a curious coincidence the most offensive verses of "The Chaldee" (iii. 36–39), are an attack on Graham Dalyell, a lineal descendant of the persecutor, old Tom Dalyell of Binns. But now, *conversis rebus*, Lockhart was the Tory, and Dalyell was the Whig.[2]

The grandson of the Covenanter of Birkhill was William Lockhart, who married Violet Inglis, heiress of Corehouse, the lady introducing the Christian name of Violet into the family. Miss Inglis's mother was a sister of Somerville of Corehouse, to which she herself succeeded. The lands of Eastshiel, Corehouse, and Birkhill were thus united. Hers was a runaway match. The pair had two

[1] "New Statistical Account of Scotland," VI. 579.

[2] What Lockhart seriously thought of the long struggle in which some of his fathers fell, and others were forfeited, may be gathered from an article in the *Quarterly Review* (December 1848), published under his Editorship. Reviewing the Duke of Argyll's "Presbytery Examined," the critic says, that not in the Established Kirk, but in the Free Kirk and among other Seceders, "we must seek the descendants of Knox and Melville, of Henderson and Rutherford, to say nothing of Cameron or Cargill. Let us frankly accept all men and all systems when we travel back into the past, in their own sense and in their own spirit." The whole passage (*Quarterly*, lxxxiv. pp. 92–93), is a remarkable instance of a truly liberal dealing with the facts of Scottish Dissent, in a Tory Orthodox Anglican Review.

sons—the line of the eldest failed; the second son was the Rev. John Lockhart, D.D., minister of Cambusnethan, and, later, of the College Kirk in Glasgow. This Dr. Lockhart married twice; in his family by his second wife the estate of Milton Lockhart still remains. His second wife was a daughter of the Rev. John Gibson, minister of St. Cuthbert's in Edinburgh, and the eldest son of this second marriage was John Gibson Lockhart.

The patient reader now sees that from the days of Malcolm the Maiden, and through the houses of Lockhart of Symonton, of Lee, of Cleghorn, of Birkhill, and of Wicketshaw, the future biographer of Scott derived a pedigree for which published documents fail, in the darkness of 1339–1440, but which, none the less, is such as Sir Walter liked to trace. The War of Independence, the chivalrous pilgrimage of the Royal Heart, the feudal anarchy, the Douglas wars, the struggle for religious domination by the Covenanters, are all among the ancestral memories of the Lockharts. Not alien, probably, are the loyal Jacobite honours of the Lockharts of Carnwath, a branch of the Lockharts of Lee, the two houses being now united. What part the Wicketshaw and Birkhill Lockharts took in Prince Charles's campaign of 1745, perhaps "'tis better only guessing." One Lockhart certainly made himself hated for his cruelties after Culloden, and a Jacobite song on the battle of Val (1747) a defeat of the butcher Cumberland, has this odd association of two names now happily united—

> " Baith Scott and Lockhart's sent to hell,
>   For to acquaint mama, Willie,
>   That shortly you'll be there yoursel'
>   To roast ayont them a', Willie ! "

The houses of Somerville and Carmichael are far off "forebears," and the Puritan strain (not very conspicuous in the son-in-law of Scott) should have been strengthened by descent from Mr. James Nimmo [1] (1654–1709), who fought and ran away at Bothwell Brig (1679), and, after 1688, getting into the Customs, smuggled in a godly fashion,—"the Lord wonderfully and mercifully guided me . . . praise, praise to Him !"   Mr. Nimmo left a curious memoir, mainly of his religious experiences, pub-

---

[1] Here is the descent from godly Mr. Nimmo—

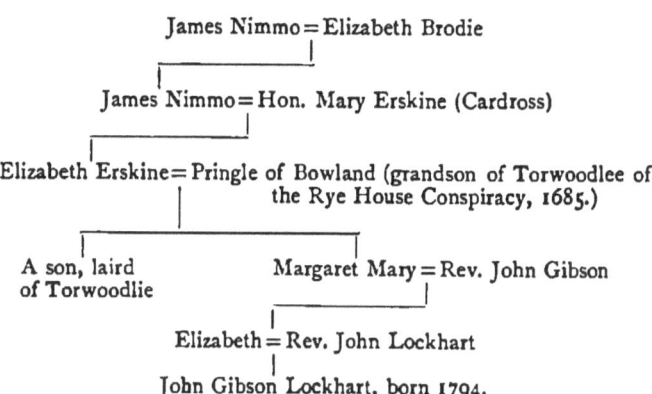

Tabulated from Mr. W. G. Scott-Moncrieff's account, in the Introduction to "Narrative of Mr. James Nimmo," Edinburgh, 1889.

lished by the Scottish History Society, and naturally never guessed that a descendant of Lockhart of Birkhill, who fought by his side at Bothwell Brig, would marry a great-great-grand-daughter of his own, Elizabeth Gibson, and so connect the subject of this biography, her son, with her paternal house, the ancient one of Pringle of Torwoodlie, Scott's neighbours and friends at Abbotsford.

Concerning the characters and attainments of Lockhart's parents, nothing of much interest has reached us.   At that time it was still not unusual for the younger sons of landed and ancient families to "enter the ministry."   Several examples are found among the fathers of young men, Lockhart's college companions and lifelong friends.   To Sir Walter Scott, in his early years, offers of patronage in the Kirk were made.   Dr. Lockhart was a scholar, and his distinguished son may have inherited from him a turn for scholarship, but it is clear that Dr. Lockhart was not a purchaser of modern books, nor a patron of the rising literature, of Coleridge, Southey, Wordsworth, and Scott.

About 1824 Lockhart's wife quotes a saying of her husband's, "Your father" (Sir Walter) "may be a greater poet, but *mine* is a greater proser." The old gentleman's letters reveal him as a serious, grave, rather narrow divine of the old Presbyterian school.   He could tell a story well, and on a story of a real set of incidents, told by him, Lockhart founded his best novel, "Adam Blair."   He had no

liking for Episcopal religion, and would grumble
a little at Lockhart's indifference as to the rival
claims of Kirk and Church.   In brief, to the
ordinary observer, Dr. Lockhart seemed a good
specimen of a large class of Scottish ministers.

About Lockhart's mother even less is to be
gleaned.   Her letters are plain, pious, and affectionate.   Probably the peculiar "Spanish" type of
Lockhart's face, which is noted by Southey, Haydon,
and Scott, was derived from her, for, when Lockhart lay on his death-bed, his younger brother,
Robert, remarked the strong resemblance to their
mother.   To both of his parents Lockhart was
warmly and devotedly attached, but his letters to
them will seldom be quoted, as they do not often
range above the everyday affairs of the family and
its friends.   It does not seem that either his father
or his mother was keenly interested in his literary
work.   Nothing in his perplexing character can,
with our present knowledge, be explained by in-
heritance from his father and mother.

John Gibson Lockhart was born in the manse
of Cambusnethan, on the 14th of July 1794.   In
his second year his father obtained the College Kirk
of Glasgow, and migrated thither.   The child was
delicate, and Mr. Gleig, who wrote the article on
"The Life of Lockhart" in the *Quarterly Review*
(October 1864), thinks that the bracing moorland
air might have been better for his health than the
smoke and fog of Glasgow.

As the result of an early malady, Lockhart was partially deaf for the whole of his life. Like shortness of sight, deafness, even in a slight degree, is apt to be the cause of shyness. A man whose hearing is not good, like one whose sight is imperfect, dares not act on his first perceptions, whether of eye or ear. He soon learns that he is very likely to make errors, as of recognising the wrong person, or not recognising the right one ; of replying to what has not been said, or of becoming tedious by requesting that a remark may be repeated. Lockhart's partial deafness may thus have contributed to cause his shyness. In a letter written at the close of his life, Lockhart speaks of himself as, with perhaps one exception, "the shyest man alive." Now shyness "is not one mental disorder, but many, and varies in degree and kind with the characters of individuals. It is afraid where no fear is ; it is humble, and appears proud ; it is sensitive, and takes the form of coldness and reserve ; it is dying to speak, and can only think of something inappropriate to say. . . . It is, in most respects, the opposite of what it appears to be ; *all sorts of false imputations are apt to be cast upon him who is the victim of it*, and the acute sense of the undeservedness of these imputations in a sensitive mind greatly aggravates the evil"—often by confirming a man consciously in the attitude which his shyness simulates.[1]

[1] "College Sermons." By Benjamin Jowett, Master of Balliol, p. 219.

These words, this protest, as we may call it, of one who knew well what shyness is, might have been written about Lockhart.   Difficult beyond common experience as his character was, his shyness yet more perplexes it.   The malady, above all when the result of a physical defect, is never allowed for, never understood by the world.   Scott speaks of Lockhart's modesty as amounting to diffidence, yet he often seemed arrogant. He himself has described shyness as "arrogance not screwed up."   His sensitiveness was taken for coldness, his "almost fierce reserve" (as Mr. Hope Scott calls it) was identified with want of heart, for the public prefers a callous heart worn on the sleeve, to a tender heart which hides its emotions.   Thus "all sorts of false imputations" were cast on Lockhart, and it is more than probable that, as Tertullian became a Montanist because he was called a Montanist, so Lockhart did assume some of the failings with which he was constantly charged.   In society Scott speaks of his tendency to be silent, or to converse with one person in a corner, where, in fact, he could hear and be heard.   This taciturnity, and his aspect, "his melancholy Spanish head," as Haydon the painter describes it, produced "the Hidalgo airs" laughingly alluded to by Scott. Cyrus Redding in his Memoirs says, "He was of a retiring, reserved habit, and by many not understood; called ill-natured, sarcastic, and I know not what beside.   I can only speak of men as I have found them, and with me he was always pleasant. . . . . An habitual cast, as of pensiveness, appeared continually over him."[1] Let it be added that, as La Rochefoucauld writes, "a wit is often more at a loss in ordinary society than an ordinary man among wits," and we have the secret of Lockhart's failure to be genial and generally popular. In him existed, in a much lower degree, certain of the qualities which made Hazlitt really unfit to succeed in human intercourse; nor is it to be denied that Lockhart seldom suffered fools gladly. Yet this manner was blended, or crossed, by a conviviality of disposition which, being rarely found in company with a shy and sensitive reserve, increases the complexity of his character.

As an undergraduate he took his part in college revels, and probably held his own with Wilson and Hogg in the suppers at Ambrose's. It is remembered that he once came unexpectedly to Milton Lockhart, when a great dinner of farmers was going on, that at first he shrank into his shell with Hidalgo airs, or, to speak *Scottice*, "with the black dowg on his back."

"Suddenly, when the sweets appeared, one of the yeomen pinched him violently on the leg, and in a voice hoarse with emotion, murmured, 'Gosh, man! *Twa puddens!* Yon'll be a kick abune the common.'

"This unexpected assault and enthusiasm sent

[1] " Fifty Years' Recollections," iii. 52, 53.

John off into a hearty fit of laughter. He shook off the black dog, and, for the rest of the evening, was the life and soul of the party."[1]

Fitful appearances of "the black dog" occur in the course of his story, and it is not to be denied that the animal was a familiar of Lockhart ; yet he lived much with gleeful folk, such as the famous Lord Robertson, the "peerless paper Lord" of his rhyme, and his after-supper lyrics retain their gaiety. Thus even his shyness was original, and unlike that of other people.

The early origin, in a physical accident, of a predominant trait has led us far from the infancy of Lockhart. We learn from Mr. Gleig, the only authority on the subject, that from four to six years of age, Lockhart "toddled to the English school, as it was called, and to the writing school, where he acquired elementary education." Of his school days, from six to twelve, at Glasgow High School, few anecdotes survive, or few have reached us. He is said to have been rather clever than industrious, often absent by reason of sickness, "but he always kept his place as dux," or head of his class, as forms are called in Scotland. Full of fun, overflowing with humour, he was yet averse to rough sports, to "stane-bickers," battles with the town boys, such as Scott's youth delighted in, and he hated quarrelling. He was a caricaturist, and if his humour hurt any one, he "sometimes could not even see the wound

[1] From H. F. M. Lockhart, Esq.

which it inflicted." This incapacity seems to have remained, more or less, through his career.

"At the same time the humorous, gleeful, merry boy was proud and reserved. A natural disposition more than commonly affectionate he kept under perpetual restraint, considering it unmanly to make any violent display either of joy or sorrow. The effort necessary to accomplish this often cost him dear, and on one occasion had well-nigh proved fatal to him. He was very much attached to a younger brother and sister, particularly to the latter, both of whom died within a few days of each other. John would not weep, as the rest of the family did, nor in any other way make a display of his feelings, and the consequence was, that he became so ill as seriously to alarm, not his parents only, but his medical attendant." The boy was indeed father of the man, and his family crest, the Heart within the Fetterlock, was the badge of his nature. The illness alluded to caused Lockhart's removal from school to the seaside. His education was now conducted by his father, a good classical scholar. Perhaps Dr. Lockhart, like the father of Reginald Dalton in his son's novel, "did not wish to have any better companion than his child." "Robinson Crusoe," the "Pilgrim's Progress," "The Seven Wise Masters," "the old genuine banquets of strong imagery and picturesque incident," were probably among Lockhart's as among his hero's early studies, and later, as editor of the

Quarterly Review, he asked Miss Rigby to write an article against "the tame milk-and-water diet," which modern dulness tried to substitute for the old immortal favourites.

In 1805 Lockhart matriculated at the University of Glasgow. He was in his twelfth year, and, though very young boys composed the junior classes in Scotch colleges, he must have been among the youngest.[1]

At that time, Lockhart says, the students of Glasgow University still wore the red gowns, which,

---

[1] Lockhart matriculated in 1805, presumably in November.

I append the official information about Lockhart at Glasgow University, which I owe to the kindness of Mr. W. Innes Addison, of the Matriculation Office, and of my friend Mr. A. C. Bradley, Professor of English Literature :—

"'Joannes Gibson Lockhart, filius natu secundus Reverendi Viri Joannis Lockhart, SS. T. D. & Pastoris Parochiæ de Black Friars in urbe Glasguensi, in Com. de Lanark natus.'

"The name is written by himself (the rest not) in a boyish but rather good hand—clear, firm, and rather large.

"In 1805—6 he attended the Humanity Class (Prof. Wm. Richardson), but took no prize.

"In 1806—7 he got the fifth prize in the Humanity Class 'for exemplary diligence and regularity,' and also a prize (second) 'for excelling at the examinations on Roman Antiquities.'

"In this session he attended the Greek Class. His name is not on the roll of the Latin Class, but of course he must have attended it.

"In 1807—8 he got a prize in the Greek Class 'for propriety o conduct, diligence, and eminent ability displayed during the whole of the session.'

"The prize-men are divided into classes or divisions (not so named). L. comes third in the second division, seventh in the whole list of prize-men.

"In 1808—9 he got one of the prizes in the Logic Class 'for the best specimens of analysis and composition on subjects of Reasoning and

during a session spent by his present biographer,
about 1864, in that seat of learning, were only
donned at the Blackstone examination. The
Glasgow gowns appear very scrimped, in contrast
with the flowing academic dress of St. Andrews.
The College, in Lockhart's time, as in my own,
was the black old quadrangle, guarded by an effigy
of some heraldic animal, probably the Scottish lion,
in whose open mouth it was thought unbecoming
to insert a bun. Blackness, dirt, smoke, a selection
of the countless smells of Glasgow, small, airless,
crowded rooms, thronged by youths at whom
Lockhart could not have scoffed for exaggerated
elegance in dress, these things make up a picture
of the Old College of Glasgow. Now there is a
new and magnificent building in a part of the town
which enjoys, for Glasgow, a respectable atmosphere. In a volume called " Janus," written by
Wilson and Lockhart in 1826, some one, Lockhart
probably, describes the changes in the Old College
since 1814. " The inner court, where I have so

Taste . . . . and for distinguished eminence and proficiency in the
whole business of the class.'

"The prize-men are divided into Seniores and Juniores. L. was
seventh among the Seniores.

"In the same session (1808—9) he got two prizes in Latin : one 'for
the best translation of the seventh book of Lucan into verse' (his is the
only prize given) : the other 'for the best Latin verses' (he is the first
of two prize-men).

"I have searched the record of the Blackstone prize-men from
1805—6 to 1811—13, but his name certainly does not appear. But
Mr. Addison tells me that the prize-lists generally have been found
not free from mistakes and omissions."

often paced, has lost its primitive Gothic air
altogether," by reason of a new building. "The
severi religio loci hardly lingers where it reigned."
In the so-called gardens (where Frank fought a
duel with Rashleigh Osbaldistone in "Rob Roy")
there were no flowers, but flowers of soot.
" The queer old lofty tenements, with small
garden courts, and occasionally a few fine stately
trees in front of them," have long ceased to
be. Doubtless the whole quarter was much less
smoky, dingy, greasy, and squalid in Lockhart's
days.

Mr. Gleig quotes from Professor Rainy early
reminiscences of Lockhart at Glasgow College.
Dr. Rainy made his acquaintance in 1805. He
had just recovered from the illness caused by
suppressed grief, was thin and pale, with feminine
features, untidy, a mocker of dandyism in others,
fond of poetry, averse from games, addicted to satire,
and to caricaturing his professors. These were
Richardson, the Latin Professor, and Young of
the Greek Chair. Richardson was a contributor
to the *Mirror*, edited by Henry Mackenzie, " The
Man of Feeling." Young, according to Lockhart
himself, was "a classical scholar unrivalled in Scotland, a master of Italian literature and of music, an
enthusiast in poetry." This scholar was not wholly
wasted on boys of twelve, he had " the art to in-
spire juvenile auditors with his own delight in the
visions of genius, as well as in the anatomy of their

records, to the minutest tint and refinement of word
and syntax."[1]

Young had " an extraordinary physiognomy, ...
a picturesque profusion of grey hairs, a brisk-look-
ing little pigtail, an enormous striped waistcoat,
and never-failing Hessian boots," all of which, and
" the sharp, shrewd, knowing, inquisitive, hair-
splitting look," a contrast to the high, melancholy,
earnest enthusiasm of the face in other moods,
Lockhart's pencil must have found attractive and
baffling.

Richardson "wore grand black satin breeches
and buckles, and sea-green or snuff-coloured silk
stockings with gorgeously-wrought clocks. He
had a delicate rosy complexion, a beautifully curled
white wig with a noble toupee in front, and a
ponderous queue behind." He was delightfully
courtierlike in manner, could " make young people
and small people happy," and he and Young were
called Billy and Cocky by their affectionate pupils.
It was the day of periwigs, cocked hats, pointed
canes, ruffled wrist-bands, prodigious Provosts, and
rum punch ; an age of Glasgow convivialities, on
which Lockhart, as a young man, made some cheerful observations.

More reminiscences of Lockhart at Glasgow
were supplied to Mr. Gleig by the Rev. Dr. Smith,
an Edinburgh clergyman. Dr. Smith, as a boy, a
bejant, or freshman, made Lockhart's acquaintance

[1] *Quarterly Review*, lxxxv. p. 37.

in his father's house, in Charlotte Street, at the
north-west corner of Glasgow Green. On October
10, 1806, the *bejants* went trembling to College.
Seeing Lockhart, whom he knew, Master Smith
wished to seat himself on the same form, but was
forcibly ejected by Master Harry Rainy, already
quoted. The truth was that Lockhart, Rainy, and
Cooper had determined to keep their bench sacred
to the sons of the ministry. On finding that
Master Smith's father was a minister, Master Rainy
received him with open arms, and the bench retained its unbroken character. Lockhart's pencil
was not idle, and he sketched Professor Young on
Master Smith's Livy. He was not fond of fights
with the town boys, miniature town and gown
rows : his amusement was to collect and recite street
ballads. As for his studies, in the Logic lecture
(a logician of thirteen) he " suddenly outstripped his
competitors." According to Dr. Rainy, he obtained
the second prize in the Junior Latin Class. The
prizes then, as I believe now, were awarded
by the votes of the students. They decided
according to the performances of each man, when
put on to construe, and by his success in answering
questions addressed to the class in general. It
used to be curious to observe the eagerness of the
ambitious on these occasions. Nothing could
possibly be fairer and more impartial than the
voting, and the system, though odd, certainly kept
up the attention of the pupils. According to Dr.

Rainy, Lockhart was disappointed by his second place, and his backers bought for him a well-bound copy of " The Lay of the Last Minstrel," one of his special favourites. This was presented to him publicly, on the closing day of the session, by Professor Richardson. Lockhart, who knew nothing of the matter beforehand, "was deeply moved. This little incident shows that, among his fellow-students, Lockhart was not only respected but loved."

There are two prizes, medals, at Glasgow, called The Greek and Latin Blackstones. A student "professes," or takes up, so many Greek or Latin authors, and is closely examined in them *viva voce*. The professor is examiner, and decides the prize. The competitors take their seats in turn, in a curious antique chair, with an hour-glass in the back, and with a seat of stone. This stone was probably, Mr. Gleig thinks, originally a "symbol of infeftment," accompanying an old charter conveying lands to the College.[1]

Lockhart's list of books was unusually long. His brother, the Rev. Lawrence Lockhart (later

---

[1] The author may be excused for mentioning two incidents of this examination in his own day. In the Latin Blackstone, a student, (*not* the winner) translated a phrase in Juvenal, "the screaming fathers." "What is the Latin for screaming, Mr. ——?" asked Professor Ramsay. "*Squalentes*, sir, *squalentes patres*, the squalling fathers." In the Greek Blackstone Professor Lushington handed his own Æschylus to a spectator, and examined without book, calling the competitors' attention to such grammatical expressions and turns of phrase as he thought desirable, a singular proof of his great memory.

of Milton Lockhart), says that, on arriving at
College after the vacation, he heard how a senior
student, a third year's man in Greek, proposed
making "a stunning profession." Lockhart, therefore, mastered the same books, and was successful.
He afterwards looked on this as "a shabby trick,"
for his opponent, had he known what Lockhart
was about, might have made a larger "profession."
But a brother of the vanquished said, "It was quite
fair, we never blamed him for it." "John, on my
telling him this, was much delighted," says Mr.
Lawrence Lockhart. Probably the examining professor was guided rather by the quality of the
work done, than by the quantity of the work
"taken up."[1]

Lockhart's success in the Blackstone settled his
career. He was offered, "quite unexpectedly," one
of the Snell Exhibitions, founded long before by
John Snell, Esq., for Glasgow students going to
Balliol. In the author's time, and now, the Snell
Exhibitions are the rewards of an examination in
written work, like scholarships at Oxford. The
income used to be about £105 per annum, a great
assistance to the purse of a Scottish parent, and
doubtless was more, when only one exhibition was
given, not two, as in later times. The exhibition has
been held by many distinguished men, as Sir William

---

[1] It is not in the author's recollection that the winners in his own
day (Thomas Shute Robertson, Esq., and Henry Craik, Esq., C.B.,
both later of Balliol,) made a single slip in their Blackstones.

Hamilton, Adam Smith, and Professor Sellar. It does not carry the privilege or burden of a scholar's or open exhibitioner's gown. Lockhart's parents hesitated to accept the prize on account of his youth, (he was not yet fifteen !). However they decided to accept, and, like Mr. Jowett, the future Master, Lockhart went up in a round schoolboy's jacket. He came to a Balliol then small, almost obscure, by no means noted for excellence in the schools, but retaining its old buildings, its chapel with the beautiful glass and Jacobean panelling, and fortunate in reckoning among its tutors, Mr. Jenkyns, "the Old Master," who really made the Balliol of to-day. We know not where Lockhart's rooms were, but Southey's, he says, were in Rat's Castle, a dilapidated old pile in the inner quadrangle.

Such are the brief records of Lockhart's childhood and boyish days. We see him with a character already formed, shy, affectionate, stoical as a Red Indian, proud, quick, industrious when he chooses to work, humorous, melancholy, mischievous, a lover of poetry, an admirer of that great man with whom his fortunes were to be linked, and whose life he was to chronicle.

CHAPTER II

IT was to an Oxford and a Balliol very unlike those of our time that Lockhart took his way, and by a very different and more expensive mode of travelling. In "Reginald Dalton" he describes the drive from Carlisle to Oxford, in "one of the largest and heaviest, but also one of the gayest and gaudiest, of all possible stage-coaches. It bore the then all-predominant name of the hero of Trafalgar, and blazing daubs of Neptunes, Bellonas, and Britannias illuminated every panel that could be spared from a flourishing catalogue of inns and proprietors."

A "beer-faced conductor" patronised the ale

offered, in a foaming can, by the rural waiting
wench, wherever the "Admiral Nelson" stopped. A
senior man, going up to Christ Church, would take
the reins, and perhaps cause one of these collisions
in which, at least, "you know where you are,"
while, in a railway accident, "where are you?"
"There is always some one either to laugh *with*
or *at* . . . . and you have excellent meals three
times a day, and snowy sheets every night. . . . .
We never hear the horn blowing without envy-
ing those that are setting out,—above all, those
that, like our friend Reginald, are starting for the
first time."

So we may imagine Lockhart starting, "eager-
hearted as a boy when first he leaves his father's"
manse. He was obviously impressed most of all
by "the richest, and perhaps grandest too, of all
earthly prospects, a mighty English plain," when,
following the route of Prince Charles, "he saw it in
all its perfection from the hill of Haynam, that spot
where Charles Edward, according to local tradition,
stood below a sycamore, and gazing with a feeling
of admiration which even rising despair could not
check, uttered the pathetic exclamation, 'Alas! this
is England!'"

It was not the Prince who despaired, nor the men
who sharpened their claymores at Derby, and who
would have followed him to death or victory, had
their chiefs not flinched. So Lockhart may have
mused on the scene of lost opportunity. However,

he probably forgot that sad memory, in the bustle
of the road, "the charming airy country towns,"
"the filthy large towns with manufactories and
steam engines," "the stately little cities, with the
stately little parsons walking about them, two or
three abreast, in well-polished shoes, and blameless
silk aprons, some of them ; and grand old churches,
and spacious well-built *closes*, and trim gardens ;
and literary spinsters," such as Miss Anna Seward,
in Lichfield. Like his hero, Reginald, Lockhart
visited the house where Samuel Johnson's father
sold books, "and walked half a mile further, on
purpose to see the willow which surly Sam himself
planted in Tetsy's daughter's garden." He met the
"men" going up, talking of "Classes, the Newdi-
gate, Coplestone's pamphlets, and the B.N.C.
Eight-oar," for already that distinguished College
was famed on the river.

In the "Admiral Nelson" fared "the young tutors,
in tight stocking pantaloons and gaiters, endeavouring to show how completely they can be easy, well-
bred, well-informed men of the world," or unbending
to sing the All Souls' ditty of "the Swapping,
Swapping Mallard." Before reaching Oxford,
Lockhart may have heard, as his hero does, about
his own college tutors, especially the recluse with
whom, a solitary pupil, Sir William Hamilton read
for a short time, "the most learned man in all our
college, but he lives retired."

To the picture of a first journey to Oxford, as

drawn in "Reginald Dalton," we may add the sketch in an early letter home (Oct. 21, 1810).

"MY DEAR FATHER,—I have the pleasure of informing you that I arrived here last night, about twelve o'clock, in all the safety that you could wish. I wrote from Macclesfield, the stage on this side Manchester, but I had not time then to inform you of any of the particulars of my journey. From Glasgow to Manchester I had the company of Charles Hagen, Doctor of Philosophy, and Professor of Agriculture in the University of Koenigsberg : Mr. Plau, a merchant in Memel, &c. : and a Cumberland traveller of whom I know nothing. Mr. Plau came with me so far as Birmingham, but I know nothing of my other companions from Manchester to Birmingham, except that one was a Welsh student, who *more patrio* wore a Welsh wig, and a Londoner of very dignified appearance, who passed himself off for a personage of no small dignity.

"I had every reason to be well pleased with my journey and everything concerning it. Upon the whole I was very much amused, and derived not only amusement but a great deal of instructive information from my two continental companions, both of whom have favoured me and all my friends with an invitation to take up our residence with them whenever we happen to visit their respective cities.

" I have just been drinking tea with Jenkyns"
(later Master of Balliol), "who is exceedingly gracious, and desires to be particularly remembered to
you all.   Hamilton " (Sir William) "has been in
college all summer, has read through Aristotle's
Organon, and all the works of Hippocrates.   I wish
I could say that I had done as much, but I hope to
make up for my idle summer by my diligent winter.
I need not bid you write, for you know your letters
are my greatest comfort in my progress.   My
travelling expenses were exactly £10 after I left
you.—Ever your affectionate and dutiful son,

                                   " J. G. LOCKHART."

To return to the old coaching days as described
in " Reginald Dalton."   At last, they drive into
Oxford, "everything wearing the impress of a
grave, peaceful stateliness—hoary towers, antique
battlements, airy porticoes, majestic colonnades,
lofty poplars and elms, . . . wide, spacious, solemn
streets, . . . everywhere a monastic stillness and
Gothic grandeur."   Alas, in the words of minstrel
Burne, which Lockhart liked to quote, alas!—

            " To see the changes of this age
            Which fleeting Time procureth ! "

We may readily imagine how fair Oxford seemed
after the black quadrangle and heavy air of Glasgow.
In one of October's crystal days, with the elms not

yet stripped of their gold, and with the crimson pall of red leaves swathing the towers of Magdalene, Oxford looks almost as beautiful as in the pomp of spring. To the freshman care is unknown, and the shadow of the schools does not overcast his new liberty.

Lockhart, in his novel, makes his hero fall in with a town and gown row, such as his own soul delighted not in, also with a Catholic Scottish priest, Father Leslie, sketched from a friend of his own. The priest had been out in the '45, according to the novel; if he really fought for the Prince he must have been a very old man in 1809, but many of the Highland army were boys. In any case Father Leslie could remember how "the Honourable James Talbot was tried in an English court, tried like a felon, for being in Catholic orders," and "good Mr. Maloney was sentenced to perpetual imprisonment because he pleaded guilty." The novel introduces us also to the actual Balliol recluse, with "the meagre extenuated hand," who read no modern and few English books, who saw no newspapers, and had no pupil but Lockhart's senior and friend, William Hamilton, not yet recognised as baronet. Lockhart shows us also the large dining-room in the Master's lodgings, still extant, and very familiar, not only to Balliol men, but to Mr. Jowett's many guests from all quarters. The Master's surroundings, his parrot and poodle, gown, "grand canonicals and grizzle-wig," may not have been those of Dr. Parsons, the actual head, but these details help to mark the differences in costume and manners between our Oxford and that of 1809.

The boy who came up to Balliol in 1809 did not, of course, enter the huge, polyglot, cosmopolitan college which Balliol has become. Except the Scotch set, in which he chiefly lived, the men were not industrious, nor perhaps much distinguished, as a rule, in any way. The modern activity is the result of the exertions of Dr. Jenkyns (Lockhart's tutor), of Dr. Scott, and of Mr. Jowett. Lockhart's friends were Mr. J. H. Christie (and a better friend no man ever had), Mr. James Traill, of the old Orcadian family (father of Mr. Traill, the well-known and accomplished living wit), Mr. Alexander Scott, a son of Scott of Benholme, and Mr. Alexander Nicoll, later Regius Professor of Hebrew, and Canon of Christ Church. Archdeacon Williams ("Caradoc," "Taffey," and so forth), who performed Sir Walter's funeral service, the Rev. G. R. Gleig (Chaplain General to the Forces), and Sir William Hamilton were also among Lockhart's intimates.

All Lockhart's undergraduate companions except Scott, who died early, and Sir William Hamilton, remained his close and constant friends for life. From Sir William Hamilton alone he was estranged, for some reason which neither could ever bear to mention. Yet in Hamilton, Lockhart never lost interest ; both "retained," says Professor Veitch, Sir William's biographer, "warm feelings towards each other." "I know not what miserable provincial differences ultimately broke their friendship," says Mr. Christie.[1] The estrangement must apparently have occurred before the writing of "Peter's Letters" (1819), in which Sir William Hamilton is not mentioned. "Lockhart more than once began to tell me the story, but the subject was too painful to him, and he always broke off without finishing. Hamilton, as far as I know, was the only friend that Lockhart ever lost, but his admiration and his real affection for him, I well know, never ceased."[2] The cause of estrangement, according to Mr. Lawrence Lockhart, was trivial : a hasty word of Hamilton's.

This is very strong testimony to Lockhart's power of gaining affection, and to his own loyalty. The man is indeed both true-hearted and fortunate, whom neither death bereaves, nor temper or circumstance deprives, of these friends who made the happiness of his youth, and with whose memory, when death divides us, it is dearer to dwell than in

---

[1] "Memoir of Sir William Hamilton," p. 40.

[2] So writes Christie, who knew Lockhart for forty years. Miss Martineau, who did not know Lockhart, avers that his friendships "were formed in flattery, and broken off by treachery. . . . Free and constant friendship he never enjoyed, nor seemed to desire"—("Biographical Sketches," pp. 349–350). This was published as soon as Lockhart was dead. Mr. Charles Sumner is in the same tale. "Lockhart has not a friend," he writes in his correspondence.

the society of the living.　For they are never to be replaced,—although

> "The primrose yet is dear,
> The primrose of the later year
> As not unlike the flower of spring."

Among these Balliol friends, the central friendship was quadrilateral, as in Dumas's famous novel. There was Lockhart, "the Hidalgo," who might stand for Athos; the clerical Williams was the amatory Aramis of the four, and, if Traill was the Porthos, Christie was the d'Artagnan of the little band.　It is touching to see how, throughout life, they who had met as boys at Balliol stood by each other in good and evil, "fall back, fall edge," ever helpful, loyal, and united.

In the *Quarterly Review*, vol. cxvi. pp. 447–449, Mr. Christie thus describes Lockhart :—

"I first saw our common friend John Lockhart at Balliol College, in, I think, the year 1809, I being his senior at the college by one year, and two years his senior in age.　But we were both boys; for I, the elder of the two, had not completed my seventeenth year.　At that age we are not critical observers of character ; we judge of those with whom we associate by the pleasure we take in their companionship, and look no further.　But I recollect that Lockhart was an excellent Greek and Latin scholar when he came to college, and immediately made his general talents felt by his tutor and by his companions.　His most remarkable charac-

teristic, however, was the exuberant animal spirits
which found vent in constant flashes of merriment,
in season and out of season, brightened and pointed
with wit and satire, at once droll and tormenting.
Even a lecture-room was not exempt from these
irrepressible sallies, and our tutor, who was formal
and wished to be grave, but had not the gift of
gravity, never felt safe or at ease in the presence of
his mercurial pupil.

"Lockhart with great readiness comprehended
the habits and tone of the new society in which he
was placed, and was not for a moment wanting in
any of its requirements; but this adaptive power
never interfered with the marked individuality of
his own character and bearing. He was at once a
favourite and formidable; his tongue and his pen
were alike ready, and both employed for merriment
and keen satire. In those days he was an incessant
caricaturist; his papers, his books, and the walls of
his rooms were covered with portraitures of his
friends and himself—so like as to be unmistakable,
with an exaggeration of any peculiarity so droll and
so provoking as to make the picture anything but
flattering to the self-love of its subject. This pro-
pensity was so strong in him, that I was surprised
when in after life he repressed it at once and for
ever. In the last thirty years of his life I do not
think he ever drew a caricature. In those days—I
mean in college days—he was a frequent writer of
verses, sometimes in Latin, sometimes in English,
and not unfrequently in both. Though Lockhart

partook with thorough relish of all the pleasures and amusements of an undergraduate, he was far from neglecting the proper business of the place. He was always a diligent reader—made himself thoroughly acquainted with the Greek Theatre, Homer, Pindar, Herodotus, and Thucydides. I mention these, because his diligent and careful study of them fell under my own personal knowledge—not as stating the limits of his acquaintance with Greek literature. He was, in fact, an excellent classical scholar, and also read French, Italian, and Spanish in the days of which I now speak : German was a later acquisition. He was curious in classical and also in British antiquities, and much attached to heraldic and genealogical questions. I think his first publication was an article on heraldry, in the ' Edinburgh Encyclopædia.' County histories were favourite reading with him. I remember his telling me of his being placed at dinner by an American lady, who explained to him that her husband (a gentleman of good position in the States) was descended from an ancient Scotch family of great distinction. 'Little,' said he, ' did the worthy lady suspect that I was a good enough Scotch genealogist to know that her husband's name was never borne by any gentleman's family in Scotland.'

" But though Lockhart was an excellent scholar and a man of great and various knowledge, he was not, I apprehend, what would be called 'a learned man.' We had only one learned man in our (in those days) small college : I mean the late Sir

William Hamilton. He was already pursuing those studies which ultimately gave him a high place among those who dwell in the higher regions of learned speculation."

On December 4, 1809, Lockhart praises Hamilton, in a letter to his mother :—

" MY DEAR MOTHER,—Since I wrote last, nothing, I am afraid, has occurred here worth the telling you. I still continue to like this place much better than I could have expected, and, indeed, as well as I could any situation whatever, which places me at a distance from my best and dearest friends. The first term of my Oxonian course ends to-morrow or next day. The six weeks have fled over my head since I came here, and I can assure you, on looking back, they appear to be hardly equal to so many hours. We have next the prospect of a six weeks' vacation, during which, if we except attendance on Mr. Jenkyns' lectures, no change whatever will take place in my mode of spending my time.

" Most of my English acquaintances leave college next week for a considerable time, and I must say that I shall have some reason to regret their absence, though the best friend I have got here, Mr. Hamilton, is more to me than all the rest put together ten times over, and I am happy to say he does not intend to be more than a few days with his mother in London during this vacation. I am just expecting a long letter from Lawrence and

Johnnie, and if they knew how happy every letter from home makes me, I am persuaded they would not delay the fulfilment of their promises.

"Yesterday the Sacrament was dispensed here. Mr. Jenkyns had a little conversation with me, according to papa's desire, in the morning. In answer to his request that I should say something about the sermons here, I have to tell you that the only sort of religious instruction which I think at all worth attending to is, the two lectures on the Creed, which Mr. Mouseley (? Mozley) gives every Saturday and Sunday evening in the chapel. They are, on the whole, excessively good and sensible; as for the sermons in St. Mary's, I think there is hardly one good out of ten. We had one last Sunday on the Catholic Bill, and another the day before on the Greek of Augustine!

"Mr. Jenkyns also lectures to us a little on the Sunday forenoons, but I am sorry to say milk and water are the articles which chiefly compose his instructions, though, I am sure, he is really a good man, and has been as yet exceedingly kind to me. I have dined once and drunk tea once at Mr. Ireland's—he is very kind and polite. He made me a very obliging offer of supplying me with money if I at any time should stand in need of his assistance in that way. Certainly his family is as original a picture as one could see. . . .

"Hamilton expects his brother Tom down to spend a few days this week. . . . If he be as agreeable as his brother we shall have a very pleasant time of it.[1] . . . I hope you will excuse this desultory scrawl, as I am very much pressed with some troublesome analyses.—Believe me, your ever affectionate and dutiful son,   JOHN G. LOCKHART."

On February 20, 1810, he writes to a Glasgow collegian :—

" I mentioned in my letters already that the Scotchmen now are not in general so much to my mind as the others—the fact is, if I except myself and two others, they are all connected with the Episcopal Church of Scotland, and a great deal more bigoted than any Englishman I have yet met with. Edinburgh and Glasgow they view in no other light than as so many nurses of infidelity and scepticism. They are all very civil to me, however, and I am very happy with one of them, a son of M'Farlane, the Bishop of Ross. I rather think you will remember a son of Cocky's—John Young—who was an exhibitioner in this college, and has now a curacy in Yorkshire. I met with him here very often in the month of December, and think him a very pleasant man indeed. His father has always behaved to him with his accustomed sourness, and I daresay he is very ill off, with a small salary of £80 or so, for not a farthing will the old boy give him, although we all know that with his wife's portion,

[1] Tom Hamilton, author of " Cyril Thornton ; " the original Ensign O'Doherty in *Blackwood*.

&c., &c., he might spare him a good deal more than he would require. Dr. Hutchinson's son is a curate in Norfolkshire, and esteemed stark mad by every man in Oxford. He made his appearance here at the election, and behaved in a most absurd manner. The truth is, there cannot be a more foolish thing than for any Scotchman in ordinary circumstances to enter into the English Church. If he does, he has little chance for any better lot than a chapel in Scotland or a curacy in England. All college preferment (and in many instances a great deal of patronage, vested in the Master and Fellows) is greedily swallowed up by those who have it to dispose of, and it would be a thing quite contrary to etiquette to make a Scotchman a Fellow. Their reason for this, they say, is, that such is the known partiality all Scotchmen have for their own country, that if they once got a footing in any college they would elect none but Scotchmen, and the whole power would shortly be confined to them.

"Nearly half of the time is now spent during which I must remain here. I have spent it much more happily than I could have expected, but I must now begin to be very anxious for the month of July. . . . —Yours affectionately,

"J. G. LOCKHART."

Scotch Fellows are no longer ruled out at Balliol, where the Master himself is a Scot of distinction (1896).

Lockhart's earliest known letter from Oxford was dated November 1, 1809. With the usual bad luck of his early correspondence it seems no longer to be extant, though, in 1869, extracts from it, and from several other epistles from Oxford, were published in Mr. Veitch's "Life of Sir William Hamilton."[1] Lockhart says "to his father," (?) "I don't know how I should have managed here at all had it not been for W. Hamilton." Six years his senior in age, and considerably his senior in standing, Hamilton, says Lockhart, "has behaved to me with all the affection of a brother. Since papa left us I have been always with him or he with me, at breakfast, tea, &c. He makes me carry over my book after evening prayers, and read it beside him all night,"—quiet work for a freshman. Hamilton advised him as to his associates, advised him in the purchase of books, and against attending balls given "to country Jennies."

In November 1810 Lockhart chronicles Hamilton's success in the schools. According to Mr. Gleig, there was a time when Lockhart took to hunting (as we might guess from "Reginald Dalton"), and probably spent a good deal of money with the Charley Symonds of the period. Hamilton remonstrated, and communicated with Dr. Lockhart, thus "diverting his friend from pursuits which might have spoiled such a nature as his." He even joined a boat club, as every one does now, but

[1] Of these letters only one is known to the biographer.

he does not seem to have been distinguished on the river, and his letters to Mr. Christie say nothing about hunting.

In "Reginald Dalton" Lockhart describes fast life at Oxford, the dinner in hall, anything but fast; the gorging of periwigged Dons (how unlike the ascetic meal of the modern high table at Balliol!); the wine in a man's rooms,—"from eighteen to twenty-two is the prime of a man's life as far as the bottle is concerned;" the "sconcing" in a silver fox-head cup, the supper of oysters and brawn; the bowl of bishop, and the final heroic feat of blocking up the chapel gate with a cart-load of coals,—they used snow in the biographer's time.

This was an out-college man's wine. Lockhart's letters tell of no such achievements, but the public expects riot in a University novel. One St. Andrew's Day he does commemorate, in a letter to Christie, then at Bristol :—

"BALLIOL, *Monday.*

"MY DEAREST CHRISTIE,—I thought to have answered your letter by our friend Tom Cornish, but a paucity of the ready detains him here, so I shall send down songs (and what not?) by him, but must allow myself to describe our St. Andrew's Eve—I forget minutiæ. I believe we went there individually without any great expectations as to the matter of fun. For (old Leslie, Hamilton, Baillie, yourself, and the Traills being gone—besides

Annan, who was hurried to London that very day, and Hannay, whom nobody missed), we looked out in reality for an evening of port and dulness. But *di meliora*. A man named Taylor of Brazennose came there, and M'Donald, and MacGowan of University ; and *Jack* Jenkyns, to make a display of his boarding-school-governess sort of authority, issued his mandate against dining in college ; so we took to Dickesons',—where nine men had a famous dinner for the small sum of £8, 8s. We went on with great harmony till about eight o'clock. Taylor, who is a bachelor and a true blue, proposed drinking in solemn silence this toast, 'The illustrious memory of the greatest champion of Scottish liberty, civil and religious,—the Rev. John Knox, minister of the gospel in the Tolbooth Kirk, Edinburgh.' Jack looked blue, and harangued *talis*. 'Sir' (on his legs)—'I hope, sir, I have lived long enough, sir, in the world to drink out of respect to you the devil—if you give it. But, sir, I would rather drink all the devils in hell than John Knox, who dung down the cathedral kirks and braw houses of all the Bishops in Scotland. For, sir, I, though not a member of this University, in so high a situation as the other members of this glorious assembly—I am an antiquarian—a very lover of antiquities! *Yet* I will drink John Knox, if you on this insist.'

" Taylor replied, and after rejoinders, replies, and replications unnumbered, changed his toast to ' The

Brigs of Ayr.' My turn came, and I gave 'The memory of the Prince,'[1] and I understand, spoke upon him and the merits of his cause with un- bounded applause—for I forgot all this in the morning. And the whole party drunk this upon their knees, and Jack reeled home, and so did we all, about half-past eleven.

" Nicoll went off at half-past seven crying—

' Oh me when shall I sober me ! '

" Tom can expatiate on all these things.

" I heard from Hamilton the other day, he is reading law at Edinburgh."

A prank played by Lockhart on a tutor is remembered and recorded by Mr. Gleig in his *Quarterly* article. The worthy tutor made a show of Oriental knowledge, so Lockhart wrote some English squibs on him in Hebrew characters, and handed them in as college exercises. The tutor did not discover the fraud, but the Master did. The pupil was once set, as an imposition, a long chapter in the *Spectator*, to do into Latin. This he accom- plished at great speed, neither missing lecture nor depriving himself of his amusements. He once mentions being " crossed " thrice, crossed in hall and buttery, so that he was cut off from meat and drink. Men were usually " crossed " if they

---

[1] The Prince Charles Edward Stuart.

failed to attend the Dean when "drawn." The old
English custom of drawing (or "hauling") is conducted under the following rules: You do not
attend chapel, or lecture, or you commit some similar
offence. The Dean then sends the messenger
for you, and he draws you, if he can, and you go
before the Dean, and there make such excuses for
your sins as circumstances dictate, or fancy suggests. But if you, detecting the approach of the
messenger, sport your oak, or hide in a cupboard
or under a table, he cannot legally draw you, but
returns *bredouillé*. The Dean's next move is to
cross you, and starve you into submission, and if
that fails, he can "gate" you. Such are the conditions of crosses, and in accumulating three at once
Lockhart gives proof of a certain lack of discipline.

Of ladies' society he probably saw very little :
nobody did in Oxford till recently. He did not
care for what he did see at parties where the men
wore cap and gown, and played cards (the Dons,
that is) in enormous wigs and flowing bands.
The fair were either elderly, or had learned "cold
cautiousness" by many transitory flirtations. In
"Peter's Letters" Lockhart talks of "spending all the
mornings after lecture in utter lounging, eating ice
at Jubb's, flirting with Miss Butler, bathing in the
Cherwell." After dinner (for which, at Merton at
least, they dressed) men drank wine in the gardens,
and then took a boat "at Mother Hall's," and rowed
improvised races to Iffley, or Sandford. Cheese

and bread, and lettuces, with a bowl of bishop (mulled port), were the modest supper. Cricket was not what it is now : there was no University match. Runs across country, with leaping poles, were a common amusement. Hamilton once rigged up a perfectly normal and "supraliminal" ghost, visible to the least sensitive, with a skull and a sheet.

Studious men read very widely and freely, especially in Aristotle and Greek philosophy at large. Lockhart also studied English, the Elizabethans in particular, Italian, French, German, and Spanish. In fact, he qualified himself for the profession of letters in a manner now very unusual. His knowledge was already such as befits a critic.

Mr. Gleig says, on the authority of Mr. Lawrence Lockhart—but the scantiness of Lockhart's correspondence does not illustrate the subject—that he wished to join the Spanish in their struggle against the French. He even offered to take Anglican orders, and go out as a chaplain, if his father would consent. But Dr. Lockhart had a son in the army already, and refused his permission. Lockhart's distaste for arms was confined to those of the flesh, which are used at town and gown rows.

The following letter to his mother displays no martial sympathy for Spain, or for Mr. Gleig, who did take up arms in the Iberian cause :—

AN OLD HAND AT THE COCKPIT, OXFORD

(From a Water-Colour Drawing by J. G. Lockhart.)

[Postmark, *Dec.* 3, 1812.]

" MY DEAR MOTHER,—. . . My life goes on in the old way—to which I am now quite accustomed, and in which I believe I may be as happy as I am capable of being anywhere, unless when certain homeward-formed recollections obtrude on the privacy. My summer sojourn here has, I hope, been very useful to me. I have acquired the Italian, Spanish, and Portuguese languages ; the two former so as to read with the utmost ease, and the last more slightly, only from the want of books ; and I am now busily engaged in Greek and Latin for my examination. I have already read everything which I mean to take up, but must do this often before I venture. . . . Who is likely to succeed Gleig here ? That gentleman has embarked into the military life, by grasping at a pair of colours in the 3rd garrison battalion, stationed at the Cove of Cork.—Believe me, as ever, your affectionate dutiful son,

" J. G. L.

" Balliol, *Nov.* 28."

Here is a rather earlier epistle :—

[Postmark, Oxford, *Oct.* 3] 1812.

" MY DEAREST MOTHER,—I would have been un-willing to delay writing to some of you so long, but have put off day by day in the expectation of letters from you. . . . Our term commences this day fort-

night, and Jenkyns has already made his appearance.
I have no pleasure in the prospect, for excepting
one or two friends, for whom I have every reason
to entertain the most sincere affection, few places
contain so few desirable to me as Balliol. At
present we have nothing here but electioneering in
all its glories—you are happily spared all such
spectacles in the North. A namesake of ours, a
glib lawyer—a silly country gentleman, who is just
about to complete his folly by a hopeless effort—a
young noble in the Marlborough interest, and a
worthy Burdettite, summoned hither by the suf-
frages of a few blackguards, are the four candidates,
and among them they continue at least to din our
ears day and night with drums and fifes, and
drunken halloos.

"I was not a little astonished to see advertised,
in the end of the last *Edinburgh Review*, 'Documents in favour of the Rev. D. D., junr., St. Cuthbert's, as touching the late election for a Hebrew
Professor in Edinburgh.' Mr. Murray, who has
succeeded, I have long heard mentioned as absolutely one of the very first Oriental scholars in
Europe. Could the fat descendant of the ———
be so presuming as to stand against such a man on
the strength of a little ill-digested Greek and Latin,
and about as much Hebrew, I daresay, as his
Aunty Betty? O vanity! If I might quote Latin
to you, *Ne sutor*, &c. Let Mr. Davy stick to the
West Kirk, and the auld wifies, and the *Religious*

Monitor. But Hebrew professorships, worthy man! I beg you would, by some means, contrive among you to let me hear a little more frequently from you; and when you do write, I wish you would give me more domestic news. I am very sure Lawrence's marrow bones need not prevent him from finding abundance of time to write me, at least every fortnight.—Yours most affectionately,

"J. G. L."

Of Lockhart's letters from Oxford, very few seem to be extant, and most of these are addressed to Mr. Christie. The date is seldom given, and the post-mark is usually illegible. In 1812 he writes— "I am going on gloriously with the Italian. I expect in about a week to attack Ariosto; meantime I have read several novels of Boccaccio and Macchiavel, and am now at the 'Del Principe' of the latter, which certainly is one of the most wonderful productions I ever read. . . . Our races are going on, but it is wet, and I could see nothing so well worth looking at as Nancy Hodges."

From Balliol (no date) he complains of Christie's absence. "Perhaps Knight is with you. Heavens! a small degree of Germanic sentimentality would be enough to make me crazy at the idea. You two, talking, spouting, scandalising, discussing and debating, and reading Southey—I, pining in a corner, without one soul worth twopence within a mile of me, that is, except Nicoll. . . . I make myself very busy, and verily believe that I shall say, *olim, ' meminisse juvat.' "*

If we possessed more of Lockhart's letters to his family, written during his residence at Oxford, or his letters to Hamilton, after Hamilton went down, many details might be added to the story of his college life.   But eighty years after date, the epistles of a man's salad days are hard to come by.   They must usually contain much the same sort of matter, records of work and play, of freaks and friendships, of studies, literary tastes, aspirations towards the future.   We do see Lockhart, by instinct, qualifying himself to be, what he became, a man of letters. His linguistic studies were wide, perhaps in modern Oxford unexampled.   The language and literature of the Latin races are now little read in Oxford, with the exception of French.   The new organisation of examinations is thought to discourage wide general reading, and to make a man the slave of his note-book, the echo of a tutor's or a coach's lectures.   In some opinions this restriction is little more than an excuse made by students who have no instinctive bent towards letters.   But in Lockhart's time men were certainly left more to themselves, and were less fretted with lectures, examinations, college exercises.   Lockhart excuses himself to Christie as a bad correspondent by reason of the scarcity of writing materials.

"It is not so easy to supply oneself with such things at a moment's notice, as it is when a hundred careless *divils* like yourself leave open doors. But now I need not say with what unpillageable neighbours I have to do, and this beautiful sheet, natty pen, and delightful Japan ink, are borrowed, *aperto die*, from that superabundant store of stationery dedicated to the manufacture of the 'Theatrum Naturæ.'

"Oh how I sympathise with all your groans! I wish the 'Miseries' had never been written" (he refers to a then popular work on the minor Miseries of Life). "You and I might have done famously as Sensitive and Testy."

He complains that, if he asks Nicoll to tea and talk, Nicoll brings three folios, and remains absorbed in them, asking with an insipid smile, "What puts you out of humour?" so that you have no resource but "sitting in the most joyless state of malignity and spleen."

So here we have an early confession to the truth of that literary commonplace, "the malignity of Lockhart!"

"I don't know what good genius whispered in my ear to begin Italian, but I am sure I owe to him every enjoyment of the last six weeks." This hard-hearted being, in fact, was pining like the poetic dove in the absence of his mate. Bristol, where Christie was living, he illiberally calls "an abominable stinking stye of artisans." "I have read two-thirds of Tasso, and a few cantos of the Inferno, besides several

sonnets of Petrarch.   I am sure if you will just
commence, you will swear that you never read
poetry so bewitching.   Spells and magicians, knights
and damsels, woods, castles, and enchanted palaces
pass before my eyes in such hasty succession that I
am most happily enabled to forget, for hours together,
the many nibbling worthless cares which continue to
render me at times the most miserable of *promeneurs
solitaires.*   My dearest Christie, if you have any
compassion in you, don't let your letters any longer
be, like angels' visits, few and far between.—Yours
most affectionately,

"J. G. LOCKHART."

    The gilded sand is still shining on "the delight-
ful Japan ink" of "these fallen leaves that keep
their green," the letters of the dead, and of the
undying affection.

    On a dateless Saturday of March, Lockhart sends
to Christie "a copy of the 'Gerusalleme Liberata,'
as a small mark of my affection, in the same
manner that Mr. Random presented to Mr. Morgan
his sleeve buttons, and I hope you will, notwithstanding that I don't admire some of Wordsworth's
sonnets so much as you, admire as much as I do
the Italian gentleman."   He announces a friend's
engagement to "Miss Sophy," and declares that
she is too pretty for a single life.   "You will know
that, however delightful it may have been to hear
Greek comedies, or Greek tragedies, acted at Athens

(which fact, like most other things, I take on trust), there is little of fun or ecstasy either in the repeated perusal of these gentlemen's writings nowadays, still less in reading long prosy accounts about skirmishes between armies, which could with difficulty mount even a corporal's guard at St. James's, and least amusement of all, in devouring Commentaries about morality and politics, subjects so much better understood since the days of Christ and the French Revolution."

From these derogatory observations on the great writers of antiquity, he turns to scandal about the Prince Regent and his wife. The schools were clearly drawing nigh, and the note, at least, indicates the books then read for the schools.

Christie seems to have suggested a venture in publishing a magazine at Bristol. But, on hearing that money would be needed, Williams and Nicoll withdrew, and Lockhart remarked that he "already owed more than anything less than a Dowager or a miracle can enable me to discharge. . . .

Hi motus animorum atque haec tentamina tanta
Pulveris exigui jactu compressa quiescunt.

Any mention of coming down with the dust is enough."

In September 1812, Lockhart apprises Christie of the death of Alexander Scott. "We must all be of one mind that for him—afflicted as he was, and good as he was—death was the best fate which his

most tender friends could wish." "Lose no time
in coming up hither," he writes to Christie, ill in
Bristol, "where you may at least have the comfort
of affectionate friends. Your arrival would be to me
a most precious relief, for I am left totally alone,"
the death of his mother having caused Williams to
go home. "This sort of misfortune makes most of
our grievances appear trifles. I am sure to go
home after such an event would be enough to
unman any of us." He again entreats Christie to
come up—"I really consider it altogether impossible
to read much, without a suitable seasoning of talk,
and talk is scarce. . . . I look for Hamilton to be
here in a week or two. Would that we might all
spend a little time, after the furnace is past, in our
old habits, lounging, bathing, port, tea, and then the
long, long nights, and every kind of jaw, palaver,
criticising, laughing, and so forth. My dearest
Christie, do come up, if it is but a month or less,
till you must come here to be examined, and do let
us have the pleasure of your company for that little
space before it." He writes of having received a
visit from Signor Belzoni, whom he did not find
amusing. This, of course, was years before Belzoni's
famous discoveries in Egypt. He chronicles the
vanity of "Cadwallader" (Williams), and his tales
of ladies who fell in love with him "long before *I*
thought of it." Hamilton, he says, has just read
through all the "Scholia" on Homer, and is perus-
ing ancient books on magic. These are an empty

study, but Sir William, in later life, declared that in mesmerism "there is a reality which deserves far more investigation than it has hitherto received at the hands of men of science," and he quotes " Die Seherin von Prevorst," as "a very curious book," which it undeniably is. " He seriously considers it as worth his while," says Lockhart, "to pore over Wierus and Bodinus, and all the believers in witchcraft from St. Augustine downwards." A fellow student *in re magica* may agree with Lockhart, who seems to have had no sympathy for pursuits which attracted Hamilton as they attracted Scott.

One Balliol letter describes a coolness with a friend, followed by too great heat. "He getting fiery insulted me most grossly. I was so fortunate as to keep my temper all the time, and he called on me next morning after breakfast, and made every apology. . . . I confess I thought myself ill-treated —but it shall not be my fault." In fact, this college friendship was only ended by Lockhart's death. " My reading has been such as gains no credit here, for modern literature is here, as you well know, a dead letter." He wishes he could get congenial work, and fears "his good father " thinks him extravagant. He wishes to support himself, while reading for the English bar. Williams has passed a triumphant examination, as Lockhart himself did in 1813. He caricatured the examiners in the schools, but this was not "unparalleled audacity," as Mr. Gleig supposed. The Master and his tutor were

full of congratulations, but there was no chance of a
Fellowship.   Indeed Lockhart is said by legend to
have inscribed, beneath a notice of a Balliol Fellowship Examination—

NO SCOTCH NEED APPLY!

He had, by the end of his nineteenth year,
in which he got his first class, read widely in
the Classics.   His habit of writing "lady's Greek
without the accents" would now be reckoned un-
scholarly ; and, though a rapid and elegant writer
of Latin, he never was a classical scholar in the
strict Oxford, still less in the Cambridge sense.
But he had learned to know the Greek mind, the
Greek thought ; he had been in Armida's bowers,
and had laid, at least, the foundation of his Spanish
and German lore.   Already, it seems, literature was
being contemplated by him, not as the task of a
life, but as a pleasant *gagne-pain* till he had qualified himself for the bar.   He had shown sense and
discretion in his Oxford life—industry, and the
power of making and retaining friends.   His letters
as yet do no justice to his humour, nor have they
the vivacity which we might expect.   A good deal
of young man's banter has been omitted, as in no
way characteristic of his style and fancy.   Hardly
one allusion to politics occurs in the fragments of
his correspondence while at Oxford ; nothing at all
points to any party leanings.   His real interests

were friendships and literature. Like Clough's hero, he

> " Went in his youth and the sunshine rejoicing, to
> Nuneham and Godstowe."

" The first step on arriving at Godstowe," says Mr. Connell (a friend of Lockhart's, later a professor at St. Andrews), " was always to see the eels taken alive out of the boxes with holes in which they were kept in the river. After that, till all was ready, we usually had a match at leaping and vaulting over gates." Both Lockhart and Hamilton were great swimmers at Parson's Pleasure, on the Cherwell.

The happy years before the entry on real life were few in Lockhart's case, but happy they were and well employed. He had won knowledge and won friends. About them, in his surviving letters from Oxford, there is no satire. They compare ill, perhaps, in his affection, with Christie. Christie and he were David and Jonathan, Amis and Amiles. There is a little good-natured banter of the personal vanity of one youth, and more quantity than quality of intellect is ascribed to him. But there is no display of the fangs of the Scorpion.

CHAPTER III

GLASGOW, 1813-1815

Early disadvantages of Lockhart.—His loneliness.—Reflections.—
Letters to Mr. Christie.—The Theatre in London.—Miss
Duncan.—The Schools.—Anecdotes of Scotch clergymen.—The
stool of repentance. — Dulness of Glasgow. — Admiration of
Wordsworth and Byron.—Mr. Christie's projected novel.—
Lockhart's novel.—Scotch manners.—Mediæval studies.—Double
authorship of "Waverley."—"Wattie a fecund fellow."—Lockhart's
own novel postponed.—" Lockhart will *blaze!* "—His neglect of
his own poetical powers. — Sordid ignorance of Glasgow.—
Hamilton and the Humanity Chair in Glasgow.—Lockhart's
novel. — " The Odontist." — Solitude. — Glasgow society. — A
commercial ball.—Count Pulltuski.—" Gaggery."—Dinner with
a dentist.—Caricature of Pulltuski.—Tour after trout.—Scheme
of an "Oxford Olio."—A pun.—Anecdotes of the clergy.—A
Holy Fair.—Lockhart goes to Edinburgh to study law.

To have gained the highest University honours at
the age of nineteen, when most undergraduates are
only entering college, may seem a fortunate beginning of life. But whether it was fortunate in
Lockhart's case is a different question. Long afterwards, in a letter to his son Walter, on the choice
of a profession, Lockhart regrets that he entered
life so young, that his resources were so scanty, and
that he had in his family, and among his friends, no
qualified adviser. The task of such a counsellor

would not, at best, have been easy. At nineteen probably Lockhart should have prolonged his education, by studying at a foreign University. But the continent was closed by war ; moreover, he had not money, as will later be seen. Possibly enough he was paying off College debts.

He had contemplated entering at the English Bar, but, except in his pen, was at a loss for means of support while qualifying. It might, in many ways, have been best for him to go to London. He would have been in contact with the central current of affairs literary, social, and political, in these important and strenuous years. Bonaparte was engaged in his death-struggle with Europe ; he fell, he was exiled, he returned, he was overthrown. Of these events Lockhart, living in Glasgow, writes not one word to Christie in the extant correspond-ence. In literature Byron was pouring out "The Giaour," "Lara," portions of "Childe Harold," and occasional pieces which caused tempests in the *Courier* and the *Chronicle*. He was marrying, quarrelling, separating, making all tongues wag, yet how little Lockhart has to say about the Byronic affairs, apart from "Lara," will be observed. Southey was publishing his "Roderick," and, in Glasgow, Lockhart could not get a sight of "Roderick." Scott produced in one year "Waverley" and "The Lord of the Isles." The former seems to have reached Lockhart late ; the latter does not appear to have engaged his interest. Leigh Hunt was being imprisoned for libelling the Regent, and was working, later, at his "Tale of Rimini." For the moment Lockhart seems unconcerned about Leigh Hunt. Moore was getting £3000 for his "Irish Melodies"; Coleridge was borrowing £100 from Byron, on the strength of "Christabel," which just paid, or might have paid, the debt. So far, Lockhart knew little or nothing of Coleridge; even "The Excursion" reached him late, and "fly-blown by reviews," to use Keats's expression, especially "fly-blown" by Jeffrey with his famous "This will never do."

Thus Lockhart was remote from the mundane movement, after getting his class, and was living in a society which shared none of his interests. He knew little of the men with whom his own name was to be mixed, and he often knew that little wrong, a cause of errors which still hang heavily on his reputation as a critic. When he went to Edinburgh, in 1815, he was affected by the violent prejudices of politics in a small, but intellectually active set, prejudices which were carried into literature. Had Lockhart been able to betake himself to the English Bar, whether he had succeeded there or not, he would have escaped many prejudices, ignorances, and consequent violences. Through his friend Christie he would have become acquainted with John Hamilton Reynolds, the "young one" of whom Byron speaks kindly (Feb. 28, 1814), the author of "Safie," the bosom-friend of Keats. Very probably Lockhart would have been in the set of Keats, Rice, Reynolds, his own friend Gleig, Bailey, and the rest. He might even have been found inditing sonnets to Leigh Hunt, and supping with Lamb, Haydon, and Hazlitt. His politics and his feud with many of these men was an affair of ignorance and accidental associations in Edinburgh. On the other hand, though Lockhart's life might have been more peaceful, and, in literature, more happily productive, had he gone to London, he never would have been, in that case, the son-in-law, the friend, and the biographer of Scott.

We cannot well compute the relative loss and gain, to Lockhart himself, of his very early, financially ill-equipped, and in many respects prejudiced and thwarted entry into life and literature. His whole career was coloured by his beginnings in Edinburgh. The town was then a brilliant rival of London as far as literature was concerned, thanks to Jeffrey, Constable, and Scott. There was plenty of activity, but it was an activity of little political cliques, agitated by violent passions. By the age of twenty-three, Lockhart was "a lion," stared at as he walked the streets, petted and dreaded. All this was unfortunate. Meanwhile, for two or three years after leaving Oxford, Lockhart was poor, lonely, almost aimless, without companions interested in his interests, learning to scorn things and men contemptible enough—to him

too easy a lesson.   Yet, as we shall see, he was
industrious, studious, and fertile in projects.   The
early adviser, whose absence he deplored in later
life, would have had a difficult or impossible task.
It was not well that Lockhart should linger in
Glasgow, nor that Edinburgh should be the scene,
and wild Edinburgh Tories the associates, of his
apprenticeship in literature.   But he could not tax
his father's resources by going abroad, or to
London, and so his fate was fashioned for him,
as for other men, by circumstances.   His letters,
those of a lad of nineteen, do not deserve the
praises later given to his correspondence.   They
illustrate, however, his tastes, his satirical observation, and his mode of life ; moreover they are, at
this time, our only source of information.   It is,
perhaps, an unavoidable reflection that Lockhart's
loneliness, and difficult beginnings, may partly
account for his tendency to a rather hostile attitude, as of one at least on the defensive, and not
prone to welcome all things and all comers with
a smile.   Throughout life we seem to see him, as
it were, on guard, observing all approaches with
the keen, wary eye of the swordsman.

The movements of Lockhart, after he gained his
First Class in the early summer of 1813, are most
easily traced in his letters to Mr. Christie.   As a
rule, he resided with his family at Glasgow (where
he had no society, but plenty of public libraries full
of old books), at Innerkip on the Clyde, in Selkirk-

shire, or wherever Dr. Lockhart passed his vacation. The following letter, dated Glasgow, June
15, 1813, shows that the anxieties of the schools
weighed lightly on Lockhart :—

J. G. LOCKHART *to* J. H. CHRISTIE.

"GLASGOW, *Tuesday,* 15*th June* (1813).

" MY DEAR CHRISTIE,—I hope you will acknowledge the veniality of my neglect in not writing
to you ere I quitted *our Athens* on two grounds.
1st, That I was remarkably hurried during the few
days intervening betwixt my examination and my
departure ; 2ndly, That, notwithstanding all the
hurry, I actually found time to write you a pretty
long epistle, which I committed to the fiery flames
in contrition for the worthlessness thereof. This
second circumstance indeed shows me and my own
modesty in such a charming point of view, that I
cannot doubt they would procure for me the for-
giveness of a heavier offence. I went up to London
with Hamilton, and stayed long enough to see new
Miss Drury, and Rae in 'Octavian.' This actor
is a very fine young man—not accurately handsome,
perhaps, but having a light, graceful, and energetic
figure, with a fine long muscular neck *surmounted*
(to talk *à la* Riddell) by a noble countenance,
shaded with long hair of the most beautiful jet
black. Miss Duncan I saw also. She is married

to a damned gamester, one Davison, and repairs
from his seat in the Fleet to Drury Lane every
evening to get him bread.   When she was in
Scotland last she refused a respectable laird of
£1300 a year, and asserted that she would have
nothing less than a title.   In our passage by sea we
enjoyed all the luxuries of a smack in perfection.

"I have had a letter from Williams this morning
in which the classification is detailed.   However,
Jenkyns is, it seems, to write me with all haste,
a favour similar to what you have, I suppose, by
this time experienced.   I have no earthly thing
to find fault with in all this affair except our
common enemy, your breast complaint, which has, I
perceive, been the sole cause of depriving me of a
double gratification——[1]   I hear Traill has *forsan
proairetically* scalded his leg by way of escaping the
little wrath of our little hero, Jenkyns.   Hamilton
has spent the last two nights with me here, and
went up this morning to his mother's.   I cannot
write to Oxford till my father comes home, and
enables me to discharge some debt contracted before
I came off to Traill.   He is in Selkirkshire, where
I mean shortly to go ; but in the meantime my
mother and the bairns, including Mr. John, are
going to Ayrshire for sea-bathing.   Address for
me nevertheless *here*, and believe me ever, your
most affectionate friend,

                              "J. G. LOCKHART.

---

[1] A couple of lines obliterated by the seal.

"*P.S.*—Hamilton has directed me to make Traill send you down several medical books left behind him, which if you have not already received, you may look for in a short time."

There are not, indeed, many happier resting-places in a literary life than the haven of a First Class, after years of work and anxiety. The benevolent sensation of repose produced in the human mind by the combination of a First Class and a Fellowship is apt to merge into a state of endless lotus-eating. There was no Fellowship for Lockhart, but there was the pleasant western indolence of the Clyde, and the humours of a country parish diverted him. On Sept. 8, 1813, he writes from Innerkip.

"INNERKIP, *8th September* 1813.

"MY DEAR CHRISTIE,—In this place of retirement you will easily perceive what a delightful variety the Caledonian Sabbath, observed *con amore*, must create. The minister of this place owed his promotion to a cause no doubt very common, although seldom so barefacedly exposed to the view of mankind. It seems the last minister left a solitary daughter of eighteen. The patron had great compassion on her light purse, and wrote to her in plain terms, that he referred the appointment of her father's successor entirely to her own judgment. The lady, having caused this munificent offer of the

laird's to circulate on the face of the earth, was
speedily attended by a true Penelopean swarm of
suitors—each eager, by a display of his various
talents, to make his calling and his election sure.
Miss S. very wisely gave the preference to him
who had the broadest back—a very Welshman as
to externals—*toto cœlo* discrepant from our friend
as to the weightier matters. This sage apostle
possesses, however, the rare power of amusing by
his sermons. He is so totally ignorant that he
professes never to have bought or borrowed a
book since he cam' to years o' discretion! He
found an old system of logic in the manse when
he was married, and has thought fit to divide his
discourses, *logice*, in consequence. He always sets
out with a definition. For instance, he has been
lecturing and preaching on the supper at Cana
for these nine weeks, and the first thing he did
was to define *wine* and *water* for the elucida-
tion of the metamorphosis performed in his text.
'Wine,' quoth he, 'is a pleasant, exhilarating
liquor, taken after dinner and at other times—by
genteel people—in moderation most excellent, but
in excess odious. Water is a pure, perspicuous
substance, useful in cleansing or purifying of things
defiled.'

"At another time, having occasion to make his
masonic audience comprehend what is meant by calling Christ the foundation of our faith—'A foundation,' said he, 'may thus be defined, "that *part*

of a superstructure which the *canny* artist first endeavoureth to make steadfast." ' So much for Presbyterian eloquence. We have the repenting stool here in all its glory. The poor man almost went out of his wits last Sunday in rebuking a damsel who appeared for the fifth time, in silk stockings. I suppose Traill is no longer with you. Connell was here lately, for a day or two, and, according to him, Traill's motions have been totally different from his original intentions. Remember me to him and Knight if they are in your neighbourhood. I am sensible that you can find (little) amusement in such letters as these. I hope I shall be able to atone in winter when I get among the luminaries of Auld Reekie. Jeffray (*sic*) —the cool-headed Jeffray—was lately, I hear, taken and released by Commodore Rogers on his way to America—from the North of Scotland—and on what errand? to marry a niece of John Wilkes, who lives at Charlestown. The Commodore knew Jeffray's kindred soul, and treated him, it seems, with singular kindness. He got a letter from Rogers to the Mayor of Charlestown, and various friends of Republicanism with whom our 'wee reekit deil' of a reviewer will, no doubt, participate in many dinners and many toasts from which—*Metu aut Montibus*—we are unhappily debarred.—Yours ever affectionately, J. G. LOCKHART."

These anecdotes were among the Presbyterian

humours which Lockhart began to collect, and, as will presently appear, he thought of combining them into a novel after (or rather *before*) the manner of Galt.

When winter drives his family back from sea and river to the blackness of darkness of Glasgow, his letters (as of a single civilised Robinson Crusoe in a world of huxtering barbarians) wax mournful, almost elegiac.

"You and the Welshman are my only true and faithful correspondents," he tells Mr. Christie, "and I don't know how I should do without you, and your letters, of both of you, come to me at certain times with great effect of comfort. They keep me up in my connection with the world, which in many respects would be but in a perishing condition, where I am.

" I have not yet read through Wordsworth's poem, from lack of opportunity only, you may be sure. I had one evening, however, the opportunity of reading several passages in it, with all of which I was most highly delighted. He strikes me as having more about him of that sort of sober, mild, sunset kind of gentleness, which is so dear to me from the recollections of Euripides, and the tender parts of the Odyssey, than any English poet ever possessed, save Shakespeare, the possessor of all.

" But then you underrate Lord Byron, I think. ' Lara ' I look upon as a wonderful production. It is like Michael Angelo completing the unfinished

rock half hewn into a giant, or like Roubillac opening the lips of Sir Isaac Newton's statue, having
originally represented them closed.

"Who but Byron would have dared to call such
a spirit from the dead as Conrad, or who that could
have dared, could have made him speak things
so worthy of himself? Upon my honour, I think
it shows more depth of insight into human nature
to invent such a terrible band of ideas, all so fitted
to this gloomy sort of being, than ever poet sur-
passed. I delight in all the great poets of our
day, and am willing to put Wordsworth and Byron
at the top.[1] But I have not yet read 'Roderic.'

"I rejoice to hear that your 'Thirlestane Leslie'
thrives."

This was a work begun by Christie: it was to
contain "the remains of the late Thirlestane Leslie,
Esq., consisting of poems and letters, with a biographical memoir." Leslie was to be "a person of
the imaginative cast, with strong logical powers
and a dash of poetry, who afterwards went religious
and died very young." Mr. Christie asked Lockhart
to give him any useful hints about the hero's
"unregenerate days"; he did not care to trust the
future *malleus hæreticorum*, and of the profane
Edinburgh Review, with the pieties of Thirlestane
Leslie.

"I hope the child may escape the illnesses common

---

[1] This, it may be remembered, is also the verdict of Mr. Matthew
Arnold.

to his time of life, and yet be one of the *Phœbo digna locuti*. Have you really brought it to any tangible size and shape? If you have, I would strongly impel you to go on, and finish and publish him with all speed. You may put a few hundreds into your pocket, and you may get a name which will push you on in life. I see plainly there is no other way of getting into notice. In this age one must be an author, and why may not you hit upon a lucky stroke as well as another? I think the shape you talk of is likely to take very well. Williams has a good many friends among the London booksellers. I would advise you to write to him before you fix anything. Murray is a most gentlemanly fellow, and most liberal.

" I don't think the novel I have in hand will at all jumble with yours.[1] I mean it chiefly as a receptacle of an immense quantity of anecdotes and observations I have made concerning the state of the Scotch, chiefly their clergy and elders. It is to me wonderful how the Scotch character has been neglected. I suppose the Kirk stood low in Smollett's early days, and he had imbibed a disgust

[1] Lockhart wrote to Constable, the publisher, from Milnburn (Dec. 29, 1814), saying that he had been "amusing himself with writing a novel," the scene being in Scotland. Important classes of Scotch society, he thought, had been "left untouched." His hero was one John Todd, a "True Blue," in London during the visit of the Emperor of Russia. The "Romance of the Thistle" was the name he thought of. The tale would, apparently, have been something like Galt's "Ayrshire Legatees." The novel was to be anonymous. See "Archibald Constable," iii. 151–152.

for it. He has given us, you see, only a few little sketches, nothing full or rich, like his seamen. Now I think there is just as great a fund of originality and humour in the Scotch character, modified as it is, in the various ranks of life, as in the English or Spanish, or any of those of which so much has been made. I think I shall have two volumes to show you when we meet, which I doubt will not be till spring. Indeed I have made up my mind to study the Scots Law here with all my might, whatever may be hereafter. I am deep in the early history of England and of this country at present. I find great use in my German, and am making myself acquainted with our Saxon remains. Indeed, I begin to think the antiquities of the Middle Ages are the most rational study a man could devote himself to, were he an idle person ; as it is, an acquaintance with these things is indispensable to a lawyer."

This letter seems evidence of a sudden intellectual advance in Lockhart. His comments on Byron may no longer be in harmony with the taste of the day ; but, whatever it was that his contemporaries admired in Byron's Conrads and Laras, that quality, now so faded, was then in universal esteem. Christie, who did not care for Byron, among lovers of poetry held a lonely position. Lockhart was always loyal to the verse of Wordsworth, though later, in private life, he smiled at the self-centred prosiness of the poet. It is curious that Lockhart, when he writes about the unexplored mine of Scotch character awaiting the novelist, says nothing concerning "Waverley," which, in the autumn of 1814, was the newest novel. We might almost think that he had not yet read Scott's opening romance, to which he refers in the following note of Feb. 28, 1815 :—

"Have you seen 'The Saxon and the Gael'? If not, you will find it a clever enough representation of Edinburgh a few years ago. A number of very capital anecdotes, mostly old here, but new perhaps to you. This much I say from having read half a volume, and from hearsay. There is come out another Highland novel called 'Clan Albin' which I have not seen, but which they say is equal or superior to 'Waverley.' Little doubt is now entertained as to the authors of that production. It seems a young friend of W. Scott's sketched the story and outlined everything. Walter Scott inserted the humour and brushed all up. 'Clan Albin's' author is not known. Old Johnny Pinkerton, on account of his notorious scurrility and hatred of Edinburgh, is suspected of 'The Saxon and Gael.' What a fecund fellow Wattie is! a long poem and two novels in the same year, besides reviews, songs, &c., &c., for they say Sir Guy the[1] (   ) is ready, or in the press. Most of my novel was written before I read 'Waverley,' but I fear the

----

[1] "Sir Guy the Searcher"? Scott liked to quote that person, for he himself was always on the search for his missing papers, &c. More probably "Guy Mannering" is intended.

rush upon Scotland consequent to that popular work is such that mine is likely to be crushed among the row. I intend letting it sleep a year or two and making use of it as a *drawable* for some more extensive thing. Now allow me to hope that I am to hear from you immediately. Remember me to any friends, will you, and believe me ever, most truly yours, J. G. L.

"*P.S.*—I heard lately both from Hamilton and Traill. They are dancing in Edinburgh."

In the matter of novel-writing, Lockhart's ambition, at the age of twenty, was to be what Galt became, the recorder of the Caledonian humours of his own, not of past romantic ages, and of " a rampageous antiquity," as Galt's Provost says. What became of Lockhart's John Todd is unknown—he may have destroyed his manuscript. "The book is damned," he wrote briefly, years afterwards, to Christie, when his "Valerius" failed, and he never seems to have fretted about the fortunes of his works. His idea of writing national fiction was bold at twenty, and his energetic attack on many new subjects is a proof of his mental vigour. That vigour, that clean rapidity in acquisition and execution, is characteristic of Lockhart. The highest hopes might have been, and were entertained for his future. " Lockhart will *blaze*," said Scott later, yet he never "blazed." We naturally ask why he did not, and we shall presently find many circumstances, often of his own making, which damped his fire, and thwarted his energies. But, from the first, we observe little promise of creative gifts. Most young men, lovers of poetry, endowed with taste, learning, and fancy, write verses, but if Lockhart did so (as Mr. Christie says he did), he never mentions the fact. That the gods had made him poetical, his rare serious pieces prove. But he perhaps criticised himself too severely, or his diffidence was too great, or, finally, he did not feel an impulse so natural to youth as the impulse to rhyme. Its presence proves nothing, but its absence may be an indication of some lack, of something wanting, which, even if Lockhart's fortunes had been different, might have deprived him of the highest literary success. His novel, even, was confessedly to be a thing based on observation, a study of character, not a romance, not a story told for the story's sake, such as a very young man, or boy, would be likely to attempt. Ambition, too, appears to have been his motive, a man who would be noticed "must be an author." He was ambitious, but, comparatively early in life, he put ambition by, for, when once he learned to renounce and resign, he resigned things lightly, as one who, after Montaigne's counsel, "made no great marvel of his own fortunes."

On November 25, 1814, we find him again writing to Christie, from his father's house in Glasgow. He has "heard from Williams, very happy at Winchester. I doubt not he will yet rise in the world, by means of his strong head, and inflexible power of nailing himself to any rough piece of timber that comes in his way. You used to be skilled in the Lakish fellows, if I remember. Can you tell me any-thing of Lambe? (*sic*) I never read his specimens of the Old Tragedians till the other day, and have been, I need not say, highly delighted with them. Really we may crack our thumbs over the departed play genius of Britain. We have lost, I think, the whole art of delineating the delicate mixtures of human character. We have now no specimens of contradictory beings such as Nature makes ; but to be sure, it is the same in real life, and what can we expect on the stage?

" I am very sorry you did not write last year on the English Essay subject " (at Oxford). " Your studies have, if I mistake not, been a good deal among our elder writers and I understand the successful effusion is a mere nothing—for I have not *seen* any of these productions for the last two or three years. I do not know yet what the subjects of this year's essays are ; if you know, be so good as to tell me, for, al-though I am not idle, I may perhaps think of writing, should the theme tempt. Last year I was too sensible of my own defectiveness in Elizabethan learning to think seriously of it, for I well knew that the knowledge one can pick up in a few weeks' read-ing is not at all of the kind necessary for explaining the genius of a set of writers such as these.

" This place is, for a seat of learning, so ignorant, that I have never yet been able to lay my hands on ' Roderick,' except for a moment, when I read the beginning, which I admire exceedingly. Tell me what sort of *whole* it is when you write next. . . . It is really a miserable thing to be without friends : out of my own family I have not a soul here I care for. The manners of men who talk perpetually of raw sugar and calicoes, and of chemical-botanical vulgar women, are intolerable to me. I am fain to take all my walks in solitude, which is as much as to say, that I walk very little, and horse I have none. . . .

" I have got abundant access to books, however, more so than I ever had either at Edinburgh or Oxon, and find, no doubt, great consolation in them, although the novelties are no longer new elsewhere by the time they come here.

" There is a vacancy at present in our Humanity Chair. I was inclined to be very desirous that Hamilton should stand, but he scorned the idea. For my part, I think he was a fool. I don't well see how they could have refused him on many accounts, although nothing is too base for them ; and I fancy I may count upon your perfect approbation for my sentiments respecting the merits of £1500 a year—an excellent house, library, &c., and six months of vacation—besides little more than two hours a day of drudging during the session.

"But *altiora petit*—and God grant he may get them, but I think if he ever gets high it will be as a writer, and I don't see where he could have had more leisure than here, and the worse the society the more.

"I think a man may tolerate even Glasgow for half the year, with the prospect of spending the other half in company of his own choice—and this is really an opinion of which I may speak with some certainty, as I know not how I should endure it at present myself, unless I had the hope of making up for the deprivations I feel by a free month's view of you all in summer.

"Traill, I understand, is to be in Edinburgh this winter. I shall be there for a day or two very soon and see.

"My novel comes on wondrously—I mean as to bulk. My fears are many—first, of false taste creeping in from the want of any censor; secondly, of too much Scotch—from the circumstance of my writing in the midst of the 'low Lanerickshire'— &c., &c., &c. But I think I have written a great many graphical enough scenes, and have really made up my mind to print two volumes of nonsense in the spring. I think of writing to Murray, but I believe I shall put it off till I come up myself. Once again let me ask you for any little odd tags, rags, and bobtails of good incidents, &c., for which you have no immediate use. They may do me great service. In the meantime, write me frequently—

frequentissime, and believe me, ever your most affectionate friend,

"J. G. LOCKHART.

"Compliments to your bantling."

The next letter (January 3, 1815), shows Lockhart taking such pleasure as Glasgow society could yield to an humorous observer. Dr. Scott, "the Odontist," was destined to appear in his *Blackwood* articles, as a butt who delighted in that office. Lockhart later composed dozens of burlesque verses, and attributed them to the dentist, nor were they seriously disclaimed. Some of the jests of the Gag club cannot be reproduced. The novel on Astrology, referred to as promised by Scott, is "Guy Mannering." Lockhart seems to have had no doubts as to Sir Walter's authorship.

"January 3, 1815.

"My dear Christie,—I am very much delighted by your letter, for it shows you to be somewhat in better humour with yourself and this world than some of the last did. This I attribute partly to your cold having subsided, but principally to the collision which you have enjoyed with Williams. Not to mention other good qualities, I think his sort of steady spirits render him a most valuable companion. What other people effect by politeness and painstaking he does by nature in this matter. He talks of composing Florilegiums, &c. I think it may be a good enough way of making £50 or so—rather better than breaking iron-stone on a road in July. I am grieved that W. takes offence at my tolerance for some of the Wordsworth school: I am not sure that I would say so much as I have said after reading the 'Excursion,' at least the Jeffreys (*sic*) give one a bad scent of it. But from their having omitted to quote any of several divine passages which I have read I doubt not they are unfair. However, you in one of your letters lately mention, among the absurdities of this age's producing, sentimental braziers and tender-hearted Jews. I daresay Coleridge has by this time added philosophising pedlars to the list. Upon the whole, I doubt we have had bad luck on the lakes this year on both sides the Atlantic.

"I have never been so solitary all my days as I am now, and have been for some months. I feel no sympathy with the mercantile souls here, and have really no companion whatever. I don't know what I would not have given to spend Christmas with the Welchman and you. I fancy Bristol may be cursedly like this place, for you—*tant pis*.

"T'other day I went to a Glasgow ball, almost, I may say, for the first time. On entering the room a buzz of 'sugars,' 'cottons,' 'coffee,' 'pullicates,' assailed my ears from the four winds of heaven. Every now and then the gemmen were deserting their partners, and rushing into the caper course to talk over the samples of the morning. One sedulous dog seemed to insist on another's putting his finger into his waistcoat pocket. The being did so, and forthwith put the tip to his lips, but the countenance was so mealy that I could not tell whether it smacked of sugar or Genseng.

"There is nobody affords me so much amusement here as a dentist—a little, fat, coarse, bandy fellow, who commonly goes by the name of Count Pulltuski. This man carries personal vanity to the most daring height I ever witnessed. It becomes quite magnanimous in him. He makes no bones of speaking it out, in a broad and open way, that he considers himself as the greatest man now alive. I won his heart one evening at a punch party. They were roasting him upon the narrow and illiberal branch of the medical trade to which he confines himself. I took up the cudgels for him, and maintained that I thought the circumstance of such a man being a tooth doctor one of the best proofs of the advanced civilisation of this age, and added that I hoped this country would soon learn, like ancient Egypt, to have no physicians who undertake all manner of cures, but restrict every practitioner to some lith or limb of his own.

"Pulltuski sported me a royal dinner the day after. He had a set of rich, vulgar dogs about him, who all pretend to the title of humorists, or, according to the local phraseology, *gaggers*.

N.B.—Gaggery, in the Glasgow idiom, means that sort of fun which consists in saying things that stop one's mouth; and the coarser the gag, they seem to reckon the joke the more exquisite. There is what they call a Gag club. I went to it one night as visitor. . . . They sang 'The pigs they lie,' in chorus, &c. Says the President, 'I was sent for t'other day to Lord Douglass. I took particular care to dress myself in silks, powdered highly, and arrived in my gig about seven in the evening. I was shown into the dining-room—dinner just over. Sat next my lady, a whisper through the room, "who's that?"—"'tis the great Scott—*the* dentist—Pulltuski—a remarkably genteel-looking man. . . ."' This chiel is President also of the Newtonian Scientific Society of Glasgow, &c., &c. But 'tis all nothing unless one could write his face. I drew him in a box great-coat with nineteen necks *and a comforter* round his neck. He has got this varnished and put in a two-guinea frame over his mantelpiece. He sent round with his dessert, after dinner, the jaw of a Roman soldier, and a set of teeth from Borodino, which last produced twenty jokes on the high profits of his import trade, &c. He drank his wine out of a glass about a foot high. . . . So much for him.

"Hamilton has lately become a member of the Antiquarian Society of Edinburgh. Traill has passed his civil law trials, as I am told, with éclat, which means without being plucked. Hamilton lately made his first attempt at a speech, but immediately lost every ray of recollection, and raved about like a madman for some minutes, and then stuck dumb. What unfortunate nerves for a barrister. He has become a great student of magic, and talks of publishing a history of Dæmonology, but I see W. Scott announces a novel on Astrology, and I fancy that will be enough of the black art for us all. Hannay, I hear, is a great dab at the bar for his time, and brought off a sheepstealer at Kirkcudbright assizes.

"Will you be in Oxon Easter and Act? I think the essay subjects are both d—— bad, but if I think of either it will be the Latin. I read during summer some of the late German histories of philosophy, and think I must make something of it.—Yours,

"J. G. L."

The following letter (Inverkip, by Greenock, Aug. 3, 1815) describes a brief Highland tour. If Lockhart went after trout, he fished with more enthusiasm for men, for traits of character. His friend to be, John Wilson, would not have left his captures unchronicled :—

"INVERKIP, BY GREENOCK, *Aug. 3rd*, 1815.

"MY DEAR CHRISTIE,—The summer is flying away, and not having heard lately from you, or anybody in the southern parts, I am beginning to be

completely Scotchified. I don't know how you go
on in the important concerns of medical lore. But
the Deity of La Paresse has resumed over me with
redoubled vigour her antique sway. The place
from which I write is a hamlet on the coast of
Renfrewshire, just where that county meets Ayrshire. The Clyde is here a noble firth of seven
miles breadth, running between the fertile hills of
Ayr on the one side, and the bleak-black mountains
of Morven on the other. The whole country is
intersected with long arms of the sea—lochs, &c.
—which render this part of Scotland the most picturesque I have seen.

Not contented with these beauties, the itch of
rambling has just been leading me away into the
depths of Lochaber. My brother and I foregathered with Hamilton on the banks of Loch-
lomond, which flows into the Clyde about ten miles
above this by means of the water of Leven, and
we have just returned from ten days of thorough
tramping. We had a horse with us for the con-
venience of carrying baggage—but contemning the
paths of civilised man, we dared the deepest glens
in search of *trout*. There is something abundantly
delightful in the naked-heartedness of the Highland
people. Bating the article of inquisitiveness, they
are as polite as courtiers. The moment we entered
a cottage the wife began to bake her cakes—and,
having portable soup with us, our fare was really
excellent. What think you of parritch and cream

for breakfast? Trout, pike, and herrings for dinner, ewe-milk cheese and right peat-reek whisky? and then at night a rushlight illuminating the smoke-dried pages of Matthew Henry's Commentary on the Song of Solomon—'The Crook in the Lot,' 'The Cloud of Witnesses, or The Martyrs' Monument— wherein are the speeches and last words of all the Presbyterian saints, burnt, hanged, and drowned for the glory of God. And lastly, but almost univer-sally—' The Light and Supple *Whang* for the Breeks of Declining Faith.' My brother being a little bit of the wag, gained the affections of all these good folks by his *graces*, each a quarter of an hour long, wherein he rang the commonplaces of young ravens crying for their food, and of men not living by bread alone. . . . I have heard not a word of any of our Oxonian friends. Don't forget in your next to give me any intelligence you possess about our friend Nicoll. Gordon MacCaul was up in Oxford, and took his A.M. just after we left it. He says Miss Ireland has at last loosed her virgin zone under the strength of Evans. Happy, happy, happy pair. What a subject for an Epithalamium. Try your hand. I see you say you are reading a great deal of French. If you can lay your hands upon the works of Gresset, I promise you exquisite pleasure. You will find a beautiful *Eloge* upon him in the first volume of the 'Discours et Memoires,' by Bailly.

" There is a famous foreign library at Greenock,

in which I find everything I can want for summer
purposes.   Compts. to Knight.—Yours most affectionately,   J. G. LOCKHART."

The letter which follows (Sept. 9, 1815, Gourock
Bay) contains an early reference to John Wilson.
Lockhart thought of making a collection of Oxford
facetiæ, and hoped for Wilson's help.   As usual,
Lockhart has a few fresh anecdotes of the Presby-
terian simplicity.

"GOUROCK BAY, GREENOCK, *Sept. 9th*, 1815.

"MY DEAR CHRISTIE,—I have been blaming
myself all this while for not writing you.   I have
put it off day after day that I might have it in my
power to tell you my agreement with the booksellers about our little production, and yet even
now I cannot do so—bless their dilatory souls.   My
dues being, according to Wardrop, thoroughly removed, and ten guineas conveyed from my breeches
pocket into his, I left London about a fortnight ago,
in company with Aristotle the second,[1] who had
been spending three weeks in rummaging a collection of letters (MS.) in the Bodleian, and egging the
tutelary angel of that mystic abode to a new flight
—*casa non detta mai in prosa ne in rima*—a translation of Schneider's Lexicon.   The little dumpling of
philology" (Nicoll) "agreed, but behold Mr. Elmsley

[1] Sir William Hamilton.

of Cambridge has forestalled him—*vide* the spare
sheet at the end of the last *Quarterly Review*—so *hæc
tentamina tanta* must sleep *in præsenti*. Hamilton
is full of strange whims and fancies—anything but
the law of Scotland—*inter nos*, I think it is likely
he may publish an 'Essay on the State of Universities, Ideal and Actual,' before long—at least his
adversaria teem with scraps concerning it, and his
talk lies much that way, though this is nothing
new.   He approves highly of the thing which
I meditate — disapproves, however, the title of
Olio ; he suggests 'the Oxford Picnic,' and by all
means recommends saying part the first.   Indeed
I already smell much matter, and expect that
the first hint of the matter to Wilson will engage
his assistance.   I understood Maudlin did not
nourish him for nothing.   By-the-bye, Reginald
Heber, you may know, printed some years ago a
Brazennose satire, the *Whippiad*, which he has
since done his best to suppress.   This of course
no one would think of meddling with *vivo auctore*,
but I understand he is the author of a number of
very good things besides.   H. heard Tuckwell repeat a good many of them.   Could you not contrive
to get at these ?   I am sure you may.   Moreover,
Jack Ireland is the repository of many old lampoons
written at the time of the war between the Balliol
exhibitioners and the college.   These might surely
be worth something—at all events, they may be
inquired after.   I mention these things because

you will soon be *there*, and can use your judgment if you think proper. Jack had so far recovered his shock as to get drunk three or four times in Hamilton's presence while he was in Oxford.

"'Pasquillus Oxoniensis' might not be a bad title. But I am not despairing but something more happy than any of these may yet occur. I made a good pun the other day (*ut dirty-Durlice loquar*). Hamilton has a law paper to write concerning a Mr. *Hume*—a poor devil—who is trying to get the title of Marchmont. I suggested for a motto—

' —— *tentanda via est qua me quoque possim*
Tollere Humo.—— '

"We are here in a beautiful situation in the Firth of Clyde, surrounded with all the mountains of Argyle, and have Benlomond right before us. I enjoy myself very much, when the weather is favourable, in fishing, boating, &c. On Sunday the Antiburghers had their *occasion* about two miles off. I went into the tent-field towards evening; the man had just finished preaching at a great rate, but something being whispered into his ear, he said just as I entered, 'Brethren, as they're aye haddin on yet in the kirk, I think we had as weel *do away the time a leetle in prayer.*' The Edinburgh Bible Society Report contains—(it is now lying before me) these resolutions on the second page :—

"11. Resolved, That the thanks of this meeting are due to Sir John Marjoribanks, Bart., for his kindness to the institution.   12. Resolved, That the thanks of this meeting are due to Bailie John Waugh for his able conduct in the chair, &c.   13. Resolved, That the fervent acknowledgments of this meeting are most justly due to Almighty Providence, for *its* watchfulness over the interests of Christ's Kingdom in general, and the British and Foreign Bible Society in particular.   14. Thanks to Mrs. Maxwell for a present of Gaelic Bibles.— Yours ever,

"J. G. LOCKHART."

In the autumn of 1815, Lockhart left Glasgow for the much more congenial city of Edinburgh, there to read Scots law, and to begin the real business of his life, miscellaneous writing.   His comments on Edinburgh, and on some of his new acquaintances, will be found, as usual, in his letters to Mr. Christie.

CHAPTER IV

EDINBURGH, 1815–1817

THE Edinburgh to which Lockhart betook himself in
November 1815, was, doubtless, already familiar to
him, already admired by him in its physical features.
" Edinburgh, even were its population as great as
that of London, could never be merely a city.
Here there must always be present the idea of the
comparative littleness of all human works." [1]   The

[1] " Peter's Letters," vol. i. p. 8.

rocks and mountains dwarf the structures erected
on them, yet the builders of the Old Town "appear
as if they had made Nature the model of their
architecture," "piled deep and massy, close and
high," as it is. To Lockhart's eye the view—

> "Out over the Forth
> I look to the North,"

from George Street, where he lodged, must have
been a delightful change from anything that Glasgow
Green had to show.

As for society, he had friends and introductions
enough, through his family and through Sir William
Hamilton. Authors he found as common in Edinburgh as tobacco or sugar merchants in Glasgow.
The book shops which he describes in "Peter's
Letters," Blackwood's, Millar's, Laing's, and the rest,
consoled him for the total absence of new works,
and of reading fellow-creatures in the capital of the
West. The time had not yet come when curls of
his raven hair were in such demand, that he expressed (to a sister) his fear of premature baldness
(1819). But his handsome face ("Landseer tells me
I was a good-looking chap twenty or thirty years
ago," he wrote long afterwards), probably made
friends for him among the maidens and matrons
of Edinburgh ; the innumerable scribbling people
learned to misdoubt "the laugh about the screwed-
up mouth of him, that fules ca'd no canny, for they
couldna thole the meanin' o't," and some very

sensitive souls may have dreaded "the bit caricatures," which he drew in pencil, on every odd scrap
of paper.[1]   "We have assemblies here, and routs,
and balls, and plays, and concerts, and dinners
without end or intermission.   I find it all very
good fun, and am quite contented," Lockhart had
written to Christie, a year before, during a flying
visit to Edinburgh.   He took Horace's advice, and
he also took what a young philosopher in Thackeray
calls "his whack."   He had made a new friend,
of the highest importance in his career, John
Wilson, who was writing poetry, angling, revelling
with Patrick Robertson, "Lord Peter," and not
practising at the Bar.   I may here quote, out of
due season, Lockhart's later remarks (Dec. 5, 1819)
to Christie, on the character of Wilson.

    "I fancy you understand him almost as well as I
do.   He is thirty-five years of age, has six children
and a charming wife, and is, I suppose, very easy
in his affairs. . . . He is a very warm, enthusiastic
man, with most charming conversational talents,
full of fiery imaginations, irresistible in eloquence,
exquisite in humour when he talks (but too coarse
in his humorous writing for the present age) ; he is
a most fascinating fellow, and a most kind-hearted,
generous friend ; but his fault is a sad one, a total
inconsistency in his opinions concerning both men
and things.   And thus it is that he continually
lauds and abuses the same person within the space

[1] See "Noctes Ambrosianæ," November 1826.

of a day, so making neither his praise nor his censure of any avail. . . . He is, I think, afflicted with much despondency as a literary man, having never been able in anything to apply his mind so as to produce satisfaction to his own judgment. But in truth his life in earlier years has been such as to give him a thousand prejudices and sore places of which I know nothing, and I have by no means penetrated his intellectual physiognomy to its roots.

" This much is certain—I have a warm and tender affection for the man, and believe him incapable of deliberately doing anything dishonourable, either in literature or in any other way ; but then it is very possible that I am unlucky in having been linked so much at my outset with such a man as this. . . . "[1]

In the troubles that followed thickly, it has been not unusual to exonerate Professor Wilson at the expense of, or in contrast with, Lockhart. The opposite course cannot be taken, even if it were chivalrous to take it, by the biographer of Lockhart. The young man who wrote the lines just quoted (lines which should be compared with Mr. Carlyle's portrait of Wilson), was clear-sighted enough to take care of himself. But these lines were written (Dec. 1819) after two years' close experience of Wilson's literary vagaries and inconsistencies : his abuse of friends and idols, his sudden returns to his old loves. Four years earlier, in 1815, when Lockhart was just

[1] Christie, in London, had heard tales to Wilson's disadvantage.

of age, the society of Wilson, wildly fascinating, *bruyant*, full of what he considered practical jokes, (though unkind persons gave them other names), can hardly have been salutary for a young student of literature and law.   There is more to be said on this topic, but we may now offer a letter (Nov. 29, 1815) on Edinburgh as Lockhart was seeing it, on his beginnings in miscellaneous literary work, and on a dinner with Wilson and De Quincey.

(Postmark, *Nov.* 29, 1815.)

"My dear Christie,—You and I are in general such exemplary correspondents that I begin to feel a degree of wonder at the two months' silence which has prevailed betwixt us, greater than a much longer cessation of any other epistolary traffic could have occasioned in me.   Since I wrote you last I have spent a few weeks at Gourock, a few weeks (including the *occasion*) at Glasgow, and now I have been for a fortnight in *this our Athens*.   Certainly if the name Athens had been derived from the Goddess of Printing—not from the Goddess of Wisdom—no city in the world could with greater justice lay claim to the appellation.   An author elsewhere is a being *somewhat* at least out of the common run.   Here he is truly a week-day man. Every other body you jostle is the father of at least an octavo, or two, and it is odds if you ever sit down to dinner in a company of a dozen, without having to count three or four quarto makers in the circle.

Poets are as plenty as blackberries—indeed much more so, unless· blackberries mean sloes. And as for travellers—good Jehovah! I think I am safe in saying that there have appeared at least twenty different lucubrations in that way concerning Paris alone within these last eighteen months. Old *crambe-recocta* stuff out of Horace Walpole and Sir Joshua—spouted by one boy of eighteen, who had never seen in his life but one or two *Edinburgh* exhibitions—and profound disquisitions on national character and Napoleon by another, who never had seen the tenth milestone from Auld Reekie, or read anything better than Jeffray and Cobbet's Parliamentary debates. I have passed my trials in the Civil Law, which cost me a little fagging, and am now seriously at work on the Scots.

"Hamilton and I have been amusing ourselves with doing into English 'the Relation' of the Battle of Waterloo. I have done my half, and H. is sitting by me at his. I have much amusement in seeing his ways—primo, he is against all French terms and fought hard for *Field-assistant, loco,* 'Aide-de-camp.' Secundo, he insists upon having the pages marked with Roman numerals, having lately imbibed a bitter spite against the d—d Arabic cipher. Tertio, he has just been reading Longinus, and would fain have an imitation of his manner in a note. We are promised half profits by Laing, and I hope to touch £25 for my quarter. I have got a few articles in

SIR WILLIAM HAMILTON BUYING BOOKS.

(Drawn by J. G. Lockhart.)

the 'Encyclopædia' which is going on, and intend
reviewing a little—being convinced that there is
nothing I want more than a habit of writing with
ease. The Picnic " (*the Oxford Olio*) "sleeps for the
present, but will assuredly begin to squall in the
spring. The Oxonian friends here are all very well,
Hannay fighting away in the usury case. Innes in
statu quo. Connel ditto. Traill I saw once—but I
have been confined to my room with a cold since,
and have heard no more of him. Tom Traill's wife
has brought him a son and heir, whereof Tom is
very glorious. Such is an epitome of our status
here. I have written it that I may provoke a speedy
answer, containing the minutiæ of your transactions
for these last two months. You are now of course
as I left you, grinding Law, and quizzing the
Balliolite B.A.'s at the dinner table—unless you have
changed your gown and your butts for *paullo majora !*
The transition is not tremendous from Everett to
Dicky. Give my love to Nicoll, and do let me hear
from you immediately.—Yours most affectionately,

"J. G. LOCKHART.

"Hamilton desires his kindest remembrances to
you. I dined the other day at his house in company
with two violent Lakers—Wilson for one, and a
friend of his, a most strange creature, for the other.
His name is De Quincey ; he was of Worcester.
After passing one half of an examination which has
never, according to the common report, been equalled,

he took the terror of the schools, and fled for it to the Lakes. There he has formed the closest intimacy with Wordsworth and all his worthies. After dinner he set down two snuff-boxes on the table; one, I soon observed, contained opium pills—of these he swallowed one every now and then, while we drank our half-bottle apiece. Wilson and he were both as enthusiastic concerning the 'Excursion' as you could wish. Wilson is just going to publish a dramatic poem—subject, 'The Plague in London.' It opens with the conversation of two shopkeepers, a trunk maker and a calender-mill mender, all whose families have caught the infection. It is in eleven (books ?), and includes many lyrics. (The two friends have gone off on a pedestrian tour to Staffa!)"

Among the articles which Lockhart speaks of contributing to the "Encyclopædia," the only one known to me as his is that on Heraldry. It is ascribed to Lockhart by Mr. Christie, and bears marks of his style. The passage on the origin of armorial bearings is careful, clear, and rather sarcastic on the learned who make classical or ancient Egyptian peoples the first beginners of the science. Much is now known about the heraldry of savages which, in Lockhart's time, was either unknown or disregarded. Mediæval blazonry was, with additional points of curiosity and display, very like a systematic development from the usages of the North American Indians and other uncivilised races. But there can be found no *catena* of heraldic blazonries from prehistoric European savagery to the earliest mediæval tombs on which coats of arms appear. The things more or less analogous to crests, and tinctures, and coat armour among the antiquities of Egypt, Greece, and Rome, are only analogous in a vague one-sided way, with casual resemblances to the mediæval usage, and essential differences from it. Lockhart elucidates all this, (except the savage side of the topic) with plenty of sense, wide and rare reading, and satirical humour. It was "meat and drink to him to see a fool" who argued in the fantastic manner of Barnabas Moreno de Vargas, who "blazons all the tribes of Israel." On one point, the arms of Jeanne d'Arc, Lockhart is decidedly wrong, but we need not enter into critical details. The essay proves that he had read and that he could write.

To return to his letters, the judicial faculties of the mind decline to accept as genuine the Latin Edict of the Glasgow Senatus, as given in the following epistle. The approving quotation from Leigh Hunt, and his paper, the *Examiner*, comes oddly from one of the future assailants of "The Cockney School":—

"EDINBURGH, 9 GEORGE STREET,
January 3rd, 1816.

"MY DEAR CHRISTIE,—I would have answered your kind and amusing epistle more in proper course, but have been spending the holidays at home, which must be my excuse. I found the good folks of Glasgow just recovering from the sensation occasioned by the visit of two Archdukes. The Faculty of the College at Glasgow issued a primitive enough edict on the occasion, thus:—[1] 'Q. F. F. Q. S. Senatus Academicus Togatis et non Togatis salutem. Ab Altissimo et Potentissimo Principe Marchione de Douglas

---

[1] May it be lucky! The Senatus Academicus salutes the gowned and the gownless. Being informed by the Most High and Puissant Prince, the Marquis of Clydesdale and Douglas, that their Imperial Highnesses, the Archdukes John and Louis of Austria, intend to-day to honour us with a visit, we are pleased to issue the following rules, by which all are to govern themselves, and whosoever fails to observe them shall be most severely punished afterwards :

1. Their Imperial Highnesses will take a cold collation, in the first Hall, with the Principals and Professors (in their gowns), and some gentlemen of the city and district, about noon, at the expense of the Faculty.

2. Students who have beards must shave them, and wash, as on Sundays.

3. All students must put on clean shirts, as when the Duke of Montrose was here.

4. Students of Theology must be combed, and wear black breeches and coats, and decent gowns, like ministers.

5. All must be in a state to be seen by the Archdukes and the honourable persons with them, and must decently and quietly form two lines between the first and the common Hall when the procession is walking. The juniors must not laugh, or make faces, when they see the foreigners.

6. In the common Hall, Professor Jardine, who was formerly in France, will speak in French to them, for Professor Richardson is dead.

7. One of the Professors of Physics will pronounce an English oration, and Principal Taylor will pray in Latin ; and then dismiss yourselves without making a noise.

et Clydesdale certiores facti, quod eorum altitudines imperiales Archiduces Johannes et Ludovicus de Austria, hodie nos visitatione honorare intendunt nobis placuit hasce regulas generales emittere quomodo omnes se sunt gerere — et quicunque eas observare non vult severrime punitus erit postea.

"'1. Eorum Imperiales Altitudines Archiduces J. et L. de Austria, capient frigidam collationem in aula priore cum Principali et Professoribus (in togis suis), et generosis quibusdam hominibus ex urbe et vicinitate circa horam meridianam impensis Facultatis.

"'2. Studentes qui barbas habent tondeant eas et lavant sese ut in die dominico.

"'3. Studentes omnes nitida indusia induant secuti quum Dux Montis-Rosarum erat hic.

"'4. Studentes Theologicæ omnes pectantur et nigras braccas et vestes induant et pallia decentia quasi Ministri.

"'5. Omnes in statu sint videri per Archiduces et persones honorabiles qui cum iis sunt—et decenter et cum quiete et ordine duas lineas faciant inter aulam Priorem et aulam communem cum Processio ambulat, et juniores ne rideant nec faciant facies cum Peregrinos vident.

"'6. In aula communi Professor Jardine qui olim in Gallia fuit Francisce illis locutus erit nam Professor Richardson est mortuus.

"'7. Aliquis ex Physicis sermonem anglicam pronunciabit et Principalis Taylor Latine precabitur et sine strepitu dismissi estotis.—Per nos,

"'DECANUS FACULTATIS,
&c., &c.'

"When Jardine's French speech was over, John observed to Louis, 'Ah! que c'est une vile langue cet ecossais——'

"By way of qualifying myself for forming a sane judgment on a subject more than once discussed between us, I have lately read over *all* Wordsworth —prose and verse. The 'Doe' is certainly wretched, but not quite so bad as 'The Force of Prayer.' The 'Excursion' I enjoyed deeply—particularly the character of the Solitary, and the description of the Churchyard and its inhabitants. One of these sketches pleased me more than anything of this day's poetry I have ever read, unless it be O'Connor's Child and Michael; it was that of the young man 'all hopes Cherished for him who suffered to de-part—Like blighted buds; or clouds that mimicked land—Before the sailor's eye; or Diamond drops —That sparkling decked the morning grass, or aught—That *was* attractive, and had ceased to be.' The whole picture is exquisite. The *Examiner* has well characterised Wordsworth as a poet—who, had he written but half of what he has, would have deserved to be immortal. He certainly has more prosing and less variety than I thought it possible for a man of genius and learning, such as his.

"As you don't read the *Examiner*, I may as well transcribe one of Leigh Hunt's last sonnets—

> "'Were I to name out of the times gone by
> The poets dearest to me, I should say,
> Pulci for spirits and a fine free way ;
> Chaucer for manners and close silent eye,
> Milton for classic taste and harp strung high,
> Spenser for luxury and sweet silvan play,
> Horace for chatting with from day to day,
> Shakespeare for all, but most society.
> But which take with me, could I but take one?
> Shakespeare, as long as I was unoppressed
> With the world's weight making sad thoughts intenser.
> But did I wish out of the common sun
> To lay a wounded heart in leafy rest,
> And dream of things far off and pealing—Spenser.'

"Was there ever such a letter as this for quotations? Expect one of a different stamp forthwith. Meantime a good New Year to you, my friend, and farewell, J. G. L.

"Compliments to Nicoll.

"*P.S.*—Riddel has just told me he heard from you lately, and that you are spending the vacation in Balliol. What means this? Is Connor with you? Write to me, and as soon as the bursar is in College transmit me the ready.[1]

"J. G. L."

---

[1] "The ready" here is his Snell Exhibition.

The following fragment (postmark Jan. 6, 1816), contains Wordsworthian sonnets to Wilson, very fair parodies of the austere singer's mode of mixing morals and mountains. If published with W. W.'s initials these noble sonnets would have received much admiration, like one of Miss Fanshawe's imitations, which deceived the Lacustrine elect.

" J. G. LOCKHART *to the* REV. J. WILLIAMS,
or J. H. CHRISTIE.

[Postmark, *January* 6, 1816.]

" John Wilson walked off to Cumberland, a fortnight ago, in the midst of the storm, in spite of his wife, whereupon Mr. Wordsworth wrote two sonnets which I have seen printed at a private press here. One of them runs thus :—

" ' And could thy gentle spirit endure no more
    The solemn prating of that ignorant town ?
    And would'st thou come in spite of frost and frore,
    And border-torrents leaping furious down,
    The spirit of the mountains to adore,
    And human converse hold with thy calm ake?
    O Wilson !   I am glad for the world's sake
    The reign of virtuous impulse is not o'er.

    Domestic duties we must all partake,
    And wife and children should to man be dear—
    But thou did'st well, my Wilson, to forsake
    Thy little ones, and bear thy spouse's tear !
    (When) holier duties call, these might not shake
    The (resolute) worshipper of this lone Mere.'

" Wilson went on the top of the Carlisle coach part of the way ; it overturned, and Wilson's head was broken—whence sonnet the second :—

" ' An outside place my Wilson did prefer,
    Tho' warmth and bodily ease within were found,
    So well befits it nature's worshipper !
    To gaze more widely o'er the snow-clad ground,
    Like the world's joys in barren coldness shining ;
    To list the unseen streamlets' innocent sound
    Beneath the snow a small path undermining.
    Like the poetic eye which moveth slowly,
    And feeds itself in darkness on things holy—
    To scatter crumbs, it may be, now and then,
    To the small redbreast and pure-minded wren.
    These things were worthy of thy soul's desire,
    And, if I know thee, spite of scoffing men,
    Who have no part in the celestial fire,
    And spite of this thy bruise, thou wilt seek these again.
                              W. W.' "

The next letter contains matter unknown to Sir William Hamilton's biographer. To see the dark dæmonologist take his stand at "the plate," and keep ward over the charitable coppers of the congregation, must have been a thing of high solemnity.

"EDINBURGH, 9 GEORGE STREET,
April 17, 1816.

" MY DEAR CHRISTIE,—Your expressions are very vague, touching everything that regards yourself. I think you intend me to conclude that you are leaving Connor, and yet neither the date of your letter, nor the way in which you talk of returning to Oxford, looks exactly that way. Pray let me know what your plans are. If you have no engagement during the summer, I would fain flatter myself with the hopes of your paying us a visit in Scotland, in which case you will know that few can be more anxious for the pleasure of housing you than myself. I am not to be in Oxford this spring. Old John gave me leave of absence very graciously, and I had reasons for preferring to pay my *last official visit* next year rather than now. Traill also, as his sister told me the other night, got leave from John; but as he is at present at Newcastle acting as supercargo to a ship of kelp, she hinted that, should the sale be favourable, he might still make a run to Oxon, where I have no doubt he may easily find a way to dispose of all his seaweed riches.

"We go on here pretty much in the old way. Innes has been made elder, and serves in this General Assembly as representative of the borough of Kintore. Hamilton also was made an elder last Sunday at a village near this town—at least, the ceremony of his taking the vows was performed, for the legality of the process is still doubtful, *a protest* having been given in against his nomination by an old farmer in the eldership there, on three grounds : 1st, Hamilton having no *domiceal* within the bounds ; 2nd, His being suspected of Episcopalianism ; and 3rd, His having no certificate of moral character, &c. The process of Presbytery, wherein the value of these objections is to be discussed, I shall certainly attend. Hamilton desires to be most affectionately remembered to you. He will write to you soon by his cousin the Freshman, and in the meantime earnestly begs you would write him. By-the-bye, do you not think *he* might have some chance for a Fellowship? and in God's name, why don't you stand yourself? There is no open *fama clamosa* against your character—electing you would not be considered as a sort of premium on idleness, blasphemy, and contempt (as electing some friends of yours might too justly be); and on the whole, as you can lose no character, either by competition with the three idiots you mention, or by any decision of those who have already lost all pretensions to justice in those matters—and as you *may* gain so much, Hamilton and I both agree that you will act very wrong if, *being on the spot*, you do not try. Taffy, I presume, will no more trouble them with his fat face and his Greek, both of which are too good for them. I met yesterday at dinner with a Cambridge man, Foster, a craniologist, whom I remember your mentioning last summer. He seems totally cracked, but cleverish withal. He is a professed infidel, but certainly has a well-made forehead above his ugly face. He is cousin to Dicky Meade, as he says—and I believe him. I will send you a copy, by the first private hand, of my Essay on the 'art noble,'—which is now in the press. If you wish to have *any* sarcasm against *anybody* inserted in a note, you are still in time.— Yours, my dear Christie,   J. G. LOCKHART.

"*P.S.*—As Hamilton is not without some thoughts of standing for a Fellowship you must not whisper to the wind that he is an elder—observe this, and consider the passage as not existing."

Lockhart occasionally accompanied Hamilton in his hunts after charters connected with his baronetcy. The following letter, after some sadder news, tells of Hamilton's success :—

"BURNBANK, HAMILTON, *July 27th*, 1816.

"MY DEAR CHRISTIE,—Hamilton came here on Friday last and stayed till this morning. He brought me the first news of Nicoll's marriage, and had himself only that morning learned by a very unfeeling paragraph (as he reported it) from the Oxford paper, the sudden calamity which so soon turned all our friend's happiness into misery. In time I have no doubt the usual lenitives of every distress among us must have their due influence in restoring him to himself—at present, of course, he must be left entirely to the working of his own feelings. The effect which this news produced in both was, I need not say, such as all Nicoll's friends will easily imagine. For myself I heard, in the

same breath, both the marriage and the death—
being saluted by W. H., 'Poor Nicoll's wife's
dead,' before I had the least suspicion that Nicoll
was married. Hamilton made after some time a
lawyer's remark, '*Patrimonially*, 'tis as well.' If
Nicoll is still in London remember us both to
him. Hamilton will write in a few weeks when
he thinks his letter may be received with calmness. I am sorry your letter did not arrive till
after his departure.

"I have surely dreamed of writing you a long
letter about ten days ago, for I remember the very
words in which I communicated to you ——'s
death. He died of two days' illness—a scarlet-fever,
much exacerbated, I am grieved to add, by the life
of dissipation which he had been leading. All last
winter he gambled and drank to excess—he was
even tipsy one day beyond decency about three
o'clock P.M., when I met him in the street. He used
to sit up all night drinking whisky punch with
some Aberdeen squires; he was fortunate at the
dice, but it drew him both into bad company and
bad habits over and above the thing itself. All this
entre nous, —— was at bottom a good, honest soul
—very affectionate in his temper, and deserves to
be lamented by all his friends.

"Hamilton, you may have observed in the
papers, has at length served himself heir *general*
to Sir Robert H. of Preston, who commanded the
Covenanting army at Bothwell Bridge, and is now

Sir William at your service. Had he followed his original profession this might have much in his favour; at present I see no great good it can do him to be set at the upper end of tables among dowagers instead of the lower end among misses. However, he makes a most respectable baronet, and may, if he pleases, make additional use of his good leg in a matrimonial way; but he is not worldly-wise enough for that, to use a *true-blue* phrase. So you are, at last, nine hours a day at a conveyancer's! May the tripling *aes* not be awanting. I beg of you to write again and more at length *on a Sunday*. My compliments to Traill. —Yours ever,   J. G. L.

"Is Connor in town, or have you entirely separated?"

In the following epistle we see something like a germ of *Blackwood's Magazine*. Christie, in early years, would occasionally suggest starting a new serial, but it never came to anything. Lockhart, as in this letter, and often afterwards, would try to make Christie exert himself with his pen. But in law Christie found a better profession than in writing for the papers; "it's seldom any good comes of it," says Captain Shandon, whom Lockhart knew very well :—

J. G. LOCKHART *to* J. H. CHRISTIE.

"BURNBANK, *Oct.* 18, 1816.

"MY DEAR CHRISTIE,—I have been tossed about
the country a good deal these six weeks past, which
is the only excuse I can think of, at this present, for
not writing to you sooner.   I wrote to Hamilton, however, touching the business of your last letter, so that
I think myself, in some sort and manner as it were,
almost out of your debt.   I have more need to make
an apology to Traill, which I beg you will do for me
in the meantime, and say I mean to do so shortly
myself.   Last week I spent in Edinburgh, not that
I am a member of the Caledonian Hunt, which then
assembled there—nor that I am a knowing one on the
turf, though the Musselburgh races were held—nor a
lover of dancing, though there were balls every night
—but I went in to officiate at the funeral of an aged
female *single* cousin, on which occasion I had the
satisfaction of witnessing a facsimile of Mrs. Bertram
of Singleside her obsequies, the parallel holding
good even as to the legacies.[1]   Kean was in Edinburgh, however, and that part of the gaieties I much
enjoyed.   Of four characters in which I saw him,
Othello was my favourite, but neither Macbeth nor
Richard were of the number.   Murray, the manager,
with whom I am a little acquainted, is a very gentle-
manlike person ; and in truth well entitled to be so

---

[1] In "Guy Mannering."

by his birth, as he is grandson to Murray of Broughton, the Chevalier's secretary in '45.[1] He wished to show Kean every attention in his power, but was given to understand that Mr. Kean accepted of no invitation wherein 'his friends' were not included—meaning two of the most despicable of Murray's own candle-snuffers, with whom Kean got drunk every night during his stay. Were I in your shoes I would fain see Kean off the stage, and I daresay you might easily manage it. Hamilton has been ill of a quinzey, and is looking as ghastly as a spectre.

"In about three weeks I shall be in Edinburgh for good, and I intend passing advocate the first week of the term, Q. F. F. Q. S. You have thrown out two literary hints this summer, neither of which has been neglected by me—one concerning reviewing, and the other touching a periodical paper. The latter is a project whereon I have long loved to dwell—even since the days of our meditated Western Star, &c., Bristol Mustard Pot, &c. &c. I think there are among my acquaintances several individuals who could contribute richly to such a thing, but it is necessary to have a stock-in-hand before we begin. Let me hear what your notions are at more length. I have a friend in this neighbourhood, by name Hodgson, an extremely accomplished man, and a great dabbler in writing

---

[1] John Murray of Broughton, the Judas of the Royal cause. See Lockhart's "Scott," i. 242–245.

some years ago, though now the quiet minister of a very small parish, who was applied to by Murray (Albemarle Street) not long ago, with a view to an undertaking of this sort—who, though he declined at the time, has been thinking a good deal of it ever since, and is anxious to see such a thing set afoot. The *worthy baronet* might contribute a few Greekified things—Taffy a few Cambrian sketches. You might be 'the young fellow in town' of the club—and I myself might depict Scottish men of this day. Oxford is a rich field common to us all and untouched.—Yours ever, J. G. L.

" Direct your next to me at Glasgow—40 Charlotte Street."

With the end of the year 1816 we find Lockhart, like Allan Fairford in " Redgauntlet," "putting on the gown, and giving a bit chack of dinner to his friends and acquaintances, as is the custom." Like Scott, Lockhart was to find that "we've stood here an hour by Tron, hinny, and deil a ane has speered our price." However, he does not seem to have foreboded this end of his promenades in the Parliament House, when he writes :—

" EDINBURGH, 73 GEORGE STREET,
December 22, 1816 (Sunday forenoon).

" MY DEAR CHRISTIE,—I am most willing to believe that your obstinate silence is owing entirely to your hard studies, so, being unconscious of any such excuse, I am resolved to make one more attempt on you. I presume I need not ask you what you are doing. You are no doubt fagging hard at the law all the day, and drinking tea and reading Greek plays with Buchanan all the evening. Now and then you have a *tavern shine* with some young fellows—perhaps with Traill, if he has in good earnest returned unto himself. I, you must know, pursue a more dignified strain of life. I am now an advocate of a week's standing—have trod the boards of the Parliament House all that time, with the air of a man wrapped up in Potier and Cujacius, and have pocketed one fee of three guineas, which I spent in punch and tobacco the same evening— so far well. I am going west in a few days to culti- vate the procurators of Glasgow.

"There is a young and itching devil here—so God speed the attorneys and damn sentiment.

"I suppose you have read before this time the new novels, supposed to be, like 'Waverley,' by Walter Scott. The 'Old Mortality' story was very de- lightful to me, as the scene is admirably laid and pre- served in that part of the country with which I am most familiar ; but I have, unfortunately, read too much of the history of that period to approve of the gross violations of historical truth which he has taken the liberty—often, I think, without gaining anything by it—to introduce. Burley has long been known by me as a short, in-kneed, squinting, sallow, snarling viper,[1] and now behold he is uselessly swelled out into a Covenanting giant, with a blue bonnet of the cut of Brobdingnag. He was drowned, on his way from Holland to Scotland, about the date of the Revolution. Claverhouse's original letters I have seen—they are vulgar and bloody, without anything of the air of a polished man, far less of a sentimental cavalier in them.[2] These productions, in which true events and real personages are blended in so close a manner with nonentities of all kinds, are only tolerable to us in proportion to our ignorance of the places and period and persons described. The novels in question have so much merit in almost every other point of view, that they naturally attract uncommon attention to those passages of history on which they are, or pretend to be, founded, and so by their very merit work their own destruction. I wish the author had either stuck close to facts—in so far as never to invent anything which could be contradicted by history—or followed fiction altogether. This last tale is far more offensive than 'Waverley,' inasmuch as Waverley is a person more obscure than Morton, and more likely to have been omitted by the contemporary writers. At the same time, the general truth of the Covenanting manners exceeds, I should think, anything the author has executed in that

[1] One is reminded of Mrs. Squeers' turned-up-nosed peacock.
[2] Here the biographer utterly dissents from this child of the Remnant.

way.   Defoe's history of that period in Scotland is,
however, after all equally picturesque, better kept
up, and incomparably better written ; with all the
other advantages that truth ever possesses over
fiction.   There is no doubt of it, that man has the
strongest imagination of any prose writer that ever
lived.   Such is his power ·that he can make plain
matter of fact infinitely brighter than all the inven-
tions in the world could ever render a fictitious event.

This is sad prosing, but we are now so much
separated that new books and old friends are the
only subjects in which we can reckon on finding
each other's attention alive.   Sir William Hamilton
is very well at the other side of my table, and
requests me to hand you his love.   Remember us
both to Buchanan.   I rejoice to hear of his being
so happy with you.   I dined yesterday with his
aunt, and they are all perfectly well.—Yours most
affectionately,   J. G. L.

" How is Nicoll ?   I wish, if you are writing him,
you would desire him to send me and Hannay
our exhibs. with all speed convenient.   Write me
quickly, at Glasgow—if not for ten days (*quod
Deus avertat*) here again."

In later life, when he wrote his " Life of Scott,"
Lockhart took a far more favourable review of that
masterpiece, "Old Mortality."   His early comments
are rather pedantic.   A knowledge of the Burley

and Claverhouse of history does not spoil for us the Claverhouse and Burley of romance. As for Morton, and the shock caused to an historical mind by his absence from history books, his position, at Bothwell Brig, was very much like that of one of Lockhart's own ancestors, the hero who hid up a tree. Yet that hero needs a good deal of research before we discover him in some obscure Covenanter's narrative.

There is an unlucky gap in the correspondence between Christie and Mr. Lockhart, in the year 1817, while, of domestic correspondence, there is but one letter. This, to Mr. Lawrence Lockhart, contains a reference to " Blacky," a servant, probably the negro of whom Hogg tells a story. Lockhart, at the time we have reached, "was a mischievous Oxford puppy, for whom," says the Shepherd, " I was terrified, dancing after the young ladies, and drawing caricatures of every one who came in contact with him. . . . Even his household economy seemed clouded in mystery, and, if I got any explanation, it was sure not to be the right thing. It may be guessed how astonished I was one day, on perceiving six black servants waiting at his table upon six white gentlemen. Such a train of blackamoors being beyond my comprehension, I asked for an explanation, but got none, save that he found them very useful and obliging, poor fellows, and that they did not look for much wages beyond a mouthful of meat."

The real explanation was simple—the coloured gentlemen were friends of Lockhart's gentleman of colour, and aided him on festive occasions.

Dining out, giving dinners, dancing, drawing caricatures, taking part in the daily babble of the briefless round the stove in the Parliament House, Lockhart passed his time merrily, but not altogether in idleness. He wished to go to Germany in the vacation of 1817, and, though funds were scant, and his exhibition was running out, he managed to pay his way. He had made the acquaintance of Blackwood, the bookseller, and Blackwood paid him £300, or more, for a work in translation, to be written later. Lockhart selected Schlegel's "Lectures on the History of Literature." Mr. Gleig says, "Though seldom communicative on such subjects, he more than once alluded to the circumstance in after life, and always in the same terms. 'It was a generous act on Ebony's part, and a bold one too ; for he had only my word for it, that I had any acquaintance at all with the German language.'" [1]

Of the German tour scarcely any records remain. In an old notebook, used again twenty years later

[1] Mr. Gleig seems to date the German tour in 1815 or 1816, but I find no mention by Mr. Lockhart himself of any date, except that he had just returned from Germany in October 1817. See, however, *Quarterly Review*, cxvi., p. 452. According to Professor Veitch, in his "Life of Sir William Hamilton," p. 89, the early autumn of 1817 was the date. Accompanied by Lockhart and a Mr. Hyndman, Hamilton examined, at Leipzig, a library which the Faculty of Advocates wished to purchase.

in composing the "Life of Scott," are a few slight drawings of German students, and a sketch, not caricatured, of Fichte lecturing to his class. We know that Lockhart met, at Weimar, Goethe, whom he describes in "Peter's Letters," and whom he defended against the sneers of the *Edinburgh Review.*

More important to him than his brief experience of Germany was his connection with Mr. Blackwood. That gentleman was commencing publisher: the first series of his Magazine had run only a few months: there are traces of Lockhart's hand in it before July 1817. His liberality to the young writer was, indeed, well judged, for Lockhart, with Wilson, gave the Magazine a success of *éclat:* by no means wholly to their own advantage.

Gratitude to "Ebony" may, perhaps, partly explain that part of Lockhart's conduct, which perplexes his biographer as much as Scott's attitude to the Ballantynes puzzled Lockhart himself. Why would Lockhart, in spite of the remonstrances of Christie, and of Sir Walter, in spite of universal disapproval, cleave to *Blackwood's Magazine?* The mere attraction of mischief should soon have worn off, but from Wilson and *Blackwood's* Lockhart seemed unable to tear himself. Christie conceived a distaste for Mr. Blackwood at first sight; Lockhart sometimes lets fall a petulant word about the complacent proprietor of "*Ma Maga*," yet he wrote occasionally for *Maga* to the end. One really begins to think of *Maga* as of a cankered witch who has spell-bound the young man, and holds him "lost to life, and use, and name, and fame."

This, of course, is an irrational sentiment, and unjust to the venerated *Maga*. She did not make Lockhart and Wilson write as they did: it was they who set their mark on her. Lockhart several times thought of breaking with her, now in deference to Christie and Sir Walter; now, in some temporary displeasure with Mr. Blackwood, in which Wilson shared. But he always "fell to his old love again." He occasionally attributes this to regard for Mr. Blackwood, and, besides, the payment for his articles was highly necessary to him. But he could have employed his pen elsewhere, though nowhere with such freedom. The love of mischief, as Haydon says, was, no doubt, one cause of his constancy. But a freedom only trammelled by Mr. Blackwood, was very prejudicial to both Wilson and Lockhart. The former is said often to have repented of his articles, when the proofs had just gone beyond recall. The latter assuredly repented, and tried to make amends in his after-life. To love of mischief, of freedom to indulge caprice, to friendship for Wilson, and regard for Mr. Blackwood, one may most plausibly attribute Lockhart's stormy, and often regretted, but never broken constancy to *Maga*.

Be the explanation what it may, Lockhart was certainly very loyal to Blackwood. In describing

Scott's relations with this bookseller, he styles him "a man of strong talents, and, though without anything that could be called learning, of very respectable information ; . . . acute, earnest, eminently zealous in whatever he put his hand to ; upright, honest, sincere, and courageous."[1] We know that, in finding fault (as he well might) with "The Black Dwarf," Mr. Blackwood "did not search about for any glossy periphrase," he was frank enough. In Mrs. Gordon's "Life of Christopher North" we meet Mr. Blackwood suppressing, very properly, some literary ferocities of Professor Wilson's.[2] Why, then—Mr. Blackwood deserving Lockhart's deliberate and duly considered praises ; and Lockhart himself being what his letters declare him ; and Christopher North being Christopher North—the magazine which they produced should have been so brutal, it is difficult to imagine. These problems, of course, will recur ; for the present it suffices to have shown how Lockhart became connected with Mr. Blackwood.

In the absence of exact information as to the first half of Lockhart's first year as an advocate, we may be certain that, like Allan Fairford and Darsie Latimer, "he swept the boards of the Parliament House with the skirts of his gown ; laughed, and made others laugh, drank claret at Bayle's, Fortune's, and Walker's, and ate oysters in the

---

[1] "Life of Scott," vol. v. pp. 154-155.
[2] "Christopher North," ii. 63-64.

Covenant Close." Though his letters, so far, have not contained one word on politics, he was probably regarded, being a friend of Wilson's and living in his set, as a Tory. Every barrister had to take a side, and we know, from Lord Cockburn's "Memorials of his Time," that Tories were dull oppressors, while sweetness, light, knowledge, eloquence, emancipation, wit, wisdom, the *Edinburgh Review*—everything good but office—were all on the side of the Whigs. The admirable, overweening, unconscious arrogance of party pride in Lord Cockburn's "Memorials" might make a man turn Tory in sheer irritation to-day. While these scarcely human splendours, Jeffrey, Playfair, Henry Erskine, Gillies, Grahame, Macfarlane, Fletcher, —*fortisque Gyas, fortisque Cloanthus*—they, or their successors, were dwelling in the serene air of perfect self-complacency ; while they had at length set going a Liberal newspaper, the *Scotsman ;* while Tories, like Scott, were calling it "a blackguard print," a few young men had grown up who were neither stupid nor Whigs. They saw, Lockhart at least saw very well, that these illustrious Whigs, with all their learned professors, and Reviewers, and political economies, were really keeping Scotland in a state of "facetious and rejoicing ignorance." "In Scotland they understand, they care about none of the three," namely, the poetry, philosophy, and history of the ancient world. Even Dugald Stewart "has throughout been content to derive his ideas of

Greek philosophy from very secondary sources."
As for the common Whigs of the debating societies
and the Junior Bar, "all they know, worth being
known, upon any subject of general literature,
politics, or philosophy, is derived from the *Edinburgh
Review.*" The *Edinburgh*, again, perpetually de-
rides Wordsworth, and all the Whigs grin applause.
"The same people who despise and are ignorant
of Mr. Wordsworth, despise also and are ignorant
of all the majestic poets the world has ever produced,
with no exceptions beyond two or three great
names, acquaintance with which has been forced on
them by circumstances entirely out of their control.
The fate of Homer, of Æschylus, of Dante, nay,
of Milton, is his."[1]

These ideas, expressed in "Peter's Letters," and
such as these, were in the clear and well-furnished
mind of Lockhart, when he looked at the intellectual self-complacency of Edinburgh's illustrious
Whigs. And he was soon to let these magnates
hear the full measure of his opinion. That a cold
superiority of ridicule did not become Whig wit-
lings when they sat in judgment on the author of
"The Excursion"; that a more exalted patriotism
than the patriotism of the author of "Marmion" was
not really theirs; that Goethe and Kant could not
be criticised through the medium of French cribs
and summaries; that a facetious and rejoicing
ignorance of Greek could not be compensated for

[1] "Peter's Letters," vol. ii. p. 144.

by a smattering of geology ; that Christianity was
a problem to be faced, not an institution to be
scornfully patronised ; these were among the lessons
which the briefless new-gowned advocate was about
to teach the Olympians of Whiggery. The spirit
of mankind, in fact, was awaking in Lockhart,
as it later awoke in a sage who had a strong
sympathy with him, in Mr. Carlyle. The Whig view
of the world, and notably of poetry, did need to be
assailed. But Lockhart, seeing almost as clearly as
Carlyle the flaws in the ice palace of Edinburgh's
intellectual despots, was very young, and was con-
stitutionally a mocker. Almost everything that he
said in a serious humour, whether as the Baron von
Lauerwinkel, or as Dr. Peter Morris, was truly and
well said, and the truth has prevailed. But with
the same pen, and in the same hour, he was writing humorous ditties as " The Odontist " ; or attacks
on men of whom, personally, he knew nothing ;
of whose politics he judged by the catch-words
and prejudices of his party, and whose characters
he detested mainly on the evidence of Tory gossip.
Many a "sham," many a "windbag" he exposed, or
pricked, but to little or no avail, so strong in him,
at that time, was the spirit of levity, and the " Imp
of the Perverse." He had great powers, much
knowledge, clear ideas, a good opportunity, but
the " Imp of the Perverse" had dominion over him.
He began to write too young, he enjoyed a latitude
far too wide, and he had, in Wilson, an elder

associate and friend whose genius was perhaps the most unbalanced in the history of literature.   Therefore Lockhart never "blazed" in the serenity of the light which assuredly was within him, but only gave forth flashes of brilliance, when he did not pass wholly under the influence of "tenebriferous stars."

CHAPTER V

EDINBURGH, 1817-1818

"There was a natural demand for libel at this period."
—LORD COCKBURN.

Blackwood's Magazine.—Account of it in letter to Haydon (1838). —Lockhart "helps Blackwood out of a scrape." — "Row in Edinburgh." — Lockhart made the scapegoat.—His regrets.— His prospects ruined.—"Intolerably grievous fate." — Parallel of Theodore Hook.—Responsibility for *Blackwood's.*—Wilson and Lockhart *not* paid Editors.—Lockhart not the assailant of the Lake Poets.—Errors in "Life of Christopher North."—The early numbers of the Magazine.—Lockhart's articles on Greek Tragedy.—Blackwood quarrels with his original Editors.—They take service with Constable.—Their new Opposition Magazine.— Scott and Pringle.—Attack on Coleridge.—Wilson, Jeffrey, and Coleridge.—Lockhart on literary Whigs of Edinburgh.—Attack on the "Cockney School."—Keats and Lockhart agree in their views of Leigh Hunt.—"Vain, egotistical, and disgusting."—His "Tale of Rimini."—His enmity to Sir Walter Scott.—He and Keats fancy that Scott is their assailant.—Persistence of this absurdity. — "The Chaldee" Manuscript. — Hogg claims the authorship.—Burlesque reply.— Lockhart's own statement.— Analysis of "The Chaldee."—"No end of public emotion."

THE often told story of the early years of *Blackwood's Magazine* has next to be repeated. It was an ill day for Lockhart when he first put his pen at the service of a journal, which for now the term of a long human life, has been eminently reputable and admirable. Frequently as the matter has been discussed, there are points which have never before been clearly stated, while there are others that still remain obscure. Perhaps the best introduction to the subject may be found in a letter written by Lockhart himself, in later days, to Haydon the painter. Haydon had been at first a victim of the *Blackwood* satirists, merely because he was an associate of their enemy, Leigh Hunt. But, as we shall see, this feud with Haydon was soon settled, and he confesses that his foes treated him with hospitality and good fellowship: aiding him to the best of their power in later life.

Nevertheless, on the appearance of Lockhart's "Life of Scott," Haydon wrote him a long epistle, complaining of his early cruelties. On Haydon's own showing this conduct was curiously inconsistent, but his unfortunate temperament, and .melancholy end, excuse much in the painter.

Lockhart replied (July 11, 1838):—"I thank you for your two letters, though the second has given me a good deal of pain. Your approbation of the 'Life of Scott' is valuable, and might console me for all the abuse it has called forth both on him and me." . . .

(What follows will find more appropriate place later.)

"But I cannot be indifferent to your severe though generous reflections about my early literary escapades. You are willing to make allowances, but allow me to say, you have not understood the facts of the case. They were bad enough, but not so bad as you make them out. In the first place, I was a raw boy, who had never had the least connection either with politics or controversies of any kind, when, arriving in Edinburgh[1] in October 1817, I found my friend John Wilson (ten years my senior) busied in helping Blackwood out of a scrape he had got into with some editors of his Magazine, and on Wilson's asking me to try my hand at some squibberies in his aid, I sat down to do so with as little malice as if the assigned subject had been the Court of Pekin.[2] But the row in Edinburgh, the lordly Whigs having considered *persiflage* as their own fee-simple, was really so extravagant that when I think of it now, the whole story seems wildly incredible. Wilson and I were singled out to bear the whole burden of sin, though there were abundance of other criminals in the concern, and, by-and-by, Wilson passing for being a very eccentric fellow, and I for a cool one, even he was allowed to get off comparatively scot-free, while I, by far the youngest and least experienced of the set, and who alone had no personal grudges against any of Blackwood's victims, remained under such an accumulation of wrath and contumely, as would have crushed me utterly, unless for the buoyancy of

[1] He had just returned from Germany.
[2] A letter of Mr. Blackwood's, to Lockhart in Germany, of August 28, 1817, gives him information as to the opposition of Constable, and the determination to begin a new series of the Magazine. Mr. Blackwood says that Wilson has promised several articles.

extreme youth.[1] I now think with deep sadness of the pain my jibes and jokes inflicted on better men than myself, and I can say that I have omitted in my mature years no opportunity of trying to make reparation where *I* really had been the offender. But I was *not* the doer of half the deeds even you seem to set down to my account, nor can I, in the face of much evidence printed and unprinted, believe that, after all, our Ebony (as we used to call the man and his book) had half so much to answer for as the more regular artillery which the old *Quarterly* played incessantly, in these days, on the same parties.[2] . . .

"As to yourself, I really don't remember that I ever wrote a line against you in my life. I don't *swear* that I never mentioned your name in some ludicrous juxtaposition, but even of this I have not the remotest consciousness. I knew nothing then either of London or artists living out of Scotland, and I believe when you came down with the picture of the 'Entry into Jerusalem,' you were received even better by the 'Tory wags' than by

---

[1] After Lockhart's death, Miss Martineau took her favourite opportunity of "a newly made grave." "Lockhart's satire had, then and always," she said, "a quality of malice in it, where Wilson's had only fun." It is "only fun" to deride the personal manners, and the poetry, of your benefactor Scott, and your friend Wordsworth—the guest who has just left your door. "Noctes Ambrosianæ," September 1825, and vol. iii., 89-95, 134-135. I select *acknowledged* examples of Wilson's innocuous raillery.

[2] The omission contains merely an unexplained reference to a distinguished person, which might be misconstrued.

your fellow-sufferers of the Whig brigade.[1]   I
believe the only individuals whom *Blackwood* ever
really and essentially injured were myself and
Wilson.   Our feelings and happiness were disturbed
and shattered in consequence of that connection.
I was punished cruelly and irremediably in my
worldly fortunes, for the outcry cut off all prospects of professional advancement from me.   I
soon saw that the Tory Ministers and law officers
never would give me anything in that way. . . .
Thus I lost an honourable profession, and had,
after a few years of withering hopes, to make up
my mind for embracing the precarious, and, in my
opinion, intolerably grievous fate of the dependent
on literature.   It is true that I now regard this too
with equanimity, but that is only because I have
undergone so many disappointments of every kind,
crowned by an irreparable bereavement, that I
really have lost the power of feeling acutely on
any subject connected with my own worldly position. . . ."[2]

It was thus that Lockhart, under a blow which
struck at his heart, the loss of his beloved wife,
reviewed his early days of raillery.   His pleas of
youth, of association with an elder friend who
should have set him a different example, and of
freedom from personal malice, may be accepted even

---

[1] Haydon's " Autobiography " leaves no doubt on this point.
[2] The rest of the letter is a vigorous remonstrance with Haydon on
his own fortunes and the causes of them.

by severe judges. What he wrote about Theodore
Hook, might be said about himself. " It is fair to
recollect, too, that in the case of Theodore Hook,
when he was making his paper so formidably
famous, there really could not have been any true
personal malignity at work. He was fresh from
a colonial life, in which few men's passions are ever
much disturbed by sympathy with the ups and
downs of the great parties at home. He had sus-
tained no sort of injury as yet at the hands of either
Whigs or Radicals. He knew little, and could
have cared nothing, about those who became the
objects of his satire. Exquisitely cruel as it often
seemed, it was with him a mere *skiomachy*. Certain
men and women were stuck up as types of certain
prejudices or delusions ; and he set to knocking
them down with no more feeling about them, as
individual human creatures, than if they had been
nine-pins. In all this there was a culpable recklessness—a sad want of thought; but, at the same
time, want of reflection is not exactly to be con-
founded with deliberation of malice." [1]

It is conspicuously apparent, from Lockhart's
letters, that he knew nothing of Leigh Hunt, nothing
of Hazlitt, for example, and nothing of " Shelly," as
he then writes the name. To him they were, vaguely,
the enemy, the other side, assailants of his party,
and, as far as Hazlitt and Hunt were concerned,
"Cockneys." He therefore attacked them with a

[1] "Theodore Hook," p. 51, London, 1853.

light heart, and with a bitterness which was merely part of the performance. But his very coolness, clearness of head, and logic made his attacks terrible, while his personalities, if not without example, went beyond even the Tory standard of the time. Doubtless the storm which he at once awoke drove him further than he had dreamed of going, and the whole results were deplorable. Yet literature was surely, more than law, his real province, though his pride appears to have resented his official connection with literature, as an editor.

To return to *Blackwood*. In a matter where the chief sinners, both publicly and privately, in later years, "took blame to themselves," an *apologia* cannot now be offered. This is not a case of which we may say, *tout comprendre c'est tout pardonner*, for all the motives could not be understood, as Lockhart frankly admitted, even immediately after the commission of one of the offences. At best we can put ourselves in the position of the culprits, try to see things and men as they must have seen them ; make allowance for prejudice, for the manners of the age, for the vivacities of youth. When all this is done there abides an amount of wrong which is not to be palliated, not to be smiled away.

As to the weight of responsibility it was partly editorial, partly, in each case, a question of authorship. About the editorial department there was division of public opinion from the first. Mr. Blackwood, the publisher, and, to all appearance, the director of the Magazine, averred (according to Scott, as cited by Charles Kirkpatrick Sharpe in a letter to Constable) that an article, the now innocuous "Chaldee Manuscript," had been inserted "against his will."[1]

Yet the periodical, if it began as it went on, was under the direction of Mr. Blackwood himself. "*Ma Maga*," he used to call it, according to Lockhart.[2] Again, in an unpublished note to Maginn, at the time of Byron's death, Lockhart says that "Blackwood will not have it," that is, an attack on Byron, proposed by the Irish writer, which Lockhart deprecates himself. Yet Wilson was, from the beginning, supposed by the curious to be actual editor. Thus Scott, in a letter to Sharpe of September 1817, says, "Wilson will be a spirited charioteer, or I mistake him, and take the corner with four starved authors in hand, in great style." Assuredly neither Lockhart nor Wilson would have publicly disassociated himself from any responsibility and fixed it upon his friend alone.

For a certain brief period, in 1818, it appears, from the "Memoir of John Murray," and from Lockhart's own letters, that he and Wilson were actually in command of the Magazine, though, (according to Lockhart) even then with Mr. Blackwood in power behind them. The arrangement proved unworkable for many reasons : among others, I believe,

---

[1] "Archibald Constable and his Literary Correspondents," ii. 349.
[2] Lockhart to Wilson, 1825.   From Manuscript.

because Mr. Blackwood was not content to be a mere constitutional monarch. The money which Mr. Murray had advanced, as partner in the venture, was returned to him.[1] Both Lockhart and Wilson denied that they had ever received money for conducting the periodical. Wilson's denial was written in 1828, after the troublous times were over, to his personal friend the Rev. Mr. Fleming of Rayrig. ".Of *Blackwood's Magazine* I am not the editor. . . . I am one of the chief writers, perhaps the chief, and have all along been so, *but never received one shilling from the proprietor, except for my own compositions.* . . . To you I make the avowal, which is to the letter correct, of Christopher North's ideal character."[2]

It thus appears that the intended editorial arrangement, like the connection with Mr. Murray, was rescinded, or rather, never "implemented," in the Scots Law phrase. A letter of 1818 from Sir Walter to Will Laidlaw seems to confirm this theory.[3] As to authorship of articles, on one point I am constrained, in fairness to Lockhart, to differ from an earlier writer. Mrs. Gordon, in her pleasing "Life of Christopher North," her father, writes, like a good daughter, "I cannot say that I have been able to trace to his hand any instance of unmanly attack, or

---

[1] "Memoir of John Murray," i. 495.

[2] "Christopher North," ii. 123.

[3] The letter is rather too familiar for publication. It more than bears out what Lockhart says as to Scott's grudge, at a certain time, against Mr. Blackwood.

one shade of real malignity.   There did appear in
the Magazine wanton and unjustifiable strictures on
persons, such as Wordsworth and Coleridge, with
whom he was on terms of friendship, and for whom,
in its own pages and elsewhere, he professed, as he
sincerely felt, the highest esteem.   But when it is
well understood that he was never in any sense the
editor, . . . it will appear that he had simply the
alternative of ceasing to contribute further to the
Magazine, or of continuing to do so under the disadvantage of seeming to approve what he really
condemned.[1]   That he adopted the latter course is, I
think, no stigma on his character; and, in after days,
when his influence in the Magazine had become
paramount, he made noble amends for its sins."

   All this is demonstrably erroneous reasoning :
the facts, too, are erroneous.   Mrs. Gordon had
access, she says, to the *arcana imperii* of the house
of Blackwood, only after the date 1826.   To the
authorship of early articles, I myself have, what
Mrs. Gordon had not, the clues of statements in
Lockhart's hitherto unpublished letters.   There is
also internal evidence of style, no two styles being
(as a rule) so easily distinguishable as the "swash-
ing blow " of Wilson, and the rapier thrust of Lockhart.   Again, in 1817–1819, Lockhart knew not one

---

[1] "Thus it is possible his desire to review Coleridge favourably in
the *Edinburgh* may have arisen from a wish to do justice to that
great man, the opportunity for which was denied in the pages of
Blackwood." (Mrs. Gordon's note.)

of the Lake School ; Wilson knew them all, and all
the ins and outs of their little domestic politics and
quarrels. Lockhart's deep and earnest admiration
of Wordsworth's poems has already been apparent
in his letters, nor was Wilson, as a rule, a less
ardent advocate. Which of the twain, then, is to
blame for personal attacks on men who were the
intimates of the elder partner, while they were
personally strangers to the junior? On December
5, 1819, Lockhart, in a letter to Christie, disclaims
any personal knowledge of any single victim of the
Magazine. "With Wilson the case is most different.
With Coleridge, Wordsworth, Jeffrey, &c., &c., in
short with all that have been attacked, he *has lived*,
at some time or other, on terms of intimacy, and,
therefore, they have all in turn complained grievously
of him." Whoever attacked Coleridge and Wordsworth, Lockhart was not the man, and one assault
on Wordsworth is included in Wilson's acknowledged works: in "Noctes Ambrosianæ," September 1825.

Lockhart, in the letter cited, refers to an extraordinary "bam" attempted by Wilson on Wordsworth,
and much talked of in London, as having occurred
during his own absence in Germany. Wilson's conduct, in fact, is attributable to his amazing lack of
consistency, his want of any "tie-beam," as Mr.
Carlyle says. Meanwhile, about Wilson's friends,
"the Lakers," Lockhart, at twenty-three, knew
nothing personally, except what Wilson told him.

It is needless to say more. The weight of responsibility for personal unfairness to the Lakers
cannot be transferred to the shoulders of Lockhart.
That excuse does Wilson injustice. A man of
thirty-two would not permit "a green unknowing
youth" of twenty-three to revile his personal friends
in a magazine where his influence was, at least, very
considerable. As Mr. Gleig wrote in a review of
Mrs. Gordon's book : " Is it conceivable that a man
at the mature age of thirty-two, already known to
fame as a poet and a critic, would give himself up,
bound hand and foot, to the guidance of a boy ? " [1]
It is not conceivable, and the facts were the reverse.
No just critic can lay all the fault on the shoulders
of the youngest person concerned, who, moreover,
as a matter of fact, was innocent of the deed. Yet,
young as he was, even in these days Lockhart gave
proofs, as will be shown, of such a clear judgment,
and sound unbiassed taste, as are not displayed by
any of his comrades. His excesses are like those of
a sober man who, finding himself in riotous company, conforms himself to their humour. One can
imagine that, within himself, he cherished a proud
disdain of the frays in which he figured, and of the
work to which he lent his hand. I do not know
quo numine laeso Mrs. Gordon penned her remarks
on her father's constant friend. In matters where
both were culpable in their degree, be it far from
me to exculpate Lockhart at the expense of his

[1] *Quarterly Review*, vol. cxiii. (1863, p. 228).

comrade, except where his own written statements
cannot in fairness be overlooked. Mr. Gleig says,
as regards Lockhart's letters, published by Mrs.
Gordon : "She must need preface them with words
of her own," which follow :

"They" (Lockhart's letters) "are as characteristic
of his satirical powers as any of those off-hand caricatures that shred his best friends to pieces, leaving
the most poetical of them as bereft of that beautifying property as if they had been born utterly without
it." Pictorial caricature, even in the pages of Mr.
Punch or elsewhere, is very seldom resented even
by the most thin-skinned of mortals, and Mrs.
Gordon herself publishes a caricature of her father.
Lockhart, who certainly had whatever "beautifying
property" a "poetical" aspect may entail, frequently
"shred" *himself* "to pieces," with his pencil. Mrs.
Gordon's "Life of Christopher North" has been
widely read, as it deserved to be, and has been
long in the field—in fact, since 1862. This remonstrance is therefore necessary. For too many years
Lockhart has been made the solitary scapegoat of
Wilson, and of *Blackwood* in general.

✓   Lockhart, though he began so young, was, I think,
a critic eminently well equipped with learning, and,
where he touched on the classics of any language,
eminently well endowed with delicacy and breadth
of appreciation. But where party prejudice came
in, and contemporaries were his themes, he was
no better, often, than other literary judges of his

time. Lest the reader, inexpert in the fugitive productions of that day, should think Lockhart a prodigy of dark critical malevolence, I would ask his attention for the notice of Coleridge's "Christabel" and "Kubla Khan," which appeared, a year before, in the *Edinburgh Review* (September 1816). Coleridge was, of course, a Tory, as Leigh Hunt and Keats were Liberals. He was also a man hardly treated by fortune, and thwarted by much that was now, "humanly speaking," beyond control in his own constitution and character. Moreover, he was very poor, and had sold his fragment, "Christabel," to Mr. Murray for a small sum, which two editions probably did not repay to the publisher. His relations with Jeffrey, the Editor of the *Edinburgh Review*, I shall take on Jeffrey's own, not on Coleridge's larger estimate. In 1810 they had met at Southey's, and, after a pleasant hour or two of talk, had passed the next day "in the fields," Coleridge dining with Jeffrey at his inn. Jeffrey, who did not care for metaphysics, "exhorted him rather to give us more poetry." "We spoke, too, of 'Christabel,' and I advised him to publish it," knowing nothing of it but four or five lines quoted by Scott, who "spoke favourably of it," and said that to "Christabel" "he was indebted for the metrical method of his 'Lay of the Last Minstrel.'"[1]

"Christabel," with "Kubla Khan," and "The

[1] Jeffrey, in a personal note to the criticism of "Biographia Literaria," *Edinburgh Review*, vol. xxviii., August 1817, pp. 509-510.

Pains of Sleep," appeared from Mr. Murray's house in 1816, and was reviewed (by Hazlitt, according to Coleridge), under Jeffrey's editorship, in the September number of the *Edinburgh*, 1816.

This odious critique is forgotten, perhaps because nobody could say that it "killed" Coleridge. It only killed his hopes of profit and fame (he being poor, ill, and in sad estate) from the most original compositions in the range of English literature. There is no critical vice which his Whig critic does not exhibit. With the blind eye, the deaf ear, the insensible heart, are allied gross and mean personal impudence, frequent imputations of insanity, and the wonted political rancour. An advertisement of the book mentioned that Byron had praised "Christabel" as "a wild and singularly original and beautiful poem." Jeffrey knew that Scott was of the same mind, but the opinions of poets on poetry were nothing to him and his reviewer. "It seems," says his man, "nowadays to be the practice of that once irritable race to laud each other without bounds; and one can hardly avoid suspecting, that what is thus lavishly advanced may be laid out with a view to being repaid with interest." This is an elegant insinuation against Byron and Scott!

"Much of the art of the wild writers consists in sudden transitions, opening eagerly upon some subject, and then flying from it immediately. This indeed is known to the medical men, who not unfrequently have the care of them, as an unerring

symptom." Under Gillman's care, Coleridge may
later have reflected on this graceful innuendo. The
poem is then burlesqued in a prose summary, and
the passage,

"But vainly thou warrest,"

is said to "have been manufactured by shaking
words together at random." Coleridge's remarks
on his own metre are "a miserable piece of cox-
combry and shuffling." Coleridge "was in bad
health when he wrote 'Kubla Khan'—the particular disease is not given, but the careful reader
will form his own conjectures." "Persons in this
poet's unhappy condition generally feel the want
of sleep as the worst of their evils." The whole
work is "one of the most notable pieces of impertinence of which the press has lately been guilty,
. . . . utterly destitute of value . . . . displays not
one ray of genius . . . . has not one couplet which
could be reckoned poetry were it found in the
corner of a newspaper." The work is not to be
tolerated, "though a brother poet chooses to laud
it from courtesy or interest." Then comes the
political spleen. "And are such panegyrics," as
Byron's, "to be echoed by the mean tools of a
political faction, because they relate to one whose
daily prose is understood to be dedicated to the
support of all that courtiers think should be
supported?"

All this Jeffrey, as Editor, published, in mature
life, in a well-established critical organ, about the

man of genius who had eaten his salt, and whom he had urged to print the very poem thus, and in this disgraceful manner denounced.   Yet nobody throws a stone at Jeffrey.   Nobody shakes the respectable head over "that wicked review of poor Coleridge," that dastardly censure of his chief treasure, his most accomplished and unequalled work.

I have introduced this digression to show the style of reviewing which was current and admired, in the most celebrated critical organ of the time, when Lockhart, almost as a boy, began to review. This was the model set him by the Whig Aristarchus, "the first of British critics."   And, if Jeffrey, mature, famous, omnipotent, could put his seal on the unspeakable meanness and stupidity, personal insolence, sordid imputations, and political clap-trap of the review of "Christabel," I ask that some lenience may be shown to political partisanship, personalities, bad taste, as displayed by a raw young Tory of twenty-three, in his remarks on poems, which no one can regard as approaching in excellence to Coleridge's masterpiece ; poems written by persons whose salt he had never eaten, whose faces he had never seen, whom he judged only by hostile rumour, or on the evidence of their own undeniable affectations.

To return from this digression :—

The *Edinburgh Monthly Magazine* (not yet nominally *Blackwood's*) commenced in April 1817. The Editors were Mr. Thomas Pringle and Mr.

Cleghorn, an authority on Farming. The prospectus announced the serial as "a Repository of whatever may be most interesting to general readers." Antiquarianism was to be made a strong point: the articles in other magazines were to be criticised: "The Register" of public events, foreign and domestic, was almost to supersede the "Annual Registers," in one of which, the *Edinburgh Annual Register*, Scott did much work. Nothing could be more blameless and pacific: the periodical, in brief, was to be an improvement on the old *Scots Magazine*, then in decay. Whether or not Lockhart was the author of the essays on Greek Tragedy, which began in the first number, his biographer has no documentary means of ascertaining. They are attributed to Lockhart by Mr. Gleig, in his *Quarterly Review* article, and they have none of Wilson's characteristic diction. They bear the signature "Zeta," later attached to the essays on the Cockney School, but such signatures were used in the early *Blackwoods* for the purpose of perplexing.[1] The translations from the "Prometheus Bound" are certainly worthy of Lockhart, and do not justify the writer's own remark, that "the inspiration of poetry vanishes at the touch of translation." An example may be offered. Prometheus is describing the state of mankind before he came, the hero of the introduction of the Arts:

---

[1] As a matter of fact, at least two writers used the signature "Zeta."

"Eyes had they, but they saw not; they had ears,
But heard not; like the shadows of a dream,
For ages did they flit upon the earth,
Rising and vanishing, and left no trace
Of wisdom, or of forethought.   Their abodes
Were not of wood or stone, nor did the sun
Warm them, for then they dwelt in lightless caves.
The season's change they knew not, when the spring
Should shed its roses, or the summer pour
Its golden fruits, or icy winter breathe
In barrenness and blackness on the year.

To heaven I raised their eyes, and bade them mark
The time the constellations rose and set,
By which their labours they might regulate.
I taught them numbers, letters were my gift,
By which the poet's genius might preserve
The memory of glorious events.

.   .   .   .

I was man's saviour, but have now no power
From these degrading bonds myself to save."

In the whole attitude of Prometheus the critic
finds "the love of independence and the hatred of
tyranny, and the unquenchable daring of a noble
mind, that rendered the play the delight of the
Athenians.   It was the bright reflection of their
own souls, and the fair image returned to them again
with all the joy of self-exaltation.   This was the
halo that shone from heaven, and shed over the
tragedy a lustre by which it was sanctioned in the
eye of freedom."

Shelley would not have thought otherwise, and
in these passages we probably discern the true self

PROFESSOR WILSON.

(Drawn by Daniel Maclise, R.A)

of Lockhart, at ease in the native air of his genius, as i₁ the cold glade of frosty Caucasus.

Thus the Magazine went its way, certainly instructive to the antiquarian, for it contained original documents, and was aided by Dr. M'Crie, author of "Knox's Life," by Wilson, and by Sir David Brewster. But in the sixth number (Sept. 1817) appeared the announcement: "This work is now discontinued." "The bookseller and Pringle quarrelled," says Lockhart briefly, and Mrs. Gordon tells us, as does the author of "Hypocrisy Unveiled," that the two editors resented Blackwood's interference. Sharpe reports to Scott the same story in August 1817. As this was the ground of quarrel, it is unlikely that Mr. Blackwood in the new series (*Blackwood's Edinburgh Magazine*, begun in October 1817) would allow himself to be interfered with by Wilson or any one else. Meanwhile, Mr. Pringle and Mr. Cleghorn betook themselves to Mr. Constable, "offering their services as editors of a new series of the *Scots Magazine*, to appear under the title of *The Edinburgh Magazine*."[1] Blackwood remodelled his own serial, and with the October number began the war of political and personal scurrilities, at least on the side of "Ebony." Mr. Pringle does not seem to have been very successful under the banner of Constable, and, as usual, we find Scott trying to help "a (literally)

---

[1] We find no letters from, and no information about, Mr. Cleghorn and Mr. Pringle in the "Memoir of Archibald Constable."

lame dog over a stile." On September 8, 1819, Mr. Croker writes to Mr. Goulburn, enclosing "a very dull and almost illegible piece of Walter Scott's composition." "One Pringle, a Scotch Tory, born lame . . . sets up a magazine, quarrels with his publisher, is turned off, abused, and ridiculed. Sets up a new magazine in opposition to the former . . . the new publisher (Constable) as bad as the old, another dismissal . . . applies to Walter Scott . . . Walter Scott . . ." as usual does all that man can do for poor Mr. Pringle, who goes to the Cape.[1]

The very first number of the new series contained three articles which illustrate at once the motiveless waywardness, the personal violence, and the boisterous humour which were to mark the periodical for years. These articles were the attack on Coleridge, the assault on Leigh Hunt, and the "Chaldee Manuscript." To consider them, and their sequels and consequences, is practically to criticise the early history of Blackwood. In October 1817 we find Jeffrey trying to enlist Wilson under the Blue and Yellow of the *Edinburgh Review.* "It would appear," says Mrs. Gordon, "that he (Wilson) had offered to review Coleridge in a friendly manner," for Wilson was of lacustrine habits, and, at Elleray, had known the Lake poets, and all the minute politics of their settlements.

Jeffrey (October 17, 1817) evaded the review of S. T. C., preferring an article on Byron. These facts

---

[1] I find an interesting letter of thanks from Mr. Pringle.

make it all the more extraordinary and unintelligible, that the October number of *Blackwood* opened with a most violent personal attack on Coleridge. " This lampoon," says Lockhart in " Peter's Letters," 1819, was "a total departure from the principles of the Magazine . . . the only one of the various sins of this Magazine for which I am at a loss to discover, not an apology, but a motive." He then praises Coleridge with enthusiasm and discrimination, ending (as to the article), " I profess myself unable to solve the mystery of the motive. The result is bad, and, in truth, very pitiable."

Possibly the motive is to be found in the end of the article. Maturin had written a tragedy, which Scott, in a letter to Terry, calls (after certain censures), "grand and powerful, the language most animated and poetical, and the characters sketched with a masterly enthusiasm." This play was " Bertram." Now Coleridge, in a critique (re-published in his " Biographia Literaria "), had described "Bertram" as "this superfetation of blasphemy upon nonsense, this *felo de se* and thief captain, this loathsome and leprous confluence of robbery, adultery, murder, and cowardly assassination, whose best deed is the having saved his betters from the degradation of hanging him, by turning Jack Ketch to himself." "Bertram" had superseded Coleridge's " Zapolya," at Covent Garden.

It was thus that men like Coleridge wrote in the brave days of old ! The assailant of Coleridge, in

Blackwood, contrasts his conduct with that of Scott, Byron, and Henry Mackenzie, who had all praised and encouraged the unfortunate Maturin. " Let me entreat you," says Scott to Maturin (Feb. 26, 1818), "to view Coleridge's violence as a thing to be contemned, not retaliated—the opinion of a British public may surely be set in honest opposition to that of one disappointed and wayward man. You should also consider, *en bon Chrétien*, that Coleridge has had some room to be spited at the world."[1]

This attack on Coleridge in *Blackwood* is a fair example, not only of the violence, but of the incalculable waywardness of the Magazine. Wilson, just before the onslaught appeared, was anxious, as we saw, to praise Coleridge ; Lockhart, in a very short space of time, is found applauding the author of "Christabel," and, in later life, liked and admired him greatly. Coleridge was no Whig, no *Edinburgh* reviewer. Yet he was set upon and mauled, apparently in revenge for Maturin, who was "no kith or kin" to the Edinburgh Tories. The proceeding, whoever the author may have been, was characteristic.[2] The vagaries of the Magazine were indeed inexplicable. Coleridge was presently taken into favour ; Haydon was insulted till he was known ; contributors themselves were as likely as any one else to be attacked. The chief writers, as

[1] The real motive for the attack on Coleridge was too vague to be traced, and too childish to be revealed here.

[2] The article was *not* by Lockhart ; he names the author in a letter to Christie.

Haydon reports a saying of Scott's, were "like bears in a china shop." As Blackwood could certainly assert himself, while Wilson was a man of mature years, with an ambition to instruct youth from a Chair of Moral Philosophy, the recklessness of their periodical is even more astonishing than its violence.

The chief enemies, while friends were insecure, were of course the Whigs, the *Edinburgh Review*, the "Cockneys," and the opposition in the persons of Constable, Cleghorn, and Pringle. In " Peter's Letters," written while the Magazine was in the flush of its unamiable youth, Lockhart speaks of the *Edinburgh Review* as offering "a diet of levity and sarcastic indifference," as discredited in the perpetual croakings of prophecy, with which it certainly laboured to chill the heart of England during the struggle with Napoleon; and as tedious and odious by virtue of its coldness in criticism. " It never praised even the highest efforts of contemporary genius in the spirit of true and genuine earnestness. . . . They never spoke out of the fulness of the heart, in praising any of our great living poets. . . . Looking back now after the lapse of several years, to their accounts of many of these poems (such as Mr. Scott's, for example) . . . it is quite wonderful to find in what a light and trivial vein the first notices of them had been presented to the public by the *Edinburgh Review*." Wonderful it is to read Jeffrey on Wordsworth,

Jeffrey on "Marmion," and to remember that he (as he seems in these articles at least) was taken for Sir Oracle. A generous young man might well resent Jeffrey's carping; his patronising manner when he praises; his cheery contented inaccessibility to what is noble, and to what is nobly spirited in verse. In "Peter's Letters" Lockhart adds to the sins of the *Edinburgh Review*, "its occasional religious mockeries." On this matter, unluckily, there is more to be said later. The *Edinburgh Review*, and the Whigs in general, were fair game, if the game was fairly played. How unfairly played it was will presently be apparent.

The excesses, to put it mildly, of the new Magazine began with the lampoon on Coleridge in the first number. They were followed, in the same number, by the opening attack on "The Cockney School of Poetry." The head of the Cockney School was Leigh Hunt, then obnoxious to Tories as Editor of the Radical *Examiner*, the libeller of the Regent, the jaunty babbler about himself, his domesticities, and the young men around him, Keats, Cornelius Webb, Hazlitt, Haydon, and many others. That they should praise Hunt, that Hunt should praise them, that Keats should furnish Hunt with an ivy crown, that they should write and publish sonnets to each other, was not odd in members of a literary "circle." But to persons at a distance, the spectacle of such endearments has always been irritating. A genius like Keats's could not long endure the atmosphere of a *coterie*. As early as May 10, 1817, before ever *Blackwood* was, we find Keats complaining to Haydon of Hunt's "self-illusions, they are very lamentable." "There is no greater sin than to flatter oneself into the idea of being a great poet."[1] Hunt has spoiled Hampstead, Keats says, by identifying it with himself. "Hunt keeps on in his old way; I am completely tired of it all. He has lately published a Pocket-Book, called the 'Literary Pocket-Book,' full of the most sickening stuff you can imagine."[2] . . . "In reality he is vain, egotistical, and disgusting in taste and morals. He understands many a beautiful thing; but then, instead of giving other minds credit for the same degree of perception as he himself possesses, he begins an explanation in such a curious

---

[1] "Letters of John Keats," London, 1895, p. 18.
[2] This Pocket-Book was rather kindly received by *Blackwood*, December 1819, after the attack on Keats. The Pocket-Book contained two sonnets by Keats, signed—I.: "The Human Seasons," and "Ailsa Rock." "As we are anxious to bring this young writer into notice, we quote his sonnets." For the first, "we thank Mr. Keats." The sonnet on Ailsa Craig is "portentous folly." It is, indeed, an exquisitely bad sonnet—

> "Thou answerest not, for thou art dead asleep;
>   Thy life is but two dead eternities,—
> *The last in air, the former in the deep;*
>   First with the whales, last with the eagle skies—
> Drowned wast thou till an earthquake made thee steep,
>   Another cannot wake thy giant size."

"Do not let John Keats think we dislike him, he is a young man of some poetry:" heavy banter about apothecaries follows.

manner that our taste and self-love is offended continually. Hunt does one harm by making fine things petty, and beautiful things hateful."[1] *Makes beautiful things hateful!* Lockhart says, " Perhaps no writer, by half so feeble, ever succeeded in turning so many beautiful things into objects of aversion."[2] This extraordinary verbal coincidence between the testimony of a friend and a foe cannot be merely fortuitous. Leigh Hunt (at that time) pawed over and vulgarised the victims of his admiration: this, with his vanity, his egotistic babble, accounts for the spleen of Lockhart, though it does not excuse his ferocities. Keats's remarks, though they abet those of *Blackwood*, are also splenetic, and doubtless exaggerated; he was later reconciled to Hunt. But if a friend thought he had cause to speak thus, we need not wonder at the scorn which Hunt provoked in the hostile conductors of *Blackwood*. Hunt is there written down vulgar, ignorant (and his education was really most incomplete); finally, as Keats says, Hunt is "disgusting in taste and morals." His religion is "a poor tame dilution of the blasphemies of the *Encyclopædia*." His dress is ridiculed; "his muse talks indelicately like a tea-sipping milliner girl." His " Tale of Rimini " is full of Cockney vulgarisms, an undeniably true

---

[1] Keats to George Keats, January 4, 1819. Mr. Forman's edition of "Complete Letters," p. 242.

[2] *Quarterly Review*, vol. xliv. p. 210.

remark. When Paolo and Francesca kiss, they are "all of a tremble"!

The criticism is not so strong as Coleridge's censures on "Bertram," but it is more personal. This kind of thing went on, and was continued in a letter to Leigh Hunt, by Zeta, in the January number of 1818. Zeta, withholding his name for the present (the *Examiner* had called him a liar, and so forth), declares that he attacks the *poet*, not the *man*, as immoral. It was of the man, however, that Keats spoke. The "Tale of Rimini" is "a smiling apology for a crime at once horrible in its effects, and easy in its perpetration," which can hardly be denied, if we are to be moral.

Leigh Hunt appears to have imagined a wonderful cause for all this animosity, which, perhaps, has been sufficiently explained on general grounds. In 1810 he had edited an abortive quarterly magazine, *The Reflector*. In this he imitated Suckling's "Session of Poets," by a piece called "The Feast of Poets": and hence, he says, came "to the Tory critics of Scotland the first cause of offence." Hunt had "taken a dislike to Walter Scott" for a singular reason. Charles II. was reported to have sent Lord Mulgrave to Tangiers in a leaky ship, along with a son of his own. In Scott's "Life of Dryden," he characterised this not very probable act of the good-natured king as "ungenerous." Hence Leigh Hunt's noble wrath. To avenge Lord Mulgrave, who reached Tangiers in perfect safety, "the future great novelist was introduced to Apollo in 'The Feast of the Poets,' after a very irreverent fashion."[1] In 1832 Hunt withdrew the "irreverent" passages, stating, however, in his preface, that they "gave rise to some of the most inveterate enmities he had experienced." We learn from Keats, that Hunt believed the inveterate Scott to have been his assailant in *Blackwood!* "He was nearly sure that 'The Cockney School' was written by Scott, so you are right, Tom!" (January 23, 1818.) Scott's desire, as he told Maturin, was ever to have his foes "*where the muir-cock was baillie*, or, as you would say, *upon the sod*, but I never let the thing cling to my mind."

What manner of man at this time was Leigh Hunt, with his belief that Scott could let an impertinence "cling to his mind" for seven years, and then avenge it anonymously, the reader may now estimate for himself. But the worst of Hunt's ignorance of a noble nature is, that he probably persuaded Keats to see *his* assailant in the most generous of men. A trace of the old incredible suspicion shows itself in Mr. Forman's note on Keats's text. "Mr. Dilke stated that it" (the article on "The Cockney School") "was written by Lockhart, Scott's son-in-law." Now, when these articles began, Lockhart had never even met Scott in society. From the first, as the motto from Cornelius Webb shows, and as Keats himself

---

[1] "The Autobiography of Leigh Hunt," 1860, pp. 215–216.

observes, the writers of "The Cockney School"
meant to pillory Keats.

> "Our talk shall be (a theme we never tire on)
> Of Chaucer, Spenser, Shakespeare, Milton, Byron,
> (Our England's Dante)—Wordsworth, *Hunt* and *Keats*,
> The Muses' son of promise."

These lines, written when Keats was the unknown
author of a small book of poems, not all worthy of
him, and when Hunt was no nearer Shakespeare
than usual, were irritating to the most lenient
observer; Keats was confused by the *Blackwood*
men with Hunt and Webb; he knew it, he expected
attack, and says that, if insulted, and if he meets
his enemy, "he must infallibly call him to an
account" (November 5, 1817).

After the affair of "The Cockney School" (which,
unluckily, had sequels), it is almost a pleasure to
reach the open buffoonery and ingenuity of "The
Chaldee Manuscript." Hogg soon claimed the
authorship of "The Chaldee." "I know not what
wicked genius put it into my head," says the
Shepherd.[1] He adds that Blackwood never thought
of publishing it, but "some of the rascals to whom
he showed it almost forced him to insert it."
"There is a bouncer!" cries a reviewer of Hogg,
apparently Lockhart, or possibly De Quincey, in
Blackwood for August 1821, and he goes on—

---

[1] "The Mountain Bard." Third edition. To which is prefixed a
Memoir of the Author's Life, p. 65.

"About the subject of 'The Chaldee,' let me now speak the truth." Christopher North, the writer himself, Blackwood, "and a reverend gentleman of this city, alone know the perpetrator. . . . It was the same person who murdered Begbie," the bank porter, whose death is an undiscovered mystery to this hour. "Like Mr. Bowles and Ali Pasha, he was a mild man of unassuming manners, a scholar and a gentleman. It is quite a vulgar error to suppose him a ruffian. He was sensibility itself, and would not hurt a fly. But it was a disease with him to excite public emotion. Though he had an amiable wife and a vast family, he never was happy, unless he saw the world staring like a stuck pig. With respect to his murdering Begbie, as it is called, he knew the poor man well, and had frequently given him both small sums of money, and articles of wearing apparel." However he decided that, by seeming to slay and rob Begbie, "there would be no end of public emotion, to use his own constant phrase on occasions of this nature. He was always kind to the poor man's widow, who was rather a gainer by her husband's death. I have reason to believe that he ultimately regretted the act, but there can be no doubt that his enjoyment was great for many years. . . . He confessed 'The Chaldee,' and the murder, the day before he died, to the reverend gentleman specified, and was sufficiently penitent; yet, with that inconsistency not unusual in dying men, almost his last words were (indistinctly mumbled to himself,) 'It ought not to have been left out of the other editions.'"

"After this plain statement Hogg must look extremely foolish. We shall next have him claiming the murder likewise, I suppose; but he is totally incapable of either."

Professor Ferrier, in his edition of "Noctes Ambrosianæ," does not wholly bear out the statements either of Hogg or of this writer. Hogg, he says, conceived the idea, and wrote, in addition to unpublished portions, Chapter I. i.–xxxvii., with two or three other verses. "The rest of the production was the workmanship of Wilson and Lockhart."

As to the authorship of "The Chaldee," *habemus confitentem reum.* On January 27, 1818, Lockhart wrote from Edinburgh to Christie, "I never certainly have been more troubled in mind than for some two or three months past,"—apparently since *Blackwood* appeared on October 20, 1817. "The Chaldee Manuscript" has excited prodigious noise here—it was the sole subject of conversation for two months. . . . The history of it is this: Hogg, the Ettrick Shepherd, sent up an attack on Constable the bookseller, respecting some private dealings of his with Blackwood. Wilson and I liked the idea of introducing the whole panorama of the town in that sort of dialect. We drank punch one night from eight till eight in the morning, Blackwood being by with anecdotes, and the result is before you. . . ."

"The Chaldee" set all Edinburgh in a flame.   The Scot is not famed for being able to take a joke, especially a joke aimed at himself.   People cried "Blasphemy," because of the Oriental character of the style, which had good Jacobite precedent in "The Chronicle of Charles, the Young Man," published in that year of grace abounding 1745.[1] The "Chaldean" text was from the "Bibliothèque Royale" (Salle 2, No. 53, B.A.M.M.).[2]   Monsieur Silvestre de Sacy (of whom the Shepherd can have known little) was understood to be occupied with an edition of the original.

It may not be superfluous to give a very brief analysis of "The Chaldee."   Blackwood "is a man in plain apparel," has "his name as it had been the colour of Ebony, and his number (17 Princes Street) was the number of a maiden, when the days of her virginity have expired."   To him come the Two Beasts (Pringle and Cleghorn, ex-editors), "the joints of their legs like the polished cedars of Lebanon," for, indeed, "they came skipping upon staves," being lame.   They brought a book, "but put no words into it."   Mr. Blackwood, therefore, called together his friends, while "the man who was crafty in council" received overtures from the Beasts.   This word, crafty, annoyed Constable, as the nickname had been given to him, says Lockhart, "by one of his own most eminent Whig supporters."

[1] The respectable Southey had already written a very dull Biblical parody on Jeffrey.   Here was precedent !

[2] Whereby is indicated *bam* or *bite*.

Blackwood, when Constable accepted the Beasts, said, "I will of myself yield up the book," that is, abandon his magazine. However, he took and snuffed up dust from a gem of curious workmanship, and called in "an aged man," Henry Mackenzie, the Man of Feeling. Mr. Mackenzie later "forbade the magazine his house."[1] However, in "The Chaldee," Mr. Mackenzie gives an evasive answer to Blackwood, "and all the young men that were there lifted up their voices and said" all manner of kind and respectful things to the venerated sage.

"The great Magician, who dwelleth in the old fortress hard by the river Jordan" was next appealed to. Sir Walter was *très Normand*, and gave identical answers to the man in plain apparel, and to the man crafty in council. "He afterwards confessed," says Lockhart, "that the Chaldæan author had given a sufficiently accurate version of what passed on the occasion." Then came Professor Jamieson, Sir David Brewster, Tytler the historian, and, alas, Charles Kirkpatrick Sharpe! Now Sharpe, at or about this time, was editing Kirkton's contemporary MS. "History of the Covenant," with notes on all the scandals about the Covenanters, for example, about the prowess of the hero of Cherrytrees. Wilson had a leaning to Covenanters, Lockhart's ancestors had been "Whigs frae Bothwell Brig," and their fellow-contributor,

---

[1] Letter to Constable, October 8, 1818, in "Archibald Constable," ii. 339.

Dr. M'Crie, was extremely Presbyterian.   Sharpe's
love of scandal, and his amusing notes to Kirkton,
may have suggested what "The Chaldee" says of
his voice, "even like the voice of the unclean bird
which buildeth its nest in the corner of the temple"
(Kirkton).   Sharpe was very angry; he complained to Scott, who said that his connection with
the magazine was through Will Laidlaw.   Laidlaw
wrote the historical chronicle of events from month
to month.   Scott, it seems, had secured for him
this appointment, and Laidlaw was his chief link
with the magazine.   Sharpe sneers at Laidlaw—
"a person of whom I never heard."   Scott added
that Blackwood had sent him an apologetic letter,
"stating that the offensive article had been inserted
against his will," and said that his remonstrances
made Blackwood omit the article in later editions.

In "The Chaldee" a Veiled Man now aids Blackwood with a list of names of contributors, "the
beautiful Leopard from the valley of the palm
trees" (Wilson), and "from a far country, the
Scorpion, who delighteth to sting the faces of
men" (Lockhart), "and the great wild Boar from
the Forest of Lebanon" (which men call Ettrick
Forest); "and the Griffin came with a roll of
the names of those whose blood had been shed
between his teeth; and I saw him stand over the
body of one that had been buried long in the
grave, defending it from all men."   The Griffin is
the Rev. Dr. Thomas M'Crie, the Biographer of

Knox, and from his part in *Blackwood* arose contendings, and the shedding of much ink.   Sir
William Hamilton (who abode not long with them)
is "the black Eagle of the desert, whose cry is as
the sound of an unknown tongue, which flieth over
the ancient cities, and hath his dwelling among the
tombs of the wise men."   Constable now appeals to
Jeffrey, "a familiar spirit unto whom he had sold
himself.   But the spirit was a wicked spirit and a
cruel," who helped him not.   Leslie (Professor of
Mathematics) is appealed to, and next the Rev.
Professor Playfair.   "He also is of the seed of the
prophets, and ministered in the temple while he was
yet young; but he went out, and became one of
the scoffers" (*Edinburgh* Reviewers).   These, too,
would not aid Constable.   Scott answered as he
did to Blackwood.   Macvey Napier, and a crowd of
forgotten folk, rallied to the man crafty in council,
including " John, the Brother of James, a man of low
stature, who giveth out merry things, and is a lover
of fables from his youth up," that is, "Leeing
Johnny," John Ballantyne.   "And there followed
many women which knew not their right hand
from their left, also some cattle."

  " The Chaldee " ends—

  "And I fled into an inner chamber to hide
myself, and I heard a great tumult, but I wist not
what it was."   A great tumult arose in little Edinburgh, "no end of public emotion."   Legal proceedings were threatened ; private *wergild* was paid

to the Third Beast, Graham Dalyell. Scott made Blackwood withdraw the article; there were excursions and alarms. Being local and personal, "The Chaldee" caused more trouble in Edinburgh than articles much more blameworthy.

CHAPTER VI

Blackwood's next scrape.—Its origin.—Cavalier and Covenanter.—
Charles Kirkpatrick Sharpe.—His edition of Kirkton.—Dr.
M'Crie assailed for contributing to *Blackwood*. — Lockhart
carries the war into Africa.—Attacks clerical contributors to
the *Edinburgh Review*.—Writes as Baron von Lauerwinkel.—
Criticises critics. — Shakespeare. — The real Lockhart. — On
Napoleon. — On Jeffrey. — Jeffrey's real insignificance. — His
ignorance. — His treatment of Goethe. — Lockhart's defence of
Christianity against the *Edinburgh Review*.—How far justified.
— Examples of religious criticism from the *Edinburgh*. — The
sceptical priest. — Sydney Smith's flippancies in the *Edinburgh*.
— "Merriment of Parsons." — Evangelicals "nasty vermin." —
Lockhart on Scottish religion.—His reprisals.—Personal attack
on Playfair. — Scott's disapproval. — Wilson and Lockhart are
attacked anonymously.—"Hypocrisy Unveiled."—They challenge
their opponent.—Jeffrey's reply.—Mr. Macvey Napier suspected.
—Denies the charge. — Extracts from his unpublished Correspondence.—Sir John Barrow's letter.—Playfair and the *Quarterly
Review*.

THE next formidable difficulty into which *Blackwood*
picked its way was Lockhart's own. The new feud
was really a sequel of the old religious Cavalier and
Covenanting struggles, at least it arose in the camp
of the suffering yet lovely Remnant. *Blackwood*,
though Tory, was not Cavalier in politics. We have
seen how Charles Kirkpatrick Sharpe was handled
in "The Chaldee." In the December number

of 1817 appeared a letter to Sharpe, "On his original mode of editing Church History,"—that of Kirkton. "We have all along the upper part of the page, the manly narrative of honest Kirkton, speaking of his suffering friends with compassion, but of his enemies as became a man and a Christian. And below that" (in Sharpe's notes) "such a medley of base ribaldry, profane stuff, and blasphemous innuendos, as at one view exhibits the character of both parties." Sharpe, in fact, had done his best to rake up the by no means rare absurdities of the Remnant, and his taste led him to revel in the few scandalous anecdotes about the godly. Whether his new assailant was Lockhart or Dr. M'Crie, the Scorpion or the Griffin, is not known.[1] It *looks* more like the Griffin's touch. Sharpe himself, in a letter to Scott, calls Dr. M'Crie "a canting rogue," speaks of "the loathsome puddle of Presbyterianism," says he is collecting M'Crie's blunders for the use of Chalmers, and is generally hostile to the reverend Griffin.

Now in these days arose one Calvinus, who printed "Two Letters to the Rev. Dr. Thomas M'Crie and the Rev. Andrew Thomson, on the parody of Scripture lately published in *Blackwood's Edinburgh Magazine*" (Fairbairn, Edinburgh,

---

[1] Mrs. Wilson in a letter attributes it to Hogg, which seems improbable. (Christopher North, i. 277.) I have reason to believe that Dr. M'Crie, in fact, did not contribute to the magazine at this time. He refrained, as he disapproved of and censured the personal violences.

1817). His engaging motto was: "Lest that by any means, when I have preached to others, I myself should be a castaway." Calvinus warned the Griffin that he was very like to be a castaway, if he did not desert *Blackwood*. The author of "The Chaldee" "makes indecent jests at his Creator," which are certainly not visible to the common eye. "And *you*, the historian of Knox and the champion of the Covenanters, are accosted, from the Scorner's chair, with the accents of good fellowship, and described in the record of his impiety as an ally." The Griffin is warned that "the companion of fools shall be destroyed." And what business, it is asked, hath the Griffin *dans cette galère*, he who "had so powerfully reprobated and chastised, in 'Old Mortality,' profanity not half so gross and odious as this." Dr. M'Crie, in fact, had made a laboured defence of Habakkuk Mucklewrath and Mause Headrig.[1] Dr. M'Crie, minister of the Auld Lichts, seems to have borne this chastisement with humorous indifference. Writing to his fellow-sinner and fellow-sufferer, Dr. Thomson, he says, "Well, and how do you relish the letter of your good friend and great admirer, Calvinus? Glad you have got off so scratch-free? Gratified with his equivocal and conditional praise, and determined to merit and secure it by never entering again the virgin-door of Blackwood, and by immediately withdrawing from him your *Instructor*, as well as your Essay on

---

[1] This long review will be found in his collected works.

Education, with all the embryo and *de futuro* productions of your brain." Neither gentleman "seems
to have considered himself called upon to answer the
summons of an anonymous writer."[1]

Calvinus, unhappily, gave the world to know that
he would "rather belong to the party that, with a
Playfair, shares the honour of possessing no quality
that can excite the complacency of so despicable a
babbler" as the Chaldæan. This was an unhappy
remark, for the Scorpion, dreading doubtless that
his, friend the Griffin, in fear of becoming a castaway, would forswear his company, carried the war
into Africa. Calvinus (a Mr. Grahame, according to
Lockhart) had called on Dr. M'Crie "to remember
the fate of that priest who associated himself with the
infidel compilers of the ' Encyclopædia.' " Brewster
was threatened in the same style. Lockhart's mischief rose to revenge Ebony. In place of wooing
the coy Griffin with fair words, he retorted by
attacking the clergy who wrote in the *Edinburgh
Review*, and he specially singled out the Rev. Professor Playfair, who then held the Chair of Natural
Philosophy, and who "had been originally intended
for the Church," according to Professor Ferrier.
He had been a placed minister. In the attack on
Playfair, which justly caused "no end of public
emotion," Lockhart called himself the Baron von
Lauerwinkel. Under this name, in March 1818,
he had written "Remarks on the Periodical Criti-

---

[1] " Life of Dr. M'Crie," p. 229.

cism of England." This admirable essay it is which justifies the opinion that, in the reserved and lofty centre of his genius, Lockhart regarded all the bickerings and feuds of literary people with impartial disdain. "These strange Reviews," says the Baron (much in the tone of Mr. Arnold's Arminius), rule the authors and readers of England with the sway "of a sportive Nero, or a gloomy Tiberius." He speaks as if Goethe had been censuring our Reviews, but this is probably part of the manner. In Germany, "a poem, history, or treatise is judged according to its merits by the critic." "On the other hand, an *Edinburgh* Reviewer is a smart, clever man of the world, or else a violent political zealot." The author may be alien to politics: "The Reviewer does not mind that; when he sits down to criticise, his first question is not, 'Is the book good or bad?' but, 'Is this writer a Ministerialist or an Oppositionist?' 'No one knows . . . but if the author has a nephew, or a cousin, or an uncle, who is a member of Parliament and votes, that is quite sufficient," for both *Edinburgh* and *Quarterly*.

What follows is eloquent.

"You remember what I have said of Shakespeare, that he is an angelic being, a pure spirit, who looks down upon 'the great globe itself, and all which it inhabits,' as if from the elevation of some higher planet. He is like Uriel, the Angel of the Sun, partaker of all the glories of the orb

in which he dwells.   Undazzled by the splendour
which surrounds himself, he sees everything with
the calm eye of intellect.   It is true that, at the
moment when he views any object, a flood of light
and warmth is thrown over it from the passing
sun of genius.   Still, he sees the world as it is;
and if the beams love to dwell longest on some
favoured region, there is none upon which they
never shine."

In the centuries of Shakespeare's praises few are
nobler, more severely great, more illuminating than
those lines, tossed by Lockhart into the medley of
a magazine—

"As rich men give that care not for their gifts."

Lockhart goes on to say that "if the world shall
ever possess a perfect reviewer, like Shakespeare
he will be universal, impartial, rational. . . . He
will have divine intellect and human feeling so
blended within him, that he shall sound, with equal
facility, the soul of a Hamlet and the heart of a
Juliet.   What a being would this be!   Compared
with him the present critics of England are either
satirical buffoons, like Foote and Aristophanes, or
they are truculent tragedians, like the author of
'The Revenge.'"[1]

Here we listen to the real Lockhart, and are
admitted to the region above the polished threshold

[1] According to Lockhart, in "Peter's Letters," this article gave
deep offence to the Whigs.

of his disdain.   He descends, he moves among the
crew of "satirical buffoons," and shares their pranks
as if the Lady, in "Comus," had frolicked with the
rout of revelling fauns and Sileni.   Here we are
with that Lockhart whom Scott loved, whom even
Carlyle praised, not with the companion of the
Leopard and the great Boar from the forest of
Lebanon.   This is the Lockhart of whom Lady
Eastlake wrote :—

" How many kind and good things I remember
from his lips—how unfailing his tribute to worth
and duty, though under the homeliest garb."

Descending from his height Lockhart compares
Whigs and Tories to the Neri and Bianchi of
criticism ; Jeffrey and Gifford are the leaders.   "The
former resembles the gay despot of Rome, the
latter the bloody and cruel one of Capreæ.   Both
are men of great talent, and both, I think, are very
bad reviewers."

Lockhart then avers that no man can be a good
critic, unless he be more than a mere reviewer.
" Aristotle and Lessing remain, but Chamfort and
all the wits of the *Mercure* have perished."   This
is hardly true of Chamfort, but, compared with
Lessing and Aristotle, his is an ineffectual light.   In
Gifford, with many better things, Lockhart notes
" ill-natured abuse and cold rancorous raillery. . . .
He is exquisitely formed for the purposes of political
objurgation, but not at all for those of gentle and
universal criticism."   *Gentle and universal criticism,*

of the masters of literature, not of contemporaries, for that end Lockhart was formed. But, in the main, he took the world and the press as he found them, and, with a stoical disdain that verged on cynicism, he subdued his hand to that it worked in.

"We often read the reviews in Gifford's journal with pleasure—such are the strength of his language, and the malignity of our nature. . . . How can one who thinks the 'Lauras' and 'Della Cruscas' matters of so great moment, form any rational opinion concerning such men as Scott, Wordsworth, Byron, or Goethe ?" Lockhart then protests against the *Quarterly's* "truly English" view of Napoleon. "Nations yet to come will look back upon his history as to some grand and supernatural romance. The fiery energy of his youthful career, and the magnificent progress of his irresistible ambition, have invested his character with the mysterious grandeur of some heavenly appearance ; and when all the lesser tumults, and lesser men of our age, shall have passed away into the darkness of oblivion, history will still inscribe one mighty era with the majestic name of Napoleon."

Jeffrey is ingeniously described, by the German Baron, as "an advocate before the parliament of Edinburgh." " The intellectual timidity of Jeffrey's profession has clung to him in all his pursuits, and prevented him from coming manfully and decidedly to any firm opinion respecting matters of such moment, that it is absolutely impossible to be a great critic while the mind remains unsettled in regard to them." He is represented as carrying the popular ways of the legal advocate into the court of the literary judge. "He can very easily persuade the multitude that nothing is worth knowing but what they can comprehend; that true philosophy is quite attainable without the labour of years" (as in reviewing Kant through the French), "and that whenever we meet with anything new, and at first sight unintelligible, the best rule is to take it for granted that it is something mystical and absurd."[1] He is acute enough to see that, however great his authority "among the generation of indolent and laughing readers to whom he dictates opinion, he has as yet done nothing which will ever induce a man of research, in the next century, to turn over the volumes of his review." On the threshold of the next century we may ask who does read Jeffrey? Mr. Saintsbury, who reads everything (except "Popol Vuh"), has indeed read Jeffrey, and in a remarkable essay has formed a much more favourable judgment of his criticisms than can be done by a writer who stills resents, like a personal affront, Jeffrey's review of "Marmion." "There may be much that Jeffrey does not see," says Mr. Saintsbury; "there may be some things which he is physically unable to see: but

---

[1] Jeffrey's letter to Macvey Napier, many years later, on Sir William Hamilton's review of Cousin, shows that Jeffrey remained impenitent.

what he does see, he sees with a clearness, and co-ordinates in its bearings on other things seen with like precision, which are hardly to be matched among the fluctuating and diverse race of critics." Thus Mr. Saintsbury ; but Lockhart writes : "When the great men whom Jeffrey has insulted by his mirth shall have received their due recompense in the admiration of our children, it will appear but an unprofitable task to read his ineffectual and shallow criticisms." In later life Lockhart took an infinitely more favourable view of Jeffrey.

"When the good and venerable Goethe," writes the Baron, "told the stories of his youth to a people who all look upon him with the affectionate admiration of children, this foreigner, who cannot read our language, amused his countrymen, equally ignorant as himself, with an absurd and heartless caricature of the only poet, in modern times, who is entitled to stand in the same class with Dante, Calderon, and Shakespeare." Jeffrey is then said to have given up his original strictly "classical principles" of Pope's and Boileau's school, not as a man converted by reading and reflection, but as a politician who sees what way the cat is jumping —"I admire his talents, I lament their misapplication, and I prophesy that they will soon be forgotten."

As to politics, it is enough to quote one sentence. "A great country, in the hour of her conflict, should not hear the voice of despondency from her children." That voice Jeffrey uttered, though personally a volunteer in the peril of England.

The Baron now defends Christianity from the *Edinburgh Review.* "This journal has never ventured to declare itself openly the champion of infidelity; but there is no artifice, no petty subterfuge, no insidious treachery, by which it has not ventured to weaken the influence which the Bible possesses over the minds of a devout and meditative people."

The Baron exclaims—"Does any man dare to speak, with the feelings and the fearlessness of a Christian, concerning God and the destiny of man? Mr. Jeffrey is sure to ridicule his piety as Methodism, and stoops to court the silly sneers of striplings against a faith which, as he well knows, neither he nor they have ever taken the trouble to understand." He must not imagine that, as a public instructor, "he can avoid being either the friend or foe of religion." The *Edinburgh* advocates Catholic claims, the *Quarterly* attacks Catholics. But the *Edinburgh* "befriends Catholicism only because it despises Christianity."

What element of truth is there in these and even stronger assertions? Had Lockhart's observations any bottom of fact? These old feuds are dead enough, but they had the deepest influence on Lockhart's future. It is, therefore, necessary to ask "how far had he any justification in fact?" It will be shown that he did denounce that chilly and ignorant scepticism, which Carlyle hated.

The *Edinburgh Review* prolonged, one may say, and even carried farther, the principles of the "Moderates" of the last century, the party which secured the alliance of Burns. This Moderation, even among the clergy, was sometimes a thing inconsistent, not only with the Standards of the Kirk, but even with the dogmatic and doctrinal essence of Christianity. In the earliest number of the *Edinburgh* some assurance is given to orthodoxy by the remark that "the presumptuous theories and audacious maxims of Rousseau, Mably, Condorcet, &c., had a necessary tendency to do harm." "Submission to lawful authority is indisputably the maxim of Christianity, and they who destroy our faith in that religion take away one security for our submission, and facilitate the subversion of governments. This is a great truth" (*Edinburgh Review*, i. p. 13). Voltaire and d'Alembert, with other Encyclopædists, are described as "pernicious writers." The value of morality is insisted upon—"We agree with our author in the importance of the doctrines peculiar to Christianity" (iv. 193).

But "good sense and morality are indispensable requisites" (in a preacher), "and if the preacher gives us these, he may be allowed, in other respects, to follow the dictates of his peculiar genius or fancy." That is, if we read through the spectacles of an orthodox Scot, a Christian pulpit may be occupied

by a Buddhist, or an Atheist, if only he has sense,
morality, and a genius to follow, a fancy to indulge
(vi. 105). In an essay on the sermons of Sir
Henry Moncreiff, an essay marked by the courtesy
of its manner, the writer says—" A preacher who
studiously keeps Christianity in the background . . .
is by no means doing his duty," a lenient censure,
yet in contradiction to the opinion about genius
and fancy. But, in the next sentence we read—
" Whether that religion (Christianity) be true or
false is another question, but surely no one who
thinks it true ought to be ashamed of it." Evangelical preaching is handled thus : " Preachers who
have not their supernatural evidences" (the power
of working miracles is referred to), "must take a
lower and more moderate tone" than the Apostles.
Preachers must remember that it is "extremely disagreeable to be kept in the trammels of mystery."

   " Too great constancy in enforcing Christian doctrines" is censured in Sir Henry Moncreiff. He laid
stress on " those doctrines of revelation which, in the
eyes of the world in general, and especially in those
of sceptics, have most the appearance of foolishness."
Still, as against Moncreiff, "the charge of hypocrisy would be highly illiberal." These remarks are
not, on the whole, reassuring to a defender of the
Christianity of the *Edinburgh Review*. Christianity
may be true, or false—it is an open question, but
a preacher who happens to think it true, should not
keep it in the background altogether. Still, he

must be very careful. He cannot work miracles, so he must not ardently uphold the doctrines of the Apostles, whom he believes to have authenticated their doctrine by their thaumaturgy. Unless he can heal the sick, and blast the apostate, he will do well to avoid expounding these doctrines of revelation (whatever they may be) which are most conspicuously absurd in the eyes of the world in general. Perhaps if the preacher, however firm his belief, burks it, and gives us only morality and good sense, his conduct is most judicious. The preacher, in common charity, must remember that, though he has been solemnly called to announce the mysteries in which he has no less solemnly avowed his belief, yet it is "extremely disagreeable to be kept in the trammels of mystery."

The sceptical priest is an object odious to an honest mind. The journal which writes as the *Review* wrote on Sir Henry Moncreiff encourages the sceptical priest, and discourages the priest of sincere faith. This much might be said by an observer who was of no faith. Much more might any man, the son and brother of Scottish ministers, if he cherished a sentiment of loyalty to a creed which his reason rejected, assail the tone, so to speak, of the *Review*. The nature of Lockhart's own attitude to religion will be manifest later. If he chose to say that the *Edinburgh Review* shuffled, and, without the courage to make open profession of "infidelity," adopted "petty subterfuges" to weaken the influence of the Bible, I do not feel certain that we could blame him. It is not a question of whether the *Review* was right in regarding "the doctrines of Revelation as 'foolish,' to the world's mind, in various degrees; but whether a journal which spoke in the tone of the *Edinburgh* had grounds for resenting the charge of what was then regarded as suppressed 'infidelity.'"

Again, the flippancies of the *Review* were in the worst taste. Few people now, it is probable, read Sydney Smith. His *Edinburgh* articles on Methodism and missionaries would not to-day be reckoned decorous. Arminian and Calvinistic Methodists and evangelical clergymen of the Church of England are to his mind "three classes of fanatics," differing only in "the finer shades and nicer discriminations of lunacy." The Scottish clergy, being on the whole "Evangelical," must apparently be inmates of the same asylum, though the reviewer makes exceptions, in the case of truly religious persons.

The reviewer of Moncreiff would allow preachers of miraculous gifts to preach the doctrine of Peter or of John. But when an evangelical preacher converts a man "of scrofulous legs and atheistical principles," and when the man "walks home with the greatest ease," Sydney Smith does not (as in common fairness an *Edinburgh* Reviewer should) make an exception in favour of Mr. Coles, the miraculously gifted divine in question. The Rev. James Moody is converted by a sermon. "The

Lord . . . was about to stop him in his vain career of sin and folly." Stopped he was (which is something), and the Rev. Sydney Smith emphasizes this ludicrous circumstance by the aid of italics. Mr. Roberts was "given to feel that God was waiting to be very gracious to him"—what a truly laughable delusion! Mr. Kestin, on his death-bed, murmured, "Come, Lord Jesus, come," and his degree and discrimination of lunacy is patent to our *Edinburgh* Reviewer. Mr. John Robinson, an hour before his death, cried, "Ye powers of darkness, begone," and was later at ease. An ejaculation so natural in the mortal strait, on the threshold of the unknown, is exquisitely comic. Miss Louisa Cooke approaches the rapturous condition of St. Francis and St. Theresa, "she often seemed to be dissolved in the love of God her Saviour,"—a rare jest indeed.

In brief, the experiences of the most saintly souls on earth, from St. Paul to St. Francis, emotions which have been familiar to the devout from the days of the Apostles to our own, are not, to the *Edinburgh* Reviewer, an awful mystery of the Soul, nor a topic in scientific psychology or pathology (and either view may be taken), but simply a ludicrous shade in a general lunacy.

A naval officer is reported to have said that there were Methodists present, and distinguished by their valour and discipline, in Nelson's ship, the *Victory*, at Trafalgar—"These were the only fellows that I ever knew do their duty without swearing." All lived to do their duty again. This testimony might conciliate a Christian divine, like the Rev. Sydney Smith, even if he had a personal partiality for profane language. But he merely says, " The army and navy appear to be the particular objects of the Methodists' attention."

"This merriment of parsons is very offensive," said Dr. Johnson. Enough of it has been cited to prove that neither the spiritual consolations which, from the beginning, have been the common privilege, or the fortunate illusion of Christians without exception of sect, nor the change from vice to virtue (if occasioned by a sermon), nor valour accompanied by decency in conduct, if displayed by "fanatics," was anything but a laughing-stock to the *Edinburgh Review*. Methodists (and Evangelical members of the Church of England) are "nasty and numerous vermin." Their protests against ridicule are like the complaints of "lice against the comb." The *Review* will clear out the vermin as it will also defend Christianity from "the tiger-spring of infidelity." But where is the promised defence ?

It did not occur to Sydney Smith and the *Edinburgh Review* that but for the spiritual conditions at which he mocked, Christianity could never have been founded, the world could never have been converted, the Faith could never among persecutions and distresses have been preserved. Assuredly "rational Christians" would neither have originated, nor perpetuated a law and a creed. As in the earth's centre, so in the core of every vital Religion, lives a fire; on occasion it will break the crust of decent routine, and will excite the terror or the laughter of the "rational." Yet without this fire there could be no spiritual life, and without its volcanic outbursts, there would be none of life's cleansing and renewal. The critic, in fact, mocked (as Lockhart wrote) at what he "had never attempted to understand."

If Lockhart had confined himself to saying that the Christian faith, in the eyes of his opponents, was a respectable form of opinion, useful in discouraging the excesses of the populace, and (if taken in extreme moderation) not unworthy of the patronage of men of taste, Lockhart might have made good his argument. He might have supported it by such quotations as his industry could discover, or his acuteness detect. But he wrote in general terms, and, with occasional reservations, he argued as if the *Edinburgh* deliberately designed the overthrow of Christianity. He added the element of personality, in a calm and clearly conceived *éreintement* of an individual. His more superficial and discernible motives are plain enough. If *Blackwood* (to descend to the vulgar facts) was to lose its Griffin because of its irreligion, the war might be carried into Africa with little expense or trouble.

Lockhart, as a child, though a strange one, of the Covenanters (whose peculiarities were precisely those of the Methodists); as the son and the brother of orthodox ministers, "an unmenseful bairn of the Manse"; as an admirer, were it but a sentimental admirer, of the Kirk and her exercises; as a man of taste above all, when prejudice did not blind him, might well dislike with heartiness the tone of the *Edinburgh Review*. We may thus account for his attacks on the "infidelity" of the *Review*, first by a sentiment of loyalty to the ancestral faith.

We can appeal, on this point, from the Baron von Lauerwinkel, in the flush of his polemical youth, to Lockhart soberly writing the "Life of Burns." He is criticising "The Holy Fair." He asks, "Were 'Superstition,' 'Hypocrisy,' and 'Fun' the only influences which Burns might justly have impersonated? It would be hard, I think, to speak so of the old Popish festivals to which a critic of Burns alludes; it would be hard, surely, to say it of any festival in which, mingled as they may be with sanctimonious pretenders, and surrounded with giddy groups of onlookers, a mighty multitude of devout men are assembled for the worship of God, beneath the open heaven, and above the graves of their ancestors."

Here we have Lockhart in his serious inward mood, and that mood, distorted and refracted by meaner passions, may have entered into his criticism of the *Edinburgh Review*.

Much more patently Lockhart was influenced by the desire to deal to the partisans of the Whig journal, the same measure as Calvinus and others had meted out to the "blasphemous" authors of

" The Chaldee," and to their learned and puritan associate, Dr. M'Crie. Mr. Saintsbury, referring among other things to the metaphysical creed of the Edinburgh Academy of Physics (to which Jeffrey and several of his staff belonged), says: "Seventy years ago it would have been the exception to find an orthodox metaphysician who did admit it ; and Lockhart, or rather Baron von Lauerwinkel, was perfectly justified in taking the view which ordinary opinion took."

He may, as we have seen, have been justified in "taking the view," but emphatically (as Scott thought) he was *not* justified in his manner of urging home his opinions.

After a letter to Dr. Chalmers on his connection with the *Edinburgh*—a letter attributed to Lockhart by Mrs. Wilson—the Baron von Lauerwinkel, in September 1818, addressed another to the " Rev. Professor Laugner," on his writings in the *Königsberg Review*. Laugner was meant for the Rev. Professor Playfair.[1]

Mr. Playfair, having begun as a parish minister, ended as a professor. What could be more blameless? Dr. Chalmers left his Glasgow parish for the Moral Philosophy Chair in St. Andrews, and such translations are common, and often laudable, never blameworthy. And Mr. Playfair wrote in

---

[1] Minister of Liff and Bervie 1773-1782. In 1805 he accepted the Chair of Natural Philosophy in Edinburgh ("Christopher North," i. 281, note). He died in 1819.

the *Edinburgh Review*, as Chalmers did, as Sir Walter Scott had done. He was now an old man, loved and respected. The Baron, to be brief, treated him as if he had been an apostate priest. He is called the d'Alembert of the Northern Encyclopædia. "You have manifested every possible eagerness to banish from the view and recollection of the public every trace of your previous habits and situation. You disclaimed every relic of that character, which in spite of, or in ignorance of, the existence of such men as you, the wisdom of the legislature has declared to be indelible."

The *Edinburgh*, however, had argued long before this date that "the supposed indelibility of the sacred character is entirely a relic of Popish super-stition," "an imposition practised upon the public by the priests of the dark ages." [1] How Lockhart's words applied to Mr. Playfair, whether he dressed as a layman and "sunk the minister," it is not now easy, nor is it important, to ascertain. He handled the learned Professor as an apostate, allied with a band of men like those whom St. Augustine calls "the Corruptors." It is not possible here, as in the case of "Peter's Letters," to say that the article "was such as only a very young and thoughtless person would write." Young Lockhart was, but the article, in its calm implacable logic, could only have been written by one who had thought deeply and clearly

[1] Vol. v., p. 315, note.

on the conditions of belief, and on the different lines of conduct open to a reluctant, an amiable, a proselytising, and a malignant sceptic. For "thoughtless," in Lockhart's apology, we must substitute "reckless." Granting the premises—namely, that Mr. Playfair's conduct had been that attributed to him,—the article is a model of polished vigour. But nobody grants or granted the premises, nobody can palliate what Scott, writing to Lockhart, calls "the personal and severe attack on Playfair, of which I did not approve." (October 29, 1818.) "I agree with you," Scott wrote to Mr. Morritt of Rokeby, "that the conductors of the Magazine have acted inconsiderately and rashly in a personal attack on Playfair. It gives too much occasion to charge them with intolerance, for although Playfair has never been suspected of orthodoxy, yet I know not that he has on any occasion made any attack upon religion, and consequently the dragging forward a charge of infidelity, which cannot be proved from any overt act, sounds very like personal scandal. . . . It seems to me not sufficiently bottomed on specific allegations of assaults committed by him on Christianity."

Scott was, at this time, a mere senior acquaintance of Lockhart's, addressed by him on the following occasion.

Wilson and Lockhart had been attacked by the anonymous author of a pamphlet styled "Hypocrisy Unveiled." It is unnecessary to make a garland of the not undeserved amenities contained in this pamphlet. Mr. John Murray, the publisher, is cited as a great denouncer of Lockhart and Wilson, which is interesting, if we remember how long Lockhart and Mr. Murray were to work together. Indeed, according to the pamphleteer, Croker had *already* reconciled Blackwood and the London publisher.

The sentence which probably gave most annoyance to Blackwood's men was : "The Scorpion has often, in conversation, expressed his disbelief of the Christian religion," while the Leopard makes "obscene parodies on the Psalms." Wilson "has praised Coleridge's 'Christabel,' which sins as heinously against purity and decency as it is well possible to imagine."

The author of "Hypocrisy Unveiled" was clearly of "a nice morality." Finally the Leopard and the Scorpion are advised to hang themselves.

They did not take that extreme step ; in letters to the author of "Hypocrisy," published in the *Scotsman* (Oct. 24, 1818)—published, of course, without their knowledge—they asked for their assailant's name and address. "If you suppose yourself to have any claim to the character of a gentleman, you will take care that I be not long without this knowledge," said Lockhart ("Christopher North," i. 283, note). The author (like Zeta) would not "make a premature avowal of his name." He was sought for so eagerly, "by fair means and *foul* if any can in such a case be foul," says Lockhart to Scott;[1] he was in such undeniably anxious request, that he did not write any more pamphlets, and even suppressed one which he had advertised. Some suspicion fell on Mr. Macvey Napier, who disavowed the pamphlet "on his word of honour." Lockhart prepared Scott for an agitated letter from Wilson. None arrived. Jeffrey broke with Wilson, in a letter which Mrs. Gordon prints, and justly describes as "manly and honourable." "I say then that it is *false* that it is one of the principal objects, or any object at all of the *Edinburgh Review*, to discredit religion, or promote the cause of infidelity. . . . I declare to you, upon my honour, that nothing of that tendency has ever been inserted without its being followed with sincere regret both on my part, and on that of all who have any permanent connection with the work." "A tone of too great levity in exposing the excesses of bigotry and intolerance " is admitted; for example, to say (as the *Edinburgh* said) that *all* Methodists would gladly "lie for the Tabernacle," may be thought rather a light-hearted statement. "But that anything was ever bespoken or written by the regular supporters of the work, or admitted except by inadvertence, with a view to discredit the truth of religion, I most positively deny, and that it is no part of its object to do so, I think must be felt by every one of its candid readers." ("Christopher North," i. 299.)

[1] Scott's "Familiar Letters," ii. 28.

The exact state of the case was well put by Mr. Morehead, an Episcopalian clergyman, in a letter to Wilson. "Nobody of sense supposes, whatever slips the *Edinburgh* may occasionally have made, that its object and secret view is to pull down Christianity, and particularly no one who knows Mr. Playfair conceives that this is one of his darling contemplations and schemes, whatever may be his opinions on the subject of Revelation, which nobody has any business to rake out." Mr. Morehead implies that Wilson and Lockhart possibly "cannot get the regulation of *Blackwood* into their own hands," and, if so, advises them to leave it. He gives both friends credit for sincerity, and allows for "the wantonness of youth and conscious power"—"this is the best view to take of you."

Unable to exchange shots with the author of "Hypocrisy Unveiled," Lockhart caricatured him, gowned, in a majestic attitude of conscious virtue, but with a villainously low forehead, protuberant occiput, and snub nose. ("Christopher North," i. 284.) He then set about finishing "Peter's Letters to his Friends."

Mr. Macvey Napier, later the editor of the *Edinburgh Review*, was suspected, as we have seen, of being the author of "Hypocrisy Unveiled." He denied the charge, and doubtless with truth. By way of curiosity, however, I add an expression of the feelings of a Tory writer, in a letter to Mr.

Napier, copied from his papers now in the British Museum.[1]

Mr. Barrow, afterwards Sir John, a *Quarterly* Reviewer, though he condemns an attack on Mr. Napier himself, feels for the wrongs of the *Quarterly* at Mr. Playfair's hands.

"ADMIRALTY, 17*th October* 1818.

" MY DEAR SIR,— . . . I assure you that your information respecting *my aid* to *Blackwood's Magazine* is wholly unfounded. I have not, in fact, once been asked to do so, and from what I have seen of it, little value as I set on anything that proceeds from my pen, I think that I should feel no disposition to enter the lists. . . . To fair and liberal criticism I have not the least objection. If a man chooses to come before the public in print, his doctrines and opinions and his style are all fair game ; but I thoroughly, and from my soul, detest those vile and slanderous personalities which are too much the fashion of the present day ; but are they not peculiarly the vice that besets the gude town of Edinburgh ? Were they not enrolled there ? Did not the *Edinburgh Review* set the example of personal attack and party rancour ? And have not your own domestic literary squabbles been conducted in that style ever since ? The attack on Professor

---

[1] (For examining these papers, and for making extracts, I have to thank Miss Violet A. Simpson, who has aided me in other researches.)

Playfair I have not seen and never heard of; but I did hear that the Professor, I suppose in some moment of irritation, declared aloud, in a public assembly, that the *Quarterly Review* was a most contemptible journal, and a disgrace to the literature of the age.   Now, if such be the fact, and the young men you speak of who are friendly to the *Quarterly* should have heard it, Professor Playfair cannot refuse them the *fair play* (vile pun) of retaliation. But I know nothing of the matter in dispute one way or other, nor do I believe it interests us of the South in the slightest degree.   For my own part, I am candid enough to confess that, in spite of the talent put forth in the *Edinburgh Review*, and the trash which the learned Professor finds in the *Quarterly*, I am stupid enough to derive more amusement from the latter than the former, and this does not arise, I can assure you, from the slightest prejudice for or against either. . . .

" Very faithfully yours."

This letter, from a future victim of *Blackwood's*, refers to the publication of the challenges *not* accepted by the author of " Hypocrisy Unveiled."

"RAITH, 25*th October* 1818.

" My dear Sir,— . . . I am glad to see from the *Scotsman* to-day, that those assassins of *Blackwood's* have been made to feel some of the pangs which

they have been attempting to inflict on others.
This will probably put an end to their plots.—
Sincerely yours,

" JOHN LESLIE."

Professor Leslie was soon to learn that his hope
was unfulfilled.   Mr. Macvey Napier's interest in
these feuds probably led to the belief that he was
the author of " Hypocrisy Unveiled."

CHAPTER VII

EDINBURGH, 1818–1820

Lockhart meets Scott.—"The Shirra."—Invitation to Abbotsford.—
Lord Melville.—Scott discourages the iniquities of *Blackwood's.*
—His chuckle.—The attack on Keats.—Mr. Colvin's theory.—
Bailey's story.—The story criticised.—Common friends of Keats
and Lockhart.—Christie on Keats.—Kindly remark of Lockhart
on Keats.—Lockhart and the scrape of a friend.—Action of
Lockhart.—His relations with his father.—Letter to Christie.—
His view of Leigh Hunt and Hazlitt.—Quarrel with Hamilton.

I HAVE just mentioned Lockhart's letter to Scott
about Wilson's agitation under the lash of " Hypocrisy Unveiled."   It is necessary to retrace a step,
and, reverting to Lockhart's private history, to
mention the origin of his relations with Scott.
This is the more needful, as Scott has been cause-
lessly implicated in a new sin of *Blackwood*, the
attack on Keats (August 1818).   But it were
impertinent, and is superfluous, to re-tell here the
story of that first interview with Scott, which Lockhart has so admirably narrated.   (" Life of Scott,"
vol. v., chapter xli.)   Lockhart had doubtless often
seen Sir Walter in public, in the Law Courts,
in bookseller's shops, even in large gatherings.
He first met Scott in private society, apparently

in June 1818, at a dinner given by Mr. Home
Drummond of Blair Drummond. Sir Walter
greeted him with his usual cordiality, and, after
dinner, while expressing a wish to "have a talk
with Goethe about trees," invited Lockhart to visit
him at Abbotsford. Lockhart had remarked that,
in Weimar, when he was there, Goethe was only
known as the Herr Geheimer-Rath von Goethe,
not at all as *der grosse Dichter*. Scott, too, warned
Lockhart that, in his own country, he must be asked
for as " The Shirra."

A few days later, Scott, through Ballantyne,
offered to hand over to Lockhart his own task of
compiling the historical part of the *Edinburgh
Annual Register*. From a letter to Christie we
learn that "the job," as Hazlitt would have called
it, was worth £500 a year. Sir Walter was eager
enough to play the historian during Napoleon's
wars; he did not love *celebrare domestica facta*.
The elder writer, it is plain, had "taken to" the
young one, who, in turn, as Scott avers, "loved
him like a son." They often met, over business,
or at Scott's table, during the summer; they often
examined together the legendary houses and heraldic
blazons of the Old Town; and Lockhart's pen, in
the chapter cited, draws the happiest picture of
Sir Walter's domestic life, in Edinburgh, and at
Abbotsford. Thither, in the following note—the
first of the Shirra's to his young friend—Lockhart
was invited.

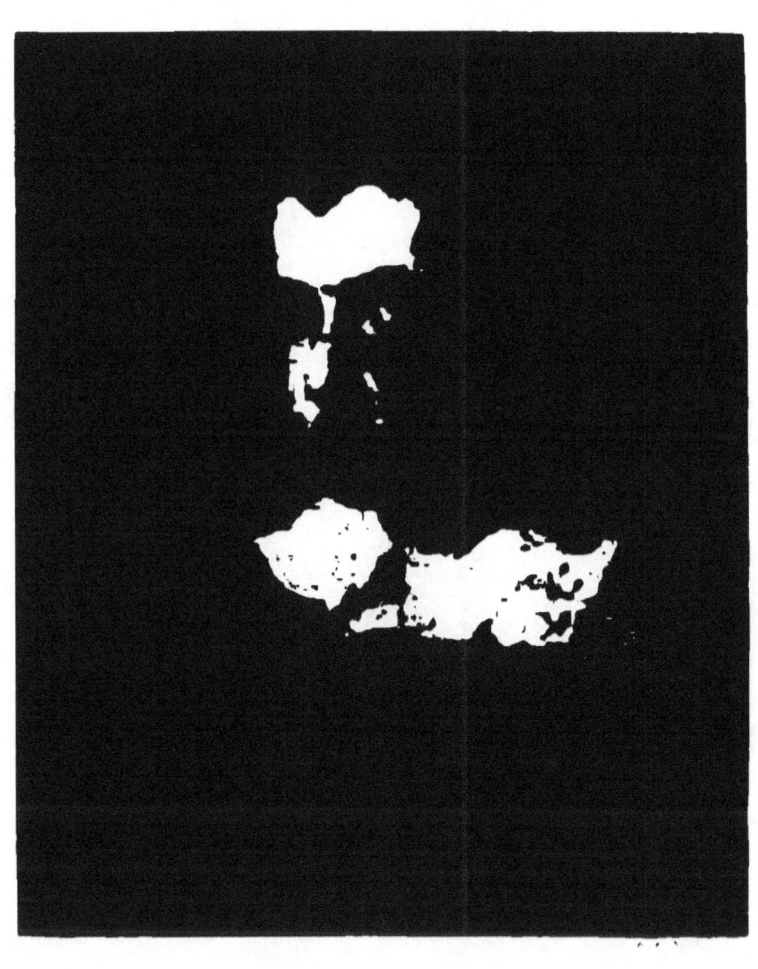

"DEAR SIR,—You were so good as to give me hopes of seeing you here this Vacation. I am very desirous that, if possible, you would come here with our friend Mr. Wilson on Thursday, 8th October, as Lord Melville is to spend a day or two with me, and I should be happy to introduce you to each other. Do not say me nay, but arrange matters so as to be with us by five o'clock, or as much earlier as you please, and to stay a day or two.—Believe me, very sincerely yours,

"WALTER SCOTT."

Lockhart and Wilson gladly accepted the invitation. They found Sir Walter in his own grounds, with some friends, and "I trust you have had enough of certain pranks with your friend Ebony," Scott said, as he introduced the Leopard and the Scorpion to Lord Melville, "the great giver of good things in the Parliament House,"—so he had described that nobleman.

Now the truth of the matter is, that, far from being an accomplice of Lockhart and Wilson in their Blackwoodian iniquities, Sir Walter, from the first, and always, attempted to wean both men from "that mother of mischief," *Blackwood*, or, at least, from personal satire therein. He began by offering Lockhart more remunerative and reputable work, as we have seen. He repeated his gentle warning while walking in one of his own young woods at Abbotsford. I shall later quote his long-lost and strangely recovered admonition, written when Wilson, partly by his aid—for he thought to turn Wilson's great powers into a new channel—obtained the Chair of Moral Philosophy. Before Lockhart's marriage, Scott returned to the charge;[1] he repeated his warning and advice, strenuously and for the last time, after the unhappy end of the affair with poor Mr. John Scott of the *London Magazine*. He would not speak as with authority. But he did keep Lockhart out of the scurrilous *Beacon*, though Lord Cockburn says that, "instead of preventing it" (the *Beacon's* libels), "he gave it his countenance. . . . His was the fault of unreflecting acquiescence." Lockhart himself (" Life of Scott," iv. 65), says that Sir Walter "had no kindness for Blackwood personally, and disapproved (though he chuckled over it) the reckless extravagance of juvenile satire " (v. 213).[2] Lord Cockburn kindly adds, " A chuckle from Scott, in the blaze of his reputation, was all that young men needed to instigate them." But Lockhart is probably thinking of Fergusson's success in breaking down Scott's gravity, and eliciting a chuckle, by a repeated, an insidious, and an innocent quotation about himself,

---

[1] There is some uncertainty on this point.

[2] A letter of Scott to Laidlaw, of 1818, entirely bears out what Lockhart says about Sir Walter's feelings, at this time, towards Mr. Blackwood.

from "The Chaldee." *That* chuckle, however reprehensible, was a year after date, and Scott had
never met Lockhart when "The Chaldee" was
penned. ("Life of Scott," v. 370.) Had Lord
Cockburn read Scott's letters to Lockhart, he could
scarcely have pressed his accusation. ("Memorials,"
pp. 316, 317.)

It is painful for a biographer to be obliged to
confess his hero's inexplicable attachment to "the
mother of mischief." But he is well assured that,
while Scott did not, indeed, regard the offences of
Maga with our modern horror, still he did most
earnestly endeavour, on every occasion, to withdraw Lockhart and Wilson from the cup of her
inexplicable sorceries. Alas, to each might have
been said—

> "*La laide dame Sans Merci*
> Thee hath in thrall!"

Before this meeting at Abbotsford, in October
1818, there had appeared, in August, the vulgar
reviling of Keats. We have already seen that
Leigh Hunt, in the spirit of conceit which offended
Keats, suspected Scott of being the author of the
attacks on himself and his associates. Leigh Hunt,
it is only fair to say, knew no more of Scott personally than Lockhart, in 1818, knew of Keats.
To Lockhart, Keats was, at first, an uneducated
Cockney adulator of Leigh Hunt; as, to Leigh
Hunt, Scott was a wicked Tory, whom he had tried

to insult in his "Feast of Poets." Hunt's opinion was absurd, but, in Mr. Sidney Colvin's excellent "Life of Keats," we hear an echo of the old belief. Mr. Colvin has changed his mind, and sung his palinode, but his "Life of Keats" remains an authority. "In the party violence of the time and place Scott himself *was drawn into encouraging* the savage polemics of his young Edinburgh friends, and that he was in some measure privy to the Cockney School outrages seems certain."

Why?

Mr. Colvin's reason is, "Such at least was the impression prevailing at the time,"—in the bosom of Leigh Hunt and his friends, for example. And again, because Severn "observed both in Scott and his daughter signs of pain and confusion which he could only interpret in the same sense," when he talked to them about "Keats and his detractors" in Rome (1832). Something more is needed than Severn's recollection of his impressions of Scott's apparent "pain and confusion!" I repeat that Keats had been selected for attack, as a Huntian, and he knew it, before Scott and Lockhart ever met. That Anne Scott, who was a lively girl of sixteen when the crime was committed, should have betrayed painful emotion, when the subject was mentioned fourteen years later, is quite incredible.

Mr. Colvin adds a tale communicated, long after date, by Keats's friend Bailey, to Lord Houghton.

Bailey had met Lockhart at the house of Mr. Gleig's father, in the summer of 1818. "He took the opportunity of telling Lockhart in a friendly way his (Keats's) circumstances and history, explaining, at the same time, that his attachment to Leigh Hunt was personal, not political, pleading that he should not be made an object of party denunciation, and ending with the request that at any rate what had been thus said in confidence should not be used to his disadvantage. To which Lockhart replied that it certainly should not be so used by him. Within three weeks the article appeared, making use, to all appearance, and to Bailey's great indignation, of the very facts he had thus confidentially communicated. To the end of his life Bailey remained convinced that, whether or not Lockhart himself wrote the piece, he must at any rate have prompted and supplied the materials for it. It seems, in fact, all but certain that he actually wrote it." Mr. Colvin instances the word *Sangrado*, for "a doctor," as a touch of his style, and I myself could add another possible example.

Accepting Bailey's account of Lockhart as a traitor, *what confidence did he betray?* That Keats's "attachment to Leigh Hunt was personal, not political"? The Reviewer asserts the very reverse: "Keats belongs to the Cockney school of politics, as well as to the Cockney school of poetry." That Keats had no classical education? Keats himself betrays *that* mischance in a dozen places, as where he rhymes "ear" to "Cytherea," and speaks of "a *penetralium*."

The single solitary fact which Lockhart *might* have betrayed is, that Keats in early life had been "destined to the career of medicine, and bound apprentice to a worthy apothecary in town." Now that fact might have been let slip inadvertently, or might well have been known through other channels. Where, in the review, are "the very facts which Bailey had confidentially communicated"? One expects to hear about the paternal livery stable, and so forth, but there is no such matter. If Bailey communicated private facts, they were not betrayed. There is not a word of Keats's private affairs, except his medical studies.

Mr. Colvin does not seem to have remarked, when he wrote the passage cited, that Lockhart had sources of information about Keats, apart from Bailey.[1] On November 22, 1817, Keats wrote to Bailey himself—"I should have been here" (at Leatherhead) "a day earlier, but the Reynoldses persuaded me to stay in town to meet your friend Christie. There were Rice and Martin—we talked about ghosts."[2]

By a curious freak of chance, Christie, Keats, John Hamilton Reynolds, Gleig, and Bailey were all "in touch," and thus Lockhart might know,

[1] Mr. Colvin's recantation, as far as Scott is concerned, is in a note to p. 60 of his edition of Keats's Letters.

[2] "Letters of Keats," 1895, p. 55.

through Christie or Gleig, anything that was to be known about the author of "Lamia." Bailey, then, was not his only source of information. Christie did write to Lockhart about Keats, though his letter is not preserved, unluckily; for, on January 27, 1818, I find Lockhart writing to him, "What you say of Keates (*sic*) is pleasing, and if you like to write a little review of him, in admonition to leave his ways, &c., and in praise of his natural genius, I shall be greatly obliged to you."

There is no "malignity" in this private reference by Lockhart to Keats; Christie, in remonstrances about *Blackwood*, never refers to the treatment of Keats, whom he obviously liked, and there my information about this unhappy matter ends. I do not know who wrote the article. On September 15, 1820, Lockhart wrote to a Mr. Aitken, in Dunbar, "I have already attempted to say something kind about Mr. Keats, in *Blackwood's Magazine*, but been thwarted, I know not well how. . . . I trust his health will mend, and that he will live to be a merry fellow. . . ."

For the rest, Keats's temper, as to literary reviling, was as manly as Scott's. "My own domestic criticism has given me pain without comparison beyond what *Blackwood* or the *Quarterly* could possibly inflict." Could Keats have read Shelley's letter to Leigh Hunt,[1] it would have vexed him far more than the stingless insults of an anony-

---

[1] "Correspondence of Leigh Hunt," i. 158.

mous reviewer.   It is needless to add the expression of the biographer's extreme regret that Lockhart was, to whatever extent or degree, connected with an unpardonable attack on a great poet and a good and brave man.   The blindness of prejudice, the infatuation of political and literary feud, and, more or less, the undeniable weaknesses, and effeminacies, and ignorances of some of Keats's immature poems, account for, though they do not palliate the deed. Yet we must not judge it as if it had been the act of a man who had before him the whole of Keats's poems, or who possessed our knowledge of the fortunes and character of Keats.

That Lockhart, whatever his literary offences at this period, kept a tender and loyal heart for the service of his friends, appears from letters written to Christie, just before and just after the visit to Abbotsford.   A young man's scrape, exaggerated by fancy, had befallen one of the old Oxford set, and was complicated by a misunderstanding with the sufferer's father.   "Your letter," writes Lockhart (Edinburgh, October 5, 1818), "has afflicted me beyond all expression.   I feel that fruitless sorrow is the only way by which any of us shall have it in our power to express our feeling of our poor friend's worth.   I am very sorry that Hamilton is out of town, which deprives me of having *any one* to speak to about it. I have ventured to drop a few lines to —— under cover to his father, and if he be at home they will reach him,—if he be not there, they will come back

to me. If anything could be done by my going or
Hamilton's going to —, I am sure I can answer
for his readiness, as well as for my own. But I
fear it is too late. After having told me so much,
do tell me more. Let me know as much as possible
of his state and its causes, and I shall burn your
letter five minutes after reading it. This story has
unhinged me for everything else."

As to the nature of the story, as to the cause of
the friend's private sorrow, not a glimmer of light
escapes the discretion of Lockhart — nor did he
keep Mr. Christie's letters on the subject. But his
benevolence and friendly courage were engaged.
On November 14, 1818, he writes from Edinburgh
—" As —'s own letter must have reached you
before you receive this, I need not tell you the step
I took in consequence of my knowledge of the
cause of —'s distress. I am apprehensive that
you may, in one point of view, condemn it. All I
can say is, that it was undertaken in consequence
of the most sincere conviction, both in Hamilton's
mind and my own, that it was a *proper* one.
The *intentions* of us both I can have no reason
to justify, because I am sure you are in no
danger of suspecting *them*.

" I have now received three or four letters from
—'s father, and were it not for the postage I
would send them, in order that you might see with
your own eyes what a pure-minded, feeling, affectionate, and estimable man he is, to whom I confided

so much. The result is sure to be happy in every point of view. It will not only be the means of releasing —— from his immediate cause of distress, but, I would trust, of opening a more entire system of confidence between him and his excellent parent, a species of confidence which, alas! the circumstances of my own life have, for some years, prevented me from entirely and undoubtingly enjoying in regard of my own father, equally good and affectionate as his, but still more averse from knowledge and participation of many feelings and views which, without being in themselves blamable, appear very much so in the eyes of secluded and venerable men.

" I trust that this is the last occasion on which I shall be put in the distressing situation of thinking myself called upon to do a thing so contrary to the common rules of friendship, and every way so hazardous. It will, however, be a consolation to me to hear from you that you do not seriously disapprove of what I have done. The affectionate manner in which —— himself writes on the occasion has endeared him to me more than ever. The longer I live" (he was twenty-four!) "the more do the ties of two or three old friendships strengthen round me. Living at a distance, and living in a different way, and with different pursuits in some respects, I always think of you as of brothers, and look forward to any prospect of meeting with you as a long absent voyager must do to a return to his home."

Such were the friendships of the antique world. In words like these, we catch a glimpse of the true, the inward Lockhart, earnest, simple, affectionate, loyal: daring, in the cause of friendship, and with the most fortunate results, to break "the common rules of friendship." This is all unlike the aspect of "the mischievous Oxford puppy," who, "with his cigar in his mouth, his one leg flung carelessly over the other, and without the symptoms of a smile on his face, or one twinkle of mischief in his dark grey eye," would beguile the good Shepherd with all manner of nonsense. " The callant never tawld me the truth a' his days but aince, an' that was merely by chance, an' without the least intention on his part," said James Hogg, who himself rejoiced greatly in a bam or bite, he being an Ettrick man indeed, in whom was (properly speaking) no guile.

The deep thoughtfulness and considerate regard for friends which shine in Lockhart's letters are alien to the reckless manner of his literary feuds. To his mind Leigh Hunt, Keats, and Hazlitt were all cockney and conceited conspirators against the constitution, common sense, and the English language. There were two aspects of Leigh Hunt; he had, so to speak, "a double personality," like Lockhart himself. Keats censured Hunt almost as severely in private as Lockhart did in public, and for the same faults. Concerning that other and admirable aspect of Hunt which shines, for example, in his regrets for Shelley, and in his letter to Severn

about the time of Keats's death, Lockhart could
know nothing.[1] As to Hazlitt, he never had a
better friend, no man ever had a more loyal friend,
than Mr. Patmore. Yet, before he met Hazlitt,
Mr. Patmore had regarded that critic as "an incar-
nate fiend." Lockhart, writing to Christie, only
calls Hazlitt "a clever profligate." Keats was
taken by Lockhart for a flatterer, imitator, and
general camp-follower of Leigh Hunt, though he
certainly learned to modify this opinion. A visit
to Christie in London might have dispelled many
of these mists, but the visit, though meditated, was
not then paid. One yet more melancholy reflection
occurs. We see that, in November 1818, Lockhart
and Hamilton were still on the old terms. There-
after I find no mention of Hamilton, and, in the
election to the Chair of Moral Philosophy, Lockhart was strong on Wilson's side. To a heart like
his, which in friendship gave itself once and for
ever, the mysterious estrangement must have been
the first of his lifelong sorrows. But he could
not speak of it, he never spoke out, even to
Christie. To his brother he was less reticent.
He lost the aid and counsel of the most learned,
pure, and estimable man among his contemporaries ; he was divided by distance from the society
of Christie, and his chief Edinburgh associates
were not likely to keep him out of mischief. In
the letter to Christie, of Nov. 14, 1818, he

[1] See Leigh Hunt's Letter in Lord Houghton's "Keats," ii. 95.

mentions his pain at the impression which the author of "Hypocrisy Unveiled" made on "the mind of Wilson, and that of his amiable wife," a lady of whom he ever spoke (and notably in his "Life of Scott") with the highest respect and affection, and, after her death, with a tender regret.[1]

[1] The Rev. Lawrence Lockhart has left a brief record of the cause of estrangement between Lockhart and Hamilton.   It arose, he says (as we have remarked), from a hasty word of Sir William's.   But he dates it at the time of "The Chaldee," and though his account is, no doubt, essentially correct, we find that, more than a year after the date of "The Chaldee," Lockhart and Hamilton were on the best terms.

CHAPTER VIII

"Peter's Letters."—Scott's bequest of his baton.—Scott's politics.—
His comments on "Peter's Letters" in *Blackwood.*—On Allan,
the painter.—Lockhart revisits Abbotsford.—Rides with Scott.—
Scott's illness.—Praises "Peter's Letters."—Analysis of "Peter's
Letters."—Mr. Wastle of Wastle.—Jeffrey.—Goethe.—A Burns
Dinner.—Wilson.—The Shepherd.—Neglect of Greek.—Lock-
hart's supposed irony.—The *Edinburgh Review.*—Jeffrey as a
critic.—Lockhart compared with Carlyle.—Defence of Coleridge.
—The booksellers.—Mr. Blackwood.—Story of Gabriel's Road.
—John Hamilton Reynolds.—Description of Scott at Abbotsford.
—His woods.—The Kirk.—Letters to Coleridge.—Reynolds
suggested as editor of a Tory paper.—Popular commotions.—
Lockhart as a yeoman.—Ballads attributed to him.—His betrothal
to Miss Sophia Scott.—Her letters.—Prince Gustavus.—Descriptions of Miss Scott.—Scott asleep.

WHILE trailing his gown in the Parliament House,
where "nae man speered his price," and "dancing
after young ladies" (or *one* young lady), and scribbling comic rhymes for *Blackwood*, and caricaturing
the lieges, Lockhart was busy, at this time, on his
singular work, "Peter's Letters to his Kinsfolk."[1]
On March 23, 1819, Scott wrote to him from
Abbotsford, where cramp held him in torment.

---

[1] The name, of course, is borrowed from Scott's "Paul's Letters to
his Kinsfolk."

"I thought of you amid all this agony, and of the great game which, with your parts and principles, lies before you in Scotland." For long Scott had been the only Tory man of letters north of Tweed, the sole writer not dazzled by the radiance of "enlightenment." This very solitude might have given Scott pause, but he deemed that he was "at least standing by, if he could not support, the banner of ancient faith and loyalty." In his physical anguish he was mentally bequeathing his baton to Lockhart, he said, and the ladies who attended him were astonished to hear him quote—

"Take *thou* the vanguard of the Three,
And bury me by the bracken bush
That grows on yon lily lea."

Why Scott had Lockhart and the dying Douglas in his mind during his torments, shall be explained later.

Sir Walter had a habit of uttering these unexpected snatches of old song, which showed his companions where his mind was, often enough in an unlooked-for situation. Thus during his last days in Italy, at a point where the Lake of Avernus, the Lucrine Lake, Misenum, and Baiæ, and the sea are all in view, Sir William Gell heard him murmur—

"Up the craggy mountain,
And down the mossy glen,
We daurna gang a milking
For Charlie and his men."

His mind's eye looked on Moidart, "and he in dreams beheld the Hebrides."[1]

So it was with him when he quoted " The Hunting of Cheviot" in his racking pains, for his heart was with his cause, as he, and he only, conceived of that cause, and the death-words of the Douglas he was applying to Lockhart, as his own successor.

There could be no such successor. Scott's peculiar Toryism, like that of his own Invernahyle, was a loyalty to the old feudal order which, though now forlorn, had once, in ideal if not in reality, been a reasoned system of life and of society. No other system to be called rational has risen on its ruins. Whiggery is the negation of a system, an inn, not a dwelling. Socialism was, as yet, incoherent. Scott's sympathies were certainly more with some of the tenets of Socialism, with many of its aims at least, than with a Whiggish industrialism. He himself, in his relations with peasants and peers, lived in the light of the ideal of Feudalism ; the friend and protector of all beneath him, his "men" ;—the friend and true "man" of his chiefs. His political creed was a transferred allegiance from the rightful kings, who (in the male line) were no more, to the king whom, by some odd cantrip of logic, he regarded as their legitimate successor. His loyalty—so hateful and so incomprehensible to Hazlitt, for example—blossomed like a white rose, among the ruins of what had been

---

[1] The explanation occurs later in a letter of Lockhart's from Italy.

a stately tower, and above the graves where the royal and exiled dead sleep after their lifelong wanderings.

This was the creed, these were the politics, of a poet and a dreamer of dreams. That airy baton of his he could bequeath to no man. And Lockhart (though, as I shall show later, his imagination could share and nobly interpret the creed of Scott), must have known the truth very well, and smiled sadly enough at the bequest. Though a free lance of Toryism, he was not essentially a party man, as he discovered before the end came. But it is plain that Lockhart had bewitched his future father-in-law from the first, and that for Rodrigue this Don Diègue had *les yeux de Chimène.*

Descending from his characteristic dream, and his snatch of minstrelsy, Scott, in his letter, thanks Lockhart for "the pleaders' portraits," in *Blackwood* (Nos. xxiii., xxiv.) sketches of Cranstoun, Clerk, and Jeffrey, which later appeared in "Peter's Letters." The articles in *Blackwood* pretended, but with a most transparent pretence, to offer extracts from "Peter's" first edition,—which never existed. In fact the Reviewer says, like Coleridge of his journal, *The Friend,* "it is as good as MS." The latest extracts were those which so much pleased Scott.

In his letter of March 23, 1819, he adds remarks (now first published) on a scheme of Lockhart's for assisting Mr. Allan, the Scotch painter.

"I am delighted with your plan for poor Allan. It would be a shame to us all were we not to make an exertion for so wonderful a little fellow. Pray put me down for *three* shares. I think I shall get two names—D. Buccleugh and Lord Montagu, for two more—indeed I am almost sure of the former. Could not something be eked to the plan in the way of engraving so as to make it still further productive? I hope to be so well as to go up to London, and trust I shall get Allan an order to paint Archbishop Sharpe's murder, of which he has made a superb sketch. If my stomach would let me exert my energies as usual, I should hope to be able to treat myself to some of his productions. But at present my nose is held to the grindstone in every way."

It was, apparently, on April 10, 1819, that Lockhart rode to Abbotsford with John Ballantyne, and found Sir Walter, his hair bleached by the stress of his malady ("Life," vi. 69; "Letters," ii. 40). In the night the family was aroused by the cries of Scott, in a recurrence of his pains, and Lockhart, naturally, intended to leave early next morning. But the indomitable Sheriff took him on horseback "up Yarrow," as we say at home, past all his dear legendary scenes, doing election business with my grandfather on the way. They rode by Carterhaugh, where the Forest waters meet,[1] and where Janet

---

[1] Ettrick and Yarrow. Lockhart afterwards gave their names to two Dandie Dinmonts, presented to the Queen.

rescued Tamlane from the Fairy Queen. They rode
by Philiphaugh, where Leslie broke on Montrose's
sleeping men, through the mist; and they passed
over Minchmoor, whereby Montrose galloped to the
Tweed; and Newark; and Slain Man's Lee, where
the Covenanters butchered prisoners taken under
promise of quarter. Next day they rode up Ail
water, and on Bowden Moor, summoned by a rising
wreath of smoke, Scott met a trembling Tory voter,
skulking, like a Jacobite, from Whig scrutiny.
Then they heard the story of "ancient Riddell's
wide domain," now dispeopled of its lords. Next
day, from Eildon crest, Lockhart was shown the
kingdom of Border romance—

> " Mertoun's wood,
> And Tweed's fair flood,
> And all down Teviotdale,"

and Smailholme Tower, and the ruined shell of
Ercildoune, where the hare kindles on the Rhymer's
hearthstone. There Scott repeated the charmed
lines of Minstrel Burne—

> " For many a place stands in hard case,
> Where blithe folk kenned nae sorrow,
> With Homes that dwelt on Leader braes,
> And Scotts that dwelt on Yarrow."

Times were blithe with Scotts that dwelt on Tweed-
side, though too soon the Minstrel's burden was to
sing sooth.

Of one charm in Abbotsford, more potent than even the Wizard's spells, Lockhart, of course, says nothing, but we may believe that already his heart was given to her from whom, in life and death, that loyal heart never wandered.

On the night after the ride to Eildon Hill, Scott suffered from another attack, and Lockhart left him "with dark prognostications" that this visit to Abbotsford was to be his last.

On July 19, 1819, Scott acknowledged a present of "Peter's Letters."[1] The letter need not be reprinted. "The Epistles of the imaginary Dr. Morris have so often been denounced" (says Lockhart, after apologising for the book, as that of "a very young and a very thoughtless person") "as a mere string of libels, that I think it fair to show how much more leniently Scott judged of them at the time. Indeed Sir Walter writes, 'The general turn of the book is perhaps too favourable, both to the state of our public society, and of individual character.' He wished Dr. Morris to revive every half century, 'to record the fleeting manners of the age, and the interesting features of those who will only be known to posterity by their works.' He 'purrs and puts up his back, like his own grey cat,' Hins of Hinsfeldt, 'bribed by the doctor's kind and delicate account of his visit to Abbotsford.'"

Indeed, had Lockhart never lived to write his

[1] "Life," vol. vi. pp. 100, 103.

famous Biography, Dr. Morris's description of Abbotsford would remain the *locus classicus.*

"Peter's Letters," in spite of its ill repute, really contains infinitely more of good than evil. Dr. Morris, a scholar of some twoscore years, is supposed to arrive in his shandrydan from Wales. He meets a Mr. Wastle of Wastle, an old Oxford friend, and an impossible, irreconcilable Cavalier Tory. Wastle's "sudden elopement from Oxford, without a degree, after having astonished the examining masters by the splendid commencement of his examination," is a trait adapted from the tradition about De Quincey. The personal description is that of Lockhart himself, grown some twenty years older, while Wastle's learned enthusiasm for Old Edinburgh is borrowed from Scott. Lockhart liked the character, and made Wastle responsible for much prose and verse in *Blackwood.* "This yellow visage of his, with his close, firm lips, and his grey eyes . . . one would less wonder to meet with in Valladolid than in Edinburgh." This is worth quoting, as there is no effort to hide, but rather to proclaim Lockhart, though he is, later, introduced briefly in his proper person. Wastle's very passion for heraldry is Lockhart's. The attitude towards the Scotch people, especially as concerns their devotions, is exactly that of Lockhart in his "Life of Burns." He sees them, at the sermon, rejoice when they detect a chink in the armour of the preacher's logic, and "bowed in the dust" before "some solitary gleam of warm affectionate eloquence,—the only weapon they have no power to resist." There occur, of course, frequent portraits of "local celebrities," beginning with Jeffrey. Dr. Morris contrasts Jeffrey's head with Goethe's (whom Lockhart met at Weimar), "the sublime simplicity of his Homeric beauty, the awful pile of forehead, the large deep eyes, with their melancholy lightnings, the whole countenance, so radiant with divinity." As to Jeffrey's own eyes, "the scintillation of a star is not more fervid." "I think their prevailing language is, after all, rather a melancholy than a merry one ; it is, at least, very full of reflection." There follows a dinner (purely Barmecide) with Jeffrey, Playfair, Leslie, and others. The sages and philosophers are described as practising leaping, a curious and by no means very humorous invention. For this the brilliant and delicate account of Jeffrey's conversational manner might make some amends. Playfair, the victim of Lauerwinkel, "left a feeling of quiet, respectful, and affectionate admiration upon my mind." The superiority of the Whigs in law is admitted, and in literature. But where now is their literature ? Aaron's serpent in the Magician's hand, hath swallowed all the serpents of the Edinburgh literary Whiggery of that day.

Henry Mackenzie, the Man of Feeling, is described very favourably. In 1823, Lockhart dedicated "Reginald Dalton" to this sometime enemy of *Blackwood*. At a Burns Dinner, in "Peter's Letters," Jeffrey does not propose the poet's memory, and Dr. Morris censures his critical severity to Burns, making a very fair and unexaggerated appeal for tenderness to the poet's failings. He tells how Mr. Maule of Panmure settled £50 a year on Mrs. Burns, and how one of the poet's sons, as soon as he obtained a medical practice in India, provided for her so well that she was able to relieve Mr. Maule from the slight burden on his kindness. Many poets were toasted, including Crabbe, Rogers, and Montgomery, but *not* Wordsworth, Southey, or Coleridge, Tory minstrels. The organisers of the feast were Whigs! If Dr. Morris fables not, this is an odd proof of Whig liberality. Here, and throughout, Wordsworth is praised "with both hands."

Wilson, of course, was present : " His hair is of the true Sicambrian yellow ; his eyes are of the lightest, and at the same time of the clearest blue, and the blood glows in his cheeks with as firm a fervour as it did, according to the description of Jornandes, in those of the *bello gaudentes, praelio ridentes Teutones* of Attila. I had never suspected, before I saw him, that such extreme fairness and freshness of complexion could be compatible with so much variety and tenderness, but, above all, with so much depth of expression." The variety, luxury, and *feeling* of Wilson's eloquence, and "the tremulous music of a voice that is equally at home in the highest and lowest of notes," are sympathetically described. He proposed Hogg's health ; the Shepherd made a brief hearty reply, and Dr. Morris "began to be quite in love with the Ettrick Shepherd." When the doctor sang "Donald Macdonald," the Shepherd, its author, confessed a kindred flame,—and toddy set in. The "dreadful tusks" and other features of the "Great Boar" are described in a manner not wholly pleasing to any personal vanity which Hogg may have cherished, but "his towering brow, and eye of genius," atone for all. The evening finished under Mr. Patrick Robertson's ("Lord Peter's") chairmanship.

Dr. Morris's view of Scotch education, of the "facetious and rejoicing ignorance" of Greek, has been already cited. It was as in Dr. Johnson's days, "every man has a mouthful of learning, no man has a bellyful." There is a really admirable defence of Greek, and of historical study. It is vain to talk of reading the Greeks in translations. "Wherein does the essence of a nation exist, if not in her mind ? and how is that mind to be penetrated or understood, if we neglect the pure and faithful mirror in which of old it has stamped its likeness, her language ? Men may talk as they please about translations, there is, in brevity and in truth, no such thing as a translation!" As for the Scotch, as compared with the English Universities, "they have different objects, and they are both excellent in their different ways."

The copious descriptions of leading advocates are incisive, and probably just; but a barrister, like an actor, has his fame in his lifetime, nor can we now care greatly to read about men who have left only names, and these, except at the Scotch Bar, well-nigh forgotten.

A very distinguished Scotsman, who remembers, "'tis sixty years since," a bad inn described by Lockhart as still deserving his description, writes to me: "Lockhart shows a good deal of malice and irony, and does not even spare the chief of his own party—witness his account of the President of the Court of Session, Charles Hope, and his address to the corrupt attorney." ("Letters," third edition, ii. 102–105.) "He manages to make the President ridiculous, while exalting his eloquence and solemnity."

Now I have read the whole passage, a most eloquent and impressive passage, carefully, and cannot detect a grain of irony, or a shade of ridicule. The piece concludes—"As I came away through the crowd, I heard a pale, anxious-looking old man, who, I doubt not, had a cause in Court, whisper to himself, 'God be thanked, there's one true GENTLEMAN at the head of them all.'"

The passage, in fact, describes the strong, almost overwhelming emotion of pain, with which "a true gentleman," in supreme place, prepares himself for the cruel task of publicly rebuking a fellow-creature, and "the haughtiness of insulted virtue, the scorn of honour, the coldness of disdain, the bitterness of pity," with which the inevitable reprimand is inflicted.

Apparently there are, and were, two ways of reading "Peter's Letters," and Lockhart may have been suspected of irony where he was serious, or the sense of irony, in myself as in Scott, may be deficient. I am, of course, inclined to prefer my own interpretation, but it is well to state (what I certainly could never have guessed), that there is another.

From the lawyers, Dr. Morris turns to the men of letters, and, of course, to Jeffrey and his *Review*. The learned doctor anticipates Carlyle's line of thought. The *Edinburgh* Reviewers are " the legitimate offspring of the sceptical philosophers of the last age," and their scepticism as to the value, for example, of thought on the great problems of thought, has resulted in petulance and *persiflage*. In truth, the Reviewers are not " earnest," as Mr. Carlyle would have said. The fact that Sir William Hamilton never contributed to the *Review*, under Jeffrey, and that when he did, under Macvey Napier, Jeffrey was vexed and puzzled, is an illustration of Lockhart's meaning. " Cousin I pronounce the most unreadable thing that ever appeared in the *Review*," says Jeffrey about Hamilton's essay on Cousin.[1] Hamilton "affects to understand the worst part of the mysticism " (of

[1] " Correspondence of Macvey Napier," p. 70.

Cousin), "and to explain it, and to think it very
ingenious and respectable, *and it is mere gibberish.*"
Jeffrey's famous letter of advice to Carlyle, analysed
by Mr. Froude, "England will never admire, nor indeed endure, your German divinities" (Goethe is in
question), supplies another example. The German
philosophers are "Dousterswivels," and so forth.[1]
Of Goethe, Lockhart had an extreme admiration.
Himself a mocker on occasion, he was absolutely in
earnest about the great works of great minds. He
found Jeffrey habitually misunderstanding, or never
trying to understand, what was not superficial. He
found him applauding vehemently "The Paradise of
Coquettes," and beginning a review of Wordsworth
with "This will never do!" He found him minis-
tering to the vanity of a nation, "which had become
at once very fond of scepticism, and very weary
of learning." He saw him "counteracting, by a
continued series of sarcastic and merry antidotes,
the impression likely to be produced by works
appealing to the graver and more mysterious feelings
of the human heart." In contemporary literature,
the *Review* was so conducted that "I do not, on my
conscience, believe that there is one Whig in Edinburgh to whom the name of my friend Charles
Lamb would convey any distinct or definite idea."
As for Wordsworth, "the reading public of Edinburgh do not criticise Mr. Wordsworth, they think
him below their criticism."

[1] "Life of Thomas Carlyle," ii. 38.

Nobody can deny the element, the much-needed element, of truth in all this censure. The world is not so clear and comprehensible as the Jeffreyan intellect supposes. Great and ultimate, if finally insoluble problems, "blank misgivings of a creature moving about in worlds not realised," cannot be sneered away. *Ernst ist das Leben*, whether we like it or not. This is, in essence, what Lockhart had to say—this is what Carlyle would have called his "message." His was *vox clamantis in eremo*, in a wilderness tempered by toddy and punch, port and claret. Carlyle, not to speak profanely, came clad in camel's hair and eating locusts and wild honey. Lockhart, amidst the complexities of his character, had the prophet's message, but not his spirit of martyrdom and renunciation.

Prophesying cannot be done on these terms, and Dr. Morris wanders off to a disquisition on that very mundane School of the Prophets, *Blackwood's Magazine*. But even *Blackwood* is under the Edinburgh spell. In the evil article on Coleridge, which opened the campaign, it is written : "If Mr. Coleridge should make his appearance suddenly among any company of well-educated people on this side the Tweed, he would meet with some difficulty in making them comprehend who he was." "What a fine idea," cries Lockhart, "for a Scottish critic to hug himself upon ! How great is the blessing of a contented disposition !"

The talk of Dr. Morris about the bookseller's

shops is now, of course, antiquated. Constable's, in the High Street, was "a low dusky chamber," without the luxuries of Mr. Murray's emporium in Albemarle Street. There was Manner's and Miller's, for a modern lounge ; and Laing's, for lovers of old books and black letter, reminded Lockhart of Parker's, in Oxford. There is a long description of Blackwood's, in Princes Street, but we have had enough of Ebony. Mr. Blackwood is praised for shrewdness, decision, and energy, and it would be "unfair" (one does not see why) to blame him for the excesses of his Magazine. "Well, Dr. Morris," exclaimed the Man in Plain Apparel, "have you seen our last number? Is it not perfectly glorious ? My stars ! doctor, there is nothing equal to it," and so on, the author's natural turn for banter getting the better of him here, at all events. They dine at Ambrose's, the tavern of the "Noctes Ambrosianæ," and Lockhart tells, very well, the tragic old story of Gabriel's double murder, wrought here when the road was a dell in a wood. There follows a history of the Magazine, a kind of confession of contrition, a defence of the Cockney articles, an eulogy on Coleridge. Keats's friend, John Hamilton Reynolds, "a very promising writer," is excepted from the general abuse of the Londoners; partly, perhaps, because Christie knew Reynolds ; partly because his really was "a very gay, humorous pen, capable, too, of charming poetry."

The painters come next, and Raeburn is pro-

nounced "in no important particular inferior even
to Sir Thomas Lawrence." The end of the volume
deals with the visit to Abbotsford, and Scott.
"There is no kind of rank which I should suppose
it so difficult to bear with perfect ease, as the universally honoured nobility of universally honoured
genius; but all this sits as lightly upon this great
man, as ever a plumed casque did upon the head
of one of his own graceful knights." Scott quotes
a ballad, his face alters, his quick eyes beneath his
heavy brows are fixed "with a sober solemn lustre.
. . . I shall certainly never forget the fine heroic
enthusiasm of look with which he spoke the lines,
nor the grand melancholy roll of voice, which showed
with what a world of thoughts and feelings every
fragment of the old legend was associated within
his breast."

One criticism Lockhart makes, which Scott may
not have welcomed. His stripling woods were
dearer than his poems to the Sheriff. Lockhart
speaks of the plantations, and the agriculture which
will take advantage of their shelter. "To say the
truth, I do not think with much pleasure of the
prospect of any such changes. . . . There hovers
at present over the most of this district a certain
delicious atmosphere of pastoral loneliness, and I
think there would be something like sacrilege in
disturbing it, even by things that elsewhere would
confer interest as well as ornament."

The Kirk and the General Assembly next en-

gaged the attention of Dr. Morris. He found the
Assembly to be little more than a kind of clerical
wappenshaw, so much had Party (as of Moderates
and High Flyers) declined in our national Zion.
Dr. Morris listened to many sermons, described
several ministers, among others the Griffin, visited
Glasgow, and dealt with its local habit of "gaggery,"
reiterated his praises of Wilson, especially as a poet,
and gave one of his best chapters to an *occasion*, or
Holy Fair, as Burns called the open-air administra-
tion of the Sacrament. These are pages marked
by an almost Wordsworthian sense of the nature of
that impressive and singular celebration.[1] They
are conceived in the best and most sympathetic
sense, and especially deserve the attention of
students of Burns's brilliant satire. Lockhart's
memory was full of comic anecdotes about rural
ministers, but his Dr. Morris repeats none of
them. To "a mischievous Oxford puppy," of
Scotch birth, the foibles of his countrymen afford
a tempting target, but Lockhart, in his assumed
character of a Welsh physician, avoids temptation,
and scarcely ever shoots at national folly as she
waddles by.

Indeed it is not easy to understand the frame of
mind to which "Peter's Letters" appeared "a string
of libels." The dinner at Craigcrook, Jeffrey's
house, was a fancy sketch, far better omitted; the
"portraits of the pleaders" were portraits of public

---

[1] These pages are *not* by Professor Wilson.

men in their public function, and certainly did not offend Scott. At our distance in time there may be sins which escape us, and others may have been invented or imagined. The introduction of himself, perhaps by the mysterious "other hand," may have been an error, but it was partly warranted, as Lockhart was already a "lion" of Edinburgh, though such a young one, and was, in fact, stared at as he walked the streets : to this Mr. Lawrence Lockhart bears witness. The disguise, it must be repeated, is designedly flimsy. Lockhart's authorship was the most open of secrets, the very drawings were a signature.

In the third edition appears a letter to Coleridge from Dr. Morris. The doctor attributes the hubbub to the arrogance of the Scotch Whigs, which is very amusingly described. After reading Lord Cockburn's " Memorials," with his description of Jeffrey as "the First of British Critics," we feel that exaggeration was impossible. Much of the book is now antiquated, but many admirable passages of living interest might be extracted. The doctor's craniological speculations are obsolete, but it is almost as true to say that a few excisions would present a useful work, as to say that many selections would be valuable. The author insists on his old private opinion, that Scotch intellect is sufficiently represented by Hume and Adam Smith, but that Scotch *character* is an inexhaustible mine. As for the personalities, the Whigs had welcomed, two or three

years before, a personal volume by a traveller, one Simond, in which Scotch Tories had suffered grievous things.[1]   It is only necessary to add that an unlucky description of the Black Bull Inn, as noisy and untidy, led to legal proceedings, and Lockhart had to pay £400 of damages, without going into court.   "Lockhart's account of the inn is very correct," says a friend already quoted, who remembers "The Black Bull," but *toute vérité n'est pas bonne à dire.*

On October 31, 1819, I find Lockhart writing to Scott, from Edinburgh, about his endeavours to obtain an editor for a new Tory newspaper.[2]   The *Scotsman* of the period was probably thought to need an antidote.   To abridge a mere letter of business, Lockhart had asked Christie to invite Mr. Murray of the *Times* to take the vacant post. Mr. Murray was in all respects well qualified, as a political writer, and a man acquainted with the material side of newspaper publication.   But Mr. Murray's connection with a well-established and successful London paper made him hesitate, and, finally, decline.   Lockhart also consulted Wilson, "who appears to enter into it with all his

---

[1] Among critics who, like Scott, did not reckon Peter's book a pestilent libel, was that respectable authority, Dr. Jenkyns, Master of Balliol.   "'Peter's Letters' have been much read in the South," writes the Master, "and with great pleasure, which I felt at the perusal of them.   I could not help recognising the connection between Dr. Morris and our portly friend of Ystraed Meirie." (Williams.)   The Master then invites Lockhart to stay with him at Balliol.

[2] Scott's " Letters," ii. 97.

characteristic ardour.   When the thing is once set
afoot, the only difficulty will be restraining his
vehemence : there will certainly be no need of any
stimulus, I mean in regard to the tendency and
scope of his lucubrations.   As to the regularity
of their forthcoming there will be a necessity for
very serious pressing indeed.   I speak, as you
know, from abundant experience.   Perhaps, if you
will pardon me for hinting such a thing, a few lines
from yourself, even at this stage of the business,
might be of great use in leading him to turn his
mind steadfastly to an examination and preparation
of his many resources. . . . —Believe me, ever
faithfully and affectionately yours,

"J. G. LOCKHART."

In an undated note, Lockhart sends Murray's
letter of refusal to Sir Walter, and admits that he can
think of no substitute in the chair editorial.   Christie,
in London, was equally at a loss.   He wisely declined,
for his own part, to abandon his prospects at the
Bar.   He could think of nobody eligible, except
John Hamilton Reynolds, the friend of Keats ; but
Reynolds was "Master T'otherside," as Scott says
on another occasion.   Reynolds had been a writer
in the *Champion* (to which Keats occasionally
refers), but the paper, Christie thought, was waning
under the editorship of Mr. John Scott, the first
mention of that ill-starred name in this correspondence.   At the same time Mr. Croker wrote

his first letter to Lockhart (November 18, 1819), trying to enlist Wilson and him in a paper to be called the *Constitution*, but, in practice, styled the *Guardian*. The Tories of these days were poor hands at journalism, and the position of an editor was not deemed worthy of a gentleman. For the inchoate Scotch paper, Scott suggested (1.) James Ballantyne, (2.) Washington Irving! In the latter case a gentleman, at all events, would have been an editor. He, of course, declined.[1]

In these months an alarm, or panic, about a Radical rising was current, and Scott was very busy with his picturesque Buccleuch Legion.

Lockhart was a volunteer, with the rest; even Lord Cockburn was enrolled in some kind of armed force. Lockhart rode about in the various unopposed marches and counter marches, the Raid of Airdrie, the Trot of Kilmarnock, but he does not seem to have taken his military character seriously. " The Songs of the Edinburgh Troop " (published in 1825), are usually attributed to him.[2]

Therein the poet sings :

> "Sometimes the thing will happen,
> The rear rides o'er the front ;
> Myself, I once came slapping,
> And fell with such a dunt !

---

[1] Scott's " Letters," ii. 57, 61.
[2] Dean Burgon assigns them to Patrick Fraser Tytler.

> I hate the gloom of Borthwick's plume !
>   There's wisdom in my tune,
>   Make your will, ere you drill,
>   Each desperate Dragoon."

Or again—

> " 'Twas at Bathgate this war might be said to commence,
>   To the tune, as was fitting, of ' D——n the expense.' "

In later days Lockhart's interest in sterile disputes of party nearly vanished ; it was never very strong, and social questions, "the condition of England," occupied his sympathies.   Even in 1819 it is pleasant to note that his heart was not all set on force as a remedy.   His "Clydesdale Yeoman's Return," attributed to his friend " The Odontist," describes a Lanarkshire farmer's view of a Radical meeting, and his readiness to rise and ride as a volunteer. But his good wife is of gentler mood—

> "Now, God preserve the King," said Jean, "and bless the Prince, his son,
>   And send good trade to weaver-lads, and this work will all be done ;
>   For 'tis idle hand makes busy tongue, and troubles all the land
>   With noisy fools, that prate of things they do not understand.
>   But if worse fall out, then up, my man—was never holier cause,
>   God's blessed Word, King George's crown, and proud old Scotland's laws."

But Lockhart's comic verse is the topic of a

separate dissertation. So varied were his pursuits, that he had already begun his well-known translations of the Spanish Ballads. The first instalment appeared in *Blackwood's* for February 1820. In the following month Mr. Wastle began a Literary Diary in the Magazine, praising, incidentally, the author of a review of the Waverley Novels, in a new serial, *Baldwin's*, or *The London Magazine*. This reviewer was the Editor, John Scott.

Lockhart had other than literary engagements at this moment. By the middle of February it had been arranged that he should marry Miss Scott. Lockhart always treasured the little notes written to him, at this time, by his future wife. The earliest begins "My dear Sir," and is written "without Papa's knowledge," a thing which must never occur again. Miss Scott had spoken to her father, and Sir Walter had hinted at a little prudent delay. "Do not, for God's sake, be so unhappy," she writes. The unhappiness did not last long. The later notes always begin "Dear Mr. Lockhart," kind, happy, playful missives, ending "Always affectionately yours." Lockhart accompanied the family on a flying visit to Abbotsford, on a Saturday, of which he has left the chronicle.[1] In a walk from Huntly Burn his future country home was fixed, the cottage of Chiefswood, on a little haugh beside the haunted Bogle burn, which flows through the Rhymer's Glen. An additional gable

---

[1] "Life," vi. 187.

has been built in the cottage, with its tiny rooms, separated only by the burn from an ancient Holy Well.   Otherwise the place is unaltered.   The bureau where Scott wrote "The Pirate" keeps its old place; the same venerable trees shade the lawn : the avenue is that which John Ballantyne wanted to mark out by a cross-country ride "on the Sabbath-day."   The glen is now haunted, indeed, by many memories.

In this February, Scott and Lockhart, with Prince Gustavus, the exiled heir of Sweden, saw George IV. proclaimed, where, in 1745, King James the Eighth had been vainly announced, at the Cross of Edinburgh.   The Swedish exile listened, with melancholy interest, to Scott's anecdotes of that other wanderer, Prince Charles, who, on this very scene, had snatched from Fate one hour of royalty.   Scott drew Lockhart to a window apart, "Poor lad, poor lad, God help him !" he said with a natural emotion.

On March 15, 1820, Scott announces to Lady Abercorn his daughter's approaching marriage "to a young man of uncommon talents, indeed of as promising a character as I know."   All his correspondence attests his satisfaction with the match.[1] Lockhart's letter, announcing to his father his betrothal, lies before me, but such documents

---

[1] "Letters," ii. 73.   A ludicrous rumour that Scott's letters to Rogers expressed "detestation" of Lockhart is published in the "Life and Letters of Charles Summer," i. 358.

deserve to be respected at any distance of time.
It is enough to say, that Miss Scott's charming
character, displayed during her father's illness, even
more than her personal beauty, is assigned as the
cause of his affection.   Mr. Christie sent his congratulations on March 17.

"Your letter has given me more pleasure than
any I ever received from you. . . . I do not question that you have better reasons to expect happiness in your wife than birth can bestow, however
exalted, either from title or illustrious character.
But surely it must be matter for congratulation
to marry the daughter of the most illustrious man
of the age. . . . Depend upon it, woman's goodness
is greater than the faultiness of our nature can
ever permit us to equal."

Of Scott's eldest daughter and dearest, "the
flower and blossom of his house," not much is
said, of course, in published memorials.   I take a
quaint vignette of her, from an unpublished letter to
Sir Walter by Mr. Edward Everett. (Cambridge,
Massachusetts, March 28, 1820.)

"Just before I had the happiness of visiting you,
a party of ladies and gentlemen, travelling into
Scotland, determined to see you, wandered into
your enclosure, and surprised you seated before
your door, in that condition into which Horace
says your great master Homer sometimes fell.
This fact I have upon the authority of Miss Sophia,
who came out and found them all standing round

you in a ring, without breaking the quiet of your *siesta*."

These were strange gentlemen and ladies, but the little picture of Scott asleep in white hat and green coat, of the gaping tourists who had calmly walked up to his door, and of Miss Scott contemplating the scene, is worth preserving.

The following page is a sketch of Miss Scott as she was in 1817, extracted from the unpublished journal of a tour by two Miss Penroses, and Miss Trevennen.[1]

The English ladies, being in Melrose, were visited by the Scotts, the Constables, and Miss Russel of Ashestiel. Naturally they were taken to the Abbey.

"In the chancel Miss Scott, a very charming lively girl of seventeen, pointed out to us 'The Wizard's Grave,' and then the black stone in the form of a coffin, to which the allusion is made in the poem, 'A Scottish monarch sleeps below,'— said to be the tomb of Alexander II. 'But I will tell you a secret,' she half-whispered; 'only don't you tell Johnny Bower' (the *cicerone*). 'There is no Scottish monarch there at all, nor anybody else, for papa had the stone taken up, not long ago, and no coffin or anything was to be found. And then Johnny came and begged me not to tell

---

[1] For this I am indebted to the kindness of my friend, Mr. Ernest Hartley Coleridge.

people so.[1] "For what wull I do, Miss Scott, when
I show the ruins, if I canna point to this bit, and
say, 'A Scottish monarch sleeps below'?" As,
however, he *had* the pleasure of saying this to *us*
the evening before, Miss Scott thought we might
fairly have *her* secret. [2]

.   .   .   .

"We now set out for Dryburgh, about five miles.
Mr. Scott placed his daughter in our carriage, that
she might point out the different places as we
passed them. We could not have had a better
director, nor a more lively entertaining companion.
Every spot was known to her, and in this fairy land
her quick imagination seemed to delight in all the
legendary lore she had heard, and could so promptly
apply, of the Goblin burn, where still the common
people deemed fairy elves and spirits loved to hold
their moonlit revels. . . . In a short time, at the
view of some distant mountains, Miss Scott suddenly
exclaimed, 'Look, there are the Cheviots ; are you
not glad to see England again?' We assured her
we were, though we should quit Scotland with
so much regret. 'Well,' she said, 'she should
not have liked us if we were not glad to return
home.' Her father had taken her to London the

---

[1] See Washington Irving on Johnny Bower, in his "Abbotsford and
Newstead Abbey."

[2] Most of the graves of Catholic Scotland have been rifled, for any
personal property they might contain. "They howkit up the Papist
corpses, and toomed them ower the brae" above the sea, in the present
century, at St. Andrews.

year before, and she was delighted to get back again, and to hail the Cheviots on her return. It was plain to see she was her father's darling, and she talked of him with enthusiasm. She has a very natural, unaffected character, with a strong tincture of romantic feeling, which seemed judiciously kept in check by *him*, as she said he did not allow her to read much poetry, nor had she even read all his *own* poems, which were never to be found *in the way*, at their house. She spoke of her sister and her brothers, with a warmth of affection very pleasing, and if we may judge by so short an acquaintance, she seems likely to become a valuable character. On asking what was become of Camp (the dog drawn in the painting of Mr. Scott), she shook her head, and said he was dead. 'You must never come to Abbotsford when any of the dogs die, for there is a sad weeping amongst us all.'"

Miss Scott, as Lockhart says, in his brief and beautiful tribute to her memory, was, of all his children, the one most like Sir Walter. It was she who nearly fainted with emotion, at the discovery of the Scottish Regalia. (February 5, 1818.) "He never spoke all the way home, but every now and then I felt his arm tremble; and from that time I fancied he began to treat me more like a woman than a child. I thought he liked me better, too, than he had ever done before."[1] She it was who

---

[1] "Life," v. 283.

sang the old songs that her father loved; she was
the Duke of Buccleuch's "little Jacobite." Her
portrait, by Nicholson, in a kind of peasant costume,
with a great hound looking up into her face, has
an expression of the sweetest humour and friendly
charm. It is barely worth noting, as an argument
in the little controversy as to Sir Walter's Presbyterian or Episcopalian leanings, that Miss Scott and
her sister Anne were confirmed in April 1820.[1]
Lockhart and Miss Scott were married at Abbotsford, in the evening, *more Scotico*, of April 29, 1820.
Among the marriages of men of letters, often far
from happy, this, in spite of La Rochefoucauld,
was *un mariage délicieux*, uninterrupted in its
happiness, save by the misfortunes of Sir Walter,
and the ill health, first of the eldest boy, and, later,
of Mrs. Lockhart.

[1] "Life," vi. 216.

CHAPTER IX

"The mother of mischief."—Election to Chair of Moral Philosophy.
—Hamilton and Wilson.—Calumnies against Wilson.—Scott's
defence.—Lockhart's "Testimonium."—Scott's letter of remon-
strance.—Promises of good behaviour.—Attacks on Lockhart in
Baldwin's Magazine.—Mr. John Scott, Editor of *Baldwin's.*—
Tims.—Christie writes to Lockhart.—Lockhart's reply.—Demand
for an apology.—Mr. John Scott's answer.—Lockhart in London.
—A challenge.—Curious evidence of Horatio Smith.—A pacific
second.—No fight.—An oversight.—Christie's statement.—John
Scott challenges Christie.—A moonlight duel.—Christie's letter to
Lockhart.—Flight of Christie and Traill.—Distress of Lockhart.
—Imputations on his courage.—Gallant behaviour of Christie.—
The trial.—Acquittal.—Reflections.

IT is with pain that we return to "the mother of
mischief," and all the trouble that came of "that
daughter of debate," *Maga.* In the end of March
1820, Lockhart wrote to Scott, who was in London,
asking him to aid Wilson in his candidature for the
Chair of Moral Philosophy in the Town's College
of Edinburgh. The University there is essentially
"the Town's College," and the electors, at that time,
were the Town Council. The electors were themselves chosen on political grounds, and the Tories
had a majority. The only formidable opponent
was Sir William Hamilton, who, as the most learned

and blameless Scottish scholar of his day, ought, of
course, to have been appointed. Wilson, on the
other side, had "great natural powers accidentally
directed" towards the subject of the Chair. But
any Scot can be professor of anything, and Mr.
Carlyle was equally ready for a Chair of Astronomy
or of Rhetoric. The best that can be said for a
struggle as fierce as any Parliamentary election,
is, that it left Hamilton and Wilson on perfectly
good terms, as it found them, and that Professor
Wilson put all his unrivalled energy into his
duties as he conceived them, kept his class
thoroughly alive, and was an elder brother to his
pupils.

The incongruity of his candidature, however, could
not escape observation. Scott, as a friend and a
Tory, and a firm believer in the candidate, took
Wilson's part. He had, not unjustly, the highest
opinion of his natural powers ; even Carlyle admits
that Wilson was "the most *gifted* of our literary
men, either then or still." Scott conceived that
the work and responsibility of the Chair would
steady and indeed redeem Wilson, which, with
time, they managed to effect. "He must leave
off sack, purge, and live cleanly as a gentleman
ought to do." [1]

The election went on, both parties putting forth
all their energies. The Whigs were so ill advised
as to charge Wilson with being "a bad husband

[1] "Life," vi. 218.

and a bad father." Here he was on perfectly safe ground, and obtained golden opinions to that effect. He was accused of singing "a careless careless tavern catch" at some revel, and Lockhart, in a letter already published in part, assures Scott that the enemy sank so low as to try to worm evidence out of hotel waiters, the minions of Ambrose, perhaps. On July 8, Scott himself wrote a remarkable letter on these heads to the Lord Provost of Edinburgh. ("Christopher North," ii. 313.) To say, however, as he did, that Wilson was "altogether incapable of composing parodies upon Scripture," argued a slight forgetfulness of "The Chaldee!" The rest of the letter is a model in its kind. As Mrs. Wilson wrote, "the Tories were triumphant," for, in fact, the election was political. Wilson set to work with a devouring energy, and, as we have seen, justified his appointment; and he had Sir William Hamilton as an enthusiastic auditor of one, at least, of his discourses.

Lockhart, unluckily, could not but raise a wild war-whoop over Wilson's success. Mr. Cranstoun, the famous advocate, had made a poem with twenty rhymes to "Packwood" (a notoriety of the day). Lockhart, under the name of his Glasgow dentist, or Odontist, Dr. James Scott, indited the "Testimonium," with some seventy rhymes to *Blackwood*, in celebration of Wilson's victory. (*Blackwood*, July 1820.) Now the *Scotsman*, edited by Mr. M'Culloch, was a vehement opposer of Wilson, and

Mrs. Gordon, in "Christopher North," prints some
of Mr. M'Culloch's amenities. The same paper, as
a matter of course, had attacked Dr. Peter Morris.
In the "Testimonium," verses xiii. and xiv. are
devoted to Mr. M'Culloch, under his nickname of
the Stot. This is needful to be known for the
understanding of the following letter from Scott to
Lockhart, and, practically, to Wilson.[1] The epistle
shows how far Scott "encouraged" the excesses of
Blackwood. He is replying to a letter of Lockhart's
of July 20, 1820. This is partly published (Scott's
"Letters," ii. 84). There is reference to the
"Testimonium," and to the passions of the hour.
There was near being a challenge to the duello
between two learned Professors. Lockhart also
speaks of beginning his novel, "Valerius." Scott's
letter follows :—

"DEAR LOCKHART,—I had your kind letter, and
congratulate you on your hard-fought battle.
Wilson has surmounted difficulties of which he
was not aware, for the worthy —— wrote to
Lord Melville on the subject of his interference,
and received a most capital answer. Moreover, all
sorts of anonymous letters were directed to little
purpose at the same quarter. The victory, however, being gained, it is greatly the opinion of Mr.

---

[1] Postmark, July 25, 1820. The letter could not be discovered for
Scott's Correspondence : I owe it to the kindness of my friend, Mr.
C. M. Falconer of Dundee, who found this, and some other papers,
by a curious accident.

Wilson's best wishers, and most especially mine, that the matter may be suffered to rest. His best triumph, and that of his friends, will be in the concentration of his powerful mind upon the great and important task before him, and in utterly contemning the paltry malice of those who have taken such foul means of opposing him. Any attempt on his part, or that of his friends, to retaliate on such a *fainéant* as poor Stookie, or on the *Scotsman*, is like a gentleman fighting with a chimney sweeper—he may lick him, but cannot avoid being smutted in the conflict. For my part, I vow to God I would sooner fight a duel with an actual scavenger than enter into controversy with such fellows.

" I am sure our friend has been taught the danger of giving way to high spirits in mixed society, where there is some one always ready to laugh at the joke and to put it into his pocket to throw in the jester's face on some future occasion. It is plain Wilson must have walked the course had he been cautious in selecting the friends of his lighter hours, and now, clothed with philosophical dignity, his friends will really expect he should be on his guard in this respect, and add to his talents and amiable disposition the proper degree of *retenue* becoming a moral teacher. Try to express all this to him in your own way, and believe that, as I have said it from the best motives, so I would wish it conveyed in the most delicate terms, as from one who equally honours Wilson's genius and loves his benevolent, ardent, and amiable disposition, but who would willingly see them mingled with the caution which leaves calumny no pin to hang her infamous accusations upon.

"For the reasons above mentioned I wish you had not published the 'Testimonium.' It is very clever, but descends to too low game. If Jeffrey or Cranstoun, or any of the dignitaries, chose to fight such skirmishes there would be some credit in it; but I do not like to see you turn out as a sharp-shooter with ——. 'What does thou drawn among these heartless hinds?' If M'Culloch were to parade you upon the score of Stanza xiii., I do not see how you could decline his meeting, as you make the man your equal (*ad hoc*, I mean), when you condescend to insult him by name. And the *honour* of such a rencounter would be small comfort to your friends for the danger which must attend it. I have hitherto avoided saying anything on this subject,[1] though some little turn towards personal satire is, I think, the only drawback to your great and powerful talents, and I think I may have hinted as much to you. But I wished to see how this matter of Wilson's would turn, before making a clean breast upon this subject. It might have so happened that you could

---

[1] Later Sir Walter says that he remonstrated before Lockhart's marriage. It is impossible to know on which occasion,—the present, or a later period,—his memory was at fault.

not handsomely or kindly have avoided a share
in his defence, if the enemy had prevailed, and
where friendship, or country, or any strong call
demands the use of satiric talent, I hope I should
neither fear risk myself or desire a friend to shun
it.   But now that he has triumphed I think it
would be bad taste to cry out—

'Strike up our drums—pursue the scattered stray.'

Besides, the natural consequence of his new situation
must be his relinquishing his share in these compositions—at least, he will injure himself in the
opinion of many friends, and expose himself to a
continuation of galling and vexatious disputes to
the embittering of his life, should he do otherwise.
In that case I really hope you will pause before
you undertake to be the Boaz of the *Maga;* I
mean in the personal and satirical department, when
the Jachin has seceded.

"Besides all other objections of personal enemies,
personal quarrels, constant obliquy, and all unchari-
tableness, such an occupation will fritter away your
talents, hurt your reputation both as a lawyer and
a literary man, and waste away your time in what at
best will be but a monthly wonder.   What has been
done in this department will be very well as a frolic
of young men, but let it suffice, 'the gambol has
been shown'—the frequent repetition will lose its
effect even as pleasantry, for Peter Pindar, the
sharpest of personal satirists, wrote himself down,

and wrote himself out, and is forgotten. The public can be cloyed with this as well as with other high seasoned food. Remember it is to the *personal* satire I object, and to the horse-play of your raillery, as well as the mean objects on whom it is wasted. Employing your wit and wisdom on general national topics, and bestowing deserved correction on opinions rather than men, or on men only as connected with actions and opinions, you cannot but do your country yeoman's service.

"The magazine, I should think, might be gradually restricted in the point of which I complain, and strengthened and enlarged in circulation at the same time. It certainly has done and may do admirable service; it is the excess I complain of, and particularly as respecting your share in it, for I care not how hard others lay on the Galwegian Stot, only I would not like to have you in that sort of scrape which, if he have a particle of the buffalo in him, might, I think, ensue. Revere yourself, my dear boy, and think you were born to do your country better service than in this species of warfare. I make no apology (I am sure you will require none) for speaking plainly what my anxious affection dictates. As the old warrior says, 'May the name of Mevni be forgotten among the people, and may they only say, Behold the father of Gaul.' I wish you to have the benefit of my experience without purchasing it; and be assured, that the consciousness of attain-

ing complete superiority over your calumniators
and enemies by the force of your general character,
is worth a dozen of triumphs over them by the
force of wit and raillery. I am sure Sophia, as
much as she can or ought to form any judgment
respecting the line of conduct you have to pursue
in your new character of a man married and settled,
will be of my opinion in this matter, and that you
will consider her happiness and your own, together
with the respectability of both, by giving what I
have said your anxious consideration.

"I am delighted to hear you get on so soon with
the Roman tale.[1] It cannot but be admirable, and is
quite new. I would have you anxiously consider the
author for a little time. The Abb. gets on ; I hope
it will do, and am greatly encouraged by your sentiments and Erskine's. James Ballantyne, a good
specimen of a certain class of readers, likes the second
volume better than the first—*Vogue la galère.*

I have at present a visit from Dr. [*name illegible*];
he has stayed with me some days, and I think him
intelligent and sensible, under a good deal of high-
church and classical bigotry—neither indeed is the
sort of bigotry which I dislike. If Charles goes
eastward ho ! I shall be glad to have compassed
his acquaintance . . .

[*This part torn off.*]

. . . which would be a beautiful thing if it could be

---

[1] "Valerius."

done, but I doubt it, and I make a point never to do anything over my poor neighbours' necks. Constable proposes £400 for the *Review* [1]—this is too little, I think, though fully what the work can afford. Write to James Ballantyne, who thinks it should be £500, what your own views are, and they will be complied with instantly. Do not let this business slumber, for in these matters one should be a man of business. I have nothing to add but my best affection to Fia, as Charles used to call her when a child, and kind respects to your father and mother. I need not say how happy I will be when your Western Circuit finishes, and you come here to see the rising towers."

Lockhart's answer is to be read in the published "Letters" of Sir Walter (vol. ii. p. 86). Both he and Wilson promised to be good, but temptation more or less overcame their resolutions. It is only just to add that the writings which led to "the most unfortunate event in Lockhart's life" (as Scott called it), were all prior to this rebuke, and to these vows of amendment. I do not trace Lockhart's hand frequently in *Blackwood* at this time. The translations from the "Faust" of Goethe, in the June number for 1820, are practically attributed to him, in an Editorial note. They are said to be "not executed by Mr. Gillies, but by another friend, whose contributions in verse and prose, serious and comic, have already very frequently honoured our

[1] The reference here is obscure.

pages." Many of them display Lockhart's great metrical skill and poetic faculty, but they will be better dealt with in some comments on his verse in general. He also now and then wrote "Wastleiana," in which the remarks on Leigh Hunt might very well have been omitted. He reviewed, with high praise, Mr. Washington Irving's "Knickerbocker's History of New York," imploring him to try his hand at a novel. (July 1820.) He acknowledges "much merit in some of the stanzas of Mr. Keats's last volume" ("Lamia and Isabella"), but still detects the "Cockney" affectation, and is blind to the Miltonic grandeur of "Hyperion," if he read it. We may remember Shelley's own strange coldness to this wonderful volume, and his opinion that Keats was imitating a greater than he,—Leigh Hunt! Shelley wrote—"Keats's new volume has arrived to us, and the fragment called 'Hyperion' promises for him that he is destined to become one of the first writers of his age. His other things are imperfect enough, and, what is worse, written in a bad sort of style, which is becoming fashionable among those who think that they are imitating Hunt and Wordsworth. But of all these things, nothing is worse than ———, in spite of Hunt's extracting the only good stanzas, with his usual good nature."[1] What is ———? The Editor, in 1862, cast a veil over the name of the piece which, in Shelley's opinion, was the worst even

[1] "Correspondence of Leigh Hunt," i. 158.

of Keats's bad poems. Doubtless it was one of his best.

It is extraordinary to find the author of "Adonais" agreeing, in essentials, though not in tone, with a reviewer to whom Keats was a Cockney, a follower (as Shelley too held) of Leigh Hunt, though withal, says Lockhart, "a fine feeling lad." Shelley offers to teach Keats Greek; Lockhart asks why, in ignorance of Greek, he writes on the legends of Greece? Lockhart hopes that he will live to despise Leigh Hunt, and be a poet, "after the fashion of the elder men of England." Shelley thinks he promises, in "Hyperion," to be one of the first writers of the age.

As regards "Hyperion," Mr. Robert Bridges, in what is probably the best criticism of Keats ever written, points out that Keats meant to desert his Miltonic manner. "I have given up 'Hyperion,'—there are too many inversions in it,—Miltonic verse cannot be written but in an artful, or rather artist's mood. I wish to give myself up to other sensations."[1] It was not in the Miltonic direction, but in his "Ode to Autumn," and "On a Greek Urn," that Keats was to "find himself," and be, without knowing Greek, himself a Greek by "grace of congruity." Shelley's letter to Leigh Hunt, with Lockhart's *obiter dicta*, prove that poet and critic alike may fail fully to know contemporary genius when they meet it, and may, as in Shelley's prefer-

---

[1] Keats's Letters, p. 380, 1895.

ence of Leigh Hunt to Keats, prefer contemporary mediocrity.

At the close of 1820, a little incident occurred which illustrates an opinion already expressed, that the Blackwoodians would never have waged war on the Cockneys, or at least on some of that camp, if they had known their foemen personally. Haydon had been sneered at as a Cockney Raphael, and the interchanges of published sonnets, and comparisons with the world's greatest, among Leigh Hunt's set, had exasperated Northern critics, just as they soon began to irritate Keats. Now, in November 1820, Haydon, for divers good reasons, left town, and took his picture of "Christ entering Jerusalem" to Edinburgh. He went to see Sir William Allan. "As we were walking, we met Lockhart. I was pleased at meeting him, though he was rather nervous. He had assaulted me as one of the Cockney clique,[1] and he seemed surprised to find that I was human. In Lockhart's melancholy Spanish head, there was evidence of genius and mischief. I dined with him. His reception was open and frank. He treated me then, and ever since, as if I was a man he had unwittingly injured. The next man I dined with was Sir Walter Scott. . . . Allan was there, and Lockhart and Terry were also of the party, with Miss Scott, Mrs. Lockhart, and Lady Scott. . . . I had a letter to Wilson, and he also made up a large party, at which we had a splendid

---

[1] This Lockhart, in his letter to Haydon, denies.

set to. Wilson looked like a fine Sandwich Islander who had been educated in the Highlands. His light hair, deep sea-blue eye, tall athletic figure, and hearty hand-grip; his eagerness in debate, his violent passions, great genius, and irregular habits, rendered him a formidable partisan, a furious enemy, and an ardent friend. His hatred of Keats, which could not be concealed, marked him as the author of all these violent assaults on my poor friend in *Blackwood.*" [1]

"The *Blackwood* set (fine dogs!), not convinced yet of my not being a Cockney, determined to put me to that sure test, a gallop," out of which Haydon thought he came very well. "John Scott predicted I should return victorious and triumphant, and so I did. . . . I felt as if for a fortnight I had been sailing with a party of fine fellows up a placid and beautiful river." Haydon's picture was lauded, and he was be-sonneted in *Blackwood!*

The tomahawk was buried. "Lockhart's whole life has since been a struggle to undo the evil he was at the time a party to. Hence his visits to me in prison, his praise in the *Quarterly*, and his opinions expressed so often, on what he thinks my deserts. This shows a good heart, and a fine heart Lockhart has; but he is fond of fun and mischief,

---

[1] This, of course, is only Haydon's inference. I do not know who wrote the *Blackwood* review of "The Poems" of 1817, and of "Endymion."

and does not think of the wreck he has made till he has seen the fragments."

Nobody but Haydon wrecked Haydon, and Lockhart, a few years later, was at the head of a subscription for this unfortunate man of genius.

For several months I find nothing of Lockhart's, unless it be reviews of no importance, and versions of Spanish Ballads, in *Blackwood*, till February 1821. But, on December 28, 1820, Christie writes that he has read an article in *Baldwin's Magazine* which "excites his spleen." "I cannot conceive what [*word illegible*] possessed John Scott to meddle with you, for, judging by that article, he is but a very ordinary man. I think you must do something more with him than kill the zinc-eating spider."[1] The letter also alludes to the generally censured faults of *Blackwood*, which provoke imputations even on its harmless portions. Christie much disliked the magazine, and Lockhart's connection with it.

Lockhart answers early in January, but without date : he writes :—

[Postmark, *January* 6.]

" I was in the country when the first of Master Baldwin's philippics was published, and, being entirely occupied with running down hares, and sticking salmon, did not hear of it for many weeks. The second distressed me very much, not on account of myself, but of Scott, of whose hitherto

---

[1] Allusion unintelligible : ink may be referred to.

unprofaned name such base use was made in it—
although, if any insult could move a man's rage,
without doubt the allusions to my marriage, wife,
&c., were well entitled to do so.   Now, however—I
mean in the January number, which has been sent
me this morning—I find myself charged with distinctness in a sort which neither present engagements, or
any thought for the future, can induce me, or could
induce any man, to overlook.   And it is in regard
to this that I am now to solicit the aid of your well-
tried friendship. . . ."

It is now necessary to say what the charges
made against Lockhart in *Baldwin's Magazine* were.
As to the motive for their appearance at this
particular moment, I know nothing.[1]   *Maga* had
spoken of *Baldwin's Magazine* as of a rival who
urged her to her best exertions.   There had been
a little word of banter on a dull number, about
the Editor being asleep, and "Tims" driving.
Now Tims was a nickname for Mr. Patmore, who
himself had contributed to *Blackwood* an impartial
account of his friend Hazlitt's lectures.   He had
also reviewed Sheridan Knowles's "Virginius."
Probably on account of the attacks on Hazlitt,
he, at some time, withdrew, and the real wonder
is how a young Londoner ever found himself in
that *galère*.   As "Tims," an ideal but harmless

---

[1] In a much later *Blackwood*, it was asserted that a London contributor, in collusion with Mr. John Scott, deliberately tried to provoke
a quarrel.

Cockney, he is often chaffed in the " Noctes Ambrosianæ," and elsewhere. All this was in sufficiently
bad taste, but Wilson, in a burlesque called " The
Kirk of Shotts," had taken graver liberties with
his friend, the Rev. Robert Morehead, who expos-
tulated with dignity and success. Thus for Mr.
John Scott's series of assaults on *Blackwood*, no
motive but general resentment of that periodical's
violences can now, perhaps, be assigned. Nothing
in particular was stirring, except that Maginn had
fallen foul of Professor Leslie's Hebrew orthodoxy,
and literary honesty, *à propos* of a Latin version
of "Chevy Chase." On this matter a lawsuit was
pending, and Professor Leslie later received
damages to the extent of £100.[1]

This being so, in May 1820, Mr. John Scott,
in his magazine, attacked Zeta, who had for some
time been silent, and who could not, in any case,
as Zeta, reply. Something, also, was said of the
treatment of the Ettrick Shepherd, which the good
Shepherd was able to resent for himself. In
November, Mr. Scott brought a charge of "a
regular plan of fraud," and "violation of the rules
of honourable intercourse in society."

---

[1] On the question of Leslie's Hebrew I have consulted the Rev.
Dr. Birrell, Professor of Hebrew in the University of St. Andrews.
He has kindly examined the matter, and informs me that both Maginn
and Leslie were right, there being two modes of indicating the
higher numerals in Hebrew. But Leslie's argument rather involved
his belief that this was *not* so, owing to "the poverty of the Hebrew
language." There were other charges of scientific unfairness.

The fraud, in brief, was the invention of pseudony-
mous characters, Wastle, Peter Morris, Dr. Olinthus
Petre (Maginn), and others. Though Mr. Scott
had much right on his side, in general, yet the
disguises of Peter and Wastle were sufficiently
transparent, and many of Dr. Morris's acts of peni-
tence were probably sincere. That Lockhart, in his
mystification, intended to deceive—that in Wastle
he did not draw a physiognomy familiar to all
Edinburgh, and to be found on no shoulders but
his own—does seem clear enough. But Mr. Scott
argued that only the few could lift the mask, that
only to the few was the mystification a joke, while
it was deliberately intended, with all the other
mystifications, to pass for truth with the multitude.
This deep-laid scheme is the *gravamen* of his
accusation, honestly made, no doubt, but no less,
I think, erroneous. Sir Walter was then brought
in as countenancing *Blackwood*. We have already
seen his letter on that subject. " It surely is
—we are sure it *ought* to be—a severe mortifica-
tion to the author of ' Paul's Letters to his Kinsfolk,' that the book has formed the archetype or
exemplar to 'Peter's Letters,' a publication sinning, both in its design and execution, against the
rules of decency and principles of honour." Peter
"gratifies the paltry and nefarious curiosity which
hovers round the enclosure of private life."

We have already seen, and for many years all
the world has known, what Sir Walter thought

about "Peter's Letters." He did not, like Mr. John Scott, think it "a most notorious and profligate example of felon conspiracy against the dignity of literature."

Sir Walter is next severely blamed for aiding Wilson in the matter of the Chair of Moral Philosophy. This one circumstance stamps him as "the zealous espouser of Blackwood's cause." He is probably a contributor. "Sir Walter has himself been lately in London, and we now find a series of papers in *Blackwood*, in which certain London parties and prayer-meetings, with the names of individuals, are exposed very much in the culpable manner of Peter Morris, but with a more delicate hand." "Surely" Sir Walter cannot have written these sketches? "We forbear to say more on this subject, because we feel that we have great power in our hands."

Much is made of Blackwood's compounding with Graham Dalyell, and with Hazlitt, who himself had published what Dr. Smiles calls "a cruel and libellous pamphlet" against Gifford (1819), and, according to Southey, "would not run the risk of having *me* subpœnaed upon a trial."[1] Hazlitt had been personally attacked; old stories about him had been raked up, and Blackwood had compromised the quarrel privately.

In December and in January appeared, in *Baldwin's Magazine*, the articles on which we left

---

[1] "Memoirs of John Murray," i. 263, 493.

Lockhart writing to Christie. The former essay, after repeating, in essence, much of what had already been said, brought in the story about the Black Bull Inn (which Lockhart had incautiously described as noisy and uncomfortable). He is now denounced as Editor of *Blackwood*, as a forger of Testimonials to his journal, and as, above all, the author of "a most virulent and offensive libel against Mr. Coleridge" (October 1817), which, as we have seen, he did not write.[1] A letter from Coleridge to Peter Morris is also said to have been printed without Coleridge's consent. Peter is called an "assassin" for his "Letters." In January the affair of Professor Leslie is introduced. Maginn's signature, "Dr. Olinthus Petre," is called a deliberate attempt to deceive. The notable discovery, that Trinity College possesses no Olinthus Petre, D.D., is proclaimed. Mr. John Scott hears that "Mr. John Gibson Lockhart has given it under his hand that he is *not* the Editor of *Blackwood*," but, under the assumed name of "Christopher North," he is well known to be so. He is covering "an organised plan of fraud, calumny, and cupidity." Allusions to Abbotsford, and its unworthy guest and dubious lord, were scattered about here and there.

This brief summary contains, I think, the gist of the essays in *Baldwin's Magazine*, for May, November, and December 1820, and January 1821. It is apparent that Mr. John Scott thought his

---

[1] Lockhart's innocence of this article is absolutely certain.

information was more accurate than it proved to be, and believed that he had hit on a popular vein of writing. His intelligence was, in many points, incorrect. Lockhart was not "Christopher North," nor was he Editor of *Blackwood*, nor author of the article on Coleridge of three years before. The "Testimonials," which he is accused of "forging," were apparently some parodies, in prose and verse, on Byron, Wordsworth, and the Odontist, composing a "Luctus," or wail for an Irish prize-fighter.[1] If so, they could not have deceived, or been intended to deceive, any mortal. Sir Walter's contributions on London prayer-meetings and breakfast parties I have been unable to discover! The general charge of a "felonious conspiracy" may be left to readers of "Peter's Letters." Mr. Scott was of Scotch extraction, a schoolfellow of Byron's at Aberdeen, and later (according to Moore), a furious assailant of Byron. Reprehensible as mystifications are, the age was rich in them, and Mr. Scott need not have taken such very high ground about "Peter's Letters." But he was Scotch, and a professed moralist. He named Lockhart, and he accused him of falsehood in setting his hand to a formal statement that he was not Editor of *Blackwood*.

We now understand the burden of the accusations, on which, early in January, Lockhart was replying to Christie. He says that Christie has already heard from him about the dual control of

[1] *Blackwood*, May 1820.

the magazine, for a brief time, when Murray and Blackwood were partners in it. We have touched on this, on the repayment of Murray's money, and on Wilson's formal denial that he "had ever received one shilling except for my own compositions." Lockhart then tells Christie, what we have previously stated, that the contemplated arrangement had in short space been rescinded, and that Mr. Blackwood "had *always* been chiefly, and since then he has been, so far as I know solely, the manager of his book, and as for myself, you would be surprised if I could show you how few pages have in so many months been supplied from my pen.

" In this state of things Mr. Leslie brings an action against Mr. Blackwood for certain articles, of the author of which I do not even at this moment know or suspect the name, and which I had never seen except in the magazine. . . . Mr. Leslie, however, claps my name into the summons as author or editor of these articles, and in particular of an article signed Olinthus Petre. It is not agreeable for an advocate to be a party in any case of this sort, so I desired my agent to tell me his opinion. It was (and I acted upon it) that he himself ought to write to Mr. Leslie's agent, stating how the thing stood, and threatening, unless my name was withdrawn, to bring a counter action. The name was withdrawn accordingly, and here is the story which has brought me the honour of being called by a name not to be repeated, by this Mr. John Scott, or whoever Mr. Baldwin's rascal may be.

" I have written the above for your satisfaction, not for his. What I expect of you is that you will, without delay, talk over the whole affair with Traill, and one or both of you go to this Mr. Scott (or whoever the editor may be) if not, to the publisher, and ask for the author.

" If he is not forthcoming, or if Scott himself be the author, you will dictate according to your own discretion, which I can trust better than my own, an apology to be inserted in the front page of his next magazine, and wherever else I please. If there is any difficulty about this, it remains only that you fix a day for the man to meet me at York, or any other place half way between Edinburgh and London.—Ever affectionately yours,

" J. G. LOCKHART."

In a postscript he repeats that he did not attack Coleridge, and is only said to have done so, because he is known to have written eulogies on him. As to Hogg, "his chief pride, and the very breath of his nostrils, are such jokes as this knave makes such a pother about." He adds that he would probably have written thus a month ago, "but to tell you the truth, my wife was then exceedingly ill from a series of cramp attacks, from which she is slowly recovering, and I had enough to think of at home, besides not being very able even to think of leaving it. . . ."[1]

As to the perplexing events which followed, after Christie received Lockhart's letter, we have three sources of evidence. We have printed statements by Mr. Scott and by Lockhart, which were written and circulated at the time of the events. And we also possess the narrative of Mr. Horatio Smith (of the "Rejected Addresses"), who was one of two seconds engaged by Mr. Scott. Usually called "Horace," he is always "Horatio" in the printed statements. Mr. Smith's narrative was published in 1847, in the *New Monthly Magazine* (No. 81). Thus it appeared twenty-six years after the occurrences, and, of course, it may be contaminated by illusions of memory. On the other hand, nobody is likely to let his memory beguile him into the belief that he and his friend cut a very poor figure, if they did not really do so. Again, Mr. Smith's narrative colligates the facts, and explains much that is unintelligible in the statement of Mr. Scott —much that, at the time, bewildered Lockhart and Christie. Now it can scarcely be by mere accident that illusions of memory, on Mr. Smith's part (if these be alleged), thus fill up and elucidate the whole confused story. I am therefore obliged to give some credence to Mr. Smith, though his tale throws a rather ludicrous light on his own conduct and on that of Mr. Scott.

[1] Mrs. Lockhart was within a few weeks of her confinement.

That gentleman's printed statement about what occurred after Christie received Lockhart's letter bears no date. It sets forth how Lockhart's friend (Christie) waited on Mr. Scott on January 10, to ask whether he avowed himself responsible for the articles in *Baldwin's Magazine?* Mr. Scott said that he would answer in a couple of hours, and his written reply, after that interval, was, that "if Mr. Lockhart's motives in putting the inquiry should turn out to be such as gentlemen usually respect, there would be no difficulty experienced about giving it an explicit answer." Of course this seemed to promise "the usual satisfaction."

Mr. Scott's statement avers that on receiving this note Christie again visited him, assuring him that Lockhart had no *legal* proceedings in view. He wanted an apology, or satisfaction. Mr. Scott asked if he was in London, and whether he would distinctly declare the nature of his connection with *Blackwood.* Christie answered that Lockhart was in Edinburgh, and had instructed him, "that no preliminary explanation whatever was to be expected from him." Mr. Scott said he must have a preliminary explanation, before he could consider Lockhart's "motives to be worthy of respect." He promised a definite reply in the evening. In the evening he wrote a note, grumbling at Lockhart's absence, and asking for "an open reference to the ground of complaint."

This is Mr. Scott's account of what occurred on

January 10. He is hesitating, it will be observed, about owning his responsibility for his articles, unless Lockhart will oblige him by a preliminary explanation. Lockhart's printed statement of what occurred on January 10, gives his reason for making no such explanation, and asserts that the reason was placed before Mr. Scott. In the second conversation of the day, between Mr. Scott and Christie, the latter, says Lockhart, "told Mr. Scott that the author of the offensive articles in the *London Magazine* had made a great number of *false assertions*, that he (the author) must therefore be conscious of having trusted either to invention, or to worthless information,—and that, to a person who had acted so, Mr. Lockhart would not condescend to offer any preliminary information whatever."

It will be observed that Mr. Scott's statement omits all this essential passage, though he does mention a general denial of some of his charges, by Christie. The writer in the *London Magazine* had made false assertions and wide inferences, and for that reason Lockhart, demanding an apology or satisfaction, would not oblige him by any explanation. Inferring from Mr. Scott's second note of January 10, that, if he would not avow or disavow the articles in the *London Magazine*, he would fight, Lockhart came instantly to London. He sent to Mr. Scott, by Christie, a letter, in which he said that Mr. Scott's "refusal to give an answer till you should be assured of my being in London admits of one explanation only, and no more," namely, that Mr. Scott would go "on the sod."

Mr. Scott, to return to *his* statement, says that he now avowed his responsibility for the offensive articles, but added that, unless Lockhart would make the demanded explanation, "he could not accept his tardy personal appeal, as entitling him to a privilege, which belongs, of right, only to the gentlemen "—who deserve it.

Lockhart merely says, on this point, that Mr. Scott, "in a shuffling conversation," tried to evade the engagement to fight. Mr. Scott himself says that he refused to "name a friend," unless Lockhart made the explanation desired.

The reader will remark that Mr. Scott's first refusal was to avow responsibility before Lockhart came to town, and informed him as to the exact proportion of truth and falsehood in his articles. He now shifts his refusal, but keeps the same pretext for it; he proclaims his responsibility for the articles, but declines to fight, without an explanation from Lockhart. And this refusal to fight without an explanation he declares that he first made, in a conversation with Christie, on January 18.

But, in "the evening of January 18" (really, perhaps, in the morning of January 19), Mr. Scott committed to writing, and presently printed his memories of what he had said to Christie. He had insisted on an explanation from Lockhart "before it could be conceded that Mr. Lockhart's motives in applying to Mr. Scott were of a nature such as gentlemen usually respect,"—a quotation from his own first note of January 10. Lockhart comments thus—" Mark the shuffle as to this phrase. Compare its meaning as used here with its plain and obvious sense when used in Mr. Scott's first note," where it seems to mean that Scott would answer "yes or no," if a duel, and not legal proceedings, were in contemplation.

Mr. Scott's paper of the evening of January 18, or the morning of January 19, ends by saying that, if Lockhart will "disavow having ever been concerned in any way in the system of imposition and scandal" of *Blackwood*, then Mr. Christie is referred to Mr. Horatio Smith, as Mr. Scott's friend,— empowered by Mr. Scott to arrange what may be proper under such circumstances.

And now we come to the astonishing narrative of Mr. Horatio Smith, which (as touching these points), I give in full. Readers may estimate his evidence variously ; it cannot, I fear, be reconciled with his conduct in 1821.

"At a late hour of the night, my friend Scott, after surprising me by a visit at my then residence in the neighbourhood of London, startled me infinitely more by its object, when he inquired whether I would become his second should he be implicated in a duel, arising from his articles impugning the conduct and character of *Blackwood's Magazine ?* I told him that I was one of the very last persons

to whom he should have preferred such a request :
first, because I despised the practice of duelling for
its gross folly, while I abhorred it for its wicked-
ness ; secondly, because I was utterly ignorant of
all the forms, punctilios, and practical details necessary for the proper conduct of such affairs. That
rival editors, instead of confining themselves to their
appropriate battlefield, their respective magazines,
should 'change their pens for pistols, ink for blood,'
appeared to me, as I frankly confessed, a species of
Quixotism totally inconsistent with their calling ;
and I reminded my visitant of the general ridicule
lavished upon Moore and Jeffrey, when they fought
a duel in consequence of an obnoxious article in the
Edinburgh Review. 'Your charges,' I continued,
'are either false or true. If the former, you must
instantly give the satisfaction required by publicly
retracting all that you have erroneously asserted,
and by making a full, frank, unequivocal apology.
If the latter, I ask you whether, as a rational being,
you are warranted in incurring the chance of being
murdered, or of murdering a fellow-creature, both
of you husbands and fathers' (Lockhart was not
yet a father), 'because you have spoken the truth,
such being at all times your duty, and a duty, moreover, which you have exercised upon the present
occasion from a conscientious conviction, that by
so doing you were consulting the best interests of
society, and endeavouring to purify our literature
from a contaminating abuse.'

" ' You appeal to me as a rational being,' was the reply, ' but in affairs of honour, am I not, in that capacity, placed out of court ? '

" ' Perhaps so, nay, certainly so, in *my* opinion ; but if your charges be true, as you doubtless believe, or you would never have advanced them, is not your opponent placed out of court, and deprived of his right of challenge ? '

" *Scott promised to weigh this question in his mind*, as well as all my other objections to his going out ; and, after a long conversation, we parted, though not until I had repeatedly and distinctly expressed my opinions just recorded, and had as often apprised him that *I would not be a party*, under any circumstances, to a hostile meeting, though I would eagerly render him my best services as a mediator with a view to an amicable adjustment of the affair. Eventually the challenge was declined, upon grounds fully set forth by Scott, in a statement which, from various notices of it, seemed to receive the sanction of public approbation."

Public approbation might have been withheld, if the world had known what Mr. Smith tells us. For Mr. Smith here avers that Mr. Scott sought him as a second, that he, himself, declined to have anything to do with a fight, that he declared his total ignorance of the laws of the duel. But, knowing all this, Mr. Scott, in a published statement, exhibited Mr. Smith to Lockhart and Christie, and to the world, as his second, or *témoin* in the arbitrament of battle! Mr. Scott, in fact, told Christie and everybody else that Mr. Horatio Smith (if Lockhart made his explanation) would act as a second, he well knowing that Smith would do nothing of the kind. He might as well have sent Christie to the Archbishop of Canterbury, or, as Lockhart said, to Aldgate Pump!

Once more, by Horatio Smith's account, the pretext for refusing to fight was not Mr. Scott's idea, but his own! The second supplies the principal with an excuse for not coming on to the ground, the principal adopts it, puts it forth under his own hand, and provides himself with a second who will not look at a pistol.

Even to the license of comic fiction could hardly be permitted such reckless burlesque. Mr. Horatio Smith's narrative explains what Lockhart calls the "shuffle" as to the phrase, "of such a nature as gentlemen usually respect." A new interpretation was now to be put on the words in harmony with the ideas of a pacific second. Nor is it possible to argue that Mr. Scott wrote the paper of " Thursday evening, January 18," before arousing Mr. Horatio Smith and hearkening to his counsel, because he could not have named Mr. Smith as his second (as he does in that epistle), without obtaining his permission, such as it was.

What follows is stranger still. Christie calls on Mr. Smith, and Mr. Smith, in a letter published by Mr. Scott, informs his principal that " I repeatedly told Mr. Christie that, if Mr. Lockhart could make the avowal required, I was authorised by you *to offer him satisfaction.*" Now Mr. Horatio Smith is in an awkward predicament, for, in 1847, he tells us that he invented a reason for not fighting, and warned Mr. Scott that, "I would not be a party, under any circumstances, to a hostile meeting." In 1821, he says the very reverse, he says that he is "authorised to offer satisfaction." It is unpleasant, and unnecessary, to draw the obvious inferences from all this. The Mr. Smith of 1821 was inducing the public to believe that "satisfaction" would be given, if a condition were fulfilled which he knew would not be fulfilled. The Mr. Smith of 1847 tells us that he never would have been a party to any such transaction, in any circumstances, and that Mr. Scott knew it.

Ignorant of all that (according to Mr. Smith) had passed between him and Mr. Scott, Christie called on the latter gentleman, "admitting that it was irregular," for no explanation would be given. And so the debate went on, Lockhart offering "any explanation upon any subject in which Mr. Scott's personal feelings and honour can be concerned." Mr. Scott now demanded that Lockhart should "declare . . . that he has never derived *money* from any connection, direct or indirect, with the *management of Blackwood,* and that he has never stood in any situation giving him, directly or indirectly, *pecuniary* interest in its sale." This note was written late on Saturday night, Mr. Smith was out of the way, and Mr. Patmore ("Tims") became a kind of substituted second, in Mr. Smith's absence.

To Mr. Scott's demand, in this new form, Lockhart's friend again answered by a *Non possumus*. Mr. Scott replied that the affair, as far as he was concerned, was terminated. Part of a letter of Lockhart's was read aloud by Christie, but Mr. Scott declined to hear more than a few words, deeming it "irrelevant to the point." Mr. Lockhart then "posted" Mr. Scott, and enclosed to him the communication, which was of the usual tenor in such cases. "Mr. Lockhart thought it necessary to inform Mr. Scott that he considered him as a liar and a scoundrel." He added that he was leaving London, after interval enough to give Mr. Scott time to change his mind about fighting. Mr. Scott promptly answered that he considered the note "as coming from the Editor of *Blackwood's Magazine*." Lockhart then hastily printed his whole statement, closing with this last note of Mr. Scott's, and adding a denial that he was the Editor of *Blackwood*. The whole paper ended thus: "*N.B.*—The first copy of this statement was sent to Mr. Scott, with a notification that Mr. Lockhart intended leaving London within twenty-four hours after the time of his receiving it." He set forth for Edinburgh on the evening of Sunday.

Now occurred, on Lockhart's part, an unfortunate mistake, such as, in ordinary writing for the press, is very frequent. A man makes an alteration in his manuscript without observing its effect on the general tenor of his argument—whatever it may be,—so that some other passage, which requires a corresponding correction, remains as it originally stood, and is obviously erroneous. An oversight of this kind happened.

On *Sunday* Lockhart and Christie visited Dr. Stoddart, Editor of the *New Times*, and showed him the document for publication in his paper. To make the narrative more intelligible, Dr. Stoddart (who was previously unacquainted with Lockhart), suggested (apart from any opinion as to the merits of the quarrel) that Lockhart should add an explicit denial, *for the public*, that he "derived, or ever did derive, any emolument from the management" of *Blackwood*. Lockhart wrote this, Christie acquiescing, and it was inserted at the head of the statement, and published after Lockhart's return to Scotland.

Nobody observed, at the moment, that the new paragraph would necessarily be taken as covered by the last sentence in the statement—"The first copy of this statement was sent to Mr. Scott, with a notification that Mr. Lockhart intended leaving London within twenty-four hours of the time of his receiving it." Thus Mr. Scott would seem, to readers, to have received an explanation in full, which he did *not* receive, at the time specified.

The new sentence, added by Dr. Stoddart's advice, demanded, in fact, a correction in the old matter which, by a not unusual inadvertence, it did not receive. This inadvertence escaped Lockhart's notice, but flashed on him after he had arrived in Scotland.

On receiving Lockhart's printed statement, as sent to him with the disavowal of editorship, but *before* he saw the statement as generally circulated with the addendum suggested by Stoddart, Mr. Scott printed his second statement. He rebutted all insinuations about shrinking from a meeting ; he had even modified his original demand for an explanation, and reduced it to a request for a disavowal of paid management or participation in profits. He repeated his charge of a mendacious denial of the editorship, in Professor Leslie's case. He made insinuations about Lockhart's " connections," namely, Sir Walter Scott. He had demanded an explanation, in order that his adversary might not clear his character by a duel. He asserted his own courage, and relied on the agreement of Mr. Smith and Mr. Patmore in his view of the case. Naturally enough, he does not contradict, nor in any way allude to, Lockhart's account of the reasons alleged by Christie for refusing to make any kind of preliminary explanation. He declares that the explanation was withheld on a " point of mere *punctilio*," without saying what that point was. Of course the wonderful pacific secondship of Mr. Smith is not described. This document is dated, Wednesday, January 31, but was published in one sheet, with and *after* another document dated February 2. In this document he takes every advantage of the error made by affixing to the published and circulated form of Lockhart's statement, the explicit disavowal of "emolument" which was not included in the first copy sent to him. No guess that this was the result of an inadvertence presented itself to Mr. Scott. He therefore argues that Lockhart is assuring the public that he sent to him the demanded disavowal which he never did send.

Of course such a manœuvre would have been the act of a criminal idiot, "a direct lie," which could attain no end but instant and disgraceful exposure. If one man could be so wicked and foolish as to practise such a helpless *ruse*, it was not likely that any other would second him in such imbecile baseness. On February 5, Christie wrote to Lockhart on the subject (Postmark, February 8). He had only that morning "with some difficulty obtained a copy of a second statement by Mr. John. In this he makes the use I expected he would make of the omission of the explicit disavowal in the copy sent to him of your statement. He goes so far as to say that the disavowal would, as a matter of course, have taken him into the field with you. On this I have taken a step of which, no doubt, you will approve. I have despatched a letter to Mr. Smith, of which the following is a copy :—

"Sir,—I have this moment seen a copy of Mr. Scott's second statement. It does not appear to me to be necessary, on the present occasion, to explain the reasons which induced Mr. Lockhart to insert the more explicit disavowal contained in the introductory paragraph of his statement, after having sent a copy to Mr. Scott of the statement as he at first intended that it should appear.

"If Mr. Scott means it to be understood that if that disavowal had been contained in the copy sent to him by Mr. Lockhart, it would have made any difference in his (Mr. Scott's) conduct, then there is no reason why the disavowal should not now have the same effect. In order to obviate all apprehensions of disappointment I pledge my word of honour that (however little Mr. Lockhart may be called upon to make such a concession), if Mr. Scott will take the same journey to find Mr. Lockhart that Mr. Lockhart took to find Mr. Scott, Mr. Lockhart will give him a meeting instantly. . . ."

Of course Christie did not know Mr. Smith's peaceful disposition. No doubt Mr. Smith never sent Christie's letter to his principal.

On February 9, Lockhart replied from Edinburgh: "I consider the step mentioned in your letter as by far the best that could have been taken, and have to thank you for the true kindness that dictated it. . . . The mistake thus seized on was a most unfortunate one, but its consequences never occurred to me till after I had come to Edinburgh. . . . Jeffrey, &c. &c., have all along espoused my cause."

On February 13, when Christie again wrote to Lockhart, no notice had been taken of his letter of February 5 to Mr. Smith. On February 8, Christie published a "further statement." It contained Dr. Stoddart's signed account of how he recommended the addition of the explicit disavowal, advice given "solely with the view of rendering Mr. Lockhart's narrative more clear and intelligible to the public;" all this without any expression of opinion as to the merits, in any respect, of the case. Christie added that the disavowal "was not made with a view to remove Mr. Scott's scruples," for it did not, in fact, cover the ground included in Mr. Scott's demand. Had Lockhart been sole proprietor of *Blackwood* he might still have made the disavowal, as it stood. Now Mr. Scott had told Mr. Christie that he would take none but a disavowal, *verbatim*, in the terms of his own letter.

Mr. Christie ended thus—"If after this statement Mr. Scott can find any persons who believe that there was anything more atrocious than an oversight in the circumstance of the two statements, Mr. Scott is perfectly welcome to the whole weight of their good opinion."

On Saturday, February 20, 1821 (Postmark), Lockhart received a letter from Christie, which, his friend says, "will surprise and distress you. I have been forced to give Scott a meeting, and he now lies (if I had written an hour ago I should have said mortally, and I must still say most dangerously) wounded. This has been the most heartrending transaction that has happened in my life: a few hours ago I would most willingly have changed places with the man I believed to lie mortally wounded.

"The circumstances were simply these. I sent a copy of your second statement and of that which I wrote, to Mr. P. (Patmore) on Saturday night. Yesterday he called upon me from Mr. Scott, with a letter demanding an explanation of the last sentence in the narrative which was signed by me, such explanation to express that I meant nothing disrespectful to Mr. Scott; this to be made public. This appeared to me to be such a complete trick to obtain something like *éclat* at the conclusion of his affair with you, that I instantly refused to do anything of the sort. Mr. Patmore then produced a challenge from Mr. Scott, which he was to deliver to me in case of a refusal. I entered a protest, in the first instance, that I could only meet Mr. Scott on the ground that I would meet any man who thought himself aggrieved by me, and to whom I refused other satisfaction, and then consented to meet him.

"We met last night, at nine o'clock, at Chalk Farm. I arranged with my second (Traill) that I would not

fire at Scott except in self-defence.   Accordingly,
I fired my first shot in the air.   Before we fired
again, Traill protested that, as Mr. Scott had taken
the usual aim at me, I should not forego that advantage again.[1]   I felt bound to follow his advice for
self-preservation, and my second shot took effect. . . .
The surgeon left him on some pretext, and did not
return, I presume thinking his case desperate.   I
cannot and shall not attempt to describe the horror
I felt.   I instantly ran to the Chalk Farm Inn, and
procured a shutter to carry him upon.   We carried
him there, and put him to bed, and then I made
my escape,—as I did afterwards (*sic*), but not till
his family had arrived."

Christie then gives the latest, and less distressing
news of the wounded man, and ends—"Pity me, I
am most wretched, though I stand acquitted in my
own mind of doing more than what, under the circumstances, was inevitable. . . ."

Christie's account of this melancholy affair is
corroborated by the statement made by Mr. Scott
to his surgeon.   "After the pistols were reloaded,
and everything was ready for a second fire, Mr.
Traill called out, 'Now, Mr. Christie, take your

[1] Mr. Traill's "exact words" were—"Gentlemen, before this proceeds, I must insist on one thing.   You, Mr. Christie, must give
yourself the usual chances, and not again fire in the air, or fire away
from Mr. Scott."—Letter from Christie (who was with Traill at
Boulogne) to Lockhart, March 3, 1821.   Mr. Christie, as will later
be seen, thinks that Mr. Scott's parallel account was not *verbally*
accurate.

aim and do not throw away your advantage, as you
did last time.' I " (Mr. Scott) "called out, 'What,
did not Mr. Christie fire at me?' I was answered
by Mr. Patmore, 'You must not speak, you have
nothing for it now but firing.'" [1]

To this distressing letter announcing the duel,
Lockhart answered :—

"MY DEAREST FRIEND,—You bid me pity you.
Pity me much more, who have to sustain the
thought of having brought you, your dear wife and
family, into such a situation as this. God grant
that this man may live!

"All the world must agree that you acted nobly,
yet all will think that you did much more than was
right. . . .

"I say nothing as to my feelings in thinking what
might have been. That thought indeed deprives

[1] Scott's "Letters," ii. 113. The account in *John Bull*, February
16, 1821, says that the suggestion of a nocturnal meeting came from
Mr. Scott. Horatio Smith confirms this, in an unquoted part of his
narrative already cited. At the inquest a carpenter gave evidence
that Mr. Scott shook hands with Mr. Christie, as he lay on the
shutter which Christie had brought. Dr. Darling, who attended Mr.
Scott, said that, according to his account, Mr. Christie, before the
first fire, called out, "Mr. Scott, you must not stand there. I see
your head above the horizon, you give me an advantage." Mr. Scott
described Mr. Christie as "very kind to him after he was wounded."
At the inquest, Mr. Pettigrew, the surgeon on the field, said that Mr.
Patmore, some days after the event, remarked, "Mr. Christie's friend
was bound, after the fire, to have communicated to him the conduct
pursued by Mr. Christie (firing in the air), of which he, Mr. Patmore,
was entirely ignorant," though Mr. Scott heard Traill's remark, and
asked a question on it.

me of all composure.   Thank God, I am not made
utterly wretched for ever."

Into the distressed house in Edinburgh, John
Hugh Lockhart, as "Hugh Littlejohn" familiar to
all the world, was born on February 14th, two days
before the fatal duel.

We have now seen the full circumstances of
a terrible event.   Throughout, want of experience
and method were observable.   There should be no
discussions, above all, no unwitnessed discussions,
between a principal and a hostile second.   There
should be no pacific seconds, who disapprove of
duels, know not the rules thereof, privately vow
they will never countenance a fight, and yet publicly
announce their readiness to go on the ground.   On
the broad merits of the question, we have Sir
Walter's remark, "The Duke of Wellington, whom
I take to be the highest military authority in the
world, pronounces you can have nothing more to
say to Scott."[1]   ("Letters," ii. 111.)   Christie's conduct was marked by every good quality.   The
quarrel so unhappily fixed on him was, as Sir
Walter says, "a sleeveless quarrel."[2]   He literally
could not withdraw or qualify, under challenge,

---

[1] Scott, in an unpublished letter, says that Lady Holland, no friend
of Lockhart's, maintained that he had done his best to make Mr.
Scott fight.

[2] See also Sir Walter's letters on the subject to Laidlaw, in Dr.
Carruthers's "Abbotsford Notanda."

an observation which was innocent in itself. By firing in the air he testified to his want of malice : he had now done all that man could do, and had left Mr. Scott's character for personal courage stainless, at the expense of risking his own life. We may attribute to inexperience, and perhaps to the darkness, Mr. Patmore's demand for a second fire, a thing, I understand, almost unheard of where one principal has fired in the air. The unhappy English addiction to the blundering pistol, in place of the sword, has always had much to answer for. Why Mr. Scott pressed his quarrel on Mr. Christie is not very clear.[1]

As to any impugnment on Lockhart's personal courage in this affair, it is enough to point to Sir Walter's letters on the subject. He, who refused to attend the funeral of a brother held guilty of cowardice, would have known how to feel and to display an implacable resentment and indignation,

---

[1] Mr. Cyrus Redding, in his "Fifty Years' Recollections," 1858, vol. ii. 225, quotes Mr. Horace (or Horatio) Smith's "A Greybeard's Gossip." "He spoke of his disapproval of Mr. Scott's conduct. . . . Scott, however, seemed determined to show that he was a man of courage, which no one doubted." Mr. Redding then tells a tale, "not evidential," of how Campbell the poet informed him that Hazlitt had been "a means of irritating John Scott to such a degree, that he was one cause of his going out in the duel in which he fell." But Horace Smith thought that Campbell was too prone to believe evil of Hazlitt, and the evidence, as offered, is worthless. Mr. Redding also says that Mr. Smith "prevented a meeting with Lockhart," that is, apparently, after Christie's letter, pledging his honour that Lockhart would meet Mr. Scott in Scotland, a letter to which Mr. Smith did not reply.

had he entertained a shadow of doubt as to the courage of a son-in-law.[1]   Twenty years after the death of the unhappy brother, Sir Walter told the story of his own wrath, and of his present contrition to Lockhart, and added that the character of Conachar, in "The Fair Maid of Perth," was intended as a kind of expiation.   By 1828 sorrow, trouble, and time had softened Sir Walter, and made him lenient to the fault or congenital misfortune which of old he had most contemned.   But in 1821, and for years after, his temper was what it had always been.[2]

The fatal consequences of Mr. Scott's wound were not long deferred.   He died on February 27.   Sir Walter Scott's letters, enforcing the lesson "not to dally with this mother of mischief any more," are already published.[3]   It cannot be said that Lockhart ceased altogether to write for *Blackwood*, though his time was now much more occupied with other work, "The Spanish Ballads," an edition of Motteux's "Don Quixote," and his four novels. I am not aware that he was ever again implicated in any of the *Blackwood* troubles, and the affair

---

[1] "Life," iii. 199.

[2] I think it necessary to insert this passage, because in so excellent a book as Mr. Colvin's "Life of Keats" (1887, pp. 124–125), we read about "John Scott, killed by a friend of Lockhart's in a duel, arising out of these very *Blackwood* brawls, in which it was thought that Lockhart himself ought to have come forward." This remark appears to be the result of imperfect traditional knowledge.

[3] "Letters," ii. 112–114.

with Leigh Hunt, in 1823, appears to have been Wilson's concern.[1]

On March 3, Christie wrote to Lockhart from Boulogne. The news of Mr. Scott's death had come upon him as a terrible surprise, for the bulletins had been so far from unfavourable as almost to relieve him of anxiety. His only consolation lay in the knowledge, "which, at this moment, nothing on this side heaven could induce me to forego," that he had not provoked the quarrel, "and that I forbore to put him in the slightest peril till I felt that my own life must be the price of further forbearance." He entreats Lockhart, with all the arguments at his command, not to consider himself responsible for what had occurred. He speaks with deep gratitude of Sir Walter's kindness, and says, "Your friend, Mr. Wilson, could not have done more than he has done, if I had been his brother twice over. His first step was to offer his house as an asylum to me, in such terms that I had no hesitation in agreeing to accept the offer." His friends, however, wished him to go abroad. "I have never yet met with a man who was so ready to make an unfortunate case, with which he need have given himself no trouble, entirely his own." Mr. Christie then repeats his consolations to Lockhart, inquires anxiously for Mrs. Lockhart, and mentions, as the thing "nearest to his own heart," Sir Walter's endeavours to be-friend the children of Mr. Scott. In a postscript

---

[1] "Christopher North," ii. 55.

he speaks of the coroner's inquest, and is glad to find that Mr. Scott's deposition, though it did not give Traill's "exact words," yet proved that Mr. Scott heard them, "though he was at a greater distance than his second."[1]

Meanwhile several of Lockhart's letters failed to reach Christie, so that they are not preserved. On March 19, Christie writes to Lockhart: he has heard of the verdict of the coroner's inquest, but is cheered by the evidence that Mr. Scott had not been left in ignorance of his firing in the air. "It was no fault of ours, if he did not take the course which one would think he ought to have taken." By his own statement Mr. Scott, being in his second's hands, acted on his second's advice. Christie (like Sir Walter in an unpublished letter) entreats Lockhart not to come to London for the trial. He reiterates his hope that Lockhart's distress will be assuaged by his assurances that Lockhart was not the cause of the quarrel. "I fought for no reason at all, except that I could not, without degrading myself, decline to comply with his demand. If his challenge had been in any way a natural consequence of anything that you had done, calculated to make him challenge me, or if I had fought for the sake of not compromising your honour, or not giving him an indirect advantage over you, then you might have had some uneasiness

---

[1] Mr. Traill's "exact words," as recollected by himself and Mr. Christie, have already been given, in the account of the affair: they are also cited in a letter to Lockhart from Mr. Traill.

in addition to what you would feel for what gave me uneasiness.   But in fact nothing of the sort was the case."   He then protests that even the kindnesses of Sir Walter distress him, because they seem to imply that Lockhart is a party concerned.

On April 14, 1821, Christie announces the acquittal of Traill and himself, and the close of an unhappy affair which clouded many lives.[1]

---

[1] Mr. Patmore did not then surrender himself, probably that his absence might weaken the evidence against the others.

CHAPTER X

CHIEFSWOOD, 1821-1824

Life at Chiefswood.—Border Scenes.—"Valerius."—Criticism of the book.—Its failure.—Letter to Christie.—Hogg, Rose, and wild-ducks.—Lockhart's love of children.—Hugh Littlejohn.—Boswell slain by Dunearn.—"Adam Blair."—Origin of the tale.—Criticism.—"Adam Blair" and "Faublas!"—George IV. in Edinburgh.—Scott's energy.—Crabbe.—Crabbe on Lockhart.—Lockhart on Crabbe.—Abbotsford.—Lockhart edits "Don Quixote."—Begins an edition of Shakespeare.—Melrose in July 1823.—"Leal Tories."—"Reginald Dalton."—Letters from Christie.—Christie on Hunt and Byron.—Report of Williams's death.—"Quentin Durward" unpopular.

THE uneventful life of a man of letters is seldom, happily, interrupted by striking personal incidents. Whether in Edinburgh or at Chiefswood, Lockhart's literary industry must now have been mainly given to reading for, and writing, his Roman novel, "Valerius." These were the days of *The Beacon*, a Tory Edinburgh paper of violent character and of huddled-up, discreditable end. Concerning this journal, I find a correspondent, Sir Alexander Boswell, informing Sir Walter that it was "too much of a gentleman's paper!" Lockhart has given his account of Sir Walter's conduct, in what Scott

himself calls "a blasted business ;" Lockhart,[1] for-
tunately, was not one of the "young hot-bloods"
concerned with the journal.

The death of John Ballantyne occurred in June,
and Lockhart has recorded how he himself attended
the funeral, and was told by Scott, "I feel as if
there would be less sunshine for me from this day
forth." There were summer visits to Chiefswood,
where "Sophia is getting stout and pretty, and is
one of the wisest and most important little mammas
that can be seen anywhere. Her bower is *bigged in
gude green wood*, and we went last Saturday in a
body to enjoy it, and to consult about furniture,"
Scott says to Miss Baillie.[2] Creepers from the
old cottage at Abbotsford, were planted by Scott's
own hands round the little porch at Chiefswood.
Lockhart has described, in a familiar passage, the
manner of life in that "bower," and Scott's occasional flight thither, on Sibyl Grey, with Mustard
and Spice, the dandies, and "his own joyous shout
of *reveille* under our windows." The cottage being
so small, they often dined in the open air, on the
lawn where the burn murmurs on its way from the
Rhymer's Glen to pay its tiny tribute to "the great
fisc and exchequer" of the Tweed. Among these
memories it is that Lockhart, for one moment half
forgetful of his cognisance, gives his heart its liberty,
and speaks of "the chief ornament and delight at all

---

[1] "Life," vi. 426, 430.
[2] June 11, 1821. "Life," vi. 337.

these simple meetings,—she to whose love I owed my own place in them—Scott's eldest daughter, the one of all his children who, in countenance, mind, and manners, most resembled himself, and who, indeed, was as like him in all things as a gentle innocent woman can ever be to a great man deeply tried and skilled in the perplexities of active life —she, too, is no more (1837). But enough—and more than I had intended."

"The Pirate" was being written, and Scott's dear friend, William Erskine, would read chapters of it aloud, under the great tree on the slope that climbs towards the Rhymer's Glen. Scott was even more than commonly busy; editing a quaint old angling book by one who thought poorly of our father Izaak as a sportsman,—and amusing himself with the "Private Letters" of the reign of James VI., afterwards abandoned for "Nigel." As for Lockhart's lighter labours, since the names of Wastle and Peter Morris were now abandoned, I renounce the ungrateful and practically impossible task of trying to follow him through the old numbers of *Blackwood.*

In summer Mr. Christie's health was so bad that he expected, as he says, "soon to know the great secret," a quotation from a person then very notorious. His native air restored him, and in September he accepted an invitation to Chiefswood. Traill also was expected. "We have *room* enough in a very humble sort," Lockhart wrote, "so I trust you

will bring your brother along with you also. . . .
Sir Walter is always inquiring for you, and desiring
to be remembered.   It is worth while to travel
some miles, I assure you, to see the Minstrel in his
glory. . . . My wife has got a donkey-cart, in which
she will drive you in great style." Meanwhile,
Williams (who was tutor to Charles Scott in Wales)
had been married, and was reported to be flourishing greatly.   Mrs. Lockhart, according to Sir
Walter (August 7, 1821), was "ordering old Cock-
a-Pistol" (the gardener) about, and directing all
things "with the solemn fuss of an old managing
dowager."[1]

At about this time, Sir Walter returned the proof
sheets of "Valerius" to Lockhart.   "They are
most classical and interesting at the same time, and
cannot but produce a very deep sensation.   I am
quite delighted with the reality of your Romans."[2]

The "sensation" produced by "Valerius" was not
wide, whether it was deep or not, and the "reality"
of the Romans probably was not in their favour.
No novel of classical times, except "Hypatia," has
ever been popular, and "Hypatia" (as Mr. Saintsbury observes) "makes its interests and its personages daringly modern."[3]

"Valerius," on the other hand, reads like a

---

[1] Cock-a-Pistol was so called from his cottage, on the site of the
last great clan battle of the Border.
[2] "Letters," ii. 125.
[3] "The Last Days of Pompeii" is another exception.

translation from the Latin, as it purports to be, an admirable translation, but remote in style from all that the novel-reader knows and likes. In Sir Walter's own novels, the historical characters, when they do not speak Scots, or converse in a kind of conventional *lingua franca* of mediævalism, discourse in the style of Sir Walter's own period. But a mind like Lockhart's was almost certain to aim at a manner not too distant from that of the Latin classics. In fact, as one reads "Valerius," one is always turning it into Latin prose!

The story tells how the son of a Roman officer and a British bride leaves the paternal villa in Albion, and visits Rome. He sups with a patrician, who says, "You would observe the palm-branches at my door. They were won to-day by a five hours' harangue before the Centumviri." Now the Centumviri (according to the Dictionary) were a bench of judges who decided in civil suits. The novel-reader does not care to pursue his studies in fiction with the aid of a Latin Dictionary. "Local colour" does not excite him, when it is borrowed from Horace, Juvenal, Tacitus, and Petronius Arbiter. A Stoic, who is present at the supper, accidentally strikes the corner of the table with his knee, "which elicited from his stubborn features a sudden contortion." It must, indeed, have been pleasant to watch a professional Stoic, when suddenly obliged to recognise that "whatsoever is agreeable to the universe,"—as a knock on the knee-pan and the resulting sensation—may be highly disagreeable to a philosophic citizen of the universe. But, in a romance of classic times, the novel-reader is constantly thrown out by want of knowledge,—*Pour entendre il fallait avoir cette lumière*—and the more learned the romance the less is the novel-reader entertained. The slave of old Roman comedy, and his amorous young master, reappear in "Valerius," but, if they now enliven only a few readers in Plautus, in a modern work of fiction their chance of success is slight indeed. The pleaders in the Forum may be Jeffreys and Cranstouns in togas, but the long sermon of an Epicurean philosopher in an arbour, has no merit beyond resembling the long sermons of Epicurean and other philosophers. They are fatiguing in Plutarch's essays, and in a novel they fatigue, though they are needed as a contrast to the early Christian views of the heroine.

Once interested in her, and by the gallant bearing of a condemned Christian, the hero has no heart for the gladiatorial sports of the arena, where the ladies eat comfits above the butchery, and the philosophers perorate and quote Greek, and the early Christian dies for his creed, after delivering an address of considerable length.

The many pictures of Roman life which follow are, in essence, correct, but somewhat cold and far away. Though the book was hardly "damned," as Lockhart briefly expresses it, still, he had not

MISS SCOTT (MRS. J. G. LOCKHART)

(From a Water-Colour Drawing by her husband.)

wholly succeeded, where, practically, every one has failed. He does not lend to his hero the psychological interest, so rare and to many minds so winning, of Mr. Pater's " Marius the Epicurean." The book is faultlessly written, but to say that of a novel is equivalent to confessing a *succès d'estime*.[1]

Lockhart took his literary fortunes lightly. Here is his letter to Christie on " Valerius," and other matters :—

" MY DEAR CHRISTIE,—My brother William has just left us after spending a couple of days, and telling us all the grand story of the coronation. He vexed me a great deal by saying that you are still looking but poorishly, but rejoiced me by his confirmation of your intended Scottish trip *twice*, because I think that will inevitably do you much good, and because I am sure it will do me much good to see you, of which pleasure I hope it is not possible I am to be deprived, if you do turn your nose northwards. Is it quite fixed that Mrs. Christie can't come with you? Might she not venture in the steamboat at least thus far? I mean to Edinburgh ?—for the journey from thence to this retirement is but a bagatelle. If she and the bairns could, I need not say how happy it would make Sophia and myself. At all events,

---

[1] Mr. Hayward, in later years, told Lockhart that "Valerius" was used as a handbook at Harvard College in America. A sagacious reviewer described it as "a religious tale by an American."

you will come.   If you come hither *first*, I will, I
think, contrive some very nice trips for you, and
I shan't care how far north I go with you afterwards.   Within very easy rides of this are Yarrow,
Ettrick, Hermitage Castle, Hume Castle—I know
not how many fields of battle, clannish and royal.
Even my gardener derives his title of 'Cock-a-
Pistol' from having his cottage on the place where
a certain knight of Buccleuch, or Cessford, was slain.
The field in front of the house is 'Charge-law.'
In short, 'tis all haunted or holy ground.   Melrose
is within half a mile, Dryburgh four miles off, Jed-
burgh fourteen.   I am sure you could spend days
here very tolerably, and sheep's head and whisky
toddy would cut short the evenings.   Sir Walter
says he won't allow me to have you all the while,
but we shall not fight about that matter, for he is
but two or three miles off.   Won't Traill and you
come together?   William tells me he gave you
a copy of 'Valerius' and abuses me for not having
sent one myself.   I put one up to be carried (with
a letter for you, and a baby's cap from Sophia for
Mrs. Christie's last gift) by Robert Buchanan—
shortly after the book was published.   But Buchanan
sent back the parcel, being obliged to defer his
journey to London till some time after.   In the
meantime I had gone into the country, and the
book had been damned, so you will pardon me for
not being very anxious to find another method of
conveyance.   William says Theodore Hook men-

tioned my being the writer. This must have been
some guess of Croker's, for (unless Blackwood
played false) nobody could know but Sir Walter
Scott and my brothers. All this is *non tanti*. I had
quite forgot the book, and all that to it pertained,
until William revived my recollection. At least, I
was trying as much as possible to forget it and
the disappointment I had met with, part of which
(but this may be the merest vanity) I cannot help
attributing to the frigidity of my publisher.

" Mr. W. S. Rose is at Abbotsford. I am going
up the water of Yarrow with him to-morrow to see
Hogg and the wild-ducks (for Rose is a great
sportsman for a palsied man, to say nothing of a
poetaster); as for myself, of course I have merely an
eye to the hodge-podge and the absurdity of such
a juxtaposition as the most sensitive of *bels esprits*,
and the roughest of all possible diamonds. If I had
thought there was any possibility of seeing the
coronation, I would have come up, but without
question there will be more of them in our day.
The Queen is, I suppose, at Edinburgh by this time.
I suppose the Jeffreys will, for Brougham's sake,
make a slight attempt, but on the whole I believe
this part of the country was never in better humour.
—Yours, most affectionately,

" J. G. LOCKHART."

Young authors are apt to attribute their disappointments to "the frigidity of the publisher,"

and perhaps Mr. Blackwood was not warmly in love with "Valerius." Lockhart, none the less, appears to have held to his belief in the possibility of the classical novel.[1]

Lockhart had consolations enough, if "Valerius" did not rival the success of his father-in-law's romances. Probably about this time Mr. Christie had an opportunity of observing a taste of his which he shared with that Prince whose memory he drank to at Oxford on St. Andrew's Day. "The love of children," says Mr. Christie, "was stronger in Lockhart than I have ever known it in any other man,—it was womanly love. He delighted to dandle and play with an infant in arms," like his own Hugh Littlejohn. "It was an early character-istic of his, and he never lost it. A little girl of four or five years of age, the child of one of the college servants, used to be his companion in his rooms for hours at a time. . . . I never saw so happy a father as he was, while dancing his first-born child in his arms. His first sorrow in life was the breaking of the health and ultimate death of this child."[2]

Indeed he had known other sorrows, the estrange-ment with Sir William Hamilton, the poignant distress of a few months before. But through the ill-health and the deaths of those nearest to him came "that expression of deep melancholy which

---

[1] See the *Quarterly Review*, lxvii. p. 352.
[2] *Quarterly Review*, vol. cxvi.

not unfrequently overspread his face, and in his later years habitually settled there." [1]

The days, however, had not yet come when he should say, "There is no pleasure in them." There was coursing, and the Abbotsford Hunt, and leistering of salmon by torchlight (a picturesque pastime not then illegal); and he writes to his brother Lawrence, "I have been making myself something of a woodman, earning my dinner by the axe." Nor did he despise the dinner when earned, bidding his brother "put his hand in the best binn," at Germiestoun. He adds some practical lessons in woodcraft, learned from Sir Walter, who had great pleasure in forestry.

These years (1821–1825) were presumably happy, for they have scarce any history. Lockhart's letters at this date are not many, or few have been preserved. We hear that the baby is "twice the weight he was," and other items of domestic intelligence, not more surprising. Letters to Lockhart's parents contain only reports of his family's health, expressions of affection, and repeated invitations to Chiefswood. Like all Scottish homes, it was very elastic, and could hold a surprising number of guests. About Hugh Littlejohn we hear that he is already a distinguished creeper, but that his ambition has not soared to walking. He is content to go on all fours, imitating the dogs, of which there are so many about the place.

[1] Mr. Christie, in the *Quarterly Review*, vol. cxvi. p. 448.

On February 13, 1822, Lockhart writes to a
relation who was aiming at some appointment un-
named. Sir Walter would do nothing, some application of a similar sort lately made by him had been
unsuccessful. " I wish you were as independent of
favours as I make myself, but cheer up and hope
the best," says Lockhart. It may be gathered from
his letter that attempts had lately been made in his
own favour, and not with fortunate results. The
reason given for not gratifying him with a legal
appointment was, that he rarely appeared in the
courts. He had not the gift of speaking in public,
and till he distinguished himself professionally,
professional rewards could not come in his way.
Such, at least, was the verdict of the givers of
patronage.

In the waste places of the innumerable letters *to*
Sir Walter, letters from English folk and foreign,
from poetasters, peers, beggars, and bores of every
species known to science,—the bore who wants
information, the bore who sends information that is
not wanted, the bore who encloses poetry, the bore
who "will be frank, and tell his private history"—
there is, in 1822, but one letter from Lockhart. It
speaks of the death of Sir Alexander Boswell, in a
duel with Mr. Stuart of Dunearn. This arose from
some ballads written by Sir Alexander in a Glasgow
Tory paper, the *Sentinel.* He had dined at Scott's
in Castle Street ; "the evening was, I think, the
gayest I ever spent there," Charles Matthews and

Boswell being full of jest and song. "It turned out that he had joined the party whom he thus delighted, immediately after completing the last arrangements for his duel." Several of the circumstances of the combat are "exactly reproduced in the duel scene in 'St. Ronan's Well.'" Lockhart's letter (dealing solely with matters no longer of interest) ends by thanks for Scott's counsel, which had kept him and Wilson out of these newspaper wars. Scott says as much in a letter of September 30, 1821, to Archibald Constable. "I expect daily to hear that some one is killed. The *Scotsman* and *Review* have much to answer for. I have kept Lockhart out of the scrape, in which some of the young men are knee-deep." The sins of the Tory papers are remembered, those of the Whig journals, (if Scott is right) are forgotten.

In February 1822, we get the first hint of Lockhart's best novel, "Adam Blair," in a note to his brother Lawrence. "By-the-bye, you must know that I have since I was with you converted a story the doctor told us after dinner one day, into a very elegant little volume, under the name of 'Some Passages in the Life of Mr. Adam Blair.' You will receive a copy one of these days. I am afraid the doctor may disapprove of some things : so take care you warn him to hold his tongue, *i.e.*, in case he suspects me (which he will do). I took it to Ebony when it was done, and he thought so highly of it that he offered me £300 at present, and £200 more on the second edition for the copyright. This I accepted modestly."

"Some Passages in the Life of Mr. Adam Blair, Minister of the Gospel at Cross-Meikle" (in the middle ward of Lanarkshire), is certainly by far the best of Lockhart's four novels. Unlike "Valerius," which demands an effort, it may still be read with pleasure, and even with that excited curiosity which only a good story can arouse. It has been said, by a friendly critic, that Lockhart had all the gifts necessary for a novelist, except the gift of novel-writing. The verdict on this point must, of course, vary *pro captu lectoris*. To myself the characters appear to be living, and powerfully drawn, while the incidents more than once, even amidst a certain exaggeration, prove a real genius for romance. The *Edinburgh Review* (October 1824) criticised "Valerius," and "Adam Blair," with six of Galt's works, and two of Wilson's, as "Secondary Scottish Novels." The *Edinburgh* had no reason to love books published by the Blackwoodians, and its notice was not enthusiastic. "They are pathetic, for the most part, by the common recipes, which will enable any one almost to draw tears who will condescend to employ them." Lockhart, of all men and writers, is perhaps least liable to the charge of "wallowing naked in the pathetic," as a great novelist freely expresses himself. "They are mighty religious, too, but . . . their devotional orthodoxies seem to tend, now and then, a little towards cant." This accusation, again, does not strike Lockhart. In all his works, from "Peter's Letters" to the "Life of Burns," and thence to his *Quarterly* articles, and his great Biography, Lockhart shows how unaffectedly he was impressed by the high, bare, austere, and heartfelt devotion of the old Scottish type. As Scott arranged a grassy walk and rural seat that he might be within hearing of "Pate's evening hymn," so, by all the traditions of early training and family legend, Lockhart was earnestly attached to a religion which makes little appeal to taste, and rejects every allurement of art.

In Lockhart, as a man of letters, nothing is more remarkable than his universal ability. Except his *éreintements* of contemporaries (and for these I confess the utmost antipathy), he did nothing which he did not do well. His criticism of classical writers in any language is warm with sympathy, acute with appreciation, and excellent, at times nobly eloquent, in style. His verse is, on occasion, nothing less than masterly, and of Biography, on any scale, he is a confessed master. It may, therefore, be worth while to point out that, in fiction too, his gifts were far indeed from commonplace, far from imitative : that he could feel with passion, and communicate what he felt with power.

The story of Adam Blair opens with the waning happiness of his married life. He has already lost several children, one little girl only surviving, and he loses his wife. His emotion, in the chamber of death, the contrast of the beautiful and cheerful scene viewed from the windows, and his one violent struggle in the lonely wood by midnight, where, as it were, he meets Apollyon, and fights for the very life of his faith, all these things are described with astonishing force and delicacy. The author's purpose is to show, beneath the black coat and Geneva bands, and the subsequent self-mastery of Adam Blair, a nature capable of sudden, violent, and overwhelming passion. The funeral, its cold naked formalities, the affection of the old elder, John Maxwell, the sympathy of that truly Scottish character, the dry, sarcastic, tender-hearted Dr. Muir, the silent kindness of the parishioners, form excellent foils to the night of spiritual conflict, and are remote from exaggeration of effect. The bereaved and desolate life of the young minister, and the gradual re-entrance into it of ordinary things and social pleasures beneath the hospitable roof of Semplehaugh, are depicted with a perfect naturalness.

One sentence is sadly prophetic. " From time to time, indeed, Mr. Blair betrayed in his manner something of that abstraction of thought with which those who have ever had misery seated at the root of their heart are acquainted, and the appearance of which furnishes at times so much amusement to the thoughtless people of the world."

These words do but anticipate Mr. Christie's description of the "deep melancholy" which, in later years, was wont to steal over their author's face.

Nothing can be better, in its way, than the portrait of the kind Mrs. Semple of Semplehaugh, with her truly Scottish hospitality. When she leaves the country for Edinburgh, the cloud falls again on the minister, and is broken by a visit thrust on the recluse by a lady who had once been ready enough to fall in love with him, and who had been the most intimate friend of his wife. Lockhart draws a "woman with a history,"—she has made a foolish marriage, has been deserted, has got (like Hazlitt) an easy Scottish divorce, has married "one of that numerous division of the human species which may be shortly and accurately described as answering to the name of Captain Campbell." This typical Captain leaves the Dutch service, buys a lonely château on Loch Fyne, wearies of it, returns to Holland, and his wife, as a "grass widow," settles herself in the manse of Cross-Meikle.

A woman sinned against, and, probably, sinning, Charlotte Campbell is affectionate, winning, passionate, and beautiful, a *brebis égarée* to be reclaimed, and Mr. Blair reclaims her. The process has its perils, and, indeed, it seems unlikely that, about 1770, any parochial society would have permitted the situation, the fair lady dwelling with the widowed minister. But even Mrs. Semple, who wishes the minister to marry the pretty daughter of Dr. Muir, makes no objection to the very unconventional arrangement, nor does the *Edinburgh* Reviewer mark the blot.

After a not quite plausible scene, in which Charlotte rescues the minister and his child from the river at Semplehaugh, and he, half unconsciously, kisses both of them, the pair, "quite safe, but very wet," have to dress in clothes from the Semplehaugh wardrobes. The minister, a handsome figure, is brave in brown kerseymere, with a very slight edging of silver, and a rich lace cravat, instead of a linen stock, while the lady seems another woman, "in pale green satin, wrought over with silken *fleurs de lis* of the same colour," and with a veil of lace over her wet black hair. So attired they are driven home, after dinner, where they sit in the warm evening, beneath an old thorn tree on the lawn, heavy with fragrance of the blossom. Thus each looks on the other, in their changed aspect, and after their hour of violent emotion, with new eyes, and in this scene there is, undoubtedly, the essence of what we call romance. Next morning an emissary from Captain Campbell carries away Charlotte to the château of Uigness. The minister leaves home, apparently with the purpose of seeing this emissary, a brutal person, in Edinburgh, and rebutting his calumnies. But "a spirit in his feet" leads him straight to the mouth of Clyde; he charters a boat for Loch Fyne, and is landed at Uigness, Captain Campbell's castle. In this second con-

flict of a wildly passionate nature, Apollyon prevails. The minister is only too kindly welcomed :
awakes to a frenzy of remorse, is smitten with a
fever, and when aroused to life, hears a lament
played on the pipes. Charlotte, who has died of
the same fever, caught in nursing him, is being
borne down to the loch to her rest in a Holy
Isle.

The rest of the story, except for the conduct of
Captain Campbell (unexpectedly honourable) deals
with the minister's confession, repentance, and final
restoration to his parish, a man untimely old and
white-haired.[1]

Such, in rude outline, is the story of "Adam
Blair." It has a faint analogy with Hawthorne's
"Scarlet Letter" (of course a later work), but is
distinctly uninfluenced, in any degree, by the
Waverley Novels. A brief tale, of times practically
modern, with a moral and psychological situation
for its pivot, with no happy humour, with no
chivalrous deeds, is as unlike Sir Walter's glowing
romances as any work can be. The characters
of Adam and Charlotte, of Dr. Muir and John
Maxwell, and the rough, yet finally forgiving and
equitable Captain Campbell, are all excellent and
veracious. The passion and the pity of this "true
story," and the clear fervent language, give an
interest which changes of taste and manner have

---

[1] An objection was taken to this restoration as impossible, but a
precedent of 1748 was produced !

not yet had power to destroy. In truth, far from relying on Scott and the past, the spirit and sense of "Adam Blair" tend onwards into the future, and to more modern developments of the art of fiction.

On March 20, 1822, Lockhart writes to Christie (the last letter preserved, except a few very many years later), asking him to Chiefswood. "Would to God we could see Mrs. Christie and the bairns here with you." He himself, having legal business at Inverary, means to ride thither "for health's sake." Traill is reported to be flourishing at York.

"'Adam Blair,' which I am glad you liked, and which I wish had been more worthy your liking, has created a good deal of rumpus, and some of the low cattle here [1] are saying, and printing, that it is fit for the same shelf with 'Faublas,'" and another book unmentionable. "If it be immoral I did not write it with an immoral intention, or in a culpable spirit, but quite the reverse. The story is a true, and, I think, a tragic and moral one, and old Henry Mackenzie, on one side, and Sir Harry Moncreiff on the other, laud it highly. The former has sent Ebony a review of it, which I hope he will insert. . . . No new romance or drama can escape the old boy. I wish you were in Edinburgh, that I might have the pleasure of showing you the *Ultimus Roman-orum*. He is, in conversation, very unlike what his books would lead one to expect, a most brilliant

---

[1] Probably *the Stot* is alluded to.

story-teller—keen, sarcastic, witty, anything but a sentimentalist. I am sorry to add, his health begins to droop of late. Scott is at Abbotsford. My wife and boy go thither when I go to the West country for a few weeks."

That "Adam Blair" should have been ranked with "Faublas" shows the length to which party spirit was ready to go. But, as the proverb saith, "people who play at bowls must look for rubs," and Lockhart had indulged freely in that pastime. He does not seem to have valued at a plack the abuse of his critics; indeed, his own indifference to such attacks was an element in his readiness to assail others.

In July and August 1822, Lockhart was a spectator, obviously an amused and critical spectator, of the visit paid by George IV. to Edinburgh. "The King *is* coming to Scotland at the end of next month," he writes, in an undated note about buying horses, to his brother Lawrence, "and the Minstrel's aid is wanted to arrange things for his reception, and I suppose everything will be done to make Holyrood as splendid as possible." He calls these splendours "a grand terryfication of the Holyrood chapters in 'Waverley;' George IV., *anno ætatis* LX., being well content to enact Prince Charlie, with the Great Unknown for his Baron Bradwardine." But, though he cannot restrain a smile at the stout Hanoverian masquerading with Sir William Curtis in the Stuart tartans, while Sir Walter appeared in the sombre Campbell colours (his great-grandmother having been a Campbell), in no part of his work does Lockhart show a more loyal admiration of Scott, and of his powers in managing men. He had to compose the differences of the Highland chiefs, which, at least in Glengarry, were as keen and bellicose as ever. He had to direct and organise everything, and to pass, from feasts and revels, to the deathbed of William Erskine, Lord Kinnedder, who was dying of a cruel and undeserved wound to his personal honour. Meanwhile Mr. Crabbe, the poet, had arrived in Castle Street, and was much discomposed in a levy of bucklers and tempest of plaids. Lockhart seems to have been attached to Crabbe's suit and service, when he was not obliged to play his own part, in a review of yeomanry. Lockhart could not "live in fantasy" like Scott, who seems to have been able to believe that the "auld Stuarts were come again." *He* could not chant—

> "To see King *George* at Edinburgh Cross,
>   With fifty thousand foot and horse,
>   And the right restored where the right should be—
>   Oh! that's the thing that would wanton me!"

But he watched, with pride and affection, Sir Walter's immense unconscious energy, his mastery over men. "I do not think that he had much in common with the statesmen and diplomats of his own age and country; but I am mistaken if Scott could not have played in other days either the Cecil or the Gondomar; and I believe no man, after long and intimate knowledge of any other great poet, has ever ventured to say, that he could have conceived the possibility of any such parts being adequately filled on the active stage of the world, by a person in whom the powers of fancy and imagination had such predominant sway, as to make him in fact live three or four lives habitually in place of one. . . . Compared to him, all the rest of the *poet* species that I have chanced to observe nearly—with but one glorious exception—have seemed to me to do little more than sleep through their lives, and at best to fill the sum with dreams;" and he is persuaded that Scott's peers can only be found "in the roll of great sovereigns and great captains, rather than in that of literary genius."

Unluckily Crabbe and Scott had but one quiet walk together with Lockhart, whose charge was "the excellent old Crabbe."[1] They visited Muschat's Cairn, renowned in "The Heart of Midlothian." "The hour in which the fine old man gave us some most touching anecdotes of his early struggles, was a truly delightful contrast to the bustle and worry of miscellaneous society, which consumed so many of his few days in Scotland."

Crabbe himself, after praising Sir Walter, writes, "I am disposed to think highly of his son-in-law,

[1] "Letters," ii. 147.

Mr. Lockhart—of his heart, his understanding will not be disputed by any one." To Lockhart's heart, that organ whose very existence has been doubted, his letter to Crabbe's son (December 26, 1833), bears ample evidence. As far as I have observed, Lockhart's kind respect for the aged equalled his affection for children. He speaks in the most pleasant and genial terms of a gentleman whom Mr. Blackwood and Wilson less humanely styled "The Old Driveller." Of Crabbe he writes that, while his recollection of the Edinburgh "mummeries" is vague, "the image of your father, then first seen, but long before admired and revered in his works, remains as fresh as if the years that have passed were but so many days. His noble forehead, his bright beaming eye, without anything of old age about it—though he was then, I presume, above seventy—his sweet, and, I would say, innocent smile, and the calm mellow tones of his voice—all are reproduced the moment I open any page of his poetry ; and how much better have I understood and enjoyed his poetry, since I was able thus to connect it with the living presence of the man."[1]

Whoever, like Lockhart, has these tender and reverent feelings for childhood and age, for babies, and for "venerable and secluded men," should be free from the imputation of want of heart.

In the autumn Chiefswood and Abbotsford re-

[1] "Crabbe's Works," vol. i. pp. 275–279, 1834.

ceived the weary entertainers of the King, the poet,
and "a' the wild M'Craws." They dined with the
weavers at Galashiels, and the "Tividale poet,"
Thomson, really a fluent writer of Scots verse.
The "plenishing" of Abbotsford was the great
affair of these months, and Lockhart records his
suspicion that, consequent on Scott's fatigues, he
had endured and concealed "a slight attack of
apoplectic nature."

In this year was finished and published a work
on which Lockhart had been engaged in 1821, a
new edition of "Don Quixote," with notes, and
translations of the Spanish Ballads alluded to in the
romance. Sir Walter himself had begun this book,
"but Lockhart, being a much better Spaniard, and
I having never been, I gave him my materials."[1]
Constable expressed his readiness to publish Lockhart's "Don Quixote," which appeared as "Printed
for Hurst, Robinson & Co., London, and Archibald
Constable & Co., Edinburgh, 1822." On February
16 of this year, Scott writes about the book to
Constable—"The notes are most curious, and I
think it cannot but supersede every other; besides,
Lockhart will *blaze* one day; of that, if God spare
him, there can be little doubt. It is good to have
an early interest in a rising author."

Lockhart (who did not put his name on the title-
page) added a Life of Cervantes. He made but

[1] Scott to Constable, September 30, 1821. "Archibald Constable," iii. 158.

few literary criticisms. "I refer to the Editor of
the Spanish Academy's Edition all those who are
unwilling to admire anything without knowing
why they admire it." The Don "is the symbol
of Imagination, continually struggling and con-
trasting with Reality — he represents the eternal
war between Enthusiasm and Necessity — the
eternal discrepancy between the aspirations and
the occupations of man, the omnipotence and the
vanity of human dreams." Cervantes wrote, not
to ridicule "the old and stately prose romances
of chivalry,—which are among the most interesting relics of the rich, fanciful, and lofty genius of
the Middle Ages,—but to extirpate the race of
slavish imitators. . . ."

Lockhart incidentally remarks, that "nobody has
ever written successful novels when young, but
Smollett," forgetting, among others, Miss Burney,
and not informed, perhaps, about Miss Austen.
He adopts Motteux's translation as "the most
spirited," for the modern reader might shrink
from "the obsolete turns of phraseology" of
Shelton. The notes are very copious, but, necessarily, in part superseded by modern knowledge
of ancient Celtic sources, and of the *Chansons
de Geste*.

I fancy that this edition met with scant success,
and a Shakespeare, to be edited by Scott, aided by
Lockhart, is said to have been sold (at least the
three printed volumes) for waste paper, after the

commercial ruin of 1826.[1]   Scott speaks of having "my son Lockhart's assistance for the fag," and Lockhart, in a later letter, mentions his pleasure in his task.   But I have never been able to find any trace of the three wasted volumes.   The notes were to be by Lockhart (who highly approved of Constable's plan), the introductory volume was the charge of Sir Walter.[2]   The enterprise was one for which Lockhart, with his admiration of Shakespeare, and his knowledge, was well adapted, and, when all failed, he might have said, with the Man who was Crafty, "Verily my fine gold hath perished."

The year 1823 has left no records of events in Lockhart's life, beyond those which he casually introduces into his Biography of Scott, and the appearance of his own novel "Reginald Dalton," and his volume of Spanish Ballads.   He has told us how Will Laidlaw suggested to Scott a novel on "Melrose in July 1823," as the three rode along the crest of Eildon, above the little town.   He has chronicled the happy days spent during Miss Edgeworth's visit to Abbotsford, and reported how he, with Scott, explored the ruined castles of upper Tweed, and upper Clyde, and how the Ettrick Shepherd, though verging on sixty, distinguished himself at the St. Ronan's Games.   "We were a' leal Tories then," said the Galashiels poet, nor would leal

---

"Archibald Constable," iii. 241.   I am not persuaded that this statement is correct.   [2] Ibid., iii. 246, 247.

Tories ever have been scarce, if there had been many lairds like Scott. What Lockhart does not tell us, Sir Walter does—"The Lockharts are now living on the smiles and babble of their single hope, which sometimes gives me uneasiness, for a failure, where a failure is so easy and probable, will make them too miserable."[1]   Hogg and Lockhart were at this time on very good terms, Lockhart bringing the Shepherd to stay at Abbotsford. Hogg had, probably, a good deal to forgive, in the possible author of "O Sus, quando te aspiciam!" and other pleasantries: if so, he forgave freely. Lockhart was constant in efforts to befriend him.

Little incidents such as these alone remain out of four or five years of happiness. As to work, "Reginald Dalton" is not a success in the same sort as "Adam Blair." Though still current at railway bookstalls, it is, on the whole, a conventional novel. The descriptions of Oxford have been already cited; for the rest, the career of Reginald, whether as a "fast," or as a reading man, whether engaged in a duel, or adopting, in debt and repentance, a servitor's gown, is, no doubt, exaggerated. The Scottish characters are not at all worthy of Lockhart's skill, and the complicated intrigue is a thing which lay outside his province. He had little gift of invention, but, given a powerful moral situation, he could do it justice. In "Reginald Dalton" the piety of the relations

_____
[1] "Letters," ii. 164.

between a wild lad and a father is perhaps the feature in which Lockhart's genius may most clearly be recognised. The book had some success, and possesses more vitality than most of the novels of its day. Lockhart received £1000 for the book from Mr. Blackwood.

A few side lights on Lockhart's thoughts and works at this time (1823), may be gleaned from Mr. Christie's letters to him. These have been more successfully preserved than Lockhart's letters to Christie. On January 24, 1823, he writes from Limoges, "Among your virtues that of being a regular correspondent is not the least." A friendship can, indeed, be kept up without frequent correspondence, but no doubt letters are rain about its roots. Christie assures Lockhart that he will "get something" by way of a legal appointment. We have seen, however, that the Scottish bestowers of loaves and fishes thought him an idle apprentice. At this moment, none the less, Christie congratulates him on "getting some business in the courts," where, at best, he was not more successful than Sir Walter had been in his day. He moralises on the outrages committed by *The Beacon*, and remarks on the unsuccessful alliance of Byron and Leigh Hunt in *The Liberal*, which they were trying to conduct from Italy. "Byron's talents, his rank, and that spirit of accusing, not complaining, will save him. . . . Leigh Hunt and he must make a strange couple, Byron as proud as H——, Hunt as vain as a peacock : Byron perpetually doing or saying something to wound Leigh Hunt's self-love. . . ." And then Christie prophesies, with much clairvoyance, the end of the connection. The men quarrelled, and Leigh Hunt, after Byron's death, wrote the history of their alliance.

Postage and news were then very vague. Christie heard in France of "the great stir made by 'Reginald Dalton,'" but to get the book was past hope ; and he was distressed by false news of Williams's death. " I cannot believe the thing, he was made to live eighty years, and be the first Radical Bishop." At last, in July 1824, Christie does obtain " Reginald Dalton," and thinks it "the most interesting novel he has read for years," probably with a mental reservation in favour of "Quentin Durward," which people abuse, he says, much to his, and indeed to our amazement. "Quentin Durward" was only revived by its success in France.

CHAPTER XI

EDINBURGH, 1817–1824

Lockhart's Poems.—Spanish Ballads.—Sources.—Weak lines.—Song of the Galley.—The Wandering Knight.—Serenade.—"The Mad Banker."—Verses on Jeffrey.—On Holyrood.—On the Stuarts.— Queen Mary.—Scott's reference to these verses.—"Take thou the Vanguard of the Three."—Criticism of Lockhart's verse.— His reserve.—Reasons why he wrote little.—His comic verse.— "Captain Patten."—The Odontist.—Trooper lyrics.—His skill in caricature.—Examples.—Fenella.—A wet day.—Charles Scott. —Miss Violet Lockhart.—A Presbytery.—A cock-fighter.— Analogy with Thackeray in verse and caricature.—Lockhart almost abandons the Art.

THE work which probably made Lockhart's name best and most widely known to the world of readers at that day, was published in 1823, his "Ancient Spanish Ballads."[1] His other writings had all been anonymous, and his novels were confused with those of Galt and Wilson.[2] The Ballads were acknowledged, and obtained a wide success, above all with the young. The printed collection of old Spanish "Lieder," mainly used by Lockhart, was that of Depping, published at Leipzig in 1817.

[1] Blackwood's.

[2] On the title-page of a copy of "Adam Blair" (1822), I find the blank for author's name filled up, in an old hand, with the words "By Professor Wilson"!

He also examined, I think, the early printed
volumes, as the "Cancionero," of Ferdinand de
Castillo (1510), containing pieces reckoned *antiguos*
at that date, after which the Spaniards frequently
published specimens of their mediæval verse.   The
natives of the Peninsula were certainly either richer
in ballads than their neighbours, or preserved more
freshly their interest in their popular or semi-popular
lays.   Like the other peoples, French, English, and
so on, the Spaniards were well contented in their
folk-songs with assonance (the similarity of terminal
vowel sounds), without rhyme.   Following "the
distinguished German antiquary, Mr. Grimm,"
Lockhart treated each stanza of four short lines as a
verse of two long lines, which Grimm supposed to
have been the original form.   His preface is an
excellent account of the development of the Spanish
language, people, and character, and he especially
insists on the chivalrous and honourable character
of the hostility between the Moors and the native
race.   The collection is divided into historical ballads,
Moorish ballads, and romantic ballads.   I shall not
attempt, for lack of the necessary qualifications, to
decide on the literal accuracy of Lockhart's versions,
being content with the favourable verdict of a judge
so competent as my friend Mr. David Hannay.   It
was my own misfortune never to see the book when
I was young, and, on the other hand, to be very
fond of "Bon Gaultier," so that "Don Fernando
Gomersalez" and the lay of Silas Fixings come

between me and Lockhart's poems. Therefore I
am peculiarly ill-fitted to defend such lines as these,
in the first piece—

> "It was a sight of pity to look on Roderick,
>   For, sore athirst and hungry, he stagger'd faint and sick."

The sword of the hero, "hack'd into a saw"
suggests, by no fault of Lockhart's, a weapon in the
same serrated condition, described by Mr. W. S.
Gilbert—(I quote from memory)—

> "And all the people noticed that the engine of the law
>   Was not half so like a hatchet as a dissipated saw."

On the other hand, many passages have a knightly
speed and spirit, in fact this is their general characteristic. The movement of the verse is almost too
catching and facile, though this comes from a strict
following of the original, and Scott himself, in one
of his letters, drops into a parody. Much more
agreeable is the versification of some ballads written
in other measures, such as the following :—

THE SONG OF THE GALLEY.[1]

I.

> "Ye mariners of Spain,
>   Bend strongly on your oars,
> And bring my love again,
>   For he lies among the Moors.

(This is from a song in the Cancionero of Valencia, 1511.
" Galeristas de Espana
Parad los remos," &c.)

II.

" Ye galleys fairly built,
    Like castles on the sea,
O great will be your guilt,
    If ye bring him not to me.

III.

" The wind is blowing strong,
    The breeze will aid your oars ;
O swiftly fly along,
    For he lies among the Moors.

IV.

" The sweet breeze of the sea,
    Cools every cheek but mine ;
Hot is its breath to me,
    As I gaze upon the brine.

V.

" Lift up, lift up your sail,
    And bend upon your oars ;
O lose not the fair gale,
    For he lies among the Moors.

VI.

" It is a narrow strait,
    I see the blue hills over ;
Your coming I'll await,
    And thank you for my lover.

VII.

" To Mary I will pray,
    While you bend upon your oars ;
'Twill be a blessed day,
    If ye fetch him from the Moors."

Here we have a genuine lyrical note, the words sing themselves with a strange yearning accent. In this metre, in all metres of short lines, Lockhart most excelled. The pearl of the volume, a flawless thing, worthy of Coleridge or Poe in its music, is—

THE WANDERING KNIGHT'S SONG.[1]

I.

" My ornaments are arms,
    My pastime is in war,
My bed is cold upon the wold,
                My lamp yon star :

II.

" My journeyings are long,
    My slumbers short and broken ;
From hill to hill I wander still,
                Kissing thy token.

III.

" I ride from land to land,
    I sail from sea to sea ;
Some day more kind I fate may find,
                Some night kiss thee."

The following serenade also cannot well be omitted ; like the others, it has a natural singing quality very rare in modern poetry—

---

[1] (In the Cancionero of Antwerp, 1555.

Mis arreos son las armas
Mi descanso el pelear.)

SERENADE.[1]

I.

" While my lady sleepeth,
    The dark blue heaven is bright,
Soft the moonbeam creepeth
    Round her bower all night.
Thou gentle, gentle breeze,
    While my lady slumbers,
Waft lightly through the trees
    Echoes of my numbers,
Her dreaming ear to please.

II.

" Should ye, breathing numbers
    That for her I weave,
Should ye break her slumbers
    All my soul would grieve.
Rise on the gentle breeze,
    And gain her lattice height
O'er yon poplar trees,
    But be your echoes light
As hum of distant bees.

III.

" All the stars are glowing
    In the gorgeous sky,
In the stream scarce flowing
    Mimic lustres lie :
Blow, gentle, gentle breeze,
    But bring no cloud to hide
Their dear resplendencies ;
    Nor chase from Zara's side
Dreams bright and pure as these."

---

[1] (From the Romancero General of 1604.—*Mientras duerme mi nina*, &c.).

The poem is not unworthy in lightness and finish of Théophile Gautier.

The Ballads were cited in the *Edinburgh Review*, and, of course, praised in *Blackwood*, where the critic bade Lockhart attempt original poetry. "Some of the translations I have got by heart," Gifford wrote to Scott, on February 13, 1823. "Where to look for a review of the book I hardly know," he adds. "Southey declines poetry and has from the first ; Reginald (Heber) the Rector would have been instantly in my thoughts, but Reginald the Bishop is out of the question." [1]

The "Spanish Ballads," like his comic pieces, prove Lockhart's command of the vehicle of verse. His very nature forbade him to be a lyrist, to express himself, his own emotions in poetry, the ancestral fetterlock was on his heart, and to this rule I know but one beautiful exception. His self-criticism, again, prohibited him from rushing in where, during his youth, so many poets, so much greater than he, were on their own enchanted ground. From a rambling set of rhymes written for *Blackwood*, in the *ottava rima* of "Beppo" and "Whistlecraft," called "The Mad Banker of Amsterdam," I extract a few stanzas. He is describing the castle of Mr. Wastle—

> " No skies have we of that unmingled blue,
>   In whose rich light Italian meadows beam :
>   But skies far dearer to a Scottish view,
>   Where thin fleet clouds for ever rack and stream.

---

[1] Abbotsford MSS.

> While here and there, the wavering mantle through
>   Small spots of azure tremulously gleam,
> Grey windy skies o'ercanopying well
> The dark pine wood, the linn, the loch, the fell."

Later he says, showing his own opinion of his own poetry—

> "To speak the truth, I neither wish nor pray
>   For fame poetic.   Once upon a time
> Perchance so high might young ambition stray,
>   My reason's mended now, if not my rhyme."

This was a true statement, and Lockhart's letters, even in boyhood, show no trace of aspirations which, at twenty-four, he thus renounces (February 1819). He turns to Jeffrey, who really occupied his mind, against his will, exactly as Sir Walter, to be praised warmly or attacked bitterly, but never to be exorcised, haunted the mind of Hazlitt—

> "Alas for Jeffrey!—if my fancy dreams,
>   Let not that dream's delusion pass away,—
> For still 'midst all his poverty it seems
>   As if a spark of some ethereal ray,
> Some fragment of the true Promethean beams,
>   Had been commingled with his infant clay,
> As if for better things he had been born
> Than transient flatteries and eternal scorn.

> "Alas for Jeffrey! for he might have clomb
>   To some high niche in glory's marble fane ;
> But he, vain man, preferred a lowlier home,
>   An easier triumph and a paltrier reign.

Therefore his book is blotted from the tome
    Of Fame's enduring record, and his gain
Hath in his life been given him, and the wreath
    That his youth won scarce waits the wintry breath

"Of the destroyer, to shed all its bloom
    And dissipate its fragrance in the air. . . ."

There is Tory prejudice here, but there is a measure of truth. Jeffrey's laurels withered with his life.

The following stanza, on Edinburgh, is not unworthy of Byron :—

"For lo ! even in the shadow of the hills
    Our fathers have their deep foundations laid,
And their old city, like a lioness, fills
    The shade that gives her shelter, and that shade
Is proud of her whose low voice wakes and thrills
    Her echoes, whose majestic couch is made
Where all things round free nature's power express,
The sea, the mountains, and the wilderness."

What follows, on Holyrood, is not less admirable.[1]

VII.

"Ay here—where narrowest is her valley's case,
    And highest is the mountain of her shade—
Here stands the mansion of that reverend race,
    Like them forgotten, and like them decayed ;
Their memory is departed, and the place
    Knows them no longer, where their power displayed
Wise splendour—where the monarch's pious pride
Adorned a shrine—a palace sanctified."

---

[1] From *Blackwood*, vol. iv. p. 730.

It would be unfair in any attempt to disengage
the charm of Lockhart's poetry, to omit his stanzas
on that hapless Royal race, of which we may say,
like Monsieur Coppée of its latest, most charming,
and most unhappy scion, *L'Écosse ne peut pas te
juger, elle t'aime.*

XII.

" Alas ! shall ne'er your glory be renewed,
    Ye palaces of antique splendour, where
Were cradled the young shoots of that high brood—
    Linlithgow, thou the pleasant—Falkland fair—
Snawdon, high throned above thy peerless flood
    Of winding glittering waters ?—O shall ne'er
St. Peter's shrine restore that Druid stone [1]
To its old haunted hermitage of Scone ?

XIII.

" Royal in all things !   O what kingly grace
    Sat pale upon their features,—what sad brows
O'erhung the mild eyes of the pensive race,—
    O well did Nature teach them to espouse
Dejected majesty in that high place ;
    O wise and well that coming fate allows
Dim forethought of her sorrows ; wisely she
Paints in the fruit the ruin of the tree.

XIV.

" And so, even he, the merriest of them all,[2]
    Whose blythe wit charmed the haughty Lewis' ear,
He, the glad reveller in bower and hall,
    Gay, gallant, courteous, all without a peer—

---

[1] The Coronation stone, now in Westminster Abbey.
[2] James IV.

Even he, amidst his brightest festival,
 Elate his royal visage—scan ye near
Those bodily lineaments, and mark ye not
The dim hereditary boding blot,

XV.

" Of misery musing over evils gone
 And evils coming, in that dark deep eye!
That forehead high and proud—it is the throne
 Of other thoughts than pride, though it be high ;—
A pining gloom sits half unseen thereon,
 That speaks of treasons past and Flodden nigh ;
And blends faint memory of the bloody heart
Of rebel Douglas, with the visioned dart,

XVI.

" Piercing his lion on the Howard's shield—
 Even 'mid the softest, most elysian notes
Which Heron's harp's luxurious strings may yield,
 A small still voice of mingling sadness floats—
Surrey's far cry upon the blasted field—
 The savage murmurings of mailed throats,—
The rush of bloody waters—and the gloom
Of the wild wind above a nameless tomb.

XVII.

" Pass over one—he died before his time [1]—
 And look on her whose beauty hath become
A bye-word to all nations—in the prime
 And flush o' her days—the rose of Christendom,[2]
Shedding such lustre over this cold clime
 As never southern knew—she struck men dumb
With the sun-like dazzle of her regal charms,
And stooped a goddess to young Darnley's arms.

---

[1] James V.   [2] Queen Mary.

XVIII.

" Fairer than eye may see or tongue express ;—
　　The sweep of centuries hath not ta'en off
The freshness of her famous loveliness,
　　The savage scowl of party hate—the scoff
Of black-souled bigots have not made her less
　　Than when she first was taught the queen to doff,
And beamed, all woman, on these halls antique,
Love's liquid eye, and mantling maddening cheek.

XIX.

" No—not all woman—woman, and yet queen
　　Amidst the very faintness of her sighs—
Wearing her majesty as it had been
　　A thing she fain would quit, but in her eyes
Enthroned immoveable, sublime, serene,
　　Woven in her essence by her destinies,
Awing her lover even in the soft hour
Of heart-dissolving passion's prime and power.

XX.

" It makes man giddy but to think upon
　　Such pride of beauty in a queen's caresses ;
Yet deem not Mary's eye untroubled shone
　　Beneath yon glorious canopy of tresses ;
Ah no ! the household fiend his curse had blown
　　Upon her radiance, and those old distresses
Had dropt their shadow on her fairest day—
Thy spectre-presage, woeful Fotheringay !

.　　.　　.　　.　　.　　.　　.　　.

XXIV.

" Alas, on cold and heartless days she fell,
　　When men threw charity from faith away ;
And even her heavenly face possest no spell,
　　The demon of their bigot rage to lay ;

And she was left to one who loved full well [1]
And practised all the privilege of sway—
And erred, perchance, as much as Mary did,
Albeit her better craft her errors hid.

XXV.

"And rivalry of charms, and love, and fame
    Kindled such wrath in that proud woman's soul,
That, when the spark had found a vent to flame,
    Nor policy nor mercy might controul
Its furious bursting, and she felt no shame
    The smouldering torrent of her ire to roll
Full on the Lord's anointed, and begun
That work of sacrilege which hath undone

XXVI.

"Old honour—which hath given men heart to ope
    The sacred sluice of the rich blood of kings,
When uninspired prophets nurse mad hope
    Which from impatient ignorance outsprings :
And popular phrenzy's shroud doth envelope
    Man's quiet light of soul ; and baser things
Are lifted higher by the pluckers down,
Irreverent of crosier and of crown.

XXVII.

"Oh ! noble is the death from noble foe
    In the free field received, when the broad star
Of day is high in heaven—yet more when slow
    The golden West receives his sinking car—
For then those mild majestic beams bestow
    Their softest splendours on the bed of war—
And soldiers close their eyelids on the scene,
Even like the sun, sad, solemn, and serene.

---

[1] Elizabeth.

XXVIII.

"But there is meekness lodged within thy heart,
  Most lovely Mary (fervid tho' thou be),
Which, when the agony cometh, shall impart
  A more than evening of tranquillity—
Tho' gloomy walls shut heaven from where thou art,
  And inward only the last light to thee,
With smiles amidst those lordlings shalt thou go,
Who come to see the blood of monarchs flow.

XXIX.

" High in her hand the silver cross she rears,
  The Lord of life is imaged there in dying—
Well pitied He another Mary's tears—
  Upon His grace, be sure, is she relying ;
Stilled every tumult—vanquished all her fears—
  With what repose she all around is eyeing ;
O see, amidst her maidens' sobs and shrieks,
O see, the blood deserts not her calm cheeks.

XXX.

" A Woman, and a Christian, and a Queen—
  What could she more or less ? she did not bare
Her neck unto the axe with the high mien
  Of pride, which mantles dying man's despair ;
Nor on her upward eyelids was there seen
  That radiant light of faith—that scorn of care—
That joy of love which virgin saints display,
When rude men take their spotless lives away.

XXXI.

" She was nor glad, nor sorrowing, proud nor cold ;
  Yet did her sex, her station, and her creed
A mingled mild serenity unfold
  Upon her forehead, when she knelt to bleed,

> Such as became her nobly; less than bold—
> And yet in nothing seemed she terrified—
> As were her life not much to be laid down,
> Being already stripped of her fair crown."

I cannot doubt that these gallant stanzas won the heart of Scott, whose Toryism is firmly and fully rendered in this lament.

> " But what avails to waste a world of sighs
> Upon the ruins of a royal pile?
> What—but perchance to tempt new blasphemies
> From men who wear one cold eternal smile
> For all beyond their vulgar ken that lies—
> For all the ancient honours of our isle—
> For all that sanctified in the old day
> The high resolves of men more pure than they?"

These lines, of course, strike at the Whigs, who, in the *Edinburgh Review*, were eternally taunting the unhappy and, one might have thought, sacred memory of Marie Antoinette with pitiless derision and "cold eternal smile." To them her sorrows, literally "too great for tears," were matter for jibe and scandal. Lockhart's verses, just cited, appeared in *Blackwood* on March 20, 1819. In a note to the poem he quoted—

> " My wound is deep, I fain would sleep,
> Take *thou* the vanguard of the three,
> And hide me by the bracken bush
> That grows on yonder lily lee."

Scott's letter to Lockhart, written *in tormentis*, wherein he bequeathes to him the banner and baton "of ancient faith and loyalty," and quotes those very words of Douglas from the old ballad, is dated March 23, 1819. Doubtless the rich, melancholy music of the stanzas on Mary Stuart and Holyrood, with the ballad burden, " Take thou the vanguard of the three," had reached Sir Walter, and haunted him in his almost mortal agonies : hence the cry which " made the women think I was growing light-headed, as they heard me repeat a rhyme apparently so little connected with my situation." In such a state of body and mind, anguished and exalted, he did not, of course, reflect that Lockhart's verses were *dramatic;* that they were attributed to an imaginary character, Wastle, the last of the Cavalier Tories, whose politics and learned love of things old are borrowed from Scott himself, while his bodily aspect is that of Lockhart "come to forty year." It was enough that the poetic imagination of Lockhart could interpret and body forth (as certainly no other living man could have done), one of the several lives of fantasy in which Sir Walter, as Lockhart tells us, habitually lived. On a later day of dark heat and brooding storm, Scott when old, and near his death, was again to quote to Lockhart, "My wound is deep, I fain would sleep."

Why, it may be asked, did Lockhart contemptuously throw away his admirable stanzas, in a fantastic, irregular, planless contribution to a magazine, in place of writing, for example, " Holyrood, A Poem"? I suppose that, first, the sentiments of

Wastle were really dramatic, not fully his own ; next, that his criticism of his own powers was too lucid and severe ; and, finally, that he had no mind to be a follower of Byron, as he might at least have seemed to be, from his use of the *ottava rima*, afterwards employed for serious purposes by Keats in his "Isabella." The poet, if he would make people believe in him, must take himself with a seriousness which, to do him justice, he usually finds no difficulty in assuming. But this implies the lack of that diffidence which Scott, no bad judge of men, remarked in Lockhart. Not unfrequently it also implies an absence of humour, which was not one of Lockhart's defects. This is illustrated by Mrs. Gordon's story of a stanza on Wilson in "The Mad Banker." "It is said," remarks Mrs. Gordon, "that my father chanced to see the proof-sheet by accident before it went to the press, and instantly dashed in—not a little to the chagrin of the author—the following impromptu lines :—

> "'Then touched I off friend Lockhart (Gibson John),
> So fond of jabbering about Tieck and Schlegel,
> Klopstock and Wieland, Kant and Mendelssohn,
> All high Dutch quacks, like Spurzheim and Feinagle.
> Him the Chaldee yclept The Scorpion,
> The claws but not the pinions of the Eagle
> Are Jack's ; but though I do not mean to flatter,
> Undoubtedly he has strong powers of satire.'"

Mr. Gleig says, "We cannot tell by whom this may have been (said), but we know that it is entirely untrue. The poem was read by Lockhart to Wilson before it went to press, in a lodging which the former then occupied in the west of Atholl Crescent, of which we have forgotten the name." (It was in Maitland Street that Lockhart then lived.) "Wilson laughed heartily at the stanza devoted to himself, and wrote on the instant, and read to Lockhart, both laughing all the while, his counter-portraiture of the individual who is assumed by Mrs. Gordon to have aimed a secret blow at his friend, and to have been very much chagrined at the exposure of his malignity."[1]

Lockhart contributed to an article by Gillies, some fragments of translation from Goethe's "Faust." Here is the Song of the Spirit of the Earth, from the opening scene of the play :—

> "In the currents of Life, in the tempests of motion,
>   Hither and thither,
>   Over and under,
>   Wend I and wander,
>   Birth and the grave,
>   A limitless ocean
>   Where the restless wave
>   Undulates ever,—
>   Under and over
>   In the toiling strife
>   I mingle and hover,
>   The spirit of life ;
>   And hear the murmuring wheel of time, unawed,
>   As I weave the living mantle of God !"

---

[1] "Christopher North," i. 275, 276. *Quarterly Review*, vol. cxiii. p. 229.

The *volkslied* of Margaret at the wheel is also very well rendered, and the blank verse throughout is worthy of the lyrics.

Of Lockhart's comic verse the most popular and best known at the time cannot well be omitted; it is the Odontist's wail for a fine old half-pay officer in Glasgow.

CAPTAIN PATON'S LAMENT.

By JAMES SCOTT, Esq.

I.

"Touch once more a sober measure, and let punch and tears be shed,
For a prince of good old fellows, that, alack-a-day! is dead;
For a prince of worthy fellows, and a pretty man also,
That has left the Saltmarket in sorrow, grief, and wo.
    Oh! we ne'er shall see the like of Captain Paton no mo!

II.

"His waistcoat, coat, and breeches were all cut off the same web,
Of a beautiful snuff-colour, or a modest genty drab;
The blue stripe in his stocking round his neat slim leg did go,
And his ruffles of the cambric fine they were whiter than the snow.
    Oh! we ne'er shall see the like of Captain Paton no mo!

III.

"His hair was curled in order, at the rising of the sun,
In comely rows and buckles smart that about his ears did run;
And before there was a toupee that some inches up did grow,
And behind there was a long queue that did o'er his shoulders flow.
    Oh! we ne'er shall see the like of Captain Paton no mo!

IV.

"And whenever we foregathered, he took off his wee three-
    cockit;
  And he proffered you his snuff-box, which he drew from his
    side-pocket;
  And on Burdett or Bonaparte, he would make a remark or so,
  And then along the plainstones like a provost he would go.
    Oh! we ne'er shall see the like of Captain Paton no mo.

V.

"In dirty days he picked well his footsteps with his rattan,
  Oh! you ne'er could see the least speck on the shoes of
    Captain Paton;
  And on entering the coffee-room about *two*, all men did know,
  They would see him with his Courier in the middle of the row.
    Oh! we ne'er shall see the like of Captain Paton no mo.

VI.

"Now and then upon a Sunday he invited me to dine,
  On a herring and a mutton chop which his maid dressed very
    fine;
  There was also a little Malmsey, and a bottle of Bourdeaux,
  Which between me and the Captain passed nimbly to and fro.
    Oh! I ne'er shall take the pot-luck with Captain Paton
      no mo!

VII.

"Or if a bowl was mentioned, the Captain he would ring,
  And bid Nelly run to the West Port and a stoup of water bring;
  Then he would mix the genuine stuff, as they made it long ago,
  With limes that on his property in Trinidad did grow.
    Oh! we ne'er shall taste the like of Captain Paton's punch
      no mo!

VIII.

"And then all the time he would discourse so sensible and
    courteous,
  Perhaps talking of last sermon he had heard from Dr. Porteous,

Or some little bit of scandal about Mrs. So and so,
Which he scarce could credit, having heard the *con* but not
    the *pro*.
    Oh! we ne'er shall hear the like of Captain Paton no mo!

IX.

"Or when the candles were brought forth and the night was fairly
    setting in,
He would tell some fine old stories about Minden-field or
    Dettingen—
How he fought with a French major, and despatched him at a
    blow,
While his blood ran out like water, on the soft grass below.
    Oh! we ne'er shall hear the like of Captain Paton no mo!

X.

"But at last the Captain sickened, and grew worse from day to day,
And all missed him in the coffee-room from which now he
    stayed away;
On Sabbaths, too, the Wee Kirk made a melancholy show,
All for wanting of the presence of our venerable beau.
    Oh! we ne'er shall see the like of Captain Paton no mo!

XI.

"And in spite of all that Cleghorn and Corkindale could do,
It was plain, from twenty symptoms, that death was in his view;
So the Captain made his test'ment, and submitted to his foe,
And we layed him by the Rams-horn-kirk—'tis the way we all
    must go.
    Oh! we ne'er shall see the like of Captain Paton no mo!

XII.

"Join all in chorus, jolly boys, and let punch and tears be shed,
For this prince of good old fellows, that, alack a-day! is dead;
For this prince of worthy fellows, and a pretty man also,
That has left the Saltmarket in sorrow, grief, and wo!
    For it ne'er shall see the like of Captain Paton no mo!"

It was my intention to quote some lively pieces from "Songs of the Edinburgh Troop" (1821-1825). But Dean Burgon has attributed them to Mr. Patrick Fraser Tytler, and the doubt makes it wise to abstain.

A singular addition to Lockhart's efforts in verse is an incomplete translation of the Iliad into English hexameters.   In one of the last of his *Quarterly Review* articles, a criticism of Colonel Mure's "History of Greek Literature," he says : "We are sorry to say that we have never been able to lay our hands upon Wolf's specimen of a translation of Homer, which remains buried in some old magazine. . . . In this *tour de force*, we are told, Wolf not only renders line for line and word for word, which Voss gives us, but he gives foot for foot, dactyle for dactyle, and above all, cæsura for cæsura —things Voss never dreams of attempting,—and yet in life, spirit, and poetry, is conspicuously above his able and industrious rival." [1]

Now in March 1843, a contributor, signing himself N. N. T., published in *Blackwood* a version, in English hexameters, of the twenty-fourth book of the Iliad.   That contributor was Lockhart.   He mentions Wolf's specimen, which he has never been able to procure ; nor had he Voss's own translation when he made his attempt.   He had not heard of the small specimen in Guest's " History of English Rhythms." Lockhart ends thus : " Should this experiment be

[1] *Quarterly Review*, vol. lxxxvii. p. 443.

received with any favour, the writer has in his portfolio a good deal of Homer, long since translated
in the same manner, and he would not be reluctant
to attempt the completion of an Iliad in English
hexameters, such as he can make them."

Mr. Matthew Arnold, when composing his
" Lectures on Homeric Translation," was mani-
festly unaware that he had been anticipated by
Lockhart in his theory that the English hexameter
is the proper vehicle.   That opinion, or heresy,
does not commend itself to me ; indeed I despair,
and say with Lockhart in " Peter's Letters,"
"properly speaking, there are no such things as
translations."   Verse in quantity is at least as much
opposed to the genius of the English, as verse in
rhyme to the genius of the Greek language.   We
have no fixed quantity, and our clashing consonants
lack the dactylic fluidity.   Mr. Matthew Arnold's
own specimens gave one word (*fire*), now as a dis-
syllable, now as a monosyllable, and his hexameters
were harsh :

"These lame hexameters, the strong-winged music of Homer!
Never did frog coarser croak upon our Helicon !"

In the following example from Lockhart, the first
syllable of "Never" is short, and is long in the
same line.   It is the dirge of Helen for Hector :—

"Hector, dearest to me above all in the house of my husband!
Husband, alas! that I name him, oh better that death had befallen!

Summer and winter have flown, and the twentieth year is
    accomplished
Since the calamity came, and I fled from the land of my fathers ;
Yet never word of complaint have I heard from thee, never of
    hardness,
But if another reproached, were it brother or sister of Paris,
Yea, or his mother (for mild evermore as a father was Priam),
Them didst thou check in their scorn and the bitterness yielded
    before thee,
Touched by thy kindness of soul and the words of thy gentle
    persuasion.
Therefore I weep, both for thee and myself, to all misery
    destined,
For there remains to me now in the war-swept wideness of Troia,
None either courteous or kind, but in all that behold me is
    horror."

It is a beautiful rendering of the words of the fairest
of women. The English hexameter, as Longfellow's
"Evangeline" proves, is not distasteful itself to
the popular mass of readers. But how it "runs in
the head!" The last line here is an unwitting
hexameter—

    " Not distasteful itself to the popular mass of readers !"

James Macpherson, Ossian Macpherson, writes a
hexameter by accident in his prose version of
Helen's dirge.

Doubtless to the Greeks, certainly to the Roman
writers, hexameters sometimes occurred involun-
tarily, as in Tacitus—

    " Urbem Romam a principio Reges habuere."

I have confessed to a dislike, perhaps pedantic, of

the English hexameter, yet in what translation—
Pope's, Cowper's, Lord Derby's—could we find
Helen's lament rendered at once so literally, and
with such spirit and poetry, as in Lockhart's specimen? Or take these lines on Niobe, after the
slaying of her children by Artemis and Apollo—

> "Yet still, far among rocks, in some wilderness lone of the
>   mountains,
>   Sipylus holds her, they say, where the nymphs in the desert
>   repose them,—
>   They that in beauty divine lead dances beside Achelous,—
>   There still, stone though she be, doth she brood on her harm
>   from the godheads."

On a close comparison of Lockhart's version with
the original, one finds, as must always be the case,
passages where one would prefer an altered phrase,
and, occasionally, a needless embellishment of the
original, as (in Helen's lament), "The *war-swept*
wideness of Troia."

Homer has only—

> "*In wide Troia.*"

But Lockhart's phrases are the phrases of a poet.
He is remarkably skilled in transferring the Greek
into the English idiom. Except, perhaps, Charles
Kingsley in lines like—

> "As when an osprey aloft, dark-eyebrowed, royally crested,"

I know no English poet who writes English hexameters more dulcet, and more rapid. Had Lock-

hart finished and published his task, and refined it into perfect accordance with scholarly requirements, certainly Mr. Arnold, at least, need have looked no further for his ideal Homer in English. *Quod petis hic est.* We cannot perhaps expect a great poet to desert original work for translation. Even if he does, his version of an author will necessarily contain too much of himself. Lord Tennyson, in his blank verse, made Homer Tennysonian. Pope made him Popeian, and only shone in the rhetorical parts, as the speech of Achilles in book ix. Lockhart had precisely the due qualifications for a translator, in sympathy, poetic feeling, and severe yet genial taste. He would have left a name for a popular yet close and spirited version of the Iliad. But he stole out a specimen or two, anonymously and unrecognised, and there left the matter, yielding to that diffidence of his which Scott had observed.[1]

These examples of Lockhart's muse may prove that he had much more of the poetic gift than many men who, in all literary periods, "commence poet," and win some few laurels. These men always take themselves, their work, and their claims with extreme seriousness. Lockhart never could do

---

[1] "Delta," the late accomplished Dr. Moir, quotes, with high praise, a poem of Lockhart's, "Napoleon," which, to speak the truth, does not rise above the vein of Mrs. Hemans. See "Poetical Literature of the Last Half Century," p. 299. Edinburgh, third edition, 1856. Lockhart refers to this "bookie" of Delta's in a letter to Wilson, in 1851.

this, and of poetry he had a very high conception and ideal. With no lofty opinion of himself and his merits, with a rarely high notion of what poetry and the poet are and should be, he could not present himself as a candidate for true poetical distinction. He rhymed for his pleasure, and only once he expressed his soul in verse. When we look round on the press of pushing poets, so concerned about themselves and their place, so avid of praise and recognition, we may admire the not untempted moderation and reserve of a better poet than most of them.

Concerning Lockhart as a caricaturist, I have scarcely the materials necessary for a judgment. To one large collection of his drawings I have been denied access. From this portfolio were taken some of the designs in Mrs. Gordon's "Life of Christopher North." It was the property of Lockhart's life-long friend, Mr. Cay. In a little old note-book of 1817, Lockhart has scrawled a few sketches in pen and ink of German students and of "meerschaumed Professors." At this time he either could not draw hands, or did not take the trouble. The stolid transcendental complacency of a Teutonic scholar, with pipe and beer, is happily rendered. Another is smoking in his night-shirt, standing, and off his balance, a fault also in Lockhart's hasty sketch of Tom Purdie, Scott's forester. The same volume contains notes for Scott's Life, and notes of law cases in which Lockhart was engaged at Inverary, Highland *hamesucken* and violent assaults and batteries.

At Abbotsford there is a little collection of his drawings, made on wet days, to amuse the family. Some are in colour, for example, Fenella meeting Charles II. in St. James's Park; the extremely artificial figurante bounds dancing in air at an impossible height; the courtiers and the cheerful monarch look on. One is reminded, by Fenella, of Thackeray's *Flore et Zephyre*, indeed Lockhart's powers in verse, and with the pencil, are related to his genius in general much as Thackeray's poems and caricatures stand related to his literary work. They are pleasant *parerga*. Thackeray had tried far harder than Lockhart to learn to draw, but Lockhart (as in his illustrations to "Peter's Letters") was wont to take more pains over the execution of a portrait. Thackeray dealt more in general fantasy, Lockhart in personal caricature. Each was fond of caricaturing himself: Thackeray often drew the flat-nosed, melancholy humourist; Lockhart, the sour, close-lipped Spanish scholar or hidalgo. Thackeray sketched beautiful faces, or, at least, *one* beautiful face, easily recognised. One has seen it again and again, in the collection at Clevedon Court, and in "Vanity Fair." From Lockhart's pencil (having had little luck in recovering his drawings), I only know two sketches of a woman, first, Miss Scott playing on the harp, a rather timidly executed but interesting piece in pencil,

Park.

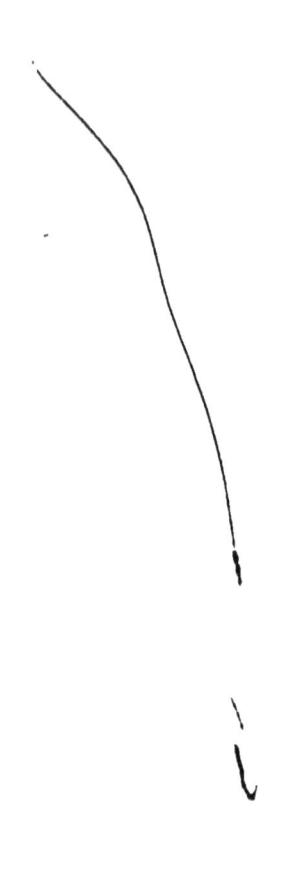

heightened with white, on brown paper. In a collection given by Tom Hamilton to Lady Brewster, there is a charming design of Lockhart's sister, Scott's "pretty Violet," executed in sepia with the brush. In the same portfolio are the Odontist, in colour on a dark ground; a brilliantly tinted group of Dons reading the *Edinburgh Review*; a laughable drawing of a frequenter of the Oxford Cockpit; several caricatures of Sir William Hamilton (in one, he is overloading a porter with books), and a large view of the Glasgow Presbytery, denouncing a Catholic Chapel. Among them—not burlesqued—is the strong, handsome profile of Dr. Lockhart.[1] In the Abbotsford set, there is also a large rough drawing in colour, of Lockhart, Scott (apparently), and another, riding in a dark rainy day, within three miles of Selkirk, as a road-post indicates. There is also a sketch of Charles Scott, as a lad, on brown paper; a little colour is used, there is a likeness to Sir Walter. Two comic old-fashioned figures of men, rather elaborately coloured, a still more finished head of a barrister in wig and gown, and a few scraps, make up the little Abbotsford collection. Lockhart had a good deal of faculty and skill in catching a likeness: there is a drawing by him of Wilson much inspired by punch, which is said to be curious, but I have not seen it, nor have I seen any caricatures of his that any but a very dull and pre-

---

[1] This fine collection is now the property of Mr. Brewster Macpherson, to whom I owe a view of it.

judiced person could call ill-natured. As Mr. Christie informs us, he gave up the practice of caricature altogether about the time when he went to London. Perhaps he knew that "fules," as the Shepherd says, dreaded his "keelavine pen," and so abstained from a source of offence. But the Dean of Salisbury says that he went on drawing, and remembers a sketch of Lady Eastlake at a party. A reference of his own to his powers of portraiture will be found in a letter to Wilson, of 1851. It is a pity that he did not leave a larger collection of his drawings of the family at Abbotsford. His colour is always very vivid and clever: reproductions in black and white do him no justice.

CHAPTER XII

CHIEFSWOOD, 1821-1825

WE have broken the continuous record of a time still uneventful, to speak of Lockhart's prowess with the pencil, and of his qualities as a writer of verse. There is, indeed, nothing of note to be said about the movements "from the blue bed to the brown," from Edinburgh to Chiefswood, where the nature of the pleasant life, with its guests, its rides, its visits to local shrines and friendly country houses, has been sufficiently described. Lockhart thought nothing, he says in a letter, of riding after dinner from Chiefswood to Edinburgh, if business or pleasure called him.

In that always dear and then still unspoiled land of many streams, where the day's ride led up stately Tweed, or Ettrick, or Yarrow, or to the lochs whence Yarrow flows, or by brown Ail water, or broadening Teviot, life indeed "for ever flowed like a river." But already there were sounds ominous of the coming straits and falls, and of the parting of the waters and the ways. In the course of the following chapter, we shall find Scott and Lockhart sundered, and the old happy time for ever ended.

In January 1824, a daughter was born to the Lockharts, and it seemed that their affections would no longer be settled on a single hope. On February 9, as Lockhart was obliged to go to Edinburgh, Scott talks of taking Mrs. Lockhart to Abbotsford. "Betwixt indolence of her own and Lockhart's extreme anxiety and indulgence, she has foregone the custom of her exercise, to which, please God, we will bring her back by degrees."[1] On March 4, writing to Lady Abercorn, Scott mentions his uneasiness about Hugh Littlejohn, who "came to this world rather too early, and, though a pretty, clever, and very engaging infant, alarms me a little from the slenderness of his frame, and a sort of delicacy of health sometimes connected with premature development of intellect. Sophia was again

[1] "Life," vii. 232.

confined about two months ago, but lost her infant, and has had but a slow and precarious recovery, which, indeed, is yet far from complete. Her face," Sir Walter says, "will soon attain its natural and most extensive circumference of half-a-crown." [1] He also attributes little Johnnie's precocity to "being much with grown-up people; . . . yet an only child is like a blot at backgammon, and fate is apt to hit it."

Lockhart himself writes, about the loss of the little girl—

"MY DEAREST FATHER,—It has pleased God to take our infant from us. The doctors despaired yesterday, but were not so kind as to say so. She died, without apparently any pain, at six this morning.

"Sophia bears this affliction with her usual firmness and gentleness,—sensible that, had it been deferred, every hour would have made it greater,—and thankful for what is left. Her calmness is such that we do not fear any ill effect upon her own state.

"Some of us will write to-morrow again. My dear mother, Violet, and Johnny are all well.—Yours most affectionately,

"J. G. L.

"NORTHUMBERLAND STREET." [2]

---

[1] To Miss Baillie, "Life," vii. 234.
[2] No date.

At this time Lockhart must have been seeing his fourth novel, "Matthew Wald," through the press, for Sir Walter writes to Lady Abercorn—" I cannot say I like it, it is full of power, but disagreeable, and ends vilely ill. . . . Lockhart is just now in London," whence we find him writing to Wilson at Elleray, and settling the question (about which Scott professes ignorance), as to whether he is contributing to *Blackwood*, or not.   He "spent three very pleasant days with Christie," and met, among other lions, Hook, Canning, Rogers, Maginn, Gifford, Irving (the popular preacher), Wilkie, and Coleridge. "The last is worth all the rest, and five hundred more such into the bargain."   Irving he calls "a pure humbug," and Sir Walter himself was not favourably impressed by that famous friend of Carlyle's.   Lockhart criticises *Maga* as if he had little part in it, and he threatens to "puff" "Matthew Wald" himself, if no one else will.[1]   He also promises a "Noctes," for they never spoke of a "Nox Ambrosiana."[2]   The original ends "burn or forget," but the recipient of such a monition usually forgets to burn.   The letter contains political surmises to be "forgotten" now much out of date, and by none remembered.

---

[1] I know not if this threat was serious. Southey, writing to Messrs. Longmans, proposes to edit a reprint of an old book, "accompanying it with preface and notes, and I would take care of it afterwards in the *Quarterly Review*."—("Selections from the Letters of Robert Southey," iii. 441. London, 1856.)

[2] "Christopher North," ii. 71, 74.

It seems possible that this expedition to London was important in a manner not expected by Lockhart. He met Canning, as we saw; he met him again in the Lake country, in August 1825, and the old writer in the *Antijacobin* may have been attracted to the young man of letters. Hence, Scott thought, might have come the suggestion of appointing Lockhart to the *Quarterly Review*. But Lockhart for the moment was concerned with his legal prospects and his novel. A novel like "Matthew Wald," as described by Scott, "full of power, but disagreeable, and ending vilely," was an obvious foreshadowing of the kind of romance which has pleased the last freak of fashion, or the last but one.[1] The hero, who tells his own tale, is a violent, and, so to say, Brontesque person. His passionate behaviour ends in a madness, from which he recovers, nor is anything of his secret suspected, it seems, till his Memoir is found, after his death. Quotations from Wordsworth on the title-page, and elsewhere, suggest that, to Lockhart's mind, he had found a Wordsworthian situation, the black tempestuous day of Matthew Wald closing in to a quiet and cheerful evening. The idea may be poetical, the execution, however, is inadequate. There are some good pictures of Scottish characters, especially the sketch of an old Lord of Session at his country house. But the construction is defective and straggling, there are far too many side issues

[1] 1896.

and digressions for so short a story.   Perhaps no
novel of that date is so modern in its disagreeable-
ness, and the unpleasant quality which was already
called "power."   If Lockhart ever again wrote an
anonymous work of fiction (Scott suspected him of
Galt's "The Omen"), the secret has never been
discovered.   Scott, writing to Lady Abercorn (June
4, 1824), says that "Reginald Dalton" "had great
success," and that "Matthew Wald" "is misery
from the title-page to the finis."

For the rest, in the absence of letters, the other
events of Lockhart's traceable history, in 1824, are
but two.   He was guilty of the false quantity, *ad
januam domini,* in the inscription for Maida's effigy:
and, in a three days' fire, which devastated the Old
Town of Edinburgh, he was "on duty, wet to the
skin and *elegant,* with a naked sword in his hand,
the very picture of a distressed hero in a strolling
party's tragedy."   The Yeomanry had been called
out, "by torch and trumpet fast arrayed."[1]

Thus a vivid light falls for a moment on Lock-
hart in the aspect of a hero of Gautier or of
Scarron, in "Le Capitaine Fracasse," or "Le
Roman Comique."

The Yule of 1824 had been peculiarly brilliant
at Abbotsford.   Captain Basil Hall's Journal, kept
there during the festivals before the marriage of
Scott's eldest son, was published by Lockhart in

[1] "Life," vii. 275-281, with Sir Walter's poem on the false quantity.
"Letters," ii. 226.

the " Life": of course he cut out all references to himself, and we know, by a letter of Basil Hall's, that such references existed. The original manuscript cannot now be recovered, but, after Captain Hall's "flourish of trumpets," and "scene of unclouded prosperity and splendour, the muffled drum is in prospect." [1]

At this time, in the spring of 1825, Scott was trying to procure for Lockhart the not very remunerative post of Sheriff of Sutherland. His letters to the Marchioness of Stafford (from Sir William Frazer's " Book of Sutherland ") are very characteristic, and explain the situation :—

"ABBOTSFORD, [2] *April* 11, 1825.

" MY DEAR LADY STAFFORD,—Allow me to express my sincere and most grateful thanks for the kind manner in which your ladyship has condescended to Lockhart's concern. I have heard nothing of the matter myself for several weeks and months. My friend, the advocate, was so intolerably wise and mysterious on the subject, the last time it was mentioned, that I vow that to be made Sheriff of all Scotland, either in a friend's person or my own, I could not have attempted again to penetrate the deep and awful gloom. The game to be played is a sort of gambit at chess. First, old Mr. Ferriar is

[1] " Life," vii. 343.
[2] From the "Sutherland Book," by Sir William Frazer, K.C.B., vol. ii. pp. 325, 326.

to be permitted to resign his office of Clerk of Session on some superannuation, the poor gentleman being upwards of eighty years old, and having wasted eyes, years, and understanding to the last dregs in writing the judgments of the Court of Session for thirty or forty (years). This old horse released from the carriage, James Fergusson, who vacates a place called a commissaryship, where he judges of all the iniquities of marrying and not marrying, and marrying once too often, and getting unmarried again altogether, is to be conferred on your present Sheriff, Charles Ross. *Et puis* Charles Ross having succeeded to all these functions of marrying and putting asunder, I have been led to entertain hopes that Lockhart may succeed in his place. I should be delighted in it, for it is always getting *pignon sur la vie*, and I think Lord Stafford and your ladyship would be gratified with his acquaintance, as he is perfectly a gentleman, and with a very uncommon share of talent and information. When this happy consummation will take place, or whether it is likely to take place at all, I really do not know. Like the old beggar with the blue cloak and the pikestaff, I can submit to make one bow, and hold my hat out once, for what is not worth asking is not worth having. But I am too old and stiff to gird up my loins and run after folks' chariot wheels till they give to importunity. But after all, this is only a petted way of taking the little diplomatic secrecy which great folks observe

on great occasions, such as bestowing Sheriffdoms;
and I dare say I am complaining without reason.
Only I cannot forget that I went expressly on
purpose to Dalkeith when the Lord Advocate
wished to be Sheriff of Edinburgh, which he got
entirely by my interest with the late Duke of
Buccleuch, and I never kept him a moment in
suspense about the matter."

.   .   .   .   .   .

"EDINBURGH, 23rd June 1825.[1]

"MY DEAR LADY MARCHIONESS,—If you give a
dog a bone, he will follow you through half-a-dozen
streets; and so it is with obligations bestowed on
the human race, they are no sooner conferred
than they are made the pretence of further
teasing. But your ladyship's great kindness encourages this species of persecution, and your
flattering inquiries about Lockhart's probable success as to Sutherland makes it incumbent on me
to mention any little progress that has been
made with respect to that Sheriffdom. . . . I own
I should be much better pleased with his having
Sutherland rather than Caithness for his own sake,
and being of a good presence, and certainly clever
enough, he would become the halls of Dunrobin
better than a thing disagreeable to the eye and
very tiresome to the ear. But the whole arrange-

[1] From the "Sutherland Book," by Sir William Frazer, K.C.B.,
vol. ii. pp. 327, 328.

ment about Sutherland must lie over until James Ferriar retires from the clerk's table, to make way for James Fergusson, who vacates a commissariat to make way for Charles Ross, who leaves Sutherland to give place, I would fain hope, to Lockhart—upon the old principle of the cat to the rat, the rat to the halter, the halter to the butcher, the butcher to the ox, and so forth. . . . My informer seems to have a superstitious fear of all this valuable information transpiring, so it is only designed for your ladyship's private ear. . . ."

.   .   .   .   .   .

In May 1825, Lockhart, as he says in the " Life," was present at a consultation, in Abbotsford, over Mr. Constable's great scheme, "the cleverest thing that ever came into that cleverest of bibliopolic heads," as Scott remarked, "that magnificent conception,"—to quote Lockhart,—of cheap literature. The manner of Constable seems to have been more excited than was in harmony with his skill in making a curious accumulation of pregnant facts. The description of the scene in the " Life " is undeniably vivid, though Mr. Thomas Constable, in his Memoir of his father, not unnaturally finds it "distasteful to his filial reverence," and believes, (as did his father) that the publisher, not the author, suggested the " Life of Napoleon." Lockhart's memory was good, but Constable spoke nearer the time of the events. Possibly both views may be correct, and Scott may have anticipated a part of the scheme already present to the mind of Constable. Lockhart was to write, as he did later, a "Life of Burns," and he suggested "a *readable* abridgment of M'Crie's 'Life of Knox,' leaving out all the controversial stuff, and much of the angry feeling," and giving "the mere personal history of a good and great man, whose name can never cease to be interesting in Scotland."[1] Lockhart also suggested a "Poor Man's Law Book." "You will agree with me that they are at present curious in regard to such subjects, that they ought to be so, and that it is a shame they have not the means of reading what concerns them all in an intelligible form."

There is a tradition that when some one once spoke of "educating the people," Lockhart said, "Educate the devil!" His suggestions do not read as if that was his mature opinion. Neither Constable, nor any one else, seems to have reflected that, if the rich did not spend ten pounds a year on books (which was admitted), the poor were not likely to spend ten shillings.[2]

Meanwhile "Taffey," that is, the Rev. Mr. Williams, had been appointed the first Head Master of the new Edinburgh Academy, and had

---

[1] Mr. Robert Louis Stevenson has written very freely on the *readableness* of M'Crie's "Knox."

[2] "Life," vii. 382. "Archibald Constable," iii. 309. Southey, as early as 1820, was proposing this idea of good books (his own) at a cheap rate.

suggested, "by his lively and instructive conversation on Welsh history and antiquities," the idea of "The Betrothed." In the introduction, Scott made merry over "a Joint Stock Company for writing and publishing the Class of Works called the Waverley Novels." In the same spirit he had, in an unpublished note, recommended Lockhart to make a company for the repair of the dam and dyke of the little burn at Chiefswood. The sorrows of Joint Stock Companies were gathering, but were not yet foreseen.

On July 8, Scott, Miss Anne Scott, and Lockhart sailed for Ireland, and the narrative of the tour exists in his published letters to his wife.[1] To have been anticipated with these bright and humorous epistles is a sorrow to a biographer. On the return of the party they visited Wilson at Elleray,[2] whence Lockhart wrote a description of the ladies of Llangollen, and "their great romance, *alias* absurd innocence." "I shall never see the spirit of bluestockingism again in such perfect incarnation."[3]

[1] "Letters of Scott," ii. 296–343.

[2] Wilson was an extraordinary being! Immediately after the meeting with Scott and Wordsworth in the Lake country, he viciously attacked Wordsworth's Poems, and personal manner, in the "Noctes Ambrosianæ" for September 1825. The "Nox" is in the collected edition of these papers. At this time, too (autumn of 1825), he used the most awful and unprofessorial language, in a letter to Lockhart, about Mr. Blackwood. The "Nox" may have been written *before* the meeting with Wordsworth, and I understand that Wilson regretted it. But, for some reason, he disliked "the Stamp-Master," as we shall see.

[3] "Life," viii. 48–50.

When the "Life" was published, some "tabbies" objected to this sketch. "Was I not," wrote Lockhart to Mrs. Hughes, "to give one sketch of blue-stockingism in the life of a man who suffered so much under it?"[1] Canning was at Storrs, near Elleray, and Wordsworth "evidently thinks Canning and Scott together not worth his thumb," which does not exaggerate the poet's self-estimate! "Wordsworth told Wilson yesterday he thought Canning seemed to have no mind at all," for the statesman evinced little interest "in these humbugs, the principles of poetry," nor had Wordsworth any other topic. They met Quillinan, Wordsworth's son-in-law, who had once contemplated challenging Lockhart for a review of his Poems, which Lockhart had not written. "Wordsworth knew all about his history in Scotland, and spoke gaily thereof." Wordsworth and Scott quoted Wordsworth's Poems all day, but the great Laker never by one syllable implied that Scott had written a line either of verse or prose. Whether these foibles amused Scott or Lockhart most, in the secret of their hearts, it would not be easy to guess. Southey "was very civil." (August 25, 1829.)

Lockhart was wearying for Chiefswood, and the privilege of "kissing Johnny red and blue" personally, not by deputy. This he enjoyed on September 1.

On arriving at Chiefswood, Lockhart returned

---

[1] Letter quoted in *Quarterly Review*, vol. cxvi. p. 472.

to literary work with even unusual industry. He was weary of *Blackwood.* Maginn was imploring him to write songs in *John Bull.* "I shall take care to keep you out of scrapes." Lockhart can hardly have cared for "Bardolph's security." "You will have perceived that I have done very little this summer," he writes to Wilson. "How could I? I am totally sick of all that sort of concern. . . ."

He was occupied with worthier things, a proposed edition of Shakespeare by Scott and himself. "I have spent five or six hours on Shakespeare regularly." He had also conceived a scheme of much less promise than his ideas for literary enterprises usually were. This was the composition, by himself and Wilson, with a little aid from Miss Edgeworth, of "Janus." Now "Janus," to be frank, might be described as a volume of magazine padding. The tome was intended to be the first of a series of Books of Sense, as it were, in opposition to "Books of Beauty." Having no seductive embellishments, it was a failure, as far as the publishers (Messrs. Oliver & Boyd) were concerned.[1] Lockhart's industry, at least, is attested by the large amount of his contributions, which have now no particular interest. A curious essay on the Ordeal

---

[1] Mrs. Gordon ("Christopher North," ii. 88) attributes the original idea of "Janus," and its publication by Oliver & Boyd, to Lockhart's impatience with Mr. Blackwood. Probably Mrs. Gordon had not read her father's letters to Lockhart. Christopher North's remarks on Mr. Blackwood in 1825 are of the most florid eloquence.

by Fire has most merit, unless we prefer an article
on Universities. Though neither in good health
nor in good spirits, Lockhart "found repose in
being busy," as was ever his way, and amusement
in the society of Abbotsford.

There, alas! things were altering. Still the flag
flew that called the countryside to "the burning
of the water,"—the salmon leistering,—still the
guests came and went "admiring, and sometimes
admired." But, in the study at Abbotsford, the
"white head erect, with the smile of inspiration on
the lips," was no more to be seen, and Lockhart
beheld, with regret, Sir Walter "stooping and
poring with his spectacles, amidst piles of authorities,
a little note-book ready in the left hand that had
always been used to be at liberty for patting
Maida." Maida was dead, and dead was old Hins of
Hinsfeldt. Meanwhile Lockhart, as he says, had
to consult Sir Walter on literary projects, involving
the abandonment of Chiefswood and Edinburgh.
"There were then about me, indeed, cares and
anxieties of various sorts, that might have thrown
a shade even over a brighter vision of his interior.
For the circumstance that finally determined me,
and reconciled him as to the proposed alteration
in my views of life, was the failing health of an
infant equally dear to us both. It was, in a word,
the opinion of our medical friends, that the short-
lived child of many and high hopes, whose name
will go down to posterity with one of Sir Walter's

most precious works, could hardly survive another northern winter ; and we all flattered ourselves with the anticipation that my removal to London, at the close of 1825, might pave the way for a happy resumption of the cottage at Chiefswood in the ensuing summer. *Dis aliter visum.*" [1]

Another domestic sorrow, of the kind which cannot but be anticipated, but may, none the less, be bitter, was approaching. His grandmother, to whom his earliest extant letter was written, lay at the point of death. Not to interrupt the story of his appointment to the *Quarterly Review*, his letter on the news of her decease may be given here :—

" MY DEAR FATHER,—Being called up to town on some business, about which I cannot, just at present, write (but which has nothing disagreeable in it), I have received here to-day" (in London), "by a letter from Sophia, my first accounts of my dear grandmother's death. Before my letter reaches you the grave has closed over her remains, and I have been deprived even of the painful pleasure of partaking in the last service. I know all reason and sense are against it, but I can't tell you, nevertheless, how much I feel saddened. You, no doubt, have still more deeply the same natural impression to struggle against. Whatever consolation the memory of kindness, excellence, and piety can give us, we surely have. I shall not write any more at present.

[1] " Life," viii. 64.

I hope to be in Scotland again in the course of a
week, and shall certainly come to Germistoun immediately unless there should be a prospect of your
coming to us. I beg my warmest love to my dear
mother and the family.—Your affectionate and dutiful son,   J. G. LOCKHART.

"6 STONE BUILDINGS, LINCOLN'S INN,
    Friday, October 14, 1825."

Lockhart's business in town was to see Mr.
Murray, the publisher, who, at first, wished him to
be, not the Editor, but the general adviser as to a
newspaper, and who also offered him the Editorship
of the *Quarterly Review*. The *Quarterly* was, and
had for two or three years, been in an unsettled
condition. Gifford's health had been very bad, and
he now spoke of retiring, now struggled on, "and
oft said farewell, yet seemed loth to depart." He
was so reduced that he had actually printed an article
of Southey's "without mutilation," a melancholy and
menacing symptom of decay. As early as October
18, 1822, Southey revealed a scheme to Grosvenor
Bedford. If Gifford died, or resigned, it was intended (unless the malcontents approved of his
successor) to start a rival Quarterly. Terms were
offered to Southey, if he would desert Murray, and
act as Editor of the new periodical. "This has
been communicated to me by John Coleridge. My
wish is that he should be Gifford's successor. . . .
Should that arrangement take place, this scheme

falls to the ground at once, otherwise . . . it is very probable that it will be tried," though Southey does not think it likely that he himself will go to town as Editor. " Murray's conduct has not been such as to make me feel bound to him in the slightest degree ; and no future Editor shall ever treat my papers as Gifford has done."[1]

The essence of the scheme then was, Mr. John Taylor Coleridge for Editor of the *Quarterly Review*, or a rival Review—"an excellent plot, good friends." Mr. Murray was, perhaps, not aware of this result of the ingenuity of Mr. Coleridge. Had he known about it, he might not have wished Mr. Coleridge to assist Gifford in his editorial duties during 1822. In May 1823, Mr. Murray, to prevent any disappointment, informed Mr. Coleridge that Gifford was very well. " During his life no change is likely to be made, and when any change is necessary it will not, as I always stated, depend on me. The subject should not, therefore, be allowed to influence in the slightest degree your other views and arrangements." On December 9, 1824, Mr. Murray offered Mr. Coleridge the appointment which, since the inception of his plan of 1822, he seems to have desired.[2] " Murray may thank me," wrote Southey to Rickman, "for having provided him with an Editor, for he knew not where to find one." In accepting the offer Mr. Coleridge made some allusions to the recent increase

---

[1] " Selected Letters of Southey," iii. 337.
[2] " Memoir of John Murray," ii. 164.

in his practice at the Bar, which was becoming considerable.

Behold, then, Mr. Coleridge in the editorial chair of the *Quarterly*, in December 1824, to the joy of Southey. Yet, on October 20, 1825, the sceptre had passed from Southey's friend, and Lockhart had been appointed in his place. How did this sudden change come about? On this point it is necessary to quote a letter of Southey to Rickman, of December 4, 1825. "I do not know for what reason Murray has thought proper to change his Editor. His own story to John Coleridge has been plumply contradicted to me by the only person who can contradict it (Sir W. Scott), and he is so well aware that I shall not like the change, that he has not yet written to me on the subject."[1]

Now, what was "Murray's story to John Coleridge"? *That* Southey does not tell us, but we do know what Sir Walter "contradicted." He contradicted the idea (which he thought might arise in Southey's mind) that he had taken any part in suggesting Lockhart as a supplanter of Mr. Coleridge. "A letter from Lockhart from London" (about October 12–15) "was the first intimation that I had of the subject. . . ."[2] And in the end of October" (in fact on October 20) "the transaction was regularly concluded. I mention these par-

---

[1] "Selected Letters of Southey," iii. 514.
[2] *Journal*, i. 27. "First a hint from Wright," says Scott. The hint was of October 3.

ticulars, because you might think it odd that when we spoke together at Keswick on the subject of the *Quarterly*, I never hinted at this transaction, in which I was so nearly connected; still less would I like you to entertain an idea that either Lockhart or I had thought of soliciting or manœuvring for such a situation while it was in the hands of another and most respectable gentleman."

It may be said that this letter of Scott's should have been written earlier. But it was written partly because a month after the conclusion of the formal treaty of October 20, 1825, Mr. Murray was perturbed by the objections, based on the old *Blackwood* brawls, of many friends of the *Quarterly*. Scott, therefore, wrote to Southey on *that* topic (without producing much effect on the Laureate's mind), and at the same time he protested against the notion that *he* had suggested Lockhart's appointment. As Scott writes in his *Journal* (November 27, 1825), " I never was more surprised than when this proposal came upon us." Again (November 29), " It was no plot of my making, I am sure ; yet men will say and believe that it was, though I never heard a word of the matter, *till first a hint from Wright*, and then the formal proposal of Murray to Lockhart announced (*sic*). I believe Canning and Charles Ellis were the prime movers. I'll puzzle my brains no more about it."

If any one is so unhappily constituted as to suppose that Sir Walter equivocated on this point to Southey, in a letter, and to posterity, in his *Journal*, the critic may be referred to a letter of Scott to Murray (November 17, 1825)—"The plan (I need not remind you) of calling Lockhart to this distinguished position, far from being favoured by me, or in any respect advanced or furthered by such interest as I might have urged, was not communicated to me until it was formed. . . ."

Now it is absolutely impossible that if the scheme had originally come from Sir Walter, he should have "reminded" Murray that he had nothing to do with the matter.[1] If these facts leave any one in the opinion which Scott himself expected men to entertain, we reserve for him something more.

The appointment of Lockhart, though obviously not solicited by Scott, is still, in some respects, as great a puzzle as Sir Walter found it. Mr. Coleridge was, it seems, advancing rapidly in his profession, and no wise barrister would prefer an editorship to such prospects of success as now lay before him. Whatever the exact facts about his demission of the *Quarterly* may have been, both Scott and Lockhart, in published and unpublished letters, agree in praising the magnanimity of Mr. Coleridge's behaviour.

As far as can be guessed, the choice of Lockhart for Mr. Coleridge's successor found occasion in a scheme of Mr. Benjamin Disraeli's, at that time a

---

[1] "Memoir of John Murray," ii. 184.

handsome, imaginative, and persuasive lad of twenty. There was then a fever of commercial speculation preluding to the "crash" of 1826. Young Disraeli had connected himself with, and had written pamphlets for, "at least one financing firm in the City, that of Messrs. Powles."[1]   Next, he, by his magical tongue, actually induced Mr. Murray to join these eminent capitalists, Mr. Powles and Mr. Benjamin Disraeli, in starting a magnificent new daily paper (Aug. 3, 1825).[2]   An editor, or at least an adviser, being wanted, Mr. Disraeli was sent to Scotland to consult Sir Walter, and to secure Lockhart if possible.[3] Mr. Disraeli's advent, and descent on Chiefswood, were heralded or accompanied by a letter from Mr. Wright.   In this letter of September 12, Wright, by Murray's wish, suggests the place of superintendent of the new paper.   He believes that Canning wishes Lockhart to accept.   He thanks Lockhart and Scott for kindness to himself in Edinburgh. He introduces "Mr. Disraeli," *not* Mr. *Benjamin* Disraeli.

Mr. Disraeli went to Scotland, and arranged with Murray a code of counterfeit names, and so forth, as if a Jameson conspiracy was toward!   Of course, in his letters all these veils are neglected or withdrawn.   Lockhart, so far, was, as he himself says in a note to Disraeli, "perfectly in the dark"

---

[1] "Memoir of John Murray," ii. 185.   [2] Ibid., ii. 186.

[3] William Wright to J. G. Lockhart, Stone Buildings, Lincoln's Inn ; September 12, 1825.

as to the purpose of his visit;[1] indeed he supposed
that Isaac D'Israeli, the well-known author, the
father of Benjamin, was to be his guest. His
natural reserve, as D'Israeli tells Murray, was not
diminished by his surprise at beholding a fair young
Hebrew boy. However, they soon "understood
each other" (which perhaps they did *not*); Lockhart
objecting, none the less, first, to leave Edinburgh
without "ostensible purpose"; next, "to the loss of
caste in society by so doing"—that is, I presume,
by editing a *newspaper*. Scott took the same
view, and Dizzy talked about Lockhart's not being
a newspaper editor, but "Director General of an
immense organ."[2] "With regard to other plans of
ours we should find him invaluable. I have a most
singular and secret history on this subject when we
meet." Mystery!

If any one hazards the conjecture (which I have
heard whispered), that by this reference to "other
plans," and "secret history," Mr. Disraeli meant
a suggestion by Scott that Lockhart should sup-
plant Mr. Coleridge in the *Quarterly*, it may be
answered that neither Lockhart nor Sir Walter,
in their letters to Mr. Murray of October 7 and
October 12, mention the *Quarterly* scheme at all.
Both merely protest against what Lockhart calls
"the impossibility of my ever entering into the
career of London in the capacity of a newspaper
editor. . . . If such a game *ought* to be played,

[1] "Memoir of John Murray," ii. 190.   [2] Ibid., ii. 192.

I am neither young enough nor poor enough to be the man that takes the hazard." On October 12, Sir Walter wrote to Mr. Murray about "the plan which you have had the kindness to submit to Lockhart. . . . I cannot conceive it advisable that he should leave Scotland on the speculation of becoming editor of a newspaper." He then speaks of Lockhart's "views" in Scotland as "moderate but certain," and adds that Lockhart "meets your wishes by going up to town."

Not a word about the *Quarterly*. The *Quarterly* is first heard of, and then only by way of the past history of a project of Mr. Wright's, in a letter from that gentleman :[1]—

"I saw Murray soon after my return from Edinburgh. We conversed on the subject of the *Quarterly Review*. He disapproved of his Editor, and I recommended, and he approved of *you*, and I was desired to write on the subject; but afterwards I was desired to suspend for a while my communication. For the newspaper business I did not recommend you as fit; but on being asked as to your fitness and inclinations, I stated my belief in your fitness, accompanied with strong observations as to its unsuitableness to your rank and feelings, and I believe Mr. Canning, on being spoken to by Mr. Ellice, said

[1] William Wright to J. G. Lockhart, 6 Stone Buildings, Lincoln's Inn ; October 3, 1825.

you could come as Editor of the *Quarterly*, but
not as editor of a newspaper, or at least as known
and reputed editor. I told Disraeli before he
left he had a very delicate mission, and that
though my rank in life was different to your
own, having no relations whose feelings could
be wounded by my accepting any honest employ-
ment, I should not receive an offer of the editorship of a newspaper as a compliment to my feelings
as a barrister and a gentleman, however compli-
mentary it might be as to my talents. In short,
I enter entirely into your feelings on this head,
and we think alike, for, whatever our friend
Disraeli may say or flourish on this subject, your
accepting of the editorship of a newspaper would
be *infra dig.*, and a losing of caste; but not so,
as I think, the accepting of the editorship of the
Quarterly Review. . . . Murray will in his letter,
I presume, offer you the *Quarterly*, but as to
bargaining, and making your contract certain and
available, when you have agreed on general principles, you may, I think, trust that to me; and
though I should like you for a neighbour, weigh
all things well, and let not haste cause you
to overrun your discretion and so bar judgment.
An editor of a Review like the *Quarterly* is
the office of a scholar and a gentleman; but that
of a newspaper is *not*, for a newspaper is merely
stock-in-trade, to be used as it can be turned to
most profit. And there is something in it (when

Disraeli has gilded and adorned it with his new notions as much as he can) that is repugnant to the feelings of a gentleman. . . . If you think of accepting Murray's proposals in any shape, leave all particulars to discussion and arrangement after you come to London, and let us talk the matter over first for a few hours oursel ves.[1]

"Disraeli, who is with you, I have not seen much of, but I believe he is a sensible, clever young fellow. His judgment, however, wants settling down. He has never had to struggle with a single difficulty, nor been called on to act in any affairs in which his mind has been necessarily forced to decide and choose in difficult situations. At present his chief exertions as to matters of decision have been with regard to the selection of his food, his enjoyment, and his clothing, and though he is honest, and, I take it, wiser than his father, he is inexperienced and untried in the world, and of course though you may, I believe, safely trust to his integrity, you cannot prudently trust much to his judgment.

"Sir Walter was so good as to promise me a little dog. Has he such a thing for me? If so, our friend Constable promised to take care of it for me. I believe you were thought of for the newspaper from what had passed as to the *Review*, and the conversations about you were between Ellice

---

[1] The lines omitted contain a criticism of Mr. Murray, conjectural, and probably baseless.

and Canning, and, I think, not between Murray and Canning directly.—I am, dear Lockhart, yours most truly,   WILLIAM WRIGHT."

Here then, in the letter from Mr. Wright, which first hinted (as Scott says in his *Journal*) at the possibility of Lockhart's appointment to the *Quarterly*, we have all that is known to the compiler as to the origin of that appointment.   Mr. Murray "disapproved" of his Editor, Mr. Coleridge, which probably means that he did not regard so successful a barrister as likely to be *permanent* successor to Gifford.   Mr. Wright suggested Lockhart's name, and Murray liked the idea.   For reasons which will become apparent later, it is improbable that Canning had any concern in the matter.   Lockhart went up to town, and on October 13 Mr. Murray wrote to Scott, that, "to obviate any difficulties which have been urged, I have proposed to Mr. Lockhart to come to London as the Editor of the *Quarterly*, also as adviser about the newspaper, and about literary undertakings in general." [1]

The deeds between Mr. Murray and Lockhart as to the *Quarterly* and the newspaper, were signed and sealed on October 20, 1825.

All now seemed to be settled; but apparently about November 15–17, young Disraeli was sent down again to tell Sir Walter that objections to Lockhart were raised, by some of the *Quarterly*

[1] "Memoir of John Murray," ii. 199.

writers, on the old *Blackwood* score. Scott replied to Murray at length, on November 17, 1825; and on November 21, Mr. Disraeli, who had returned to town, wrote to Lockhart. Murray "has spoken to Coleridge" (that is, John Taylor Coleridge, Editor of the *Quarterly*), "and nothing could go off better. It is perfectly settled." But poor Mr. Disraeli himself is in great disgrace. He ought, it seems, to have mentioned the matter of the objections, not to Lockhart, but only to Sir Walter. However, in a couple of days Mr. Disraeli congratulates himself and Lockhart that all is well, and that "while Mr. Murray has cash in his pockets and blood in his veins, he stands by John Gibson Lockhart even unto the death."[1] Nothing can be more eloquent! Mr. Murray, writing on November 23, was equally explicit, but less ornate; or not so much less ornate after all. "Heaven and earth may pass away, but it (*sic*) cannot shake my opinion."[2] By December 2, Mr. Murray wrote about Lockhart's arrangements as to coming permanently to London. Lockhart had written to him, on November 19, as to the objections urged against him.[3] Thus, after being firmly fixed by the deed of October 20, 1825, the appointment had been, as far as such a covenant could be, imperilled by the opposition of several old *Quarterly*

---

[1] Scott's "Letters," ii. 414.   [2] Ibid., ii. 415.
[3] The letters are in "Memoir of John Murray," ii. 219, 230, and in the Appendix to Scott's "Letters."

Reviewers, such as Rose, Barrow, apparently Croker, and the junta in the Admiralty, whom Murray does not seem to have consulted. Few things could be more unsatisfactory. At length, in December, everything was settled.

The circumstances of Lockhart's accession to the *Quarterly* chair were, according to Scott, unembarrassed by any doubt as to Mr. Coleridge's position. "He put the question as to whether Mr. Coleridge's retiring was a thing determined on, and he received a positive answer in the affirmative. . . . I have only to add that Mr. Coleridge has most handsomely offered to continue his support to the *Review*, by the contribution of articles, a circumstance which is valuable of itself, and will be most grateful to Lockhart's feelings."[1] Sir Walter also thanks Southey for his own promise, in spite of his dissatisfaction, to continue his support by way of articles. He was a contributor till 1839.

Of Mr. Coleridge, so suddenly superseded in his editorial position, it must be repeated that he displayed the perfection of conduct in a very trying situation.

How, or why, or by whom Lockhart was selected as Editor of the *Quarterly*, unless it was by Mr. Murray's mere motion on Wright's suggestion, I am unable to say. The *Blackwood* stories were against him; he had done nothing serious in political writing; he was known, in letters, merely

[1] To Southey, November 28. "Letters," ii. 377.

as a scholar, a translator, an editor of "Don Quixote," and as a novelist. Moreover, the original idea was to make him a kind of general adviser, and occasional writer of political essays, in the magnificent organ projected by that young capitalist Mr. Benjamin Disraeli. Being at once eager about his newspaper, and uneasy about his Editor's (Mr. Coleridge's) professional work at the Bar, Mr. Murray was probably taken by what he saw of Lockhart, and it is obvious enough that he did not consult Southey, or Barrow, or Rose, or others of his usual associates, till he had signed and sealed the deed appointing Lockhart to the *Review*.

The nature of Lockhart's new duties is set forth in two legal documents of October 20. He is to edit the *Quarterly*, "and otherwise assist in the publishing business." For this he was to receive (for three years) £250 a quarter, or, if five numbers of the *Review* were published, £1250 per annum. William Wright and B. Disraeli witnessed the deed.

The second deed stipulated that for "hints and advice," and occasional articles in the contemplated newspaper, Mr. Murray should pay Lockhart £1500 a year. In case Lockhart prefers to exchange this salary for a share in the paper, that transaction is regulated by certain stipulations. Mr. Murray seals with a griffin, rampant; Lockhart's seal is not his crest or coat armour, but a profile of Byron, probably a seal lent by Mr. Murray. Byron, in his letters, says that this work of art makes him look like a negro. Lockhart's functions were obviously vague ; a newspaper editor he was not, nor was he qualified for that truly arduous and thankless life of laborious days and sleepless nights.

When all was finally settled, or even before, Sir Walter advised Lockhart to "take devilish good care of your start in society in London." Especially he was counselled not "to haunt Theodore Hook much. . . . He is *raffish, entre nous.*" Again, "You will have great temptation to drop into the *gown and slipper* garb of life," which Sir Walter hated with a righteous hatred, "and live with funny, easy companions," such as Theodore Hook and Maginn. It is one of the contradictions in Lockhart's character that, with a great deal of apparent "Hidalgo airs," he did take pleasure in "funny, easy companions." But society in general went far beyond him in a passion for the company of Theodore Hook—by all reports, a fellow of infinite fancy, whereof the sparkle is dead long ago.

Commercial affairs now looked ominous in London. Lockhart heard, in mid - November, disquieting rumours, which he communicated to Scott, who replied in a long letter, setting forth his grounds of confidence in Constable's house.[1]

On Lockhart's return to Chiefswood, Mr. Wright (who witnessed the deeds of October 20) informed him, by letter, of a report (unfounded in fact) that "Constable's banker had thrown up his book."

---

[1] Lockhart refers to this in the " Life," viii. 83.

Lockhart rode over to Abbotsford with the news. Scott made light of it, but next morning Lockhart found Scott's carriage at his door, and Sir Walter feeding the ducklings, with little Johnnie. He had driven to Polton, seen Constable, been reassured, and had driven back again. Then for the first time Lockhart suspected that Scott was deeply concerned in the fortunes of Constable. " The night journey suggested serious alarm," the more as the rumour sent previously by Lockhart from London had been of a very grave nature. Yet both reports were " such refraction of events as often rises ere they rise," and, in actual fact, baseless.

It is at this time that Scott (Nov. 23) " bespeaks " Mrs. Hughes' " affection for Lockhart," an affection which never failed him. " I know you will love and understand him, but he is not easy to be known or to be appreciated as he so well deserves, at first; he shrinks at a first touch; but take a good hard hammer (it need not be a sledge one), break the shell, and the kernel will repay you. Under a cold exterior Lockhart conceals the warmest affections, and where he once professes regard he never changes. . . ." He never did change—loyal himself where he loved, and a centre of loyalty in others.

So Scott wrote November 23, but apparently did not post his letter at once. On December 5 he told his son Walter about the *Bonspiel*, or farewell dinner to Lockhart. " About fifty people were present

—Solicitor-General, preses; Dundas of Arniston, croupier; and much wine shed. Many songs and speeches to the honour and glory of the said Don Giovanni, who fell asleep in his chair, about one in the morning, to the sound of his own praises. . . ."

Scott, on the same 5th of December, finished his letter of November 23 to Mrs. Hughes, expressing his fear of spine-complaint in little Johnnie, a forecast verified too soon. On December 5 the Lockharts left Abbotsford for London, "without any formal adieus, for which I thank them. They were off before daybreak." Scott then recommends Mrs. Lockhart to the maternal kindness of Mrs. Hughes, who gave all her affection, as Sir Walter had hoped. The family occupied a house in Pall Mall, though Mr. Murray had offered his hospitality. Probably they did not care to bring an ailing child under Mr. Murray's roof.

A little needful cheer is given to the exiles by a letter from Scott on Hogg, in which I make a few omissions. The story has been told before, but here is the original version.

"Hogg of the mountains made a descent this morning, perhaps in order to make a Bardic convention 'of huz Tividale poets,' and brought with him Thompson the song-making, not 'psalm-singing, weaver' of Galashiels. This was rather cool on the said Hogg's part, but Thompson is a good enough fellow, so it all went off well. Talking of Moore, or according to his mode of accentuation *Muir*, Hogg

said his songs were 'written wi' ower muckle melody
—they *gied* him,' he said, 'a *staw*[1] of sweetness.'
'Aye,' said Thompson, 'his notes are ower sweetly
strung.' 'Na, na,' said the partner, 'ma ain notes
are just right strung, and it's his that are clean ower
artificial.' Don't you think you hear this? I thought
Lady Anne would have spoken, but, thank God, she
gave a gulp and was silent. After all, Hogg is
kindly, very grateful to you."

By a rather high-handed act of editorial authority,
though under strong temptation, Lockhart had engaged Sir Walter to write on Mr. Pepys' Journals,
then newly published. Mr. Hughes, by Mr. Coleridge's desire, had already begun a review.[2] Sir
Walter's, however, occupies the first place in Lockhart's first number. The last article in the number
was on Moore's and other books about Sheridan.
Sir Walter writes :—

"EDINBURGH, 20*th December* 1825.

"MY DEAR LOCKHART,—I had your letter this
morning, and observe with great pleasure that you
are settled, or in the act of being so. It is better
you have got a good house, for there is scarce
anything in London so necessary to comfort and
credit. . . .

[1] Satiety.
[2] Mr. Murray, however, writes, "Mr. Croker has given up the
'Pepys' Papers,' and Mr. Bankes, the Member for Cambridge, wrote
to undertake them a few days ago. Of course you will induce Sir
Walter to persist in his kind intentions."—November 23, "Scott's
Letters," ii. 415.

" I observe, with very great interest, what you say concerning Tom Moore and Sheridan. It will be one of the most noble opportunities for an opening and leading article which you could have had. You will, I know, give Tom his full merits, and treat him with that sort of liberality which may show that the censure which you bestow comes out of no narrow party feeling, but is called forth by the occasion. I would have you take an opportunity to consider briefly his poetical rank. He may be considered as reformed in the point of his Erotiques, and I would not rake up old sins. There is one especial reason for candour in respect to his merits, because in order to blame him (which there is every reason for doing) for lending himself to circulate calumnies respecting the King, you must show that you are neither an enemy of genius, nor the tool of a party. I am aware that high-flying Tories will not be pleased with this. Nevertheless, fair pleading is the real way to serve a good cause. If a critic were to begin by treating Moore as a passing singing poet of the boudoir, whose works were to be considered as trifles or worse, and then to bring a charge of calumny against him, it would be blending falsehood with truth in such a manner that your argument would lose the benefit of the one, without gaining any credit from the other. Everybody will be sensible that the frivolity is not proved because the critic cries *trifler*, and will therefore argue that the calumny is as little proved when he cries *slander*.

'A critic was of old a glorious name,
  Whose sanction handed merit up to fame;
  Beauties as well as faults he brought to view;
  His judgment great, and great his candour too.'

"Constable goes up to town in next week to launch his 'Miscellany,' by which I have no doubt he will make a great deal of money. . . .

"When I read your letter, I missed an important fact, *videlicet*, that the article on Tom Moore is not to be *yours*. I am *very, very* sorry for it. I do not like Croker's style in such things in the least; he is a smart skirmisher, but wants altogether the depth of thought and nobleness of mind where the character of a sovereign is to be treated. If you can get it into your own hands, or can modify this article your own way, I shall be much better pleased. He blunders about his facts too, and indeed will never be more than a very clever confused sort of genius.—Yours always,   WALTER SCOTT.

" The more I think of Moore's article the more I wish you would do it yourself. At any rate, let no condescension to Croker or any one else prevent you from shaping it your own way. I foresee from your natural modesty of nature you will have difficulty in ruling your contributors, but you must in some cases be absolute."

About Lockhart's management of the *Quarterly Review* as a political organ, I have little to say.

I do not enjoy access to the archives of Albemarle Street, and any occasional information about the political conduct of the *Quarterly* which may be found in private letters, belongs rather to the history of Mr. Murray's house than to that of Lockhart. It is, therefore, a subject on which I do not intend to trespass. As to Lockhart's relations with Mr. Murray during nearly thirty years, it must be said, once. for all, that they were not invariably smooth, as it was hardly probable that they could be. Mr. Murray himself, of course, took a very lively interest in his own periodical, so did Mr. Croker, and many other old contributors, and official persons. Hence it came that Lockhart, on occasion, expressed dissatisfaction with "interferences." I offer an example, as it is already published, and violates no confidences. One or two other cases occur later. Southey reviewed what he calls "Hallam's essence of Whig vinegar," his "Constitutional History," published by Mr. Murray. On reading the critique, Mr. Hallam wrote to Mr. Murray (June 27, 1828), "protesting against the pique of Southey and the hostility of the Editor" —Lockhart. Murray answered, with spirit, that books published by himself should be reviewed with fairness. "I do not mean to offer the slightest apology for the appearance of the article, because I am conscious that I have nothing personally to do with it. . . ."[1]

[1] "Memoir of John Murray," ii. 264.

Turn we to Southey's correspondences (February 23, 1828): "There is a large interpolation in my reviewal of Hallam's book,—all that relates to Cromwell, the Whigs of Charles II.'s reign, and William III. Some friend of Murray's (Edwards, I believe, is the name) is the author, and some tender consideration of Murray for Hallam, extraordinary as it may seem, gave rise to the insertion. It was sent to me in slips . . . for my sanction, with a letter from Murray, and another from Lockhart, who, I believe, was a good deal annoyed by Murray's qualms on the occasion. . . ."

This is a very fair example of an editor's *tracasseries*. His publisher puts out a book ; Southey reviews it, *more suo;* Lockhart (according to Southey), approves ; Murray has a huge essential interpolation made in Hallam's interest, and, after all, the author of the book, Mr. Hallam, complains !

Thus it may be guessed that many circumstances, many interests, trammelled and troubled Lockhart in his new office. On the whole, it seems very desirable that the proprietor of a serial should either be his own editor, as Mr. Blackwood was, with irresponsible assistants ; or that he and his friends should leave a responsible editor entirely alone. The former set of conditions is the more readily secured. In neither set did Lockhart find himself. He was not, as Editor, entirely his own master.

Though it is not easy to say what precise situation in life would have been best fitted for Lockhart, and would have most potently disengaged the full force of his faculties, I cannot think that the Editorship of the *Quarterly* was that situation. It bound him to a task, and to a task much thwarted by many influences from without. To edit a Review now, may be, for all that one can guess, a light occupation of elegant leisure. In Lockhart's days it demanded incessant intercourse with people in power, and perhaps a good deal of what is called "lobbying." Croker would bring "the whisper from the throne," and be tedious about "his Royal friend." Enormous importance was attached to the affairs of the *Edinburgh* and the *Quarterly*, when newspapers were small, not numerous, and not "respectable." The deed of appointment speaks of Lockhart's "labours," and the word was then appropriate. There were endless consultations, correspondence, suggestions, people to be satisfied or conciliated. Lockhart also acted, occasionally, as a literary adviser to Mr. Murray.

To a very proud man I do not think that the whole position could be agreeable. Personally he and Mr. Murray, and Mr. Murray's son and successor, remained, throughout life, on the best of terms. I find, in his correspondence, none of Southey's incessant mutineering and *dénigrement* of Murray; and financially, I understand that Lockhart was treated with perhaps unexampled liberality. Still, as people talked of "Bacon's man" and "Bungay's man" (in "Pendennis"), I doubt not that they spoke of Lockhart as "Murray's man," and the situation could never have been wholly congenial. It had great advantages; society, literary or political—or "society" simply—was open to Lockhart. His occupation was with letters, which he loved. Power he had, if not absolute power. Leisure enough he possessed for the writing of his great biography, his own monument as well as Sir Walter's. In all this there was much to envy, and much that was envied by many. But in London Lockhart was transplanted from the scenes and the friends most dear to him, though he now had the company of Christie. For social intercourse on a great scale he never, perhaps, cared much, though he played his part in it, and, finally, he ceased to concern himself with crowds. My impression, derived from his letter to Haydon, is that he did not always feel sufficiently independent, enough "his own man." But this sentiment may have come upon him in his later years of bereavement and regret. He soon gave up his hopes of political patronage, as we shall see; he soon resigned himself to the neglect of his party, and devoted himself to editing, reading proofs, reading manuscripts, steering the *Quarterly* among the passions of contributors, a fierce generation. Lockhart's one great work, his biography of Scott, was dictated (like his toilsome editorship of Scott's works) by a sense of duty; the profits went towards the extinction of Sir Walter's debts.[1] Other ambitions he ceased to cherish. I would not represent him as dissatisfied and discontented : rather he was resigned. In the interests of his family and its fortunes he had obtained probably the most desirable of literary positions. He was not a recluse, like Southey or Wordsworth. But there was more in him, more of genius and power, than ever found full and free expression ; he never realised all his energies, and not to do so is not to be happy, even as far as happiness is meant for mortals. Yet I know not with what occupation he could have been better fitted. It was not Lockhart who lamented his destiny ; but a student of his life feels that, in his case, there was "something in the world amiss." For Lockhart leaves, on a mind long and closely occupied with him, an impression as of thwarted force, of a genius that never completely found its proper path. In life, and in literary history, such foiled energies are not uncommon. That Lockhart was expected by Scott to do very great things is certain ; on him the living personality made that impression to which, here and there, a reader may still be sensitive. But his greatest work by far Lockhart was to lay, where all of him that was mortal, by his own desire, was laid, "at the feet of Sir Walter Scott."

[1] I gather, from a letter of Mr. Cadell's, that Lockhart received a considerable fee from the trustees.

CHAPTER XIII

LONDON, 1826

To Lockhart's ultimate frame of mind—content
with his daily task, and patience under the implacable assaults of fortune—the events of the year
on which we now enter, namely, 1826, probably
contributed their full share. At this period, and
indeed generally, while Sir Walter lived, Lockhart's
career cannot well be contemplated or chronicled
apart from that of his father-in-law. For this
reason, and because Lockhart's own letters at this
date are so scarce, I must ask permission to insert
in this chapter some unpublished letters of Scott's.
These often indicate, better than any other acces-
sible materials, what was passing under Lockhart's

roof. That he was editing the *Quarterly*, of course
we know, and need not perpetually refer to his
business in detail. In a later chapter ample evidence will be given as to Lockhart's genial and
humorous correspondence with a contributor after
his own heart. At present we are to consider
his private anxieties and regrets.

The year 1826 was laden with misfortunes for
Lockhart and those dearest to him. First, and
to him least important, came the total failure from
its very beginning of the "organ" whence he had
expected to draw a great part of his income.
Then arrived, about January 17, the news of Sir
Walter's financial ruin, and shortly after came
the opinion of the physicians, that poor Master
Hugh Littlejohn really had a disease of the spine,
and must be removed to Brighton. Anxiety was
increased by the condition of Mrs. Lockhart, who,
somewhat prematurely, gave birth in spring to a
son, christened Walter. Meanwhile, in Scotland,
the health of Lady Scott was undermined, and
the worst was feared. Even the Shakespeare on
which Lockhart had laboured, went down and
practically vanished in the wreck of Constable's
house. Thus ill tidings pressed hard upon ill
tidings, and a new career, in a new society, could
not have been more inauspiciously begun. The
bad omens, moreover, were fulfilled, for few years
henceforth ran their course without bringing to
Lockhart a stab or a blow from destiny.

About Mr. Murray's newspaper, christened by
Mr. Disraeli the *Representative*, the story has been
told in the "Memoir of John Murray," and needs
but brief summary.   As soon as things came to
the point, these ardent capitalists, Mr. Benjamin
Disraeli and Mr. Powles, were no longer seen or
heard of in this enterprise.   Mr. Murray had
already spent much money, and made many
arrangements, but he had no editor !   Practically,
he never had an editor.   Mr. S. C. Hall has left
a few anecdotes of the forlorn, bewildered journal,
staggering about "in worlds not realised," now
perhaps decorated with an "academic" political
essay by Lockhart, now discredited by what Scott
called some "genteel-blackguard, touch and go "
effusion of Maginn's.   That Irish wit, after writing
much in *Blackwood*, under the names of "O'Doherty,"
and "Olinthus Petre," and so forth, joined the
Representative as Paris correspondent, and afterwards was attached to the editorial staff (if the
words "staff" and "editorial" are appropriate) in
London.   "Had there been no other morning
paper, the *Representative* might have succeeded,"
says Dr. Smiles ; but really, even if no rival had
existed, its chances appear to have been very
dubious.   On February 7, 1826, Lockhart wrote
to condole with Mr. Murray on the melancholy
estate of the "organ" : "That I should have been
in any measure accessory to bringing you into the
present situation weighs, I assure you, more heavily

on my spirits than even the mass of domestic melancholy by which I am surrounded. . . . I hope you have never for a moment supposed it possible that I should add to your embarrassments by being willing to touch unearned gold. The *Quarterly Review*, I think, promises well. Let us hope for better days. . . ."[1]

We need not follow the *Representative* to its grave. The child of Mr. Disraeli's boyish fancy, it was never duly organised, never edited by a practical man : the Tories, in these times, seem to have been incapable of finding or buying an editor. The "organ" expired on July 29, 1826, entailing, if not "dishonour," certainly "infinite loss." Mr. Murray "returned," as he said, "to reason and the shop."

In Edinburgh the cloud which had begun to gather in mid-November was, in January, already darkening all the sky. Constable left Edinburgh for London on January 13. It is no longer of importance to ask whether he should have started a fortnight earlier, whether he was delayed by his health, whether he could have availed to stave off ruin if he had come to town with the New Year, and so on. Constable's purpose, of course, was to raise money, by selling copyrights or otherwise, so as to meet the demands on his allies, Hurst and Robinson. Lockhart was made "privy to all" by Constable. These few words, and a similar passage written by Constable "under harassed feelings,"

---

[1] " Memoir of John Murray," ii. 212.

on January 18, 1826, represent from his side the strange scenes and proposals described by Lockhart.[1] "It was then," says Lockhart, "that I, for the first time, saw full swing given to the tyrannical temper of 'the Czar.' . . . I will not repeat his haughty ravings of scorn and wrath. I listened to them with wonder and commiseration. . . ."[2] In Mr. Constable's Memoir, by his son Thomas, we are informed that "though passionate and irritable, if any one who understood his nature had patted him gently on the shoulder, and said, 'Dear me, Archy, what is all this about?' you would see the usual kind and benignant smile return in an instant."[3] Perhaps, indeed certainly, Lockhart did not sufficiently understand Constable's nature, for he abstained from patting him gently on the shoulder, and saying, "Dear me, Archy!"

Concerning the excited manner of the publisher, on occasion, at this distressing moment in his fortunes, unpublished letters of Sir Walter to Lockhart entirely corroborate Lockhart's own statements. As Lockhart says, and as Constable's letter of January 18, 1826, agrees, the publisher wished Scott "to join, as additional cover, to the amount of £20,000."[4] Lockhart had already left Con-

[1] "Archibald Constable," iii. 418. "Life of Scott," viii. 174–178.
[2] Constable, January 17, describes himself as "nearly unfitted for business."
[3] "Archibald Constable," iii. 464.
[4] Ibid., iii. 418. The date of the letter, by an error of the press, is given as January 18, 1825.

stable once "in stern indignation" after declining
to take a wild financial step in a matter where he
had no right and no power to interfere. There
was "another scene," when Constable wished
Lockhart "to back his application to Sir Walter to
borrow £20,000 in Edinburgh, and transmit it to
him in London. I promised nothing but to acquaint
Scott immediately with his request, and him with
Scott's answer. Sir Walter had, ere the message
reached him, been made aware that his advances
had already been continued in the absence of all
ground for rational hope."

Lockhart's opinion as to this "mad proposal" of
Constable's is unconcealed. When Constable and
his partner, Cadell, separated, Sir Walter held by
Cadell, because he had lost confidence in Constable.
"And he had lost confidence," says Lockhart,
"especially because of the invitations to borrow
large sums of money for his support after all chance
of recovery was over." By acting as Constable
desired, in a mood and moment of great excitement,
Sir Walter would have thrown good money—*æs
alienum* too—after bad.

This was Lockhart's opinion, and this, to myself,
seems plain on Constable's own account, written on
January 19, 1826. "Hurst, Robinson & Co. have
not succeeded" (in raising money) "to the extent
necessary, and therefore the plan is at an end; they
could have got to one half of the amount, which
would not be at all what would have done the

deed."[1]   Now we know the amount for which Hurst
and Robinson failed, dragging down Constable with
them.   And we know that if Scott had borrowed
£20,000, as he was asked to do by Constable, the
sum would not "have done the deed" and saved
the two firms.   The biographer of Mr. Constable,
however, writes : " Had Sir Walter Scott agreed to
the guarantee suggested by my father, his " (Scott's)
" creditors would not indeed have received more than
the twenty shillings in the pound which he honour-
ably paid them ; but those of Constable & Co.
might have had good cause to differ from Mr.
Lockhart as to the insanity or soundness of the
suggestion."[2]   How this could have happened, if
the £20,000 demanded by Constable from Sir
Walter was totally insufficient "to do the deed,"
I am unable to conceive.

Constable's proposal, that Sir Walter should raise
£20,000, being written in London on January 17,
could not reach Mr. Cadell in Edinburgh till the
evening of January 19.   By that time Mr. Constable had abandoned hope of raising the money,
and was leaving town.   He reached his home on
January 22, and had thrown up the game before
Sir Walter could have accepted the "mad proposal,"
had he wished to do so.   Obviously nothing that
Scott might have done, could have saved Constable,
and Constable recognised the fact.

This proposal of Constable's may, among other

---

[1] "Archibald Constable," iii. 421.   [2] Ibid., iii. 430.

causes, have induced Lockhart, in his "Life of Scott," to adopt a tone towards the publisher which cannot always be defended, which must be regretted. But that is a matter apart from the soundness of Constable's suggestion about Scott's raising more money, and from the wisdom of the hypothesis, that had Scott agreed to the plan the firm might have been saved! These two ideas appear to be absolutely untenable.[1]

Throughout this dark month of January, Lockhart was in frequent communication with Scott, apprising him, for example, of Constable's designs and demands. "I was so very unwise," Lockhart writes, "as to express surprise at the nature of Sir Walter's commercial engagements." He prints Sir Walter's answer, so gentle in terms, yet so far from being really satisfactory as an explanation. It came to this, "with my little capital I was too glad to make commercially the means of supporting my family." In this letter occur the sentences, "I have been

---

[1] Mr. Thomas Constable occasionally complains that Lockhart does not quote Scott's *Journal* in full. Here is an example against which he takes no exception :—

"EDINBURGH, *January* 16.—Came through cold roads to as cold news. Hurst & Robinson have suffered a bill to come back upon Constable, which, I suppose, infers the ruin of both houses. We shall soon see." So Lockhart, in "Life," viii. 197. He does not quote the passage in full. It runs on : "Constable, it seems, who was to have set off in the last week of December, dawdled here till, in all human probability, his going or staying became a matter of mighty little consequence. He could not be there till Monday night, and his resources must have come too late." These remarks of Scott are omitted by Lockhart : to be sure, Scott repeats the ideas elsewhere.

far from suffering by James Ballantyne ; I owe it to him to say that his difficulties, as well as his advantages, are owing to me. I trusted too much to Constable's assurances of his own and his correspondents' stability, but yet I believe he was only sanguine. The upshot is just what Hurst & Co., and Constable, may be able to pay me : if fifteen shillings in the pound, I shall not complain of my loss, for I have gained many thousands in my day." [1]

These manly words of Sir Walter's are quoted here, because they ought, I think, to have been the keynote of Lockhart's comments, in the "Life," on Constable and the Ballantynes. Lockhart did not, it must be confessed, maintain the tone. Yet we must remember how Scott himself said about Constable, to his own friend Skene of Rubislaw, " He paid well and promptly, but, devil take him, it was all spectral together. Moonshine and no merriment. He sowed my field with one hand, and as liberally scattered the tares with the other." [2] It is also not to be forgotten that when Scott wrote the letter just cited (Jan. 20, 1826) he still hoped that Hurst & Robinson would pay fifteen shillings in the pound. They and Constable really paid about ten per cent. [3] Lockhart himself, as he toiled at

[1] "Life," viii. 232.

[2] Mr. Skene's "Reminiscences." Scott's *Journal*, i. 95.

[3] Scott's *Journal*, i. 99. Notes. As to the sanguine temperament of Constable, see the accounts of his relations with Mr. Murray's house, in 1806–1808, given in Murray's " Memoir," i. 80–84, and in "Archibald

his great biography, was prolonging the task which killed Sir Walter : he was writing not to reap the fruits of his labour, but to pay off the debt of Scott and the Ballantyne firm. He was not without excuse for acrimony, and one point must here be defended.

At the close of his Memoir of his father, Mr. Thomas Constable prints a letter from Sir James Gibson Craig. In this letter (November 25, 1848) Sir James says that, in 1813, Sir Walter, *by Constable's advice*, applied to the Duke of Buccleuch for a loan of £4000. At the same time, and "on the faith" of this loan, Sir James says that Constable gave Sir Walter bills "to a very considerable amount," a beginning of bills from Constable to Sir Walter, and from Sir Walter, by way of counter-security, to Constable. Later, Constable, says Sir James, grew uneasy, and was obliged to meet his engagements for Sir Walter by discounting *his* bills. And all this "could not fail to produce, and did produce, the ruin of both parties."[1]

Constable," i. 380–382. In April 1807 "Constable began to draw heavily on Murray, and the promissory notes went on accumulating until they constituted a mighty mass of paper money. . . . But repeated expostulation was of no use against the impetuous needs of Constable and Co." "The bill transactions with Constable had become enormous : they amounted to no less than £10,000. . . . Murray found it necessary peremptorily to put an end to it."—"Memoirs of John Murray," i. 81–83. Mr. Thomas Constable's version of these affairs, *loc. cit.* i. 382, is not quite so explicit (he may not have known the facts), and is only to be understood in the light of Murray's "Memoir." All this was long before the year 1813, when, it is stated, the transactions of Constable and Scott first became so sadly entangled.

[1] "Archibald Constable," iii. 457.

As a matter of fact, in 1813 Constable did suggest that Scott should ask aid from a friend, and
Scott himself selected the Duke of Buccleuch.[1]
And Lockhart remarks that any success which fell
to Scott's measures was due to Constable, "who
did a great deal more than prudence would have
warranted."[2] There is, in fact, on essential matters,
no difference between Lockhart's account, here, and
Sir James Gibson Craig's. By a common logical
artifice, or unconscious fallacy, an impression is
given that Sir James Gibson Craig corrects, whereas
he really corroborates, Lockhart's statement as to
the origin of the dealing in bills and counter-bills.
It is when Lockhart describes Constable's reckless
use of Scott's bills (viii. 95–101) that, I suppose,
his opinion is attacked. What I know about the
matter will be stated later. But I have shown that,
as early as 1807–8 (long before the affair of Scott's
distress and Constable's aid in 1813), Constable
was already dealing with bills, and paper money of
the brain, in a manner which Murray found intolerable, and declined to endure. When we remember,
in addition to the sanguine temperaments of Constable and of Sir Walter, Scott's own pathetic
remark to Ballantyne, "I can't follow details which
would be quite obvious to a man of business,"[3] ruin
seems to have been bound to arrive by pre-estab-
lished harmony.

The letters of Sir Walter to Lockhart at this

---

[1] "Life," iv. 99–102.   [2] Ibid., iv. 120.   [3] Ibid., iv. 102.

time, when so many anxieties pressed hard on both
of them, mainly repeat reflections already published
in the " Life," or in the complete edition of Scott's
Journal. A little extract may be made from a
letter of January 26, 1826. Scott mentions his
design of taking lodgings, or rooms in a Club.
" What a relief it would have been to have had one
of your attics, and to have seen affectionate faces at
your daily meal, which must now be solitary enough.
. . . As for myself, I look with perfect firmness
and calmness on the life before me, and though I
have no delight in the circumstances which have
led me to adopt it, yet in respect of the life itself
I like it well.

" I shall have Abbotsford to walk about in, Tom
to lead me, and a pony to carry me. We will keep
Pete " (the coachman) " and the old horses, if by any
sacrifice it is possible ; and study must be at once
my amusement and my business, as indeed it has
always been. For I never knew the day that I
would have given up literature for ten times my late
income.

" I am afraid you will suffer about the Shakespeare ;
but surely you will have retention on the book so
far as it has gone, for recompense of your labour.

" I am, with kindest compliments to Sophia and
good and kind wishes to poor Johnnie, very truly and
affectionately yours,   WALTER SCOTT.

" Do not let Johnnie forget poor old Ha papa.

Talking of the *Review*, can you help me to the place where is found the curious passage about the pickling the quarters of criminals, *tempore Caroli secundi*, and the blow-out which the hangman gave on the occasion ? It was the *Retrospective Review*, perhaps.

" I am sorry to send away an unsatisfactory letter ; but I think you would be glad to know that I feel as firm as the Eildon hill, though a little cloudy about the head now and then, like him. My mind tells me I will get above these things in two or three years."

The Shakespeare, on which Lockhart had expended much labour, is occasionally spoken of, as in the letter just cited, and its fate remains a literary mystery. One would have expected to find copies of the three volumes finished, at Abbotsford. It was much later abandoned by Lockhart, Mr. Cadell distrusting its success.

In January (no date), Scott says, "We relished the *Representative* very much," but the "relish" was short-lived. On February 25, Sir Walter refers to Lockhart's severe indisposition, and he encloses his Malachi Malagrowther pamphlets on the English interference with that palladium of Scottish liberties, the One Pound Note. "I think the sooner Murray gets rid of his paper the better. It is, as I feared it might be from the beginning, *heavy ;* wants the touch-and-go blackguard-genteel which distinguishes the real writer for the press.

"Am I wrong in detecting you in 'The Omen,' a very beautifully written but melancholy tale just published here? I had not read two pages when I said to Anne, 'Look, *Erasmus aut Diabolus*,' or something equivalent. She told me it had (been) advertised as by Wilson, but we all thought it much more like you—more elegant and simple than he is when he sets about sentiment. First proved hand I will send you 'Napoleon,' and 'Woodstock,' so far as they are done."

"The Omen" was a tale by Galt, with whose novels those of Lockhart were apt to be confused. Some remarks on Constable show an increase of asperity.

The next letter deals with Lockhart's domestic cares : and adds a reminiscence of Sir Walter's own childhood :—

"*3rd March.*

"My dear Lockhart,—I had Sophia's letter yesterday, and your kind note to-night. I rejoice to hear of Johnnie's health and his grand flip towards instruction. I hope Mrs. Mactavish, whom I like not the worse, you may be sure, for her name, will be mild in her rule, and let him listen to reading a good deal without cramming the alphabet and grammar down the poor child's throat. I cannot at this moment tell how or when I learned to read, but it was by fits and snatches, as one aunt or another in the old rumble-tumble farm-houses could give me a lesson, and I am sure it increased my love and habit of reading more than the austerities of a school could have done. I gave trouble, I believe, in wishing to be taught, and in self-defence gradually acquired the mystery myself. Johnnie is infirm a little, though not so much so as I was, and often he has brought back to my recollection the days of my own childhood. I hope he will be twice any good that was in me, with less carelessness."

He now speaks of his patriotic and very dis-interested efforts in the " Malagrowther " Letters.

"Old Gardiner, when wounded at Prestonpans, almost dying, himself rode up to the infantry when the cavalry were broken, and saying, 'These poor lads will be destroyed without a leader,' called out, ' Fire away, my lads, and fear nothing ; ' a wiser man would have galloped off. But my heart will not brook— ' fall back or fall edge '—to leave the cause of my country, as I do sincerely conceive it to be, in a state so precarious, without doing whatever one poor voice can to sound the alarm. If my power had been answerable to my will, I would, like old Hardy-knute, have

> ——'blown a blast so shrill,
> The trees in greenwood shook thereat,
> Sae loud rang ilka hill.'

It is pretty well as it is, though—for you never saw *braid Scotland* in such a humour."

It was now Sir Walter's turn to be the recipient

of bad news, as to his beloved little grandson.   He
writes :—

"ABBOTSFORD, 17th March 1826.

" MY DEAR LOCKHART,—I am almost stunned with
the melancholy intelligence I have this morning
received.   It appears to be God's pleasure that
this year shall be a most melancholy one, but
other considerations were trifles compared to the
anxiety communicated by your intelligence.   Most
unhappily, Morritt is, I understand, just leaving
Brighton " (whither Hugh Littlejohn had been sent
by the physicians).   " I own I have had always a
deep-rooted anxiety on account of that poor dear
infant, and have sometimes thought there was too
much mind for the corporeal strength.   I can scarce
conceive a situation more melancholy than yours—
thinking and feeling as you do.   Even Sophia is
easier, because she is at least constantly present
where her anxiety is most anxiously fixed.   What
can I form for you but vain wishes ? or what arguments can I use that will not occur to yourself,
and when they have thus occurred, be of very little
avail ?   We would send up Anne with pleasure if
her presence could be useful.

" As for the political part of your letter, Scotland
will, in twenty years, perhaps much sooner, be
revolutionised from head to foot ; and then let
England look to herself, for she may have some
reason to resume her own old proverb, ' All
ill comes from the North.'   The present time

reminds me strongly of 1638-9, when useless and uncalled-for changes unsettled the minds and irritated the temper of the Scotch, who were not long in communicating the infection to England. Then the opinions were religious, now they are political, but the effect may—indeed, I think, *will*—prove the same.

"Within these twenty years, nay, within these ten years, there have been so many alterations made, that law seems to be treated like religion, according to Hudibras—

> ————'as if intended
> For nothing else but to be mended.'

In the meantime the Burghers have been assembled into popular meeting of Commissioners and so forth, and have most effectually modelled themselves in such a manner as will make it impossible long to refuse them the popular representation they demand. They will probably send up clever men, for the time is so near, and the prospect so tempting, that some of our clever friends in the Parliament House will never quit so pleasing a harvest. Bold, speculative, able men, long-headed, too, beyond the length of the Southron noddle, they will propose and carry through more general measures of alteration, all leaning to the popular side of the question. These will be given way to as concerning Scotland. Fiercer innovators will arise behind in the usual course of such events—England will catch fire in her turn—

and all this from encouraging a spirit of innovation in the most quiet and peaceful country in Europe. . . .

"As for myself, what reason on earth can I have to affront all my friends in power" (by his "Malagrowther" Letters), "but the deep consciousness that there is a duty to be discharged? If they can argue me out of the world, as they say, and into Liddesdale, I have not the least objections.

"I have written more than I intended, but I am not sorry that any of our private friends should know why I do not answer my friend" (Croker) "at the Admiralty. Mr. Canning is mistaken if he supposes I appealed to the populace. On the contrary, I resisted every proposal to put the 'Letters' into a shape for general circulation. If ever there should be an occasion to address the people, I fancy I might have a guess how to set about it. But it should not be against the present men, although I am so unfortunate as to disapprove of the present measures.

"My heart sinks at writing all this stuff on a subject so different from that which at present occupies us both. It is what, however, we would likely have talked about, to divert for a moment our thoughts from that which must be uppermost. I am alone at Abbotsford, and have spent one pleasant day here, but that which follows is after the manner of Sezed with a witness. Pray write often.—Yours truly, W. SCOTT."

This letter, in which the political prophecies are only a relief from private sorrow, was written on March 17. In Scott's *Journal* for the same day Lockhart, long afterwards, read the lament for "the child almost too good for this world; beautiful in features, . . . having one of the sweetest tempers, as well as the quickest intellect I ever saw; a sense of humour quite extraordinary in a child," with all that follows. "The poor dear love had so often a slow fever, that when I pressed its little lips to mine, I always foreboded to my own heart what all, I fear, are now aware of."

Next in the series of calamities comes the fatal illness of Lady Scott; Sir Walter writes at first in good hope.

"ABBOTSFORD, MELROSE,
22nd March 1826.

"MY DEAR LOCKHART,—The return of mama and Anne to this place gave us yesterday a pleasant reunion, the more so as Lady Scott was much better than I had ventured to expect. The medicine which she is taking (digitalis or foxglove) seems to agree with her and do her much service, and I trust with care her health may be in a great measure restored. She is so well, and in such a good way, that she and I have a serious plan to send her up to be with Sophia during her illness."

Far worse intelligence rapidly follows:—

" I grieve to say, my dear Lockhart, that we have but bad news to send up from this country in answer to your deplorable intelligence of my dear Johnnie's health. Lady Scott is far from well ; the asthmatical complaint has assumed the character of hydropsy, and Dr. Abercrombie, who has been consulted, looks very grave on the subject. They work by some new medicine, but I own I am not very hopeful of the result, at least as to perfect cure."

The Lockharts were now at Brighton, whence, on April 16, the birth of a little boy was announced. "He is a very little one," writes Lockhart to his mother, "for he comes three weeks ere his time." The child was to be that Walter Scott Lockhart Scott, the young laird of Abbotsford, whose inconsiderate youth and early death clouded his father's latest years. On April 18, after "a day of some anxiety about the baby," Lockhart writes to his mother : "Sophia, even although she knew our fears in the early part of the day, is quite as well as any one could wish her to be—cool, calm, entirely placid in spirit, and easy in frame." He writes hopefully, too, about Hugh Littlejohn.

Just before the coming of the new baby, appeared another bantling, the first number of the *Quarterly*, edited by Lockhart. In his *Journal* for April 9, Scott says that he does not like Lockhart's article "on Sheridan's Life. There is no breadth in it, no general views, the whole flung away in smart but party criticism. Now, no man can take more general and liberal views of literature than J. G. L." However, Scott's chagrin as to the treatment of his friend Moore is not expressed in his letters to Lockhart. He sends thanks, as regards his own article on Pepys, for "Mr. Murray's generosity, but frankly the half was more than it" (the article) "is worth, and I make it a condition of future labours that I have no more than an adequate compensation for my time; and the present is extravagant. I will do 'Cranbourne Chase' with pleasure."

On April 22, Scott was obliged to send to Lockhart the worst news of Lady Scott's condition. For the *Quarterly* he undertook the long article on theatrical matters ("Life of John Philip Kemble"), which appeared in the June number. Lockhart himself reviewed some translations from Goethe, including those in Shelley's "Posthumous Poems." All that Lockhart says about Goethe is excellent; as regards Shelley, he touches only on the translations. "He wanted little to be a distinguished original poet but distinctness of conception and regulation of taste." The *Quarterly* was too much hampered by the politics of Mr. Matthew Arnold's "beautiful ineffectual angel."

As an editor having authority, Lockhart ventured on some "criticisms of style," which, indeed, Sir

Walter's article about Mr. Pepys (written when
under the influence of doctor's drugs) rather clamo-
rously demanded. Scott replies that he "literally
never learned to read, far less has studied composition. . . . You will unceremoniously point out
whatever you object to, which will be a great
favour, and I hope you will not confine it to style
alone."

The health of Lady Scott failed day by day, but
better hopes were entertained at Brighton, as
appears from this letter of Sir Walter's :—

"*May* 1826.

"My dear Lockhart,—Your truly acceptable
news gave me as much pleasure as circumstances
make me at present capable of receiving. I am
happy to think Sophia and the baby are doing well ;
and for dear Johnnie, as I remember myself on my
back, and shrouded in a new sheepskin, taken hot
from the back of the animal to communicate some
genial warmth to the wearer, I have strong hopes
that his present confinement may not prevent his
enjoying robust health at a future period of life, and
his lively temper and disposition to collect information will make the necessary confinement less irk-
some than one would guess. I who recollect much
of a sickly infancy and childhood can judge well of
this.

" I have no good news to send you in return—*none*
—and you must take your own time and manner

of communicating to Sophia that mama's state of health admits of little hope.

" I send enclosed the greater part of the dramatic article ; you will readily excuse the lateness and the quality when you read what is gone before ; but I think it is unmanly to sit down to fold one's hands in helpless regret, when exertion may do good to yourself and others. My philosophy, if it can be called such, is that of the porch " (stoicism).

" If Charles chooses to fall back on the Church, of course I may be of use to him ; but it is *entre nous* a sneaking line unless the adoption of it is dictated by a strong feeling of principle, and one which, with good prospects in that career, I renounced.[1] I would not go to the altar for a bit of bread unless I could do so with a strong conviction that I could adopt, in the fullest extent, the doctrines which I was to teach.

" I will put off Chaffin (Cranbourne Chase) to another occasion, unless you want it much.[2] I cannot write anything about the author unless I know it can hurt no one alive, and your well-intended offer would not mend the matter, because it is not that I care for the consequences of such a thing personally, but because I do not think it right. What I consider right to do I am not anxious to conceal from any one, and what is not right should not be done at all."

---

[1] This seems not to be generally known.

[2] From delicacy towards the possible feelings of Mr. Chaffin's surviving relatives, Scott never wrote this article.

These letters display a good man in accumulated misfortune, an example already needed by Lockhart. Unlike Southey, Scott exclaims, " Use the scissors as freely as you like," that is, on his contributions to the *Quarterly*. On May 15 he announces the death of Lady Scott. Lockhart was unable to leave his wife and attend the funeral. Sir Walter writes :—

"ABBOTSFORD, 23*rd May* 1826.

" MY DEAR LOCKHART,—Anne has suffered, and still suffers, much from weakness. She is, contrary to her manner under trifling vexations, extremely quiet and patient, but every now and then Nature gives way, and she has swoons which last perhaps ten minutes.

" For me I must bear my loss as I can ; at any rate, I have no want of comforters, for both old Botherby and Sir John Sinclair have volunteered to play Eliphaz and Bildad on the occasion—such is some folks' delicacy. A better comfort is the regret expressed by great and small for the good qualities of the deceased. My poor labouring people affected me much by insisting on supplying a night guard in Dryburgh Abbey till such precaution should be totally unnecessary. There was something very delicate in this peculiar expression of attachment.

" I beg my best love and affection to Sophia. Tell her not to be in the least anxious about me. I am of that age and temper which endure misfortunes the more patiently that they have ceased to look on the world with the same evident sensations of pleasure and pain which it presents to those who enter it. Kiss little Johnnie for me, and also little Walter. My best love attends Violet.—I am always, dear Lockhart, most faithfully yours,

"WALTER SCOTT."

Lockhart himself communicated the ill news to his wife, then at Brighton :—

"LONDON, *May* 16, 1826.

" I know you too well to hesitate about letting you see exactly how matters stand ; and you know me well enough to be sure that it is a great misery to me to have to *write* instead of speaking such tidings. You must exert yourself and be, as poor Anne seems to be, satisfied that prolongation of life under such circumstances is a cruel prayer. Your father also writes to me, and much in the same tone ; but he still preserves all his firmness, and in the midst of his sorrow has found time to give me an admirable review of ' John Kemble's Life,' telling all his old stories about the man and his manners in the best style."

On May 26 he adds,—" Your father writes with all his old composure. . . . What a blessing to have such a regulated manliness of heart and mind ! The possession is even more enviable than his genius."

On May 30, Scott writes,—"My love to little Walter, and especially to poor Johnnie; . . . he was one of the last persons mentioned by his poor grandmama, which will always make him the dearer to me.

"What do you about Shakespeare? Constable's creditors seem desirous to carry it on. Certainly their bankruptcy breaks the contract. For me *c'est égal:* I have nothing !to do with the emoluments, and I can with very little difficulty discharge my part of the matter, which is the Prolegomena, and Life and Times.

> "So speak your wishes, speak your will,
> Swift obedience meets them still."

On June 30, Scott wishes Lockhart joy of the *Review*, "which is not only unexceptionable, but commands general praise. I am sorry you have trouble with Murray, but it was foreseen, and you must just be steady with him." A letter of July 20, shows that Scott's remonstrance against being overpaid for his *Quarterly* articles was successful. The "rapacity" lamented by Macaulay was not really a marked feature of Sir Walter's character.

On July 6, Lockhart wrote to his brother Lawrence, from 16 Bedford Square, Brighton :—

"MY DEAR LAWRENCE,—Here we are now settled for three months more, certain—for the doctors all united that, as Johnnie was so much improved

by the air and bathing, it would be madness to
remove him from the coast before October. We
shall pass October and November in London, and
the winter months in some of the villages near it,
for the doctors say that it would kill the poor boy
to be *in* town during the dark and foggy season.
Our present plans are to be at Chiefswood in the
beginning of June, for the whole summer of 1827.
But who can speak boldly about so distant a
period?

"We have met with many sore disappointments
since I saw you last. But there is no use in re-
pining; we must e'en take the world as we find it;
and I would fain hope for better days hereafter,
though I have thoroughly ceased to have any very
sanguine dreams. My wife's even and firm temper
accommodates itself wonderfully to changes and
chances, and if Johnnie recovers, and the baby
continues to thrive as it is doing, we ought to be
satisfied at home. . . .

"Violet will soon be at home now.[1] I fear my
dearest mother has a poor dull life when she is
away, and I have felt for her extremely, leaving
Germiston at the very bloom of the season. . . ."[2]

Writing on the same day to his brother William,
Lockhart says,—"I do not wish to *write* about my

[1] Miss Lockhart had been with Mrs. Lockhart since the settlement
at Brighton.
[2] The rest of the letter deals with purely domestic affairs of Mr.
Lawrence Lockhart's.

own concerns. The change of situation has taken place under circumstances of unlooked-for difficulty and disadvantage, and things have turned out poorly indeed compared to what I had been led to expect. . . . I see no help, nor prospect of it, except in time, labour, and patience."[1]

Writing to his father, on July 10, Lockhart expresses his anxiety to hear about his brother Dick, who had gone to India, with a letter from Sir Walter to a Mr. Swinton. "He wrote in a very particular manner, of which, having seen the letter, I can safely say it was beyond what we could have hoped, or even wished, almost."

A very short time had passed before Dick was drowned in India, so resolutely did misfortune pursue Lockhart and his family. He ends by a description of the noise, heat, and glare of Brighton. "But the air is certainly most healthful, and the children are all day long on the beach, which is everything for them, and therefore for us."

There exists a letter, written a few months later, by "Hugh Littlejohn," to his "Aunt Violet," as Scott says he used to call her. The handwriting is wonderfully good for a child not yet six years old :—

"My dear Aunt Vi,—You left me in your letter five shillings, and I am very much obliged to you

---

[1] Lockhart refers to the failure of the *Representative*, and of his hopes in that quarter.

for them. I have still fourpence left. Walter is
growing a fine boy, and baby is a little beauty. I
have got a great many new books since you were
here last time. I hope Grandpapa and Grandmama
are quite well, and my Aunt Louisa, also my uncles
and cousins. Give my love to them. I am to go
to Scotland next year, and I shall have the pleasure
of seeing you.—Your affectionate nephew,

"JOHN HUGH LOCKHART."

On October 7, Sir Walter announced his intended visit to London and Paris, in search of
materials for his "Life of Napoleon." From his
Journal (October 17, 1826), we hear of this April
weather meeting with his daughter and Lockhart.
"Too much grief in our first meeting to be joy-
ful; too much pleasure to be distressing. . . . I
am childish with seeing them all well and happy
here," though poor Hugh Littlejohn "was kept,
as much as possible, in a recumbent position."
With the Lockharts Sir Walter inspected Windsor
Castle; they dined with Terry, the actor; and an
hour was passed in teaching Johnnie the history
of his namesake, John Gilpin. They dined with
Dr. and Mrs. Hughes, and their son, the disin-
herited of Pepys. Mr. Pringle, the Lamb of "The
Chaldee," of all people, paid a visit, the Lamb
who, with the Bear, came skipping on staves.[1]

---

[1] Lockhart later did what he could for a book by his old victim,
reviewing it in the *Quarterly*.

On Scott's return from Paris in November, Croker and Theodore Hook came to breakfast, and "we had, as Gil Blas says, a delicious morning, spent in abusing our neighbours." They dined at Croker's "with five Cabinet Ministers, Canning, Huskisson, Melville, Peel, and Wellington," such a party as more modern times could not bring together. Sir Walter thought that "the presence of too many men of distinguished rank and power always freezes the conversation." "I wish I could turn my popularity amongst these magnificoes to Lockhart's advantage, who cannot bustle for himself. He is out of spirits just now, and views things. *au noir :* I fear Johnnie's precarious state is the cause."

Lockhart persisted in not being able to "bustle" and push his fortune with magnificoes. One task for which he was eminently fitted nearly came to him; he was overlooked, and, as we shall see, the work which he could have done admirably *has not been done even until this day.*

In. brief, the year 1826 did much to break the spring of hope and to destroy ambition in Lockhart. His industry remained unimpaired, but was seldom set to tasks that elicited his highest powers.

Lockhart at this time did not allow his troubles to interfere with his work. To his first number of the *Quarterly* (No. LXVI.) he contributed the Sheridan article, justly disliked by Scott, and a "cold-blooded" plea for reflection and discrimination in dealing with slavery and the West Indies.

Many a bright popular delusion, many a vulgar but moving error was exposed here, of course to very little purpose. In the next number he only wrote the article on translations from Goethe, already mentioned. To No. LXVIII. he contributed an interesting and reflective essay on the art of fiction, taking for his topic Scott's "Lives of the Novelists," then pirated by Galignani, who ingeniously abstracted Sir Walter's introductions from "Ballantyne's Novelists' Library."

Lockhart argues that the novel is the only form, or *genre*, of literature which modern times have invented. Materials and genius were not wanting in Greece and Rome. "Who, to take an example, can read Horace, and doubt that Horace might have written a novel?" he asks. We are unconvinced: might Pope have written a novel? "Why," he asks, "did Froissart's age produce no novel?" Why, it *did;* Froissart wrote an immense historical romance, lately discovered among the MSS. of the "Bibliothèque Nationale." Among the illiterate peasants of Domremy, one woman (giving her evidence at the Rehabilitation of Jeanne d'Arc) declared that she had learned some facts about the Fairy Tree from hearing them read aloud *in uno romano, dans un roman.* Lockhart, unobservant of these circumstances, argues that tragedy, comedy, satire, lyric and epic verse could exist where readers were few, but that novels can only flourish in a reading public. But the Rome of

Horace's days read much, and romances, as a matter of fact, were extremely common in the Middle Ages. Froissart, as a young man, borrowed novels from, and lent them to, a young lady whom he admired, in the most modern way.[1] Probably Lockhart is thinking of our contemporary novel of manners ; but, even so, Apuleius, and Longus, and many late Greeks practised the art of fiction in prose.

Among Sir Walter's followers, Lockhart selects Cooper as the best, because " he has employed a style of delineation which he could never have invented, *upon a fresh field*, and, which is of still more import- ance, on a field of manners and feelings familiar to his own observation." Scott's English successors, on the other hand, " trust to reading and imagination for the best part of their materials, and being in- ferior beyond measure to their master, both in the accomplishment and the faculty, they have pro- duced, at the best, the mere *corpus exsangue* of the historical romance." Yet there is a general improvement, a higher common level has been reached. "One genius, in a word, has made many clever artists," but "the imitating romancer shrinks at once into his proper dimensions when we ask— what new character has he given us?"[2]

In this number Lockhart also bantered, in brief space, Monsieur Parseval, who carried on the tradi-

---

[1] See " Froissart," by Madame Darmesteter.
[2] Dumas, of course, had not begun to write romances.

tion of Chapelain in "Philippe Auguste, Poème Héroique"; and he reviewed "The Subaltern," by his friend Mr. Gleig, with some other "Military Memoirs." Mr. Gleig had left Balliol to fight in Spain, in 1813, when Lockhart also was eager to take up arms for Iberian liberty, as we have seen in an early chapter.

END OF VOL. I.

Printed by BALLANTYNE, HANSON & CO.
Edinburgh and London

www.ingramcontent.com/pod-product-compliance
Lightning Source LLC
Chambersburg PA
CBHW022028110726
47901CB00006B/1690